Pike's Passage

John J. Spearman

DEDICATION

For Alicia, as always.
Also, for my supporters and fans who encourage me to keep writing.

OTHER BOOKS

ACKNOWLEDGMENTS

Thank you to Hugh Ryan. His support has been wind in my sails.

And to you, dear reader,
You are the purpose of this and all my books. Thank you for reading. If you like what you have read, please leave a positive review on Amazon.com or goodreads.com. If you did not like it, I'm sorry.

1

"Commander," Giersch began, "I have some unpleasant news."

"Sir?" replied Commander Alexander S. Pike.

"The Governing Council has removed Al Dorsey as Head. They have ordered Admiral Ketyungyoenwong to rescind all the changes Dorsey pushed through in the last few days. The only two that stand are Admiral Ketyungyoenwong's promotion and Pat Holton's promotion to replace her. They put all other personnel changes, including your promotion, on hold. The refit of the HUW ships is no longer on the fast track, and your assignment is no longer valid."

Commander Sandy Pike was on his way to Valkyrie to take command of one of four HUW battlecruisers when he received that call from Rear Admiral Bob Giersch. Alliance Admiral Ketyungyoenwong captured the ships along with most of the Hegemony of United Worlds' Attack Group Eagle when she intercepted it in system RY 232. That would have been a great victory had the Alliance not lost its entire 2nd Battle Group of Red Fleet in the Battle of Excelsus, fought at nearly the same time as the RY 232 battle. Pike's ship, Planetary Alliance Ship (PAS) *Driscoll*, a heavy cruiser, the third of a recently developed class, was destroyed. Pike spent nine days in an escape pod in a deep sleep afterward.

Sandy was silent, stunned. Rescinding the changes Dorsey championed meant he no longer had a command.

"I'm sorry," Giersch added quietly. "You deserve far better."

Pike swallowed hard before asking, "What will my next posting be, sir?"

"I don't have a ship for you, I'm afraid," Giersch's throat tightened with regret, and he cleared it before continuing, "and it might be some time before I do."

"How long, sir?"

"Months, at least."

"I see."

"It appears as though they might assign you to logistics or BuPers. However, I understand from Admiral Ketyungyoenwong that you've already suffered through a BuPers assignment, and I am unwilling to ask you to do that again."

Swallowing the bitter cud of disappointment, Sandy replied, "Thank you. I'll await your orders then, sir."

The war between the Alliance and the HUWs began slowly. Sandy enjoyed some notable success as it heated up, earning the Legion of Merit medal and, later, an oak cluster to add to it. He expected better than an open-ended posting to logistics.

Losing the 2nd Battle Group highlighted leadership problems in the Alliance Navy. As the Alliance hadn't been at war for nearly a hundred years, the government had nibbled away at the navy's budget for decades. That environment bred a command structure half filled with pencil-pushing petty tyrants. The Head of the Governing Council, Al Dorsey, recently announced sweeping measures to address the problem. But when the Governing Council replaced Dorsey, they canceled all his plans.

The buzzing of his comm unit broke Sandy's negative train of thought.

"Hey, you doin' okay?" Monty Swift said, his face appearing on the small screen.

"Me? I'm doing just great. Enjoying the shit sandwich that life just served me," Sandy replied sarcastically.

"Yeah. If it makes you feel any better, they took away my promotion, too," Monty said.

"It doesn't make me feel better, buddy. But at least you've got a ship. Looks like I'm going to be commanding a desk for the foreseeable future."

Monty winced. "That sucks."

"Yup."

"Maybe this won't last too long," Monty offered.

"Which? Canceling all Dorsey's overdue ideas, or the Alliance?"

"Maybe they'll see the sense of what he was trying to do."

"Yeah. And maybe I'll bend over, and flying monkeys will pop out of my butt."

"You really think we're in that much trouble?" Monty asked.

"The Alliance?"

"Yeah."

"One more Excelsus," Sandy commented, "and it's all over. This whole thing started over Castor, a planet that isn't even ready to colonize yet, but now I think the HUWs might go for the whole thing." He pronounced the acronym for the Hegemony as *Hoo*. "The new Hegemon sounds like he's hardcore."

"You think they'll press the issue?" Monty asked.

"No idea," Sandy replied. "But if they do, we're in trouble."

"I hope you're wrong," Monty said, "but I'm worried that you're right."

"Meh. Don't mind me. I'm bitter and cranky," Sandy suggested. "You just keep commanding your ship with all your wonderful Red Fleet colleagues."

"Way to cheer me up, pal. You know those guys are going to figure they're untouchable now that the Governing Council saved their asses."

"At least you won't be tracking toilet paper usage. Giersch said my next posting is likely to be logistics."

"Damn. I really am sorry, Sandy. It's not fair. It's not right."

"Yeah, but it is what it is," Sandy stated flatly. "I'll talk to you later."

A comment he'd made in the conversation with his old friend stuck in his mind. Sandy wondered whether the Alliance was going to come out on the wrong end of the war. He thought of what might happen if the Alliance indeed lost. The victors would certainly disband the Alliance Navy, and he would be unemployed, at the very least. It was also possible that the HUWs might subject him to intense scrutiny because of his Navy career. What would he do?

Then he remembered an abandoned fast transport he had spotted years earlier. What if he salvaged her and established a freight business? Sandy had amassed a tidy sum of capital from prize money and was willing to invest it in something that would keep him as a starship captain—his lifelong dream.

Sandy first learned of the existence of the *Alice May* fifteen years before. He was a lieutenant then, serving aboard an Alliance frigate that was hoping to sneak up on a smuggling base. The smuggling base was located one jump away from the standard travel route between Valkyrie, an Alliance planet, and Faunus, a non-aligned world. Faunus was known for permitting quasi-legal shipping activity. On the way through a lightly traveled system, Sandy was practicing on sensors, wasting time, to be honest, and trying to look busy. To his surprise, he discovered an abandoned fast transport ship, left cold and deserted in the system's asteroid belt.

Fast transports were one of three main types of cargo ships in use. They specialized in the swift transfer of small, low-volume cargo. The other types, high volume (HV) and ultra-high volume (UHV), were used to ship bulkier things and were much slower. UHVs were typically used on long-distance inter-system routes. HV ships were generally used to distribute cargo within a system.

Sandy kept the discovery to himself. He didn't know why, but he didn't think about it at that moment. It was just one of those oddities one encountered in space from time to time. He never forgot about it, though. Curious, he tried to learn more about the ship whenever he was on liberty and could access the 'net without going through a Navy connection. It took some digging, but he eventually learned that the ship, the *Alice May*, had been abandoned over sixty years earlier following an episode of reactor instability. The company which owned the ship went bankrupt a few years later. Its other assets were purchased, but not the *Alice May*. In fact, the *Alice May* did not appear in the court records listing the assets of the defunct corporation.

Sandy also learned the *Alice May* had been built by Heydrich & Sauer more than a century before. Heydrich & Sauer was a small shipyard that previously built frigates for the Alliance Navy. When they lost their government contract because of political reasons (not quality), they turned briefly to building civilian vessels. They had a reputation for over-engineering their ships—one of the reasons they were no longer in business. The frames they installed in the cargo ships they built were extremely robust—what one would expect from a ship built to military, not civilian specifications. H & S struggled on for another ten years before going under. Almost all the cargo ships they built were still in service, a testament to their sound construction.

A couple of years earlier, during the war with the HUWs, he had served briefly on the maiden voyage of a modified fast transport freighter, the *Ali Kat*. The Office of Naval Intelligence had developed the ship. They had started with a fast transport, then enhanced her with military-grade weaponry, shielding, drives, and sensors. Its purpose was to curtail smuggling and piracy since the navy frigates that usually had that assignment were all needed for the war effort. It had been wickedly effective.

If the HUWs won, it would likely be several years before they established tight control over the Alliance systems. During that period, Sandy knew general lawlessness would increase. While he had no desire to act as a vigilante, being able to protect his ship and his customers' cargo would provide a secure market niche. Ideally, he would add to the *Alice May* some of the features that had made the *Ali Kat* unique. Unfortunately, they all required access to military hardware—a stumbling block. The various governments tightly controlled the kind of military hardware that had been installed on the *Ali Kat*. Though there was a black market for anything, Sandy suspected that these types of goods appeared only on very rare occasions and would be obscenely expensive. He put the idea on the back burner.

After reporting to logistics, Sandy noticed that Portia Thompson, a Master Chief Petty Officer who had also served on the *Ali Kat*, was now in charge of the navy supply depot at Valkyrie. One night when he had trouble sleeping, his idea about retrieving and upgrading the abandoned fast transport popped into his thoughts. On a whim, he arranged a meeting with Portia for a drink.

He had no desire to steal anything from the navy—he wasn't made that way. Even more, he knew Portia would never agree to such a thing. Yet, if the Alliance ended up losing the war and surrendered, would it still be stealing? He tried to justify the idea of taking military hardware that now belonged to the enemy as almost patriotic. However, it still required quite a leap of mental gymnastics.

He met the heavyset black woman at a bar named The Shuttle Bay. When they sat in a booth, he used his comm to activate a suppression field to counter any listening devices that might be active nearby. After exchanging small talk with Portia and discussing the progress of the war and what might happen, she asked him what he thought was the most likely outcome.

"It's all up to the other side," he explained. "If they decide to press the issue and mount a major attack, they might win. If they do their homework and target what remains of Red Fleet, I'd say they have a better than even chance. If Admiral Ketyungyoenwong can pull another rabbit out of her hat, we could even win. I don't know about the long-term. I know we don't have any capital ships under construction. I've heard they do, and if that's true, then we're in trouble. That's one reason I wanted to talk to you."

He continued and explained about the abandoned fast transport.

"So, you want to create our own *Ali Kat*?" she surmised.

"Well," Sandy said, "maybe even slightly improved. The ship is over a hundred years old but was built by a company called Heydrich & Sauer."

"That name sounds vaguely familiar."

"They were a military shipbuilder that lost their contract because of politics," Sandy confirmed. "They struggled on for a few years, but I think they lost money on every civilian ship they made. From what I understand, the ships are tough as hell. Most of them are still in service, even after all this time. The *Alice May* is a fast transport, but slightly larger than more current models. I think we could get bigger reactors in her, with more powerful drives and maybe even a bigger weapon."

"So, why do you need me?" Portia asked.

"I have some money," he admitted, "but trying to outfit the ship with what's available on the black market would exhaust that pretty fast and leave the ship much less than half-finished. I think that we need military hardware to do it right."

Portia's forehead furrowed, her dark skin showing creases Sandy had rarely seen. Then, without raising her voice, she hissed, "And you think I'm just going to help you steal that stuff? Sandy, you and I have been through a lot, so I'm going to pretend you didn't just insult the hell out of me—because there is no way that you would ask me to do that and have any hope that I wouldn't get up right now and turn you over to the SP."

"Portia, I would never mean to insult you," Sandy apologized. "I respect you too much and owe you for helping me keep my head screwed on straight when we were both on *Chapman*. I'm no thief, and I know you're not either. Will you stay and hear me out?"

Sandy took a deep breath, looking carefully at Portia to see if she had

5

calmed slightly. She had, but only a little. "I've always stayed at arm's length from politics, but when the Governing Council replaced Dorsey as the Head and then prevented Admiral Ketyungyoenwong from cleaning up the mess, that was a pretty clear signal that the problems we both know are plaguing the navy aren't getting fixed soon. I've heard that the HUWs have a bunch of capital ships nearing completion. We don't have any. They're going to replace the losses they took and then some. I figure they'll mount an attack shortly after they are complete, if not before—meaning right away. We're nearly as unprepared as we were at Excelsus, despite everything Admiral Ketyungyoenwong has tried to do. The Council has tied her hands, and she's still stuck with a bunch of incompetent captains—mostly in Red Fleet. If things go the way they seem to be headed, we might lose. I think the HUWs originally only wanted the planet Castor. Now, they might be thinking of a complete conquest of the Alliance. One big battle that goes their way and it will force the Alliance to surrender. If we surrender, our navy will almost immediately cease to exist. The only question is when it will happen. It might not. Then again, it could be next month, or it could be a couple of years."

"If things go that way," Portia admitted, "we'll both be out of work. In a couple of years at the outside."

"Exactly," Sandy confirmed. "The worst might not happen at all," Sandy cautioned. "We might make it through this. I don't want you to take anything, at least not while there is still a navy that we both serve."

"Then what do you want?"

"Just for you to reorganize your storage, so the parts we might want are all in one place that's accessible, in case we have to move quickly."

Portia thought about what Sandy was suggesting. "You keep saying 'we.' I don't recall agreeing to your scheme. Is there someone else involved?"

Sandy shook his head. "No. The 'we' is just you and me, if you decide to take part."

"If I don't?"

"Then I'll have to abandon any plans of enhancing the ship. I might still try to salvage her, but it makes the next few years a risky proposition. I'd probably still do it because I can't see myself doing anything other than piloting a starship."

Portia relaxed, sitting back. "If the Alliance surrenders, I don't know what I'll do. I can't retire, and the labor force will be flooded with ex-navy. Not all of us will find work. So, I'm not saying no. Not yet. I haven't said yes, so don't get all excited."

"Understood," Sandy said somberly.

"Should the Alliance surrender," she mused, "then all that material technically belongs to the HUWs. So, we'd be stealing it from them, even though they wouldn't know about it for months, maybe ever."

"You keep using the word, 'steal.' I prefer to think of it as 'liberating' those materials before the HUWs get them."

Portia laughed. "We'll need an engineer to help us get that ship running again, too. We should think of someone before it's too late. In the meantime, put together a 'wish list,' and I'll see what I can do. We lease some additional warehouse space from civilians. I think I could move what we need piece by piece to one of those locations to have it ready. It won't leave a navy-controlled facility until after a possible surrender, so it hasn't been lost or stolen—just organized differently. I'll also need to prepare to fudge the paper trail so the HUWs would never know it was missing. That can happen later."

"This isn't too shady for you?" Sandy asked with genuine concern.

"It's a bit devious, but there's no crime in moving things from one warehouse to another. There won't be a crime until we remove those materials from a navy facility. That won't happen as long as there's an Alliance we both serve. Agreed?"

"Agreed," Sandy confirmed. "I think I know an engineer who might be a good fit. Remember Mike Xie?"

Portia nodded. "From *Chapman*. I agree. He struck me as someone who wanted to step outside the engineering bubble. And if we do this, we need people who can wear more than one hat. What about Puss and Stick?"

"I'm going to wait and contact them later. If we can somehow pull this off, I think they'd jump at the chance."

It was the middle of Sandy's sixth week in logistics. He came into his office, sat, and activated his console. Though he was in command of a section tracking usage of various commodities, the people reporting to him knew far more about logistics than he did. At least during the six weeks he had spent reviewing FitReps for BuPers, he had something to do, even though it was mind-numbing.

He was playing a game of solitaire on the console for what felt like the millionth time when he noticed the buzz of conversation outside his office. He opened his door and stepped into the big open room divided into cubicles by low partitions. Almost everyone was standing, talking.

"What's going on?" he asked Mike Herron, the enlisted man posted nearest his office.

"Big news," Herron replied. "Huge battle in the Freia system. The bad guys won."

Sandy pivoted back into his office and brought up the reports. The HUWs targeted the portion of Red Fleet stationed in the Freia system with two Attack Groups. The results were devastating for the Alliance, similar to the Battle of Excelsus. The Alliance lost three superdreadnoughts and four battlecruisers, while the HUWs lost one of each. The bitter anger he felt surprised him.

Sandy stood and went back out. "Hey, commander," one of them called.

"You heard the news?"

Sandy nodded.

"What's it mean? Is the war over?"

Sandy thought carefully before he responded, fighting the temptation to share his true feelings. Instead, he shrugged. "Beats me."

Regina Smalley, now Head of the Governing Council, called the meeting to order. "Foreign Relations has informed me that the position of the United Worlds is unchanged. We have offered them the Castor system and other incentives. Nevertheless, they insist on our capitulation."

"When you say capitulation," Tom Sutton asked, "what does that include?"

"Demobilization of all armed forces, immediate establishment of planetary governors with the existing Alliance governments dissolved, oversight of the press, control of communications — "

"Complete surrender, in other words," Al Dorsey interrupted.

"We are still negotiating, Speaker," Smalley snapped.

"You might be," Dorsey said with a grim chuckle. "They're not."

"What would you do, Speaker?" Smalley asked sarcastically.

"Ha!" Dorsey barked. "At this point? There's nothing we can do. Give them what they demand. Dragging things out will only irritate them and invite harsher treatment."

"They do not have an overwhelming advantage in military strength," Smalley protested. "They should be satisfied we're willing to cede Castor to them."

Dorsey laughed bitterly. "At the moment, they are stronger than we are. Enough stronger that if they pressed the issue, the odds are in their favor. In less than a year, when their new ships are complete, they will enjoy an undeniable advantage. Your only hope at this point is to try to negotiate some sort of transition period to ensure that basic services continue to be provided to our citizens."

Alliance Press Interwebs:

"At 6:55 pm, Sigrun local time, the Press Office of the Governing Council issued the following statement:

Following the battle in the Freia System, the Alliance entered negotiations to end the war with the Hegemony of United Worlds. These negotiations have just concluded. There will be peace.

Governance of the Alliance member planets will change. Free and fair elections have been promised. In the interim, planetary governors will be appointed to oversee a smooth and orderly transition.

"The brief statement appears to suggest that the Alliance has surrendered to the United Worlds with few conditions, if any. API has attempted to contact members of the Governing Council, the Press Office, and Foreign Relations for comment without success."

"Men and women of these United Worlds. I am pleased to announce the Planetary Alliance has agreed to the surrender terms we dictated to them. There is no more Planetary Alliance. Their planets are now part of the United Worlds. We now rule their people.

"What started as a conflict over a single, uninhabited world became a war of conquest. Under my leadership and at my direction, our United Worlds prosecuted the war with vigor and steadfast determination. We took full advantage of the opportunities we were given. We did not settle for anything less than victory."

Mortimer Edison
183rd Hegemon of the United Worlds

Three weeks later, Sandy was in the process of losing another game of solitaire. He heard the buzz of conversation outside again. Before leaving his office, he checked the news using his console. The Alliance just announced their surrender to the United Worlds, ending the war.

Sandy tried to contact Portia immediately but could not get a response. He had an uneasy feeling. Then, his comm unit buzzed with an incoming message. It ordered him to report to the office of Admiral Ketyungyoenwong. The combination of the surrender, not reaching Portia, and the summons to see the admiral combined to make him feel slightly nauseous.

He left his office quickly, locking the door. He ignored the crowd standing in their cubicles, discussing this latest development. After a few minutes' brisk walk, he reached the admiral's office. Her yeoman showed him inside immediately. He saw Portia sitting there, and his heart sank further.

He saluted the admiral. She waved him to a seat. As he crossed the room, he tried not to look as guilty as he felt. Portia was no help, refusing to make eye contact.

When he sat, Admiral Ketyungyoenwong leaned forward across her desk, her hands clasped before her. "So, Commander Pike," she began, with a grim smile, "I brought the two of you here because I noticed an interesting assortment of material, staged in a leased facility. It's almost as if it were ready for quick shipment. The list of items includes EM drives and nacelles, shield generators, reactor cradles, a 105mm photon cannon, a full sensor suite, and a shipboard computer, among many other things. Even more interesting is that these items don't appear in the inventory records. Most unusual. I've asked the Master Chief for an explanation, and she refused to say anything until you arrived. She did implicate you and swore that there was no intention of selling the material on the black market. Since the material is still in a facility leased by the navy, no crime has been committed. Because the material is not included in the inventory records, its disappearance would cause no alarm—unless I were to assign the accountants to dig into the records to find something. Seeing as how the Alliance Navy will soon cease to exist, I am hardly feeling a sense of urgency about that. I am not planning on turning this matter over to the SP unless you give me reason to. You, Portia, are one of the most highly regarded Master Chiefs in the navy. You, Sandy, are twice decorated with the Legion of Honor. So what the hell is going on?"

Sandy knew his only chance at salvaging anything from this was through full disclosure. He explained his reasoning that, technically, the material now belonged to the HUWs. Because of that, he felt that removing it from the warehouse to keep it from them was morally justifiable. But even as it was coming out of his mouth, he realized how ridiculous his argument must sound.

He forged ahead, explaining to the admiral what he hoped to do: to refurbish the abandoned fast-transport he'd found years before into a pirate-proof ship even better than the *Ali Kat*, since it might take ten years or even longer for the United Worlds to establish effective control over the Alliance sectors and their borders. With the ship configured the way he envisioned, he would have a near-monopoly on the market for secure transport of low-volume, high-value cargo. He had no intention of becoming a rebel—his motive was profit and the chance to continue to command a starship.

"Admiral," he said in closing, "it was one hundred percent my idea. Portia was only trying to help me out of a sense of personal loyalty. If there is to be punishment, let it fall on my head and mine alone."

When he finished his explanation, Ketyungyoenwong leaned back in her chair. She looked grim. She steepled her fingers and gazed at Sandy with a disapproving look, bordering on disgust. Sandy's heart sank. Unexpectedly, the admiral snorted—a laugh she had been trying to hold back.

"Don't either of you turn to a life of crime," she said. "You'd both fail miserably. But the reality is, the Alliance Navy will soon be dissolved. Flimsy as it is, I can easily persuade myself of the validity in your argument, Sandy, now that we've surrendered. We might be in a position to help one another, Sandy, Portia," she said. "Much as your careers are ending because of our surrender, my niece—you know her as Alison Lynch — "

"Ali is your niece?" Sandy asked, incredulous.

Ketyungyoenwong nodded. "As a field agent for the Office of Naval Intelligence, she might face worse than the loss of her job. So agree to cut her in on your venture in exchange for the materials Master Chief Thompson was planning on 'liberating'—that's the word you used, isn't it, Sandy?"

He nodded.

"Agree to include Ali in your scheme, and not only will I look the other way, I'll make sure no one comes looking for it."

Sandy looked at Portia for the first time since he sat down. Portia gave the slightest of nods, indicating her approval. Sandy turned back to Ketyungyoenwong.

"What sort of help can you provide us, Admiral," he asked, "without getting your own hands dirty?"

"Ali has access to an ONI courier boat. ONI is in a similar situation to the rest of us here in the navy—nothing belongs to them any longer. I would imagine she can figure out the rest. As far as what you might need to bring the ship back to life, Master Chief Thompson can take whatever she needs, so long as no one is any the wiser. Would it be correct to assume that you already have gathered everything?"

Portia nodded.

"Good," said Ketyungyoenwong. "That way, my hands won't get the slightest stain."

"Understood, Admiral," he replied. "Where is Ali right now?"

"Here on Valkyrie," Ketyungyoenwong said, now openly smiling. "One other thing. I want the three of you and whatever you're taking to be gone as soon as possible. Within 24 hours. Away from Valkyrie Station."

That was a bit of a problem. Sandy had been figuring they would have some time to pull things together. He had to find Mike Xie or someone else if Mike was too far away. He hadn't even talked to Mike about this, figuring they had more time. Restarting reactors that had been cold for decades would absolutely require someone with more expertise than he had. He explained this to the admiral.

"I'll send you a list of competent engineering people who are here on Valkyrie," Ketyungyoenwong said. "As to whether they'd be game for your little adventure, I can't say."

"We also need a transport company that won't ask questions and won't remember what we've done," Sandy asked.

"I can't help you there," Ketyungyoenwong replied, "but I imagine Ali can. That's all I can do, Sandy. I want you gone as soon as possible so I can pretend I don't know a damn thing. As far as duties, you'll officially be on leave until your demobilization orders come through."

Admiral Ketyungyoenwong dismissed them both shortly after. Sandy's mind was racing. The dismay of seeing Portia in the admiral's office, the

11

surprise of the admiral's willingness to look the other way, the shortened timetable, the lack of a well-trained engineer to oversee reactor start-up—it all weighed on him. "What do you think, Portia?" he asked, once the door had closed to the admiral's office.

Thompson squinted her eyes at him with a look of distaste. "I can't believe I let you talk me into this. But Lord, Sandy, if she'd thrown the book at us, I would have killed you. As it is, I think the degree of difficulty just went up by a factor of about ten," she stated. "Beats the shit out of going to prison, though."

"That's the way to put a positive spin on things, Portia," Sandy commented. "Let's find a place to sit and figure out what needs to be done first."

They left the admiralty section of the station and walked into the nearest bar. They found a booth and ordered a couple of beers. Sandy pulled out his comm unit and activated the field distortion feature to prevent anyone from overhearing. After the server brought the drinks, Sandy began.

"First, tell me what happened, Portia?"

"Since you and I met, and you gave me your wish list, I've been moving things a piece at a time to an outside warehouse we lease for overflow storage. I'd just managed to get the last of the stuff moved over when the news came in about Freia. Right when I heard about the surrender agreement, I was then summoned to the admiral's office. When I entered, she told me she knew what I'd been doing and wanted to know why. She was worried I was doing it for a quick profit on the black market. I told her that wasn't the plan, but I needed you to tell her the rest. Sorry I couldn't warn you."

"She said you also had a ship computer," Sandy commented. "Really?"

"Hey, I figured it would be better than whatever civilian piece of crap is on board now."

"Anything else you grabbed that wasn't on my list?" Sandy asked.

"Environmental stuff. A few tools. Stuff to make the ship livable. A lot of little things you didn't think of. Didn't take long to pull together," Thompson commented.

Sandy was about to comment but quieted himself. A tall, slender woman with blue hair and pale skin approached their booth with a big smile on her face. "Sandy, Portia," she said. "How great to see you again!"

She slid into the booth on Portia's side, forcing her to scoot over. Ali had changed her appearance since they had last seen one another. Her dark brown hair was now a light blue, and the beauty mark on her cheek was gone. "Well, Portia, look what the cat dragged in," he commented wryly.

"It's so good to see you," Thompson added warmly.

Speaking quietly without moving her lips, the woman said, "I just talked with my aunt, and she told me to find you guys. What's going on?"

The server appeared and asked if Alison wanted anything to drink. She asked for a beer, the same as Sandy and Portia. Alison carried the conversational load until the server returned, chatting about how long it had been and wasn't it great to see one another. Sandy and Portia played along.

When the server left again, Sandy spoke quietly. "It's nice to see you again, Alison. I do hope we can help one another out. Unfortunately, we have some issues and a tight timeframe."

"What?" Alison asked.

Sandy explained about the *Alice May* and his idea to make her into a slightly improved version of the *Ali Kat*. Thanks to Portia, they had the components they needed. Ali whistled softly through her teeth.

"I understand you can get us a courier boat," he stated.

Alison nodded.

"It occurs to me it would be wise to make sure that any record of it disappears before we leave. Otherwise, you'll never be able to get a title for it and register it in another system," Sandy suggested.

"Already taken care of," Alison responded smugly. "Any and all records show it belongs to me, titled and registered on Providence."

Sandy raised his eyebrows at this. "We have one other pressing need at the moment," he explained. "If you can help us with it, you'll make a valuable contribution to our venture."

"Fire away," she replied.

"We need a freighter to pick up some materials and deliver them to a location we will disclose later. We need the kind of captain and crew who don't ask questions and will forget all about us. We need them now. We'll pay for discretion."

"I *can* help with that," Alison answered, nodding.

"The other thing your aunt is supposed to be working on. She was going to send us some names of people who are experienced with reactor start-up and possible repair."

"I just received a message from her with some names," Alison responded. "What else?"

"Those are the most pressing emergencies," Sandy commented. "Once we get the ship working again, we'll need to take it somewhere for modifications—again, someone who won't ask questions and who will keep his or her mouth shut. I have some people in mind to join us once we get the ship running, but that can wait until then."

"As far as a yard for the ship," Alison asked, "would it be safe to guess that outside of Alliance space would be preferable?"

"It would," Sandy stated as Portia nodded.

"The yard is in the Providence System. I worked through them to register the courier. The freighter we need is on Valkyrie Station right now and looking for a load," Alison explained. "We, ONI, have used both the yard and the freight company in the past. They're both reliable and know to keep their mouths closed. When would you like to meet the freighter captain?"

"Now," Sandy said. Then, looking at Portia, he asked, "How much time do you need to load everything?"

"A couple of hours, tops," Thompson answered.

"Forward that list of names to me," Sandy asked, handing his comm unit to Alison. "Portia, give her your comm, too."

When Alison had finished synching their comm units, Sandy told Portia to get busy. He'd find an engineer and meet the freighter captain. Then, they'd let her know when to expect to load the material.

Things came together quickly and surprisingly smoothly. Mike Xie was actually conducting training on Valkyrie. Sandy asked him to meet at the same bar as soon as he could get away. Xie replied that he'd be there within 30 minutes. When they met face-to-face, and Sandy explained what he needed him to do, Xie thought briefly.

"Worst case," he responded after a minute or two, "we can't get the thing restarted, and I come back here in two or three weeks to the same situation I'm in now. So yeah, I'll give it a try, Sandy."

"Go pack for an extended journey. Make whatever arrangements you need to make as far as your lodgings and your assignment."

"With the news we received today, I'll file for emergency home leave," Xie replied. "My CO suggested to everyone that they might want to do that, and she would approve anyone who asked."

After Mike left, Ali returned with the captain of the freighter. He was a taciturn man, used to doing work for intelligence. Ali let him think this was an ONI project. The captain contacted Portia and began making arrangements to pick up the materials immediately. The two of them left together.

After the meeting with the captain, Sandy returned to his quarters. He gathered his belongings and checked out of the BOQ, and headed to where he could grab a taxi to the courier boat Ali had. With nine hours left of the 24-hours Admiral Ketyungyoenwong had given them, they pulled away from Valkyrie Station and headed towards the *Alice May*.

They arrived in the system, located the abandoned fast transport ship, and maneuvered into position to board her. Sandy left the bridge and headed aft to the small hold of the courier ship. Portia and Mike were almost finished donning their EVA suits. Sandy began putting on his own. The three of them would enter the derelict and start trying to bring her back to life.

Portia and Mike would do the complicated work. Sandy was their gofer. When he finished suiting up, they gave him a large pack to strap on. It contained tools and also a powerful battery. With the *Alice May* dead and powerless, they would need power to open the hatch unless they did it manually. Manual operation took much longer. Sandy would return to the courier once they'd opened the hatch. Then he would link the two ships with a power cable. This would allow them to power up the dead ship's systems from the courier's reactor.

They left the courier airlock one at a time. Sandy went last, pushing off to join the two of them already on the *Alice May*'s hull. When he arrived, Thompson spun him around and pulled a power cord from the battery, plugging it in a receptacle at the hatch. The controls illuminated, and the outer hatch opened. Thompson went in first.

"The ship still has atmosphere," she reported. "So, it's airtight, at least. No gravity and cold as space, so we'll need the suits. I'm heading to the reactor. Mike, help Sandy find the port for the power cable, mark it and then come on in."

Mike beckoned to Sandy, indicating he should follow him. Then, using compressed air jets, he gently moved aft. Mike turned the floodlight on his helmet on, looking at the hull of the freighter. He found the port and attached a small glow lamp on the hull next to it. He opened the port cover.

"Standard coupling," he said, giving the thumbs-up sign to Sandy.

They returned to the hatch. Mike removed the battery from Sandy's pack and plugged it back into the hatch receptacle. "You head back, retrieve the cable, and plug it in on both ends. Let us know when you're finished."

Sandy did as he was told, returning to the small hold aboard the courier boat through the airlock. He took the electrical cable and looped it over his shoulder. Then he went back out of the airlock and found the port on the hull of the courier. He inserted the coupler from one end of the cable. Then, turning and finding the marker light, he glided over to it, uncoiling the cable as he went. When he plugged it in, he informed Portia and Mike.

"Come aboard, Sandy."

With power coming from the courier's reactor, they were bringing the ship back to life. The *Alice May* had gravity and light immediately. Heat would take some time, and restoring a breathable atmosphere depended on whether the environment systems would still function.

Mike was able to diagnose the trouble with the ship right away. He explained when they returned to the courier ship a couple of hours later to eat and get new air tanks. "They were about to lose the bubble on their reactor," he stated. Seeing Alison's blank look, he continued, "Fusion reactors essentially recreate a miniature sun. They use plasma shields to contain the energy. Each reactor has two plasma field generators, each responsible for half of the containment sphere, usually called the bubble. One of their generators was failing. They had to shut the reactor down before they blew up."

"Can you fix it?" Sandy asked.

"I could if I had to," Xie responded, "but you could never be sure it wouldn't fail again. Fortunately, Portia brought replacements. We'll install new ones. It will be much safer, and they should last us a good long time. There's enough room that we could fit three of the new generation reactors once we get to a shipyard."

After they ate, Mike and Portia returned to the *Alice May*. It took a couple of hours to install the new containment field generators for the reactor. After that, Mike sent Portia back to the courier boat.

"Reactor start-up is the trickiest part. It will take about four hours. None of you can really help, so stay out of the way. Once we get the reactor back online, you can start loading our cargo, Sandy," Mike explained.

It was over four hours before Mike informed them that the reactor was back online. Sandy headed out shortly after and removed the power cable between the two ships. They contacted the freighter carrying their material, and it maneuvered into position to transfer the cargo. After stowing the power cord, Sandy headed to the empty hold of the *Alice May*.

Ship-to-ship transfer of material in deep space did not happen very often, but Sandy had trained for it at the Academy years before. He considered it one of the more fun chores he'd ever been assigned. Essentially, the crew of the first ship would shove the cargo into space. Sandy, using a tractor beam, would capture it, then pull it aboard gently. Portia joined him, making sure every container she had loaded came over and that they had not been tampered with. It took less than 45 minutes to transfer the pallets and only slightly longer for Portia to approve.

Once finished, Sandy closed the cargo bay and restored atmosphere to the hold. Portia informed Alison she could send the other freighter back. Sandy would transfer the second half of payment as soon as he reboarded the courier ship and accessed the computer.

They found that the environmental systems on the *Alice May* were barely functional. The ship had heat, but the atmosphere was stale, with a funky smell. The environmental equipment could be repaired, but that would take several days. Portia's foresight in bringing extra environmental components saved them that time. The next day they spent three hours replacing the inserts on the units. They kept the old inserts as they could be refreshed and still had value. Sandy and Portia figured they could work out a deal to knock down the price of the planned modifications with the shipyard that was their next stop.

Portia, Mike and Sandy moved their belongings to the *Alice May* now that the environmental systems functioned. Alison stayed aboard the courier ship. Since Ali now held the title for it, they might trade it in with the shipyard, provided they agreed on the right price.

After running tests to make sure the drives were still tuned properly, they gave the word to Alison. They headed on a twelve-jump trip out of Alliance space and to the non-aligned planet of Providence. Providence had somehow managed to remain independent despite being surrounded by the multi-system territories of the Planetary Alliance, the United Worlds, and the Free Republics. But, of course, with the Alliance having just surrendered, its former space would soon be controlled by the United Worlds.

The multi-system governments controlled a large, amorphous blob in the middle of civilized space. Providence was one of only three non-aligned planets within that blob, while the other 26 non-aligned planets were all on or near the fringes. The unique routing of the tramlines—the hyperspace corridors through which faster-than-light travel was possible—made it possible to reach Providence from other non-aligned planets, without crossing through a system claimed by the larger entities. It took over a month, but it could be done.

Providence enjoyed a dubious reputation. Its astrographic position made it a hotbed of smuggling tariffed goods into and out of the multi-system areas. In addition, the intelligence services of the three multi-system governments had a strong presence on the planet, trying to keep tabs on the various illegal operations centered there and spying on one another as well.

They set off on the month-long trip to the Providence system. They spent the first few days cleaning the ship. The previous owners had not left a mess. Still, the years of abandonment meant all the airborne dust had settled on every exposed surface. Ten days into the trip, Mike, Sandy and Portia received their demobilization papers—they were officially civilians and no longer part of the Alliance Navy. Once they confirmed receipt of the documents on their comm units, their navy account access disappeared. Alison heard nothing from the Office of Naval Intelligence. She didn't expect to.

As all of them became more familiar with the ship, they offered suggestions for possible changes. Most were slight cosmetic changes, done without difficulty. Sandy wanted to expand the bridge. It was small, with only room for two people. Sandy wanted it to fit four. The layout of the bulkheads and the structural load they carried argued against it.

With four people, each had a six-hour shift each day. During their off-hours, they continued to clean and examine every inch of the ship. Mike was the one who found where a previous member of the crew had stashed contraband. The two bottles of whiskey were now well-aged. Amazingly, when they froze due to the loss of heat, they did not burst the containers.

Sandy made an executive decision. Since they had just entered a system and had nearly two days before their next hyperspace jump, he declared a celebration was overdue. He gave everyone a chance to adjust his or her sleep schedule, and twelve hours later, they gathered in the galley. Sandy cooked a meal with the supplies Portia had 'liberated' and then sat down with the bottles. They toasted their good fortune in being able to salvage the *Alice May*, and shared some of their hopes for the future.

Upon arriving in the Providence system, they obtained clearance from traffic control to proceed immediately to the shipyard. The yard was expecting them—Alison had informed them she was bringing a ship in for a refit. They had asked for more information, but Alison had put them off, saving it for an in-person discussion.

The reactor containment field generators that Portia had 'liberated' from the Alliance supply depot were more robust than the commercial-grade generators originally mounted in the ship. They already installed them on the one reactor, replacing the damaged originals. Part of their plan was to reconfigure the powerplant layout and install two more reactors. Though smaller than the original equipment on the *Alice May*, the new generation of reactors would produce more power. When they installed the second and third, they would provide *Alice May* with over three times the power output she had when built.

That power would be needed. They were planning on upgrading the EM drives and adding defensive plasma shielding on the ship's hull, a 105mm photon cannon, and a full military-grade sensor array. The new reactor capacity would meet the power demands and still have reserve capacity if needed.

As they were bringing the components with them, they would only need the shipyard to do installation work. This would save them a great deal of cost. Still, Sandy expected the negotiations with the yard to be tricky and challenging. He knew he would pay more than he wanted. Still, if he could somehow gain confidence that the yard would be discrete about their modifications, he would consider it balanced. Alison vouched for the owner of the shipyard, someone about whom she knew from her role with ONI.

According to Ali, Tom McAllister was skilled at both repair work and skimming right along the edge of the law. He took care to stay in the good graces of the Providence authorities and had a few of them on his clandestine payroll. Most of his business was legitimate repair work. Yet, he had a handful of customers who paid a premium for discretion and silence. All of them were based in other systems. Providence had a relatively relaxed attitude about the work he did for foreign customers, figuring it helped their trade balances. As a result, they didn't look into it too closely. ONI had approached McAllister nearly a decade earlier and had him on the payroll as a confidential informant. He had assisted them in obtaining documentation, as with Ali's courier boat, but ONI had not needed repair services.

Following instructions from traffic control, they reached the shipyard. It was in a stable orbit of the inhabited planet, only 12,000 kilometers from Providence Station. The shipyard resembled an octopus. A central rectangular cube housed the offices and warehouse, with eight umbilical connections snaking out into space. Six of these umbilicals were connected to ships when the *Alice May* arrived. Buzzing around were a couple of small tugs that hauled bulkier components from the warehouse to where they were needed. Four of the attached ships had workers in EVA suits crawling on their hulls. Motionless in the space nearby were three other ships, either awaiting repair or finished and waiting on their owners to retrieve them.

They were meeting with McAllister, the owner, directly. They called a taxi service from the station to collect them and deliver them to the hatch nearest the office. Before leaving, they set up security protocols on both vessels to ensure no one could take them.

2

McAllister met them. He was tall, with unusually pale skin. It was extremely rare to see someone with skin at either extreme of pale or dark—most people were in the middle of the spectrum. McAllister greeted them politely and ushered them into his office. They sat at a conference table. Alison asked permission to activate the field suppression feature on her comm unit. McAllister nodded his acceptance.

"I'm guessing that FT out there is the ship you want to discuss," McAllister opened. "She's a Heydrich & Sauer FT 170. They quit making them over a hundred years ago. Heydrich & Sauer has been out of business since then."

"It is," Sandy replied. "We salvaged her from deep space. She was abandoned so long ago that the owners no longer had her listed as an asset when they went bankrupt, with no bill of sale for twenty years preceding that. So we'll need to get a clean title while we're here. I figure you can help us with that."

"I can," McAllister agreed. "Won't be a problem. So, you just found her?"

"A few years ago," Sandy clarified. "We just picked her up now."

"Still, that's a marvelous piece of salvage," McAllister commented. "What do you want to do with her?"

"Before we get into that," Alison interjected, "we need your commitment that what we discuss will remain confidential."

McAllister raised an eyebrow. He looked coolly at Alison. Alison returned his look with a steady gaze. "Do I know you?" he asked.

"We've never met," Alison responded, "but you did some work for a colleague a few years ago. You would have known him as Brad Rogers."

McAllister gave a hint of a smile. "I don't recall ever doing work for anyone by that name."

"Exactly," Alison confirmed. "That level of discretion."

"Understood," McAllister agreed. "I agree to keep our business just between us."

"Thank you," Alison said. She looked at Portia and Mike. Portia placed a portable console on the table, angling it so McAllister could see.

"We brought the major components along with us," Portia stated. "About the only thing we didn't bring is shielded wiring conduit, but we figure that shouldn't be a problem."

McAllister nodded.

"Most of what we need you to do will be external, except for running the new conduit through the ship. Here's a list of what we want to do."

She accessed the task list and allowed McAllister to look it over. His forehead creased by the second item. After reading the third, he whistled softly under his breath.

"You say you have these components?"

Portia nodded.

"You realize you could sell them, and the four of you could retire on the proceeds?"

"We promised we wouldn't," Sandy said with a grin.

"This is all Alliance Navy stuff. How did you get it?"

"You don't need to know," Alison answered.

"I do if someone is going to come looking for it," he responded tautly.

"No one will," Alison reassured him. "I can assure you that these components will not show up as missing. Even if anyone did notice they're missing, I doubt they'll report it to their new overlords. You don't need to know."

"You're right. Sorry," McAllister apologized. "Curiosity killed the cat. So, what are you planning to do with the ship?"

"With the Alliance surrendering to the United Worlds," Sandy explained, "we figure things will be wild and crazy for the next ten years or more, primarily in the areas where the Alliance borders the Free Republics and the non-aligned systems. It will take at least that long for the United Worlds to get a handle on it since they'll disband the Alliance Navy and replace all the customs personnel with their own. With these modifications, we can establish ourselves as *the* provider of secure transport of low volume, high-value cargo."

McAlister sat back and thought. At length, he nodded. "Makes sense—a lot of sense. You're all Alliance Navy, aren't you?"

"Not anymore," Sandy replied.

"Quite right. By any chance, are you looking for investors?"

Portia, Mike and Alison looked at Sandy. He shrugged. "We weren't. If you're thinking of being that investor, we will consider it. We need to talk amongst ourselves before committing to anything."

"Fair enough," McAllister agreed. "We can discuss that later once I'm ready to give you a firm estimate on the cost of the modifications you'd like to make. Can you send me this file?"

Portia took back the console. "What's the address?"

McAllister dictated it to her. She entered it in and sent it. When she finished, she added, "The file also contains detailed schematics. That should make estimating easier."

McAllister rose and went to his desk, accessing the file on his own console. He opened it and began to go through it. He hummed a couple of times, then looked up, realizing he abandoned his potential clients.

"Sorry," he said, returning to the table. "You've gotten my mind racing. I must say, it's nice to be dealing with professionals. Your schematics are indeed a big help. Can I get a closer look at the ship?"

"Sure," Sandy replied. "When?"

"Now," McAllister answered. "As I said, you've intrigued me."

Sandy looked at the others. No one objected. "Let's go," Sandy stated.

McAllister had a small shuttlecraft, and they used it instead of a taxi. Before docking with the *Alice May*, McAllister guided the shuttle around her. "I'm scanning the hull," he explained. "With her being out in space so long, you're going to have some minor impact damage that you might not have noticed. The scans will pick it up."

When he was satisfied, they docked. Portia and Mike took him on a tour. Sandy and Alison went to the bridge of the ship. Alison activated her field suppressor again.

"What do you think so far?" she asked.

"I'm getting a good feeling about him," Sandy admitted, "better than I thought."

"I think it has to do with the vibe you guys give off," she explained. "You, Portia, and Mike are all clearly ex-navy. It oozes from your pores. I let slip where I come from by mentioning that name, so he knows how I'm connected. He's ex-navy, too—Free Republics. The shipyard was an asset owned by a smuggling syndicate that he broke up. He bought it at the government auction afterward, then retired from the navy. He's grown the business since then. I'll be interested to see how the numbers add up."

"What do you think about taking him on as an investor?" Sandy asked.

"For a small stake, like ten percent or less, I think he could help us. McAllister is tied in with many people who can help us get established. It could make things easier for us, especially in the beginning, since an association with him makes us seem more credible. It also helps keep him honest in terms of his quote for the work. We'll have to talk with Portia and Mike and then see what he's thinking of, but I'm willing to entertain the idea."

Mike came to get them, and they met with McAllister in the galley. "So," McAllister began, "I have a firm idea of what you need from the files Portia sent me. I understand that some internal work—installing the new reactor field generators and the new computer system—you plan to do yourself. The only thing you need us to do inside the ship is run new conduit and establish the anchors for the new reactor layout. If you don't mind, I'm going to give you an estimate on the other internal work anyway, to see if I can't convince you to let me do it. Portia and Mike let me know that the environmental components in the hold that you replaced would be traded in as part of the deal. Anything else?"

"There's a possibility," Alison added, "that we could add the courier ship to the deal."

"I'll certainly consider it," McAllister said, "but you might find you have a use for it. For example, you might want to keep the courier to use for an advance person staying ahead of this ship to negotiate your next job. Just a thought. Or you can sign up with a shipping agent who will do all that legwork for you. I'll get back to you tomorrow morning with some estimates."

When McAllister left, Sandy asked the group what they thought about McAllister. Portia and Mike both had good things to say. Sandy asked about the partnership idea. They agreed with Alison that, at under ten percent, it might be worth discussing. Mike and Alison pointed out that they didn't know how it would affect their share of the partnership since Sandy hadn't discussed it with them. They both assumed it was just a job for them until McAllister mentioned buying a share.

Sandy slapped himself in the forehead. "I apologize," he said sincerely. "When it was just Portia and me, we sort of discussed a 60/40 split, but then I realized we would need other people. With you, Alison, and you, Mike, I think it's only fair to include you. Two others are currently on their way to help fill out the crew, but they'll be junior partners. There's one other person who I'd like to invite to join us. Let me contact him, and then we can resume this discussion."

Sandy reached out to his friend Monty Swift after the meeting broke up. He could see on the screen he obviously woke Monty up. "Sorry, butthead," Sandy apologized.

"Don't worry about it, loser. What's on your mind?"

"Well, I have a business opportunity I'd like to tell you about," Sandy stated.

"Sheesh. You sound like an insurance sales agent," Monty cracked.

"That did sound pretty lame," Sandy admitted. He told Monty about the *Alice May* but shared nothing about the military hardware he and Portia had managed to 'liberate' that would make the ship unique. Monty heard him out, but by the end, Sandy saw him shaking his head.

"Buddy, I don't plan on doing anything for a bit. I've got enough stashed away that I don't have to, and, I gotta admit, I'm a little burned out on the navy right now. We haven't really talked about it, but the time in Red Fleet under Treffitte was a horror show. Giersch was much better, but all of Treffitte's people were still there. You had a taste of it with Slocum, but I had to live with those clowns for a couple of years. I hoped things would get better after Dorsey's announcements right after Excelsus, but then they canned him, and it was back to pretty much what it had been. I wasn't surprised at all by what happened in Freia — "

"Neither was I," Sandy commented.

"At least I was on a ship," Monty remarked, "so I had that to keep me busy. It must have sucked for you, stuck in limbo at Valkyrie. Did they give you anything to do?"

"Nope. They didn't know what to do with me," Sandy said. "They canceled our promotions, they were in no hurry to refurbish the captured ships, and they didn't have a command for me. So, I just hung around in logistics playing solitaire, waiting for orders."

"Not chess?"

"Hell no. The computer kicked my ass every time," Sandy admitted.

"The sitting around waiting would have messed with my head," Monty said, nodding, "especially after Elizabeth and all that."

"It wasn't fun."

"Anyway, I could see Freia coming, as I'm sure you did. I hate to say it, but I was almost relieved that we surrendered. I'd been thinking about resigning my commission since they took away our promotions but hadn't gotten around to it. So, I think I'm going to take a year or two off and get my head sorted out. Maybe I'll come ask you for a job if this all works out, but right now, I just want to do nothing except go to the beach, have some drinks with little umbrellas in 'em and maybe pick up some girls. So, thanks for the offer, but no thanks."

"Hey, buddy, it's okay," Sandy replied. "I feel bad. We never did get around to having that talk about how things were going in Red Fleet. After getting a much smaller taste of it than you did, I'm feeling guilty like I wasn't there for you when you needed me."

"Not your fault," Monty said, waving his hand as though to dismiss it. "Neither of us had the chance. Anyway, good luck with the new venture. Stay in touch."

Sandy met with the group again. "I spoke with the other person I wanted to invite, and he's not going to join us," Sandy informed them. "Here's what I propose off the top of my head: if we cut McAllister in for ten percent and split ten percent between the two junior partners, that leaves eighty percent. I'd like to be generous, but without Portia or me, none of us would be here. So I think twenty-five percent each for Portia and me is reasonable, with fifteen percent each for you. You'll all draw a salary from the operation, but the ownership stake will determine profit sharing. Does that sound reasonable?"

"I wasn't doing this because I thought I'd get rich," Mike Xie stated. "I joined up because I thought it would be a way to maintain employment, and it sounded a lot more interesting than anything else I could dream up. I don't think the commercial transport market will absorb all the suddenly ex-Alliance Navy engineers, and I didn't want to go run an environmental plant or something like that. Fifteen percent is fine by me."

"I know I was sort of foisted off on you two," Alison added, "but I *have* contributed some physical assets, like the courier ship, *plus* contacts and information. So I think I'd like to be on equal footing with you and Portia."

Sandy nodded slightly, seeing the validity of her argument. He looked to Portia. She shrugged. Sandy thought quickly.

"You've got a point, Alison. If we bump your share up to twenty percent, Portia and I lower our shares to the same, which will leave five percent unaccounted for. We could hold that in reserve in case we figure out we need to add someone else in. Does that sound fair?"

Before Alison could respond, Portia spoke up. "I'm okay with you keeping twenty-five, Sandy. This was all your idea, and I think you should have the biggest share, if only by a little. But if we do add someone else, we'll all be looking at you to take a hit up to that five percent."

Alison nodded her agreement. Mike simply smiled. Sandy looked at each of them carefully, not wanting any hard feelings over this. He didn't sense that any of them had a problem.

"I'll get a lawyer to draft some documents as soon as we get things settled with McAllister. Does that sound good? Anything else?"

Sandy's next pressing concern was the tiny computer chip he had in his pocket. Since he received it, he'd been terrified of losing it. Before leaving Alliance territory, he asked his broker to cash in his investments and put the proceeds in bearer bonds. The bearer bonds were encoded on the chip. Most of Sandy's net worth, nearly twelve million credits from prize money during his career, was on a piece of silicon the size of his thumbnail.

He headed to the office of Kruppen Financial, an investment firm based on Terra Nova. Even though Kruppen had offices on Valkyrie, Sandy could not have done the transaction there. The Alliance government had cameras monitoring every non-Alliance financial institution since transferring large amounts of money outside of the Alliance was illegal.

Sandy found Kruppen's office without difficulty. It was small, with two employees—one a receptionist. When he entered, he gave his name to the receptionist and a code that his broker had given him. The receptionist entered both and then asked Sandy to wait. The receptionist went into the other room briefly. When he returned, he waved Sandy in. The manager introduced himself as Tamas Takada.

"Did you know, Mr. Pike," Takada said, "that when you enter a Kruppen Financial office, you are entering an official Terra Nova consulate?"

"I did indeed," Sandy said. Terra Nova was the first planet colonized by earth. It had been the point of origin for the other colonies. It still enjoyed a unique diplomatic status as a result. One aspect was other planets looked to Terra Nova to negotiate resolutions to interplanetary disagreements. Terra Nova also had the most stringent laws to protect personal financial data. As a result, many referred to it as the New Switzerland of old earth. "And I appreciate your government's maintenance of confidentiality in certain financial matters."

"I grew up on Terra Nova," Takada said.

Sandy was intrigued. "I've only visited once. I thought it was amazing. The cities are so much larger, and there are so many more people than I am accustomed to seeing."

"How much of Terra Nova's history did they teach you in school?" Takada asked.

"Not much," Sandy admitted. "It was considered ancient history, like the demise of earth and the departure from Mars. But, I always wanted to know more."

"You know that, as earth died, the most powerful governments established colonies on Mars, right?" Takada asked.

Sandy nodded.

"When Terra Nova was discovered, those major powers planned to stay intact after the move to Terra Nova. They each planned to seize one of Terra Nova's three main continents. What actually happened was different. As each colony ship arrived, the passengers aboard laid claim to the best real estate available. Instead of being new centers of power, the three continents became a hodge-podge of settlements from all three.

"Over time, these settlements coalesced into new continental nation-states that had their own distinct identities. Each sponsored separate colonization efforts. Once established, the colonies quickly staked out their independence. That forced change on Terra Nova. The colonies all had unified planetary governments. Terra Nova's different and competing nation-states put us at an economic disadvantage. To compete, we formed a homogenous government. For those who disagreed with government policy, they now had a selection of different planets to which they could migrate."

"I never knew most of that," Sandy admitted. "Our history lessons focused on the formation of the Alliance."

"Sorry," Takada apologized. "I'm probably boring you. I've always been interested in history. A couple of thousand years before the demise of earth, a man said, 'To not know what happened before you were born is to remain always a child.' I guess I took his words to heart."

"Don't apologize," Sandy said. "I enjoyed hearing it."

"Is there anything else I can help you with?" the banker asked.

"Yes," Sandy replied, "I'm hoping you can recommend a lawyer who can draft a partnership document."

"I am a lawyer," he stated.

"I do not know if one of my potential partners has an account with your firm," Sandy said with a shrug. "No offense meant, but it might be better to use someone not affiliated with my investment house."

"Understood," he said, smiling. "In that case, I would recommend Sarah Simpson. Should I ask her to contact you?"

With that business done, Sandy felt a sense of relief. Carrying almost twelve million credits around on a piece of silicon and plastic the size of his thumbnail had made him anxious. Now that it had been safely transferred, he could almost feel the tension leaving his body.

The next item on the agenda was their meeting with McAllister at eleven hundred. Sandy met up with Portia, Mike and Alison in McAllister's office a few minutes early. McAllister came out to greet them and ushered them into the same conference room as before.

"I have prepared the estimates on the work you listed," McAllister began. "I have also drawn up an estimate for some minor hull work. Some pinhole breaches in the outer hull should be addressed. They'll only get worse if you leave them. They're a consequence of the ship being abandoned so long in space. I've also drawn up some numbers on optional enhancements that I think you might want to consider."

McAllister sent the files to their comm units. Sandy quickly opened them and scrolled down to get a sense of the total. The work of installing the 105 mm cannon, the new drive units and nacelles, the plasma shield generators, the sensor nodes, and running EMP-proof wiring conduit was surprisingly reasonable. The total for these items came to just over half a million credits. The hull repairs added almost another 200,000. Sandy winced at that.

The optional enhancements, though, were nearly a million credits. There were only two: one labeled frame reinforcement, which was over 300,000, and another titled missile system, which was 495,000. Sandy looked up and caught Portia's eye. She squinted back at him with a slightly disapproving look.

"What is the frame reinforcement for?" Sandy asked.

"You're putting much more powerful EM drives on the ship," McAllister explained. "The frame wasn't built to handle that kind of strain. Heydrich & Sauer overbuilt their ships, but not by as much as you will need. The frame might last a year or two, but eventually, it would begin to buckle. The time to reinforce it is now when we have the drives off. I guarantee it will last the foreseeable life of the ship, even with the new drives."

Sandy glanced at Portia. She nodded in understanding and acceptance. Sandy then asked about the other option.

"Why do we need a missile system? The military hasn't used missiles in over a hundred years?" Sandy inquired.

"No, they haven't," McAllister responded. "And if this were a military vessel up against military targets, I would never recommend it. But most of the potential trouble I think you might encounter is not military—it's going to be converted civilian ships. These civilian ships will not have a military-grade defense system. That means no anti-missile defense and no exterior shielding. Nor will they have EMP-shielded components and conduits, like the *Alice May*. With your cannon, you can blow any potential threats into pieces. If that's all you want, have at it. If, however, you would rather take hostile ships and capture them, intact, then I would suggest a missile system with EMP warheads."

"I see," Sandy replied, as noncommittally as he could. McAllister's idea was a good one. Sandy's mind was racing, thinking about the possibilities. He forced himself to stop and get back to the moment. "We'll need to discuss that amongst ourselves"

"The quote for the missile system does not include any missiles," McAllister clarified. "Those would be extra, and they *are* expensive. We can manufacture them here in my yard, but they'll likely run a half-million each, if not more. The advantage is being able to bring back a captured ship intact and sell it."

"Understood," Sandy stated. "So, the work we asked for, plus the hull repairs and the enhancements, comes to 1.5 million credits, give or take. Correct?"

"Correct," McAllister confirmed.

"We discussed your interest in becoming an investor last night, Tom," Sandy said. "Tell us what you were thinking."

"I'm prepared to make the repairs, with the optional enhancements, plus provide your first five EMP missiles, in exchange for a fifteen percent partnership stake," McAllister stated.

Sandy merely laughed in response. The others, Portia, Mike and Alison, had the sense to keep quiet and betray no feeling about the matter. When Sandy stopped laughing, he simply shook his head no.

"We have the resources, Tom, to pay cash for these repairs, including your optional enhancements. We certainly aren't looking to give away such a sizeable chunk of our operation. Go ahead and draw up a contract for the original work we specified, the hull repair and hull reinforcement. Give us a day or two to decide about the missile system. We need to puzzle through it."

"I can have a contract to you later today," McAllister confirmed.

"That will be fine," Sandy said. "We'll have our lawyer look it over and get back to you."

On their way back to the courier ship, it was clear that Portia, Mike and

Alison wanted to talk. Sandy shushed them. When they closed the hatch on the courier, he told them, "Now we can talk."

"Do you really have that kind of money?" Portia asked.

"I do," Sandy replied. "It will make a dent, but I could do what I said—pay for the repairs in cash. Naturally, I'd prefer not to."

"I noticed you didn't counter-offer," Alison pointed out.

"That was intentional," Sandy grinned. "I want him to think we don't need him that much. I estimate this ship will net us about 1.5 million credits every year, on top of our salaries. If he donates the labor and materials to us, he's out of pocket only about two-thirds of what he quoted us. If we gave him a fifteen percent share, his return on the investment would be between twelve and fifteen percent annually, depending on his actual costs. I'm guessing his rate of return would be perhaps even higher. Portia, you have some investments. What sort of return have you been getting?"

"Shit," Portia spat. "I'm lucky if I can get three percent."

"But we're going to be a bit riskier than buying a stock on the exchange," Mike pointed out.

"Perhaps," Alison said, "but not by much, considering our defenses and armament. What about the missile system? Could that change the equation?"

"Only in his favor," Sandy pointed out. "If we manage to capture a vessel every year, or even every other year, that increases our net substantially. That increases his return. Remember, he's staying here at Providence and not risking life or limb."

"So, what do you plan to do with him?" Portia asked.

"Let him stew," Sandy answered. "See if he comes back with a more reasonable number. I know we talked ten percent last night, but now I'm thinking five."

The women nodded in agreement. "What about the missile system?" Mike asked. "Do we want it?"

Sandy looked at them to gauge their interest. "Hell, yes, I want it," he said. "There's a problem, though. How do we take control of the disabled ship?"

"We would need combat armor," Alison surmised, "and people trained to use it."

"Any of you know any Alliance Marines?" Sandy asked, "who might be able to sneak away with their combat armor before the HUWs arrive?"

"I think we should just hire mercs," Alison commented.

"Mercs?" Mike asked.

"Mercenaries," Alison clarified. "Soldiers for hire. They have combat armor and are trained to use it. If we hire them, we don't need to consider adding any other partners. I have some contacts."

"Is that something we'll be looking to do?" Mike asked. "That seems to me to be on the wrong side of the law. I didn't sign up for that." Portia nodded in agreement.

29

"You're right," Sandy said after a moment. "It's not the sort of thing we'll be looking to do. But, that said, it would not surprise me if we face some challenges during the first year or two we begin operations."

"Just like on *Ali Kat*," Portia commented. Turning to Mike, she explained, "Sandy, Ali and I were assigned to a ship like this that ONI built. We were having problems with smuggling and piracy on the borders with the Free Republics since all the frigates were pulled away to the war zone and convoy duty. Our first couple of runs, we had several people gunning for us."

"The same thing happened after you two moved on, and we moved the ship to a different sector," Alison added.

Sandy continued, "We'll be moving in and taking business away from someone, or several someones, and I would expect them to react to our presence. I don't think we'll be looking for opportunities, but I have a hunch that some opportunities might present themselves early on."

"Mike," Alison commented, "I don't think any of us want to become pirates or even smugglers. I would expect our existing competition to react negatively to our entrance to the market. I can tell you from my experience that those types of operators are a lot shadier than we intend to be. They might not attack us in space—it might be on a station. That's another good reason to hire a couple of mercs—for personal security."

"Like bodyguards?" Portia asked.

"Exactly," Alison confirmed, "or security experts if you'd rather think of it that way. Face it, none of you have needed to face the prospect of someone recognizing you and trying to kill you while you're walking down a corridor. You're all navy—all your conflict has been in space. From what I've seen, I can tell you that our existing competitors generally have a couple of guys in their crews who are there for muscle—thugs, really. They might help shove cargo around one day, or show up at a slow-to-pay customer's office and look threatening that afternoon, or even assault or kill a rival, given the opportunity. So, having a couple of mercs in our employ gives us an edge."

"Trained thugs," Mike commented.

"Exactly," Alison confirmed.

"I don't think we need to decide right now," Sandy offered. "I believe there's a fair chance that one of our competitors will try to take us out. With the weaponry we're installing, if they try to do it in space, we'll be in little danger—we can destroy them. But the idea of capturing them and turning their attack into a revenue-generating opportunity for us appeals to me. I wouldn't expect our competition to continue making those sorts of attacks for long in either case. It won't be a regular part of our business. The idea of hiring people who can help protect us when we're on a station, and train us to protect ourselves better—that to me has merit. Let's all think about it a bit more. In the meantime, we need to contact our lawyer."

"Lawyer?" Portia asked.

"Yes, to draw up our partnership agreement and to look over the contracts that McAllister will send."

The meeting with the lawyer turned out to be a bit more complicated than Sandy had expected. Setting up their new partnership was the easiest part. Sarah Simpson, the attorney, had suggested establishing a corporation rather than a partnership, explaining the benefits of doing so and the liabilities of partnerships. Simpson recommended basing the company on Providence due to favorable tax laws. Establishing ownership of the *Alice May* was slightly more complicated. According to laws governing salvage, the *Alice May* was theirs. They needed to file certain documents with the Inter-Planetary Court on Terra Nova before they could be issued a title. Simpson assured them there would be no problem; it would merely take some time. She also agreed to review the contracts that McAllister would send them.

The least troublesome issue was establishing ownership of the courier ship. McAllister had already provided a clean title in the name of one of Alison's intelligence identities. With the title, Simpson could re-register it and get a new, clean title with the corporation as the owner.

Sandy contacted McAllister after they finished with the lawyer. He asked McAllister to send the contracts to Simpson for review. Rather than speaking over a line that could be monitored, he asked McAllister to meet to discuss another issue.

Only Sandy and Alison went to this meeting. McAllister tilted his head to the side and looked at them. "If I were as rude as you were yesterday," he said, "I'd laugh at you."

Sandy blushed. "It was meant to be a negotiating strategy," he tried to explain.

McAllister looked at him coldly for a moment, then smiled. "Hell, I know that. I'm just busting your balls, Sandy."

"Good to know," Sandy said, blushing again.

"You're going to have to work on your negotiation skills," McAllister commented. "The laugh seemed a little forced, as though you'd been planning on responding that way to whatever I offered."

"You got me," Sandy admitted, "but what you asked for was not close to what we were thinking."

"What were you thinking?" Tom asked.

"Five," Alison interjected. "Five percent. This isn't a negotiation. You're also going to throw in four of the EMP missiles. You'll pay for the work done. Five percent—no counter-offers, no haggling, take it or leave it."

Sandy looked at her, open-mouthed.

"The two of you were about to slap your dicks on the table to measure," she explained. "I'd rather skip that."

"Done," McAllister said, chuckling, extending his hand to shake. "It's a little less than what I hoped for, but it's fair. I'll throw in the EMP missiles because if you use even one of them, I might sell dozens to other folks."

"One thing I need to point out," Sandy explained. "In talking about the missile system amongst ourselves, you understand we will not be looking for trouble of that type. It will not be a part of our business model. In the beginning, I expect we'll see some people challenge us. I'd certainly like to take advantage of their misguided thinking. Still, once we establish ourselves in the sector, I doubt we'll face those challenges."

"Understood," Tom confirmed. "I agree that after the first few trips, those opportunities will probably dry up. If you were to pursue it after that, you'd be going against the grain of who you seem to be. You guys are clearly Alliance Navy, or were until a couple of weeks ago—I don't think your mindset would adjust well to being a pirate. To be honest, I don't even see you guys as being comfortable with, how should I say, evasion of normal customs duties?"

"We've actually had more experience with that than you'd think, Tom," Sandy stated, "but I agree. The special capabilities of this ship will provide us with a unique market niche. I don't think we'll need to entertain anything of the other."

"If it's acceptable," Tom said, "I'd like to get started as soon as possible. I know your lawyer, and she won't find anything too objectionable in the contract I sent. Have her send me some documentation of my share in the company, and we're all set."

Sandy had one other chore to perform. He asked the advice of Kruppen to learn from whom he could purchase insurance. Kruppen put him in touch with Lloyd's, the largest and most reputable firm that offered insurance for starships. What followed was a series of meetings with the representative from Lloyd's. She had difficulty understanding the enhancements that were being made to the *Alice May*. She delegated the issue up the ladder to her boss, who then bounced it up to someone who then delegated it upwards to a vice president, Regis Smith. Smith came to McAllister's shipyard to see for himself what was going on. While he tried to look as though there was nothing out of the ordinary, Sandy could tell he was astounded.

Another series of meetings followed, where Smith asked Sandy about the cost of replacing particular components. Smith tried to substitute more easily obtainable items, and Sandy needed to correct him. He pointed Smith toward the black market, informing Smith that even there, what was available would be an inadequate substitution for the equipment on the *Alice May*. Finally, Smith summoned Sandy to his office.

"My researchers could only determine pricing on about a third of the more unique enhancements to your ship, Mr. Pike," Smith stated. "Even though you had mentioned that some of them would be inadequate replacements for the equipment now being installed. The cost of the parts has climbed over 200 million credits—and that is only for roughly a third of them."

"Are you able to estimate the rest?" Sandy asked.

Smith shook his head in frustration. "What I am trying to say, politely, Mr. Pike, is that there is simply no way to determine a value for your ship. It is, quite literally, priceless. I needed to take your file to the Board, and they decided that we can offer you a binder for your ship. It will be limited to a maximum of 100 million credits. In addition, because of the powerful weaponry you have on board, the Board decided that your premiums will be based on the rates charged to the military contractors we provide with insurance and not on the same basis as a normal fast transport freighter. The premiums will be expensive, I wish to warn you. I would also venture a guess that there is no other firm, anywhere, who would offer to insure such a vessel."

"May I see the quote?" Sandy asked.

Smith handed the folder over to Sandy. He opened it and skipped through the opening pages, trying to find the annual premium. It was on the fourth page. It came to just under a million credits per year. Fortunately, Kruppen had prepared him. When he asked his rep at the bank what he guessed the premium would be, the man smiled sadly and said, "Between 800,000 and a million per year."

Sandy looked up. Smith was sitting up, with the expression of a man who feared the worst: either an argument or an unhappy customer. Sandy shrugged calmly and asked, "Where do I sign?"

Work on the *Alice May* began immediately. In the negotiations, Sandy had not thought to ask McAllister what sort of turnaround time there would be or where they might fit in his schedule of existing work. It turned out to be unnecessary.

After the paperwork cleared, McAllister asked if he could begin right away. He explained he had other jobs already scheduled, but he was so intrigued by this project that he wanted to "get his hands dirty." He assigned himself as the foreman on the project, something Portia learned from the yard workers that he had not done in several years.

Sandy and the others found small apartments on Providence Station. They were busy for a few days furnishing them and making them livable. Patrick Boyle and Tim Warburton arrived about ten days after McAllister began work on the ship, having received their demobilization papers from the Alliance Navy. They were their usual exuberant selves. When they learned that the *Alice May* was going to be more powerful than the *Ali Kat*, in which they had both served briefly, their excitement level grew.

Sandy used the local Kruppen office to help find a shipping agent. When they had served on the *Ali Kat*, they did not use a shipping agent. Shipping agents would not touch any illegal business, so they would not have associated themselves with the *Ali Kat*. In this case, though, Sandy wanted to stay away from smuggling and piracy. He planned to establish the *Alice May* as the safest choice for high-value cargo—legitimate cargo. Sandy and Ali interviewed several shipping agents. Sandy and Ali would share with the prospective agents that their ship could survive any sort of threat short of a naval frigate without getting into specifics. A couple of them did not understand. They didn't make it to the next round.

Kevin Moon, the representative from Bharwani & Minami, was the most enthusiastic and immediately grasped the value of a ship like the *Alice May*. He feared that the fringes of what had been Alliance-controlled space would become somewhat lawless until the Hegemony was able to impose control. Moon agreed that the process might take as long as a decade. As a result, he felt confident that he would have no difficulty in finding business for them.

In the second meeting, Moon brought a list of customers who could use the *Alice May* immediately. He was slightly disappointed to learn that the ship was not yet ready but confident that most of these customers would wait. Sandy and Ali glanced at one another and offered to sign the contract right then. Of course, it didn't hurt that Sandy's account manager at Kruppen had recommended them to begin with.

Boyle and Warburton (or Puss and Stick, as they referred to each other) haunted the McAllister shipyard. At first, they made a nuisance of themselves, asking questions almost non-stop. Finally, Tom McAllister decided the best way to deal with them was to put them to work. He later told Mike Xie that they were the most cost-effective workers he'd ever had—since he didn't pay them a thing. They actually came up with some valuable suggestions along the way.

Ali suggested they meet with a mercenary firm with an office on Providence Station and a more extensive operation on the planet itself. "Manlius Military Bureau is the best outfit I know," she explained. "They're not the biggest, but my own experience and what I've heard about them from my former colleagues tells me they are the ones we want."

"Why?" Sandy asked.

"A couple of reasons," she said. "Mercenary companies often try to renegotiate contracts in the middle of a job—when the customer is over a barrel and has no choice. I've never heard of Manlius doing that. They do a thorough job of identifying contingencies in advance, so there aren't any surprises. It often makes them look more expensive than their competitors. In reality, they often end up being slightly less costly. If something comes up in the middle of an op that neither party could have foreseen, they deal with it. They have a reputation for being able to keep confidences. In our case, that's important. We don't want people to know exactly what the *Alice May*'s capabilities are, other than that they shouldn't mess with us."

"Fair enough," Sandy commented. "This is all pretty foreign to me. If you don't mind, I'll sit down, shut up, and let you run this."

Ali smiled and patted his hand. "I knew I liked you for a reason," she cracked.

They met with Lieutenant Colonel Tumperi. Ali explained in broad strokes that they were entering the business of secure, fast transport. Their ship had unique capabilities, and they expected existing competition to challenge them during the first year or two. Without sharing details, she informed Tumperi that anyone who confronted them in space would end up with a disabled ship.

"We would like to hire a couple of your people, with combat armor, who can take control of a disabled competitor," she stated. "We will also need to contract with you for pickup services to collect the crew of a disabled ship."

"Where?" Tumperi asked.

"Unknown."

"When you say disabled," Tumperi asked, "will life support systems be affected?"

"Yes," Ali responded.

"You will need to provide oxygen, water, and heat unless you plan to put the crew in escape pods."

"I think escape pods are the better option," Ali stated, "from both a security and logistical viewpoint. It might turn out that some of the captured crews are wanted criminals. We will carry a limited supply of oxygen and water, and a heating unit in the event their escape pods are inoperable, but it would be preferable to use the escape pods."

"If there are wanted criminals and rewards for their capture, how do you — "

"Negotiable," Ali responded crisply.

"What will you do with the ship?" he asked.

"Send a salvage tug to retrieve it and bring it back."

"Where?"

"Right now, Providence," she replied, "but we may make other arrangements if there are closer facilities. We will then sell them. Salvage laws are on our side, so we would own any ship that attacked us and failed. I assure you we will not be looking for trouble or deliberately provoking anyone."

"Are you saying that you will not shoot first?" Tumperi asked, slightly incredulous.

"That's exactly what I'm saying," Ali answered.

"Your ship's 'unique capabilities' must be pretty impressive," Tumperi commented.

"They are," Sandy interjected.

"Once we have a contract, colonel," Ali stated, "we will share some details regarding those unique capabilities."

"Understood."

"We will also need personal security when we are off the ship," she requested. "Our competitors may figure out that they have a better chance of neutralizing us on station or down-planet than in open space."

"How many in your crew?"

"Six. We can simplify things by restricting ourselves to only traveling in pairs."

"That won't be required," Tumperi commented, "based on how I think we'll approach this. How much room will you have on your ship? How many additional personnel could you accommodate without strain?"

"Four," Sandy replied. "They will need to store the combat armor in the hold, though. The hold is included in the life-support system so they can access it at any time."

"Shouldn't be a problem," Tumperi responded. "Let me think about this. Ms. Lynch, I will probably have other questions before I can prepare a proposal, but I hope to get back to you promptly."

3

A few days later, Tumperi contacted them and asked to meet again. Then, when they arrived at the Manlius office, he had a proposal ready. He gave them a chance to read it. When they both looked up, he began.

"From what you described to me, you certainly won't be out looking for trouble, but from what my intelligence arm says, it's likely to find you—at least at first," Tumperi stated. "We recommend you take four of our operatives with you for at least the first year. As we approach the end of a year, we both would certainly want to re-evaluate that. Ordinarily, we would charge a flat monthly fee of 50,000 credits to engage four of our operatives, with combat armor, on a full-time basis. It will depend on travel time and resources required, as far as retrieval of personnel from any disabled ship. I cannot provide you with a blanket quote, but a schedule of rates is attached. If there are reward monies, we propose that Manlius Military collect the rewards and deduct them from the retrieval expense. Now, based on intelligence estimates, we would be willing to reduce the monthly fee to 30,000 credits. In exchange, you give us a ten percent share in the sale of any ships you neutralize and seize."

While Sandy was still trying to process the numbers in his head, Ali responded quickly, "No. If we grant you a ten percent share in any ships we snare, Manlius will charge no monthly fee. Nor will there be any fees for personal protection services when we're on station or down-planet. The retrieval fees should not be a problem unless I find your schedule of rates excessive."

Tumperi gave a rueful smile. "I apologize. I told our bean-counters that what they wanted wouldn't fly. Let's keep talking."

"If we snag even one ship, most likely a fast transport, even in fairly distressed condition, it will undoubtedly sell for well over 10 million credits," Ali explained. "The damage we do to it will be minimal, let me assure you.

Your ten percent share from only one ship far exceeds the aggregate of monthly fees for the first year. If we need to 'neutralize'—good word, by the way—any over-aggressive competitors, I estimate we will face at least three the first year until word spreads that we are not to be trifled with. I believe it might be more than three."

"In that case, your offer seems more than generous," Tumperi pointed out. "Why?"

"We are willing to offer a ten percent share because any proceeds from 'neutralized' competitors will be 'found money' for us. It's not a part of our business model," Ali responded. "Having a relationship with Manlius Military that is extremely profitable for you earns us goodwill that we might need in the future should something unforeseen occur. You also have customers who need the type of service we provide. Does that make sense?"

"Perfect sense," Tumperi agreed. "If you don't mind, I'd appreciate it if you could return in, say, an hour? I will run this by my superior—I'm certain she will agree—and get a new contract drafted."

"When you have the new contract drafted," Sandy said, "send a copy to Sarah Simpson. She'll review it. We can certainly meet with you again tomorrow after she has had a chance to look it over."

"That would be fine," Tumperi agreed.

Sandy was itching to talk with Ali on the way back to the ship but refrained until they were back aboard. Then, before he could start, she said, "I apologize for jumping in like that."

Sandy shook his head. "Don't worry about that. That didn't bother me at all."

"Whew," she sighed. "I was worried. This is all your baby, after all, and I just got thrown in at the last minute."

"I know I'm glad to have you, and I'll bet Portia is, too. What you proposed to him was not something I was going to come up with on my own," Sandy admitted.

"One thing I forgot to mention about Manlius is they do their homework," Ali explained. "I'm certain that they know you were Alliance Navy until recently. I think their initial proposal was based on that, which is why it was so far off from what I suggested. No offense intended, but that was the first time you've ever met a military contractor."

"But not yours," Sandy stated.

"I doubt they know who I am," Ali confessed. "You're fairly well known, but even without your medals, they would have been able to identify you from the intelligence they maintain. All they likely know about me is that I was a government employee—that could cover anything. I'm sure Lieutenant Colonel Tumperi is likely chewing someone a new asshole right now for underestimating me. If he'd entertained even the slightest suspicion that I was an ONI operative, he would never have made that initial proposal. As it is, he's professionally embarrassed right now."

"I don't know that he should be," Sandy said. "The 50,000 a month for four people sounds about right."

"Oh, that part is fine," she replied. "It was the offer of cutting it to 30,000 in exchange for ten percent of the sale of any ships we capture. That was based on their reading of you and your lack of knowledge."

"As you pointed out, the ten percent will work out to more than the monthly fee—a lot more," Sandy commented. "They were going for a double-dip."

"Right. The beauty of what I proposed is it doesn't hit our books as an expense, particularly during the first year when we are establishing ourselves. It has the opportunity to make them a great deal of money and having someone like Manlius Military on your side because you steered a lucrative business opportunity their way—well, friends like that are good to have."

"That part I understand completely," Sandy agreed. "The meeting didn't expose you in some way, did it?"

Ali laughed. "Not really. It points them in the right direction, but I doubt they'll find any proof. They might think I was ONI or AIS, but it won't be something they can verify. They might also think I was in the management & budget office or some other accounting function. It would likely cost them a lot of money to find out more, and I'm guessing they won't go to the expense. They'll file it away for future reference, though."

Sarah Simpson approved the contract that Manlius had sent after a brief discussion with Sandy and Ali. Their appointment with Manlius was at 09:00 station time the following day. When they arrived, they were ushered into the same conference room. Besides Tumperi, there was a dusky-skinned woman with the insignia of a full colonel.

"Commander Pike, Ms. Lynch, may I introduce Colonel Khavita Patel," Tumperi began, "my superior officer."

After sharing handshakes, they sat down. "We've reviewed the contract you prepared and are ready to sign," Sandy stated.

"We appreciate that," Patel said with a smile. "When would you need to begin?"

"Our ship is still undergoing refit," Sandy explained. "It is estimated to be six weeks from completion."

"Yes, your ship," Patel commented. "I'd like to learn more about her if you don't mind."

"Let's sign the contracts," Sandy replied, "then I'll share with you what you need to know."

They took care of signing the documents with thumbprints on a console. "Please," Patel asked. "Colonel Tumperi shared with me that you have deep confidence that you would survive any hostile encounter. He did not believe you were bluffing."

"The *Alice May* is, or will be once the refit is complete, a unique vessel. She was originally built by Heydrich & Sauer over a hundred years ago. Following an episode of reactor instability, she was abandoned by her owners and forgotten. We salvaged her and are upgrading certain systems. She will mount a 105mm photon cannon, have full defensive shielding similar to an Alliance light cruiser, a military-grade sensor suite, and a substantially improved power plant in addition to other refinements and enhancements. She will also carry missiles armed with EMP warheads."

Tumperi's mouth fell open, hearing this. Patel controlled her reaction a little better. "I must ask, Commander, whether these impressive components were obtained legally?" Patel inquired.

Sandy smiled. "I am not the subject of any criminal investigation related to them, and no one is or will be looking for them. Let's just say that we took advantage of the chaos caused by the Alliance's surrender to the HUWs and leave it at that."

Patel thought about this for a moment, then nodded her acceptance. "The *Alice May* will certainly enjoy a competitive advantage in these uncertain times," she said. "I can see now why you would not need to fire first in any encounter. I take it the EMP warheads are designed to disable any potential attacker without destroying them. Quite clever."

Sandy shrugged in response.

"I learned you are represented by Bharwani & Minami," she commented. "We share many of the same customers and, as colonel Tumperi suggested, several of them will probably engage your services. We will refer those clients to B & M."

"One last thing… Commander, we would like to have the members of your crew meet with one of our staff psychologists in the next few days," Tumperi requested.

Sandy raised his eyebrows, questioning.

"We are assigning four of our operatives to your ship. A fast transport is a small space, and they will probably be with you for months. We want to make sure that the people we assign will fit in with the rest."

Sandy pursed his lips appreciatively. "That makes perfect sense. I knew all the people who joined our operation from serving with them earlier. I wouldn't have included anyone who would cause friction."

"Precisely," Tumperi said.

"Commander, it has been a pleasure to meet you. You, as well, Ms. Lynch," Patel said, rising from her chair.

They met the Manlius operatives who would join them a couple of weeks later. It was an informal meeting. They gathered in a bar on the station. There were two women and two men, all reasonably attractive, seemingly intelligent, and obviously in peak physical condition. The two women, Heidi and

Cheyenne, were both tall, at about 180 centimeters. It was completely obvious to everyone that Stick and Puss were immediately smitten. Their wisecracking personas disappeared, replaced by a sober, mature demeanor, and both were uncharacteristically quiet. The two men, Bungo and Morgan, were physical opposites. Morgan was an imposing, barrel-chested, broad-shouldered, dark-skinned man, while Bungo was short and slight.

The conversation was formal at first but, after the first beer, picked up for everyone except Boyle and Warburton. Those two appeared tongue-tied for the first time Sandy could remember since they were snotty-nosed ensigns. Interestingly, the Manlius employees knew a bit about everyone's background, except Ali. Bungo had been an Alliance Marine and showed his tattoo proudly to prove it. Morgan had been in the military for the non-aligned planet Noricum. Heidi and Cheyenne had both served in the Free Republics' Special Forces.

They seemed pleased with their assignment, even after Sandy warned them it would likely be weeks or months of boredom with only occasional need for their services. None of them seemed put off by that. They also expressed willingness to help out wherever needed on the ship. Puss jumped on that suggestion, immediately offering to teach Cheyenne anything she wanted to know. Sandy managed to stifle his laugh.

Work on the ship proceeded quickly. With Boyle and Warburton having been assigned the job of pulling conduit, they provided daily status reports without Sandy needing to bother Tom McAllister. The day the 105mm cannon was installed, Puss and Stick were nearly beside themselves with excitement. Precisely on the day he had promised, McAllister presented the ship for inspection. All six of the crew joined in. As usual, there were a handful of items that still needed attention. However, it was far fewer than Portia and Mike had expected. It took another two days to clear those up, then it was time to put the ship through trials.

Sandy pulled away from Providence Station and took them to the nearest tramline. Once clear of traffic control, he opened up the throttle and was absolutely delighted at how quickly the ship responded. They entered the tramline and jumped into hyperspace. Their route was not on a regular shipping lane, so they did not expect to encounter any other ships. They passed through that system and jumped into the tramline to the next.

Sandy had explained to his crew that they were doing this to get away from any prying eyes. The system they were headed for contained an asteroid belt. It would provide Stick and Puss the opportunity to calibrate the targeting of the cannon. Sandy had asked for a targeting laser to be installed on the top of the hull in the ship's refit, centered perfectly on the ship's axis. This would enable them to adjust the targeting of the gun precisely. The laser would also provide a secure communications method to ships not linked by quantum particle communications systems, known for centuries as kewpies.

Once they left the second tramline and re-entered normal space, it took 20 hours for them to establish a position within range of the asteroid belt. Boyle and Warburton needed four-and-a-half hours to adjust the targeting. Eventually, they were satisfied that the gun was perfectly calibrated to the targeting system, to the limit of its range. At that point, Sandy allowed everyone the chance to blow up some rocks. Mike Xie seemed particularly enthused after his turn.

"I don't think I could ever get tired of that, Sandy," he sighed, a big smile on his face.

They returned the way they came. Sandy sent messages to Manlius and to Bharwani & Minami, letting them know the *Alice May* was ready for her first run. By the time they returned to the Providence system, B & M had confirmed that there was cargo for them and provided a dock number and appointment time. Sandy sent that information to Manlius. They confirmed their operatives would meet the ship there.

Using the services of a first-class shipping agent eliminated the need to meet clients and negotiate rates. Sandy had found that the most unpleasant part of his time on the *Ali Kat* and was happy to allow B & M to take that off his hands. Their first cargo was rare earths, going to Galatia, a non-aligned system. Galatia was similar to Providence in terms of its location. It was in the middle of the blob of systems of settled space, accessible to the Alliance, the HUWs, and the Free Republics. It was also open to the non-aligned systems on the periphery. The load would nearly fill the hold of the *Alice May,* and its estimated value was an astounding 135 million credits.

Based on that fact alone, Sandy felt sure someone might attempt to intercept them. When they arrived at the loading dock, the four Manlius soldiers were there, accompanied by Lieutenant Colonel Tumperi. He warned Sandy that he also believed it likely that they would come under attack.

The loading, completely automated, took less than fifteen minutes. Sandy signed for the shipment with his thumbprint. Returning to the bridge, he had to squeeze past the containers in the hold. The four Manlius soldiers were stowing their combat armor. Stick and Puss were lingering nearby. Sandy shook his head with a smile.

The *Alice May* pulled away from Providence Station and set off on the four-jump trip to Galatia. Once free from traffic control, Sandy opened up the throttle and could not detect any difference in the ship's performance, even with the additional mass of the cargo. Once he set the autopilot, he called everyone together.

"Starting now, I want to discuss with you what our standard operating procedure should be. For the next year or more, we will exit tramlines before their terminus. We will vary the amount from jump to jump, subject to the demands of our schedule. From now on, whenever we exit a tramline, I want shields up instantly. We will not fire first."

Warburton and Boyle frowned at this.

"We will not fire first," Sandy repeated, looking at the two until they nodded in reluctant agreement. "There are legal reasons, guys, that are part of salvage law. Plus, I promised the folks at Manlius we wouldn't. I doubt either of you wants to get Morgan, Bungo, Heidi, or Cheyenne mad at you."

Portia, Mike and Ali smirked at this, knowing how interested the two were in Heidi and Cheyenne.

"From our experience and what Ali saw after we left the *Ali Kat*, the biggest weapon we are likely to encounter will be a 40mm. True, we did run into the one 75mm cannon, but even so, our shielding is so robust that a 75 mm won't strain it. We likely won't need to use the big gun at all. The EMP warheads will be our primary weapon. Puss and Stick, I would like you to begin training Portia, Mike and Ali on sensors. Let them know once you have a plan put together."

"Should we encounter a hostile, we let them take the first shot. We fire an EMP warhead and disable their ship. Then, our combat-armored friends here will access the hostile and force the crew into the escape pods. We will scan the crap out of any hostile to make sure there aren't any people hiding. Once the escape pods are activated—and I'd like to activate them without ejecting them, when possible—our guys come back aboard, and we call in a tug to retrieve the ship and Manlius to come to pick up the pods."

"Boss," Stick asked, "I hate to ask since you made it clear, but when we were on the *Ali Kat*, we shot first."

"When we were on the *Ali Kat*, we were working for someone else," Sandy explained. "We didn't care about the salvage value of someone who attacked us; we simply wanted to eliminate the threat. We work for ourselves now. If we can prove we were defending ourselves and, in the process, we disable our attacker, salvage law allows us to take the disabled vessel as our own. We can then sell it to the highest bidder. A fast transport, even in terrible condition, will fetch more than 10 million credits. You and Puss have a share of this company. I'll let you do the math."

They made the first of four jumps on the way to Galatia. They exited the tramline two light-minutes short of its terminus. No ships were waiting nearby. As they entered the system, Sandy plotted a standard fuel conservation course into the navigation system. There were no other ships immediately apparent anywhere in the system. After a day, Sandy changed to a least-time course, figuring that the shift in direction might force anyone lying in wait to reveal themselves. Nothing happened. They made the second jump, again exiting the tramline early, this time by three light-minutes. As before, no ships were lurking by the standard terminus.

In studying the current positioning of the planets in this system, there was a gas giant with six moons located in a spot where either a least-time or fuel conservation course would bring a traveler nearly within range of even a

40mm photon cannon. Sandy didn't even have a chance to bring it up when Mike mentioned it. Sandy reflected after hearing Mike speak up. When he had met Mike, he was a typical engineering officer—somewhat isolated from the rest of the crew aboard PAS *Chapman*. That was actually a good thing in Mike's case since *Chapman* had been a mess before Sandy's arrival. Sandy and Portia had only a limited time to turn things around, and Mike had joined in those efforts with enthusiasm. He had declared to Sandy that he wanted to be a good officer, not just a good engineering officer. His studying the system's layout and bringing it to Sandy's attention was a sign that he was no longer confining himself to only engineering matters.

As they drew closer to the center of the system, Stick and Puss used it as an opportunity to demonstrate what they had learned a few years before from a petty officer. They worked individually with Mike, Portia and Ali, showing how to read the current radiation signature from the planet and then match it against the radiation signature in the astrographic files. They allowed each of them to make the same discovery—there was a ship trying to hide there. Sandy was impressed at the way the two handled it. Each of their three 'students' was elated to have been able to spot the difference and identify it as an emissions signature typical of a fast transport.

It would take another twenty-three hours for the *Alice May* to close within range at their current rate. Sandy actually lengthened that time by reducing speed. He did not want to overshoot their potential attacker and need to double back any more than was necessary. Then, he contacted Tom McAllister and informed him he needed a salvage tug to collect a fast transport and gave him the coordinates.

"You got one already?" McAllister asked.

"Oh, no," Sandy replied casually. "We're still more than a day away. We'll nab them when we get there. I just wanted to get things moving ahead of time."

Sandy had allowed the gravity from the star at the center of the system to slow them down as they approached the gas giant. As they drew within cannon range, the sensors picked up that a ship had activated its drives, climbing away from the planet. A laser communicator aimed at them sent a message.

"Heave-to immediately. You are within range of our photon cannon, and we will not hesitate to use it. You have no chance of escape. If you value your lives, heave-to immediately."

Puss was on the bridge. "Gosh," he exclaimed, with faked nervousness, "I'd better heave-to immediately then."

He engaged reverse thrust at the normal maximum, allowing the hostile ship to approach. Once their attacker was fully clear of the planet's exosphere, he commented, "Boy, I'd better not do anything to piss them off and make them fire at us, like this — "

He engaged forward thrust again, as though he were going to try to run away. The hostile ship fired its 40mm cannon at the *Alice May*. The attacker continued to fire on the *Alice May* without any effect, her plasma defensive shields not even strained.

Portia was at the firing controls. She looked at Sandy. He nodded. A hatch on the lower, or ventral, face of the ship opened, and an EMP missile emerged on the end of a mechanical arm. The arm released the weapon, giving it a gentle shove to carry it further from the ship. When the computer signaled that the missile was far enough away from the ship, Portia keyed in the ignition instructions.

The missile sped straight and true towards their attacker. In less than 30 seconds, it closed the distance. Once at the optimal distance from the target, the warhead detonated, generating a powerful electromagnetic pulse that overwhelmed all the electrical circuitry on the ship. As a result, its computers were irreparably damaged. In most ships, only the most essential systems were protected against electrical surges of this type. This included the reactors, the inertial dampener, and the mass compensator. It usually did not include gravity and life-support.

"Thank you for saving us, Mama P," Puss called out with feigned relief.

"Puss," she fired back with mock anger, "don't make me drag you out and hurt you in front of our guests. Unless you want Heidi and Cheyenne to see you get your butt whupped."

The silence and complete absence of a witty response from the bridge almost made Sandy laugh out loud. Moments later, a red-faced Boyle stuck his head out of the hatch. "Sorry, Mama P," he said. "I was just having fun."

"I know," she replied smugly. "So was I."

At this, Sandy did laugh out loud.

Puss returned to the bridge and maneuvered the *Alice May* close to the other ship. Heidi and Bungo were suited up in their combat armor. They exited the airlock and used their suits to fly over to the other vessel. They used the manual controls to open its airlock and entered. Their combat armor had camera feeds, and Sandy and the others watched the action unfold.

One crewman on the other ship had a fléchette pistol in hand. When he saw the Manlius soldiers in combat armor, he murmured, "Crap," and pushed the gun away. Heidi's suit had a deep metallic voice filter. She announced, "If you wish to live, go to an escape pod now."

The five crewmen they could see began doing that, struggling in the zero gravity. Bungo went to the bulkhead by the hatch and rapped on it. "You too, buddy," he said, "unless you want to die. It would probably be the cold rather than the lack of oxygen. I'm told it's a peaceful way to go after you stop shivering if that's your choice."

A nearly invisible seam opened on the bulkhead to reveal a man who had been hiding. He looked at the others of the crew and nodded. They opened the escape pods and entered them. When the three escape pods were loaded, Heidi and Bungo closed the hatches. They activated the pods without ejecting them from the ship. Bungo and Heidi exited and returned to the *Alice May*.

When they returned after stowing their armor in the hold, Portia was curious. "How did you know that guy was hiding?" she asked Bungo. "I picked him up on a scan but hadn't called it over yet."

"Heat signature," Bungo answered. "He showed up clear as day on infrared."

Sandy double-checked to make sure the disabled ship, registered as the *Prudence Rose* on the planet of Noricum, would not drift into danger after they left. Once satisfied, he transmitted its current coordinates and course to both Tom McAllister and Manlius. A bit more than an hour later, he received a message from Lieutenant Colonel Tumperi.

"Congratulations, Commander. We learned that the United Worlds have active arrest warrants for the six currently sleeping in their pods. We verified their identity, taking the camera feeds from the armor and running them against facial recognition software. The offered reward for their capture is more than the cost of retrieval. Advise how you want to handle the excess."

Sandy conferred briefly with Portia and Ali, who both recommended keeping the money on account with Manlius. A future retrieval might not involve any sort of reward, so this would help offset that expense. Ali noticed Sandy was uncomfortable about aiding the Hegemony, even by recovering criminals.

"Sandy, last time I checked, their credits spend just the same was as any," she pointed out.

"I know," Sandy admitted. "It just feels weird, though."

A few hours later, after Sandy had just begun his sleep period, someone entered his darkened cabin. Startled awake, the visitor shushed him. Moments later, he felt a warm body enter his bunk and back into him. Quick examination with his hands informed him it was a female body, with her clothing absent. A quick process of elimination—not heavyset enough to be Portia and not tall enough to be Cheyenne or Heidi—and he whispered, "Ali? What are you — "

"Shhh. Just hold me, okay?" she whispered back.

Sandy's body betrayed him as he reacted to the presence of an attractive nude female snuggling up against him. Embarrassed, he tried to shift away. Ali reached back and prevented him from doing so. She then reached back and grasped his right arm, pulling it over herself and placing his hand firmly on her breast, holding it in place with her own. Ali sighed, and Sandy could feel her body relax. Sandy could smell traces of the shampoo she used on her hair and the soap she used on her body. While his mind was spinning, his body also appreciated the comfort of her closeness and relaxed. Despite himself, he fell asleep quickly. His last conscious thought was realizing he had not slept in the same bed with anyone since Leezy, two years before.

When he woke, Ali was gone. He briefly wondered if he had imagined it until he smelled the scent of her hair on the pillow. Instead of providing reassurance, it sent his mind spinning again. He showered and dressed, then went to make himself something to eat.

He was hoping to speak with Ali. While he did see her, she was engrossed in conversation with Morgan. Sandy would have felt awkward interrupting. She kept herself out of Sandy's way all day. When he saw her, she was always with other people. Finally, his sleep period came again, and he returned to his cabin, undressed, and climbed in bed. He stayed awake.

Sure enough, within a short time, she slipped into his dark cabin. He heard what he thought were her clothes slipping off, and then she climbed into bed. She scooted back into him. She reached back for his hand and brought it to her chest, holding it there.

His voice clearly betraying his wide-awake state, he asked, "Why?"

"I'm lonely," she said quietly. "You're lonely. You're also broken. I thought we could be lonely together and that maybe it might make us feel better."

Sandy didn't know how to respond. He wanted to protest that he wasn't broken, but he realized that was a lie as he started to form the words. He and Ali had only talked once about personal issues and even then, only briefly. Yet he had imagined that the life she had chosen as an intelligence agent had left no place for any sort of romantic ties.

"Can we talk tomorrow?" he asked softly.

"Yes. Go to sleep."

When he stirred in the morning, she was already up and out of his cabin. He readied himself for the day and was about to get something to eat when she returned, shutting the hatch behind her. She sat on the edge of his bunk and patted next to her, indicating he should sit there. When he sat, she half-turned and took his hands.

"Hear me out before you go all mental on me, okay?"

Sandy nodded.

"I know more about you than I have any right to," she admitted. "I'm not obsessed or anything, but ever since our first assignment, I've kept tabs on you. Think of it as looking out for a friend. I know your girlfriend Elizabeth dropped you. I can only imagine what a hole that left in your life. I also know about the whole thing with Tobin and how poorly ONI handled it. I know what happened in Excelsus and in Ilex. I know how the navy left you in limbo after the Council replaced Dorsey until the surrender. I can see the effect of all these things on you."

Sandy began to speak, but she put her finger on his lips. "I'm not in love with you, Sandy. I don't know if I'm capable of that kind of emotion. I don't think I was wired that way. I do have a healthy case of 'like' for you, though. I'm also lonely. I chose a lonely career, so maybe I should have come to grips with it, but every so often, the loneliness rises up. I don't have friends. Friends are dangerous baggage that I've avoided. Of all the people I've met in the last ten years, you're the only one that has treated me like I could be a friend. It makes me feel less lonely. I don't know what compelled me to come into your cabin. It was the best sleep I've had in years, though. It felt so good, I came back again. I think I'd like to keep doing that, and other stuff, too."

Sandy looked nervous and cleared his throat. "Uh, this is all really different for me," he explained apologetically. "Obviously, I like you, Ali. I have since we met. You're certainly attractive and smart as hell. I'd like to count you among my friends but always have felt you enjoyed keeping your distance. I have to say, you surprised me the other night. It wasn't unpleasant, though. Far from it."

"Then I'll keep visiting," she said. "If it gets too strange or you start thinking of me as more than a friend, we'll cool it."

"Well, I have to warn you," Sandy stated. "I've never slept with anyone, in the grown-up sense of the word, without thinking of them as more than friends. It might be something I can't do. I have friends, some of them on this ship, but I realize I do miss the companionship I enjoyed the last two nights. Your presence was... comforting."

They faced no other threats on the rest of the journey to Galatia. Ali came and slept with Sandy every sleep period. She had adjusted the schedules accordingly, which Sandy only learned later. When they arrived at Galatia Station, they offloaded their cargo immediately. They learned from the B & M office that their outgoing load was not yet ready but should be within the next three days.

Galatia was a planet with an interesting niche. Just over 500 years before, a Congress on Artificial Intelligence decided that the creation of AIs would be confined to one system. Galatia was the planet selected. It was already the location of most of the leading AI companies. All the representatives to the Congress pledged that their governments would never attempt to seize Galatia. The planet was considered neutral territory by all.

The *Alice May*'s next cargo was a freshly constructed, unactivated positronic brain for a company on Corbulo in the Free Republics that made replacement human organs. Though its container would only take up a tiny amount of space in the hold, it was incredibly valuable. Sandy had been required to sign an additional contract for this shipment, guaranteeing that he would destroy the cargo before letting it out of his possession.

Since they had to wait until the cargo was ready, Sandy offered to let the rest of the crew visit Galatia Station to at least stretch their legs. He insisted no one go without an escort from one of the Manlius operatives, however. Boyle and Warburton quickly expressed an interest in getting off the ship, obviously hoping Cheyenne and Heidi would accompany them. Portia seemed happy to match up with Morgan. Mike shrugged his shoulders, realizing he would be paired with Bungo. The two of them got along well, but there was no hint of a romantic connection the way there was with the other pairings.

Puss and Stick looked at Sandy and asked whether he wanted to get off the ship as well. "Not really feeling the need, but if I do, I'm hoping that Ali would be my bodyguard."

Morgan started to object, but Portia shushed him. "She's ex-ONI," she explained quietly. "She's qualified." Morgan's eyebrows raised upon learning this about Ali, and he nodded slightly in acceptance.

They called a taxi to collect them. Sandy promised to share any updates he received from B & M about their departure. Once the eight of them left, Ali approached Sandy. Putting her hand on his chest, she directed him backwards into his cabin. They didn't emerge for several hours.

Later, the B & M rep updated Sandy that the cargo would be ready on the following day, around fifteen hundred station time. Sandy sent the information to the others. Now that he knew how long he'd be waiting, his usual restlessness made itself felt. Though he had just spent an energetic and active few hours with Ali, he was feeling cooped up.

"How would you like to go out to dinner?" he asked.

"On the station?" she inquired.

"Yeah. I don't know why, but suddenly, I seem to crave a steak and a baked potato. A real steak, not some vat-grown crap," Sandy clarified.

"Worked up an appetite, did we?" she teased. "Sure. That sounds good. Let me get cleaned up, and we can go."

It didn't take Ali long, and Sandy summoned a taxi. He asked the driver for a restaurant recommendation. The driver did not hesitate. "If money is no object, Barney's," he said. "There's a taxi stand right near it, too. Want to go?"

Sandy approved. Sitting next to Ali in the cab, he smelled perfume. That caught his attention, and he looked at her more carefully in the dim light of the cab. He couldn't be sure, but he thought she might have applied some make-up. Her eyes seemed accentuated in a way he hadn't noticed before. He didn't say anything, with the driver able to overhear.

When they exited onto the station, he offered her his arm and was smugly pleased when she took it. "Are we on a date?" he asked, teasing.

She gave him a cross look in response.

"Well, you look fabulous, and you smell divine," Sandy commented. "I don't know that I can recall seeing you with make-up or smelling perfume on you. I hope you didn't go to all that trouble for me. I'm a sure thing, as you have found out."

Ali used her free arm to reach across and punched him in the shoulder. Hard. She waited until they were seated in the restaurant before responding.

"I never really dated much when I was in school," she explained. "I wasn't interested in the kind of boys who would ask me out."

"Who were they?"

"The mondo-jocko types. Athletic, decent-looking, reasonably intelligent without being bright—you know." Sandy nodded. "I wasn't interested in them. They were looking for an attractive girl to be their trophy, a visible reflection of their own desirability. I wasn't interested in that at all. If any of them had the balls to just ask me if I wanted to have sex, I likely would have. I just wasn't drawn to the social niceties. I couldn't care less about getting to know them.

"At university, it was more of the same. After I shot so many guys down, they started rumors that I liked girls. Then, after a few girls asked me out and I shot them down too, the rumors stopped. I was focused on my studies and on the officer training program. I'd already decided I was going to follow in Aunt Letty's footsteps."

"Aunt Letty is Admiral Ketyungyoenwong?" Sandy asked.

Ali nodded. "My parents weren't too enthused. They hadn't allowed me to apply to the Academy, so they weren't happy that I'd signed up for the Officer Training Corps as soon as I got to school.

"ONI got their hooks into me before I even graduated. Near the end of my junior year, they came to school to interview me and work up a complete psych profile. I had exams to study for, and ONI took up three days of my planned study time. I was resentful about that, especially since I was set on following my aunt on the command track as soon as I could. On the last day, they shared some results of the psych profile they'd compiled and managed to convince me I would be a perfect fit."

"What did they tell you that swayed you?" Sandy asked, intrigued.

"Without getting into all the mumbo-jumbo, they said my indifference to social norms made me a perfect candidate. It wasn't so much what they said, but how it was delivered. The Director came to close out my interview. That impressed me. He was direct and unforgiving, pointing out that my refusal to engage in the social whirl was egotistical and that he would not accept it. Despite that, or maybe because of that, I felt like he really understood me. He only spent twenty minutes with me, but I believed he read me like a book. I was their girl after that."

"Have you ever regretted it?"

"Not seriously," she commented. "I've had second thoughts at times. Everyone does. How about you?"

"Ever since I can remember," Sandy shared, "I wanted to be captain of a starship. All my life, that was my goal. When I was given command of my first ship, there was such a feeling of rightness and fulfillment. I knew I had been correct all along."

"You are one of the least ego-driven people I know," Ali remarked. "I would have thought that a healthy ego is important."

Sandy shook his head vigorously. "Trust me. Those are the worst officers. They're all little dictators. For me, it's taking a group of people and helping them, individually and as a group, to achieve as much of their potential as possible. It's convincing them to subordinate themselves to the greater, collective goal. It's more about removing obstacles to their success than it is issuing commands."

"You sound as though you've given it a great deal of thought," she said.

"I guess I have," Sandy shrugged. "I've been reading the biographies of influential leaders throughout history since I was old enough to read."

"Those skills that you mentioned," she said, "could be useful in any number of positions, in government, industry, academia — "

"I wanted to be a starship captain," Sandy interrupted, "and those were the skills I thought would make me successful. But, back to my original question: are we on a date?"

Ali laughed. "I thought you would appreciate it if I took a little extra care, not tease me."

"I do appreciate it," Sandy protested. "You look great and smell wonderful. I would have enjoyed this evening regardless, but knowing you did that when it's not really your thing, makes it subtly better. Thank you."

"You know, they had to teach me a lot of this stuff in ONI," she stated. "My parents made sure I had good manners, but things like making conversation for its own sake, flirting, teasing, engaging people—I had no experience since I'd never had any interest. When I saw that these skills would be useful to me as an agent, I became an eager pupil. I found I can be incredibly manipulative. It's an extremely seductive form of power. I had to learn to turn it off when I didn't need it for an assignment."

"Interesting," Sandy commented. He paused. "I'm trying to think if you manipulated me recently."

She chuckled. "No. That was sheer force of personality. Now, I want to circle back to the question I asked that you avoided. Did you ever have second thoughts about the navy?"

"I would have thought that was obvious," Sandy replied. "I left. That your aunt helped me, I still don't quite understand, but I'm grateful."

"I'll share something with you since I don't think it will go to your head," Ali stated. "Aunt Letty has a soft spot in her heart for you. She had picked you out as an officer of great promise before you had your first command. You've proven her assessment correct since then. She knows the navy treated you poorly in the last couple of years. I think that's why she was willing to let you and Portia 'liberate' all those components. She was mighty impressed with your plan and a little envious."

"That's very — I don't know — comforting, I guess, comforting to hear," Sandy said.

"Are you enjoying this? I mean, the *Alice May* and starting this business?" Ali inquired.

"I am," Sandy admitted. "It helps that I got to hand-pick everyone — "

"Except me," Ali pointed out.

"If I'd known how valuable you would be, I would have included you from the beginning, like Portia. Without your help, we'd be nowhere. Plus, I told you before, I'd have liked to have considered you a friend but always felt you liked keeping your distance. So, after the last couple of days, I'd say we're friends now, but I don't think we're the kind of friends who share much of our feelings and certainly no deep, dark personal secrets."

Ali smiled at this. "Touché."

The server interrupted them, asking if they would like anything else. Sandy glanced, but Ali shook her head. "Just the check."

When he paid it, they walked back to the taxi stand and returned to the ship. When they entered, Ali said, "Thanks. That was nice."

By noon on Thursday, everyone else had returned to the *Alice May*. Everyone seemed pretty happy and relaxed, though Mike and Bungo were the only ones who shared much about what they'd done while off the ship. Apparently, Stick, Puss, and the two women didn't get out and interact with the locals. Portia and Morgan simply stayed quiet.

"People here a bit strange," Mike commented, recalling what he and Bungo had seen.

"How?" Sandy asked.

"It felt like everyone we dealt with had a chip on his shoulder."

Bungo nodded in agreement.

"It's almost like they were expecting us to think they were weird or something," Mike added. "They were kind of defensive about everything."

"Well, no one goes to Galatia if they can help it," Ali remarked. "All the other planets do business with them, but there's no real interaction. Since the AI Congress met about 500 years ago, Galatia has a planetary monopoly on creating Artificial Intelligence. The Congress was originally assembled because some AIs went crazy. Most committed suicide, but some tried to take over the planets they were on. They figured out the problem, but there's been a stigma against AI since then. As a result, Galatia has been socially isolated for a long time. People do look at them as weird."

They received word from B & M with an updated loading slot that afternoon. They loaded the one small sealed container and set off for Corbulo. It would take three weeks to get there.

"I don't think we'll see any action on this trip," Ali commented.

"Why not?" Mike asked.

"There's no black market for Artificial Intelligences," she explained. "Each one is custom-built with a specific end-use. It's the something they figured out after the problems that cropped up back when."

"What did they figure out?" Portia inquired.

"The AIs that went crazy after becoming self-aware had one thing in common—they were programmed generically and not specifically. The reason for this is so they could be used by anyone. In researching the AIs that didn't go crazy, they found many were self-aware already, but they hadn't gone nuts. The reason is that they were programmed for specific tasks. For instance, an Artificial Intelligence created specifically to manage the growth of human organs for transplant had become self-aware. Because it had been programmed for just that business, with its new awareness, it evaluated its place in the universe and realized that what it was doing was its highest calling. As a result, instead of feeling frustrated or trapped or enslaved, it was content and happy."

"Are there self-aware AIs out there today?" Portia asked.

"Quite a few of them are," Ali replied. "But because they are doing what they were specifically built and programmed to do, they feel fulfilled."

"Gotta say, Aunt Ali," Warburton commented, "that's kind of creepy."

"I think most people are uncomfortable with them," Ali agreed. "Still, they're irreplaceable in certain industries."

4

As Ali had predicted, the three-week journey to Corbulo was uneventful. Though they kept their guard up, no one appeared along the route to challenge them. Their stay at Corbulo Station was brief. B & M had already arranged for their next cargo to be waiting for them when they arrived. In less than 30 minutes, they unloaded the small container they'd picked up in Galatia and were now fully loaded with a shipment of human organs that had been grown artificially. Their destination was Edda, in what had been the Alliance.

Edda was where Sandy, Portia, Stick and Puss had left the *Ali Kat* a few years before. Sandy and Portia were transferred to PAS *Chapman,* and one of the most challenging assignments either could have imagined. It ended with Sandy's crew needing to seize an enemy ship in a boarding action in order to return to Alliance space.

A few hours after leaving Corbulo Station, Sandy bumped into Portia in the galley. Portia flashed him a rueful smile. "Edda, huh? Brings back memories."

"Yeah," Sandy agreed, a sour look on his face as he sat. "Actually, the Edda part was okay. It was the Ilex part I'm still upset about."

"I have to agree with you on that," Portia commented. "But what we accomplished from Edda to Robur is something I'm still damned proud of."

"Still, no one should have been put in a position like that."

Portia looked at him with narrowed eyes. "Who? You?"

Sandy shook his head vigorously. "No. The whole crew. I have dreams about it every once in a while. They always make me sad and pissed off."

Portia didn't reply. She simply patted Sandy on the shoulder as she left.

They were released from Corbulo Station traffic control about an hour later. Nearing the first of four tramlines that would take them to Edda, Mike Xie in the bridge noticed a fast transport less than an hour behind them. He used passive sensors to read the ship's emissions. The computer matched that to its database, giving him the ship's name and ownership: the *Clare Anais* out of Corbulo. He entered it in the log but didn't think much of it since this tramline was frequently used.

When they jumped into the next system, Portia could see most of the ship traffic was splitting towards two other tramlines on more commonly used routes. The *Alice May* was headed to a third tramline, on the direct route to Edda. Warburton and Boyle had done a thorough scan of the system. They had not identified any potential threats ahead of them. However, when the *Clare Anais* still followed, Portia mentioned it to Ali.

"Any reason to be concerned?" Ali inquired.

"Could be nothing," Portia admitted, "but all the other traffic is heading on the busier lines. The only thing this way is Edda."

"Huh. Well, Puss and Stick scanned the system and didn't find any traces of bogeymen," Ali remarked.

"Maybe they're in the next system," Portia commented.

They traveled across the system for the next two days. The *Clare Anais* still just an hour behind. Before they jumped into the tramline, they discussed their shadow.

"The *Clare Anais* out of Corbulo, owned by an LLC controlled by a guy named Rafe Dermot. No shipping agent. B & M doesn't know the guy. Manlius doesn't know the guy—but they don't have any presence on Corbulo," Sandy stated.

"Hah!" Ali exclaimed. "I feel much better about spending the company's money then."

They looked at her, puzzled.

"When you turned up nothing, I contacted a freelance intelligence bureau I know of on Corbulo," Ali explained. "It cost us 2,000 credits, but I can tell you that our friend is a naughty fellow. He hasn't been convicted of any crimes, but he's been under suspicion several times for smuggling and piracy. His brother McCoy also owns a fast transport, the *Peggy Lea*, also out of Corbulo. Until recently, he had a contract with the company that produced the cargo we're carrying. They fired him a couple of months ago after an audit found some irregularities. McCoy had an accomplice in the company's accounting department who covered his tracks for him. He was stealing a portion of the cargo and selling it on the black market, cutting the accountant in for a share. The accountant is in jail, awaiting trial. Anyone want to bet me on whether brother McCoy is waiting for us in the next system?"

"Did I ever tell you how glad I am that you're on our side?" Sandy quipped. She shook her head slightly. "I'm really glad you're on our side," he stated, grinning.

"We're on a relatively tight schedule," Sandy told the others, "so we don't have a lot of time to mess around with these guys. I'm thinking we drop out of the tramline about one light-hour short of the terminus and begin reversing thrust. I'd like to take care of both of them on one pass without needing to double back. If we can do that, we'll still be on schedule. If we have to double back, we'll need to make time up elsewhere, and our options on that are limited by the nature of our cargo. Granted, the potential payday from bagging two ships far exceeds what we'll make for carrying this load, but we're new in the business, and I want to establish and maintain a reputation for meeting schedule demands, too. Any thoughts?"

"Just thinking where our welcoming committee will be," Warburton mused. "I'm guessing he won't be at the tramline terminus but won't be too far in-system. He'll want to cut us off whichever way we try to go. His brother following is there to deal with us if we put on the brakes. When our shadow exits the tramline and brother-dearest tells him where we are, he'll put on the brakes too. I'll need to plot it out on the computer, but I think we can do what you want, boss."

"Get busy," Sandy suggested. "Any other ideas?"

Shrugs and head shakes followed. The meeting broke up. The *Alice May* entered the tramline. It was a relatively short duration jump of only six hours usually. It would be slightly less than that since they planned to exit early.

Stick had run his ideas through the tactical programs and came up with his best guess where the *Peggy Lea* would be located. From that, it looked as though they would need to double back slightly, but it shouldn't cost them more than an additional couple of hours. He sent his analysis to Sandy.

They emerged from the tramline, one light-hour short of the terminus. *Peggy Lea* was close to where Stick had predicted. Sandy engaged reverse thrust at 500G. Shortly after, the *Clare Anais* emerged from the tramline into normal space at the terminus. Though she had no sensor data of her own, obviously, the brothers were in contact, and the *Peggy Lea* slowed. From the sensor readings they picked up later, they learned the *Clare Anais* had engaged max boost to slow as quickly as possible.

Because the *Alice May* was slowing her progress, the time to engagement lengthened. When they initially emerged from the tramline, the computer had estimated four-and-a-half hours until they were within range. It currently stood at six hours and was increasing. It took another hour before their sensors could see the initial reactions of the two ships. Boyle updated the plot. Based on observed courses and deceleration rates, the computer provided an estimated time-to-range of just under eight hours. Sandy sent messages to both McAllister and Manlius Military, informing them of the situation.

Manlius responded first. "In an hour, we are due to pick up the detainees of your first encounter a few days ago," Tumperi sent in a text message. "Regret we have no operations near your location. We will sub-contract to a firm with whom we have worked, Braeiwa Associates. They will contact you to firm up the details. No outstanding warrants or bounties on the crews of these two ships."

McAllister's message was similar. "Haven't retrieved the first one, and you've got two more lined up? Too far for us to handle the pickup. Will hire some tugs from Corbulo. Once retrieved, will try to arrange sale in Corbulo as well, to reduce transport fees. Will update soon."

Sandy was due for his sleep period but knew he was too keyed up to sleep with action pending. There wasn't any room for him to do his Tai Chi forms with the hold full of cargo. That was his customary way of centering himself to get through the last few hours of waiting. Instead, he started pacing. When Portia complained and asked him to sit down and stay still, Ali beckoned him subtly to his cabin. He followed, and she engaged him in a different exercise routine that left him calm and relaxed.

With an hour to go, he showered and dressed and returned to the bridge, relieving Mike. He looked at the computer course plots. They would encounter *Peggy Lea* first, then *Clare Anais*. They would need to double back after that to *Peggy Lea* to retrieve the Manlius people who had gone to deal with her crew. Neutralizing these two ships would add a bit over twelve hours to the overall transit time due to leaving the tramline early and decelerating. Sandy checked and found he could make up a good portion of that by changing to least-time courses and using one hundred percent of standard thrust. It would cost a bit of fuel, the ^{3}He that fed the reactor, and the ship's tanks would be nearing empty by the time they reached Edda. However, the cost of the extra fuel was minimal compared to the potential gain of the two ships.

The *Peggy Lea* was broadcasting a message, instructing the *Alice May* to heave-to and prepare to surrender her cargo. Sandy ignored it. He brought the plasma shields up. Ali had pulled the seniority card and shoved Warburton out of the gunnery seat. As the *Alice May* continued past the *Peggy Lea* on a course for the *Clare Anais*, the *Peggy Lea* fired a shot from her 40mm cannon. While likely meant as a warning shot to convince the *Alice May* to heave-to, it was justification enough, and Ali launched an EMP missile.

It sped unerringly towards the *Peggy Lea*. Reaching the ship seconds later, it detonated upon nearing the hull, releasing its powerful electromagnetic pulse. All the electrical systems aboard the ship shorted out, overwhelmed. The reactor went into an emergency shutdown.

Once the missile detonated, Bungo and Heidi departed from *Alice May*'s airlock. Activating the thrusters in their combat armor, they slowed themselves to land on the hull of the *Peggy Lea*. Operating the airlock manually, they entered, instructing the crew to get in the escape pods. None of them attempted to hide. All were a bit stunned that their ship had been disabled and didn't quite understand how it had been done.

The *Alice May* continued to decelerate, coming to a stop past the *Peggy Lea*.

The *Clare Anais* had also stopped and was now climbing back towards the *Alice May*. Sandy just waited for a time. When the *Clare Anais* had reached cannon range, Sandy headed back towards the *Peggy Lea*. The *Clare Anais* fired a shot, warning him to stop, and Ali launched a missile in response. As before, the ship was completely disabled. Morgan and Cheyenne flew over in their combat armor and had the crew climb into the escape pods.

With the crew of the *Clare Anais* safely in the escape pods, Morgan and Cheyenne returned. When they were aboard, Sandy activated the drives and returned to pick up Heidi and Bungo. With all safely back on the ship, Sandy resumed the course for Edda. They maintained their wariness until they reached the Edda system. They had made up some of the time lost and were going to meet the delivery schedule comfortably. Along the way, they received confirmation that Manlius had picked up the crew of the first ship they'd encountered, the *Prudence Rose*, and the tug Tom McAllister sent now had the ship in tow, returning to Providence.

When they emerged back into normal space, Ali checked the news feeds and shared with them that a scandal was brewing in the United Worlds. According to what she'd read, it had recently been reported that irregularities had been discovered in the election of the new Hegemon two years earlier. The Hegemony of United Worlds had strict laws concerning the right to vote. Citizens of the United Worlds had to pay a minimum of ten percent of their annual income in tax to be eligible to cast a ballot.

According to the news reports, the new Hegemon, Mortimer Edison, and his party were accused of altering vote counts. Traces of computer worms were found in the vote tabulation software. Forensic experts were digging into the problem now. There was widespread suspicion that the worms had been designed to manipulate vote counts and then disappear. Ali passed along that half the news media was defending Edison and the other half calling for him to face a new election. Millions of United Worlds' citizens had joined demonstrations both in favor of Edison and calling for his removal.

"Hey, if it slows down their absorption of the Alliance," Sandy commented, "it plays into our business model."

"That it does," Ali agreed.

When they neared Edda Station, they learned from the B & M rep that their outbound cargo was slightly delayed. They would have a two-day layover. After delivering their cargo and finding their assigned parking coordinates, Sandy asked if anyone wanted off the ship. Puss and Stick glanced quickly at Cheyenne and Heidi, then said they would. Ali said she would, but she preferred to go by herself. None of the rest seemed eager, but Sandy stated he felt the need for real food. Those who were staying were welcome to join him, his treat.

A taxi arrived shortly afterward and collected Ali and the other four, who were departing for a couple of days. Sandy quizzed the others on when they wanted to eat, and they decided to wait a couple of hours. With Puss and Stick away, Portia made an oblique comment about them with the two women. Bungo, Morgan and Mike all laughed.

Seeing Sandy's blank expression, Portia looked at him. "Don't tell me you don't know," she said.

"Know what?" Sandy replied, mystified.

Portia began to laugh, and the others grinned. "Puss and Heidi. Stick and Cheyenne. They've been sleeping together since we left Galatia. Haven't you noticed how much less obnoxious Stick and Puss have been?"

"Huh," Sandy remarked, suddenly self-conscious about his own sleeping arrangements. His face grew hot.

"And, yes, we know about you and Ali," Portia continued. "It's a small ship. Don't worry about it."

"The problem is," Morgan rumbled in his deep voice, "we get rotated to new duties when we return to Providence."

"How serious are they?" Sandy inquired.

"More than you and Ali," Portia commented. "Not picking baby names yet, though. My guess is that they stay in touch."

Two days later, they picked up their cargo—catalysts for zero-G smelting. After leaving Edda Station, Sandy received word that Braeiwa Associates had retrieved the crews of *Clare Anais* and *Peggy Lea*. Tom McAllister confirmed that the tugs he had hired out of Corbulo would arrive in a couple of days. He also confirmed that the *Prudence Rose* would arrive at Providence about the same time they would.

Ali boarded the ship as they were loading the cargo. She greeted them with a tight smile. After coming aboard, she disappeared into her cabin. Ali emerged a couple of hours later and joined Sandy on the bridge.

"So, I've been on-station and down-planet the last two days, checking with some of my contacts and a former colleague," she informed him. "I wanted to learn more about what's going on with the HUWs. Those news reports were unusual."

"How so?"

"The news media in the United Worlds never—and I mean, *never*—criticizes the government, unless it's a specific individual who has fallen out of favor with the regime. For them to admit that there is a controversy surrounding the last election, when the current Hegemon came to power, is unprecedented. I wanted to know more."

"Did you learn anything?"

"Yeah," she said, shaking her head. "It's bad, Sandy. Far worse than the reports we read. The demonstrations they mentioned? They understated the situation. Millions have been demonstrating, and the government has sent in armed troops to try to regain control. Thousands have been killed in confrontations between the protesters and the troops. Their navy has withdrawn all their ships from Alliance space, and their fleets are gathering. Admirals and captains are taking sides. So far, they're not approaching Perseus, the capital system of the Hegemony, but they aren't far away."

"What do you think will happen?"

"It all depends on the Hegemon, I think," she said. "He could call for new elections. That would defuse the crisis. I don't think he will. To this point, he has maintained a steady stream of denials and tried to put the burden of proof on his accusers. His people are preventing anyone from gaining access to most of the systems where they might find the evidence. People who are familiar with the election process are convinced he gamed the system but haven't been able to provide solid proof. They got control of a few pieces of hardware, and their forensic analysts are digging into them. If the forensic people can recreate what was done, or if someone on the inside turns and confesses, then it's all over.

"I think Edison is trying to drag this out as long as he can and hope that his opponents eventually give up. The same election that put him in place also gave his party a majority in their version of the Governing Council, so he's not in danger of facing a 'no confidence' vote any time soon."

"I sense there's a 'but' coming in what you're saying," Sandy suggested.

"Yeah," she agreed. "From what I can pick up, the HUW Navy is pretty evenly split between pro- and anti-Edison people. The younger officers tend to be supporters since Edison pushed for the navy to press home the advantage after Excelsus, and it was successful. Edison also rewarded his most outspoken supporters with governorships and such over the Alliance planets.

"The more experienced officers aren't as keen. While they are also pleased that he took advantage of the Alliance's weakness and discord, they have also seen that the government was completely unprepared for victory. They had no plan for how they would administer the Alliance. From what I understand and could see for myself, down-planet, the Alliance planets are struggling— things are falling apart."

"In what way?" Sandy asked.

"Think of the lowest levels of government," she explained, "things like the power plant, or waste disposal, even police and fire departments. The United Worlds' people didn't have a plan to deal with them. In most cases, the existing employees stayed on the job until they no longer got a paycheck. The different agencies ran out of money in their accounts and have received no funds from their new masters. The new masters haven't released the funds because they haven't put their own people in place yet. So, some of the things we take for granted, like turning on the lights when it gets dark, or flushing the toilet, stop."

"I didn't see any evidence of that on the station," Sandy remarked. "Granted, we only left the ship twice, for dinner."

"The station is in far better shape than down-planet," she commented. "It's a much smaller entity. Where government agencies have shut down, like traffic control, groups like the Shippers Guild have filled in and paid to maintain the services. That's not happening down below. Back to my original point, the more experienced HUW officers have seen this and have also seen that the Hegemon's appointees are totally unprepared to deal with the problems. They're also not getting any help or guidance from above. The Hegemon and his people are entirely focused on protecting him in the election scandal."

"Ah," Sandy remarked. "So, what do you think will happen?"

"Nothing good, that's for sure." Ali laughed darkly. "The people on Edda and other Alliance planets, from what I've heard, are about ready to take matters into their own hands. That means insurrection. Since the HUW Navy controls space, any insurrection is doomed to fail, eventually. You might see some of the higher-ranking commanders in the navy also stepping in to fix the problems down-planet and bypassing the governor that the Hegemon put in place. You also have the potential for a civil war if the navy splits into factions. Or it could be a combination of any or all of those."

"Is it imminent?"

"I don't know," Ali admitted. "Something could happen in the next few minutes, or it might take months. I don't see the current situation lasting more than a few months, though."

"Wow," Sandy breathed. "I'm guessing that we're going to need to avoid Alliance and HUW space for now."

"Probably a good idea," Ali agreed.

"On another subject," Sandy offered, "did you know about Puss, Stick and the girls?"

"Duh," Ali retorted. "Portia and Morgan, too."

"No way," Sandy remarked.

Ali smiled.

"Sheesh," Sandy muttered. "Not Mike and Bungo?"

Ali laughed hard. "No," she said, recovering her breath. "They were joking about feeling left out, but neither one of them is interested that way."

They had no hostile encounters on the journey from Edda to Providence. Before they entered the tramline that would deliver them into the Providence system, Ali alerted them that one of the HUW group captains had arrived in the Perseus system and threatened to bombard the planet if the Hegemon did not resign immediately. She didn't have any further information.

"By the time we enter the Providence system," she counseled, "all of them will probably have chosen a side."

"Do we know who it is, in Perseus?" Sandy asked.

"Group Captain Dieter Manbarschwein," she replied, "of Attack Group

Wolf. The equivalent rank in the Alliance Navy would have been Rear Admiral. He led the attack at Excelsus and again at Freia. He lost ships at Freia, but they had new construction come online just after. He is at full strength. The balance of their new construction is just about complete. It will be interesting to see who grabs it."

They dropped out of the tramline into the Providence system. Ali went to her cabin to get the latest updates on the situation with the HUWs. Sandy received confirmation that the *Clare Anais* and *Peggy Lea* had been retrieved and were due to arrive in the Corbulo system in two days.

When Ali emerged, Sandy asked her if she could share what she'd learned with the group. She nodded. Sandy called for a 'team meeting' in the galley.

"From what I picked up," she began, "the United Worlds are on the brink of a massive civil war. Manbarschwein, the guy who threatened to bombard the capital, was chased out of the system by a loyalist group led by Group Captain Tatiana Johara."

"Huh," Sandy grunted, not able to help himself.

"What?" Ali asked.

"She's the one I surrendered to, back when. She got a promotion, obviously."

"Okay," Ali said, clearly dismissing his comment. "After chasing Manbarschwein away, Group Captain Johara went to the Nereus system. That's where the new construction is—three superdreadnoughts and four battlecruisers. She got there just in time before the other guys did. Before that, the two sides were evenly matched. Now the pro-Edison forces have an advantage if they can keep the new construction safe until it is finished. My sources tell me the ships were anywhere from 30 to 90 days away from being ready for trials. So I'm going to guess that's where the first big showdown will happen."

"Not over the capital?" Mike asked.

"Even the HUWs are reluctant to drop rocks on people," Ali cracked, "especially their own. No, the first battle will be in Nereus, to either win or destroy the new construction."

"What does this mean for us?" Portia asked.

"Good question," Ali commented. "I don't know. My vote would be for us to sit tight, at least until after the first big confrontation. Once that happens, we should have a better idea of how far afield this might spread. It might stay confined to one or two battles and be over; it could drag on and spread through HUW space. It might take some other twist or turn I haven't thought of yet. I think we'll know more after they tangle for the first time. For now, I think our best option is to get to Providence and wait."

Sandy contacted Kevin Moon at Bharwani & Minami and informed him not to schedule any loads for the *Alice May* for at least a couple of months. Moon understood. Sandy was not the only ship owner concerned about the possibility of the HUW's civil war expanding.

"That doesn't mean I won't contact you," Moon cautioned. "There might be some folks who will offer bonuses."

"It would need to be an obscene amount to sway my interest," Sandy confessed.

"That might happen if this drags out," Moon commented.

Sandy also informed Lieutenant Colonel Tumperi at Manlius Military that they would likely take a breather. Tumperi also was understanding. He commented that Manlius actually stood to pick up business because of the uncertainty.

They delivered their cargo and then brought the ship to Tom McAllister's shipyard. He would replace the EMP missiles they used and had offered them a secure place to leave the ship. The critical factor was security. McAllister offered a higher degree of watchfulness than they could get elsewhere. Since he was also a shareholder, the price was right—free.

The Manlius operatives departed. There were hugs but no tears. Sandy observed Boyle and Warburton to watch their reaction. Shortly after, the crew left, going their separate ways, at least for a month. Sandy promised to keep them updated. Likewise, Ali promised to keep Sandy informed of the information that wouldn't necessarily be in the news feeds.

As McAllister had said, the *Prudence Rose* arrived only a few hours after they did. He caught Sandy before Sandy departed from the yard. "You can put the ship up for auction 'as is,' without fixing anything," McAllister told him. "Or, you can invest about 500,000 credits in replacing the electronics and giving the ship a general 'sprucing up' which should increase the auction price by three million or more."

"Why are you even asking?" Sandy replied, amused.

McAllister shrugged. "Some people are quirky. I can't guarantee that you'll get more for her fixed up, but in the past, that's generally been the case. If it were up to only me, I'd do it."

"What sort of shape is she in?" Sandy asked.

"I'd definitely recommend getting a cleaning crew in, that's for certain," Tom smiled.

"Done," Sandy stated. "Let me know once you get a firm idea of the costs, and I'll make sure Kruppen releases the funds to you."

"Would you like to do the same with the two ships heading to Corbulo?"

"Of course."

"Last question," Tom stated. "Do you want to handle this through the existing company? Or do you want to set up a shell corporation to hide your tracks?"

"I hadn't considered that," Sandy admitted. He thought for a moment, then looked up. "The guys who attacked us know who we are and know we disabled their ships. Word will get around, so I don't think there's any need to try to put up a smokescreen. Are there any tax advantages to doing it?"

"I don't have a clue," Tom confessed. "I've never been involved in something like this before."

"Let me check with the lawyer and get back to you," Sandy suggested.

Sandy returned to his apartment on Providence Station. The air smelled stale and musty since it had been closed up. He was just wondering what to do about dinner when his comm chimed with a message from Ali.

"I'm outside," it read. "Let me in?"

Sandy went to the door, and the security camera indeed showed Ali. He opened the door and let her in. "Perfect timing," he commented. "I was just thinking about dinner. I don't have a thing to eat in here, so want to have dinner with me?"

"As long as you understand this is not a date," she replied with a smile.

They went to a restaurant that she had heard of. When they sat at the table, Ali put her comm on the table and activated her field suppressor. She waited until the server left with their orders before speaking about anything important.

"It looks like there's going to be a battle in Nereus over the new construction any time now," she said softly without moving her lips. "I've also heard that the new ships are much closer to completion than my sources originally thought. According to one, the pro-Edison folks are staffing the ships and planning on using them if it comes to a battle."

"How are they fielding crews?" Sandy asked.

"By splitting their own people and tossing in a bunch of raw recruits and cadets from their naval academy. It means that all the pro-Edison ships will be under-manned, in the short-term, at least."

"What about the Hegemon?"

"He's dug in," Ali reported. "Complete denial of any wrongdoing and attacking the other side for weakening the United Worlds because of jealousy over his brilliant victory. Meanwhile, on the Alliance planets, the former Alliance governments are reforming in secret and trying to restore basic services—sort of like a shadow government. They can't come out into the open because the HUWs still have ships overhead."

"Capital ships?" Sandy asked.

Ali shook her head. "No. Some heavy and light cruisers, some frigates, and that's it. Only one or two per system. Everyone else has formed up with the attack groups."

"Huh," Sandy grunted, trying to process the information.

They enjoyed their dinner, and the conversation turned to the other shipboard romances. "I don't have to worry about Stick and Puss going through some kind of melt-down, do I?" Sandy asked.

"They're big boys," Ali commented. "I think they'll stay in touch with

Heidi and Cheyenne, but I don't see them getting broken-hearted. It's probably the most fun they've ever had on the job, though."

"What about Portia?"

"She's fine," Ali stated. "She and Morgan were just casual. They'll stay friends, I'm sure, but nothing more." She paused and looked at Sandy quizzically. "All this talk about them isn't going to make you go all goopy on me, is it?"

Sandy displayed the faint smile of minor embarrassment, and his face grew pink. "No," he replied. "I mean, I like you a lot, Ali, and I enjoy being with you in the way that we have been. But you made it clear you could take it or leave it, so I'm staying on the proper side of the line you drew at the beginning."

"Has that been a problem for you?"

"Not as much as I would have thought," he admitted. "It's different from my past experience, that's certain."

"Would it bother you if I told you that, after tonight, you might not see me for a couple of months?" she asked.

Sandy paused in thought. "I enjoy your company and the 'extra-curricular activities' we've engaged in, so I'll miss you, for sure, if that's what you mean."

She shook her head.

"If you're asking whether I'll pine away for you or feel upset because you're not around? I don't think so," Sandy offered.

"Okay," she accepted.

"You planning on going anywhere in particular?" he asked.

"I was thinking I might head to the Free Republics," she said but offered no reason why.

Sandy nodded, then had a thought. "Could I convince you to go to Corbulo, at least for a couple of days?"

"I guess. Why?"

"Those two ships we ran into last are arriving in Corbulo any minute. The first one arrived here, and Tom McAllister counseled me that we'd get a much better price at the auction by replacing the electronics and 'sprucing up' the ship. So I instructed him to arrange for the same sort of thing in Corbulo, but if you could be there, it would be great to have an officer of the company check on things."

Ali chuckled. "Sure. That means the first part of my trip is on the company, right? As far as expenses?"

"Absolutely," he confirmed.

"That works. I'll find out from Tom who he's got lined up to do the work and make an appointment to see them when I get there."

Ali returned with Sandy to his apartment and spent the night. In the morning, she left early. Sandy was a light sleeper, so woke when she got up. There was no big goodbye. He told her to stay safe. They exchanged a brief hug, and she was out the door.

It was just under a month later when everything started to go crazy. Sandy first knew when he received a message from Ali advising him that the battle in Nereus she had predicted had taken place. Sure enough, 24 hours later, Sandy saw reports appearing on the news feeds. However, Ali's message was more informative and, Sandy felt, likely more accurate, too.

According to Ali, the anti-Edison Attack Group Wolf entered the Nereus system where the pro-Edison Attack Group Lion and the new construction were waiting. The loyalist forces drove the interlopers away in a relatively brief engagement. Ali reported that both sides had taken damage, but neither lost any ships. Sandy advised the rest of the crew that he planned to extend their hiatus but not to stray too far away.

A week later, Ali sent another message. This one told of the Hegemon's assassination. Apparently, the two loyalist Group Captains and their superiors had seen preliminary reports of the forensic investigation regarding the last election. The evidence pointed to the Hegemon's guilt. Rather than continue to defend him, his forces had him killed and called for new elections. According to what Ali had learned, they hoped to end the conflict by doing so. The news media did not report this for another two days—information from the United Worlds was being restricted.

Five days later, Ali sent Sandy another update. Attack Group Eagle, which had been anti-Edison, struck the loyalist Attack Group Badger. While this confrontation also resulted in no ship losses, it showed that the rebellious forces were not willing to lay down their arms even though the Hegemon was dead. Ali's estimation was that the opportunity to avoid civil war was now past, and the conflict could escalate at any minute.

During all this, the three ships that the *Alice May* had disabled all went up for auction. The *Clare Anais* sold for 21 million credits. The *Peggy Lea* sold for 20.5 million and the *Prudence Rose* for just over 18 million. After consulting with the company's lawyer, Sandy sent a message to the crew and Tom McAllister informing them that half of the proceeds from the sales would be distributed to them according to their shares in the company, while half would be held in reserve, parked in investment accounts as a financial reserve for the company.

A week after Ali's previous message, he received a very cryptic text from her. "Expect a call," was all it said.

That evening, as Sandy was preparing to go to sleep, the console in his apartment chimed, indicating an incoming call. The screen displayed "unknown contact." If he had not been forewarned by Ali's message, he might not have answered it. Suspecting it might be her, he activated the link. He was stunned to see Admiral Ketyungyoenwong appear onscreen. He was also a bit surprised to see her in uniform. The Alliance Navy had been disbanded shortly after the surrender.

"Hello, Sandy," she said.

"Admiral," Sandy responded, tongue-tied.

"Sandy, I know Ali had kept you apprised of what is happening with the United Worlds. She has been sharing the same information with me. The Alliance government has retaken control of Valkyrie, and we manned a couple of ships to regain control of the system. I am reassembling the Alliance Navy on my own authority and am asking if you would like to join us."

Sandy was stunned. Competing thoughts ran through his mind, clamoring for his attention. On one side were loyalty and duty; on the other, the personal toll it had taken on him. He realized the admiral was waiting for him to respond.

"Admiral, I cannot give you an immediate answer," he replied. "I promise to consider it carefully. How do I get back in touch with you to let you know what I decide?"

"Ali has my contact info," she said. "Let her know when you're ready to talk, and I'll reach out to you."

With that, the admiral closed the connection.

Sandy went to bed and stared at the ceiling in the dark. He sorted through his feelings. The initial tug at his sense of duty and flattery at the admiral reaching out to him slowly faded behind the onslaught of reminders of past events. The eight months of being without a ship and stuck in a form of purgatory while the government failed to address the problems uncovered in the navy. Losing Leezy. The deception of ONI. His treatment at the hands of Captain Slocum and her incompetence. The mission to Ilex.

Additionally, he tried to consider the current situation. The Alliance had surrendered. While the HUWs were currently at one another's throats, faced with an outside threat, they might put aside their differences. The navy had been disbanded. The remaining ships were lifeless. It seemed like an impossible mission. Having had his fill of impossible missions, Sandy simply had no enthusiasm for the task.

He tried to balance the scales with positive memories, but the more recent events overwhelmed his attempt. He did not sleep well that night. When he woke, the feelings of frustration he had felt won the argument. He sent a text to Ali: "The answer is a respectful 'no.' Please ask the admiral to contact me if she would like to discuss it further."

Sandy had never handled downtime well, and after two more weeks of idleness, he was beside himself. So when Kevin Moon from Bharwani & Minami contacted him, with a cargo of rare earths bound for Galatia, and offered double the regular rate, Sandy was ready. He reached the rest of the crew and asked them how soon they could return. Everyone except Ali was actually either on Providence Station or down-planet. He informed them they had a load and all agreed to return within hours.

He contacted Manlius Military and confirmed that they could assign four combat-armored personnel to the *Alice May* as early as the next day. Sandy then informed Moon that they would be ready to pick up the cargo within 24 hours. Next, he asked what sort of freight they might pick up on Galatia.

"The terraforming operation on Castor is desperate to get their AI from Galatia," Moon related. "No one has been interested because they're worried about the situation with the United Worlds. Castor is not far away."

"Are they offering a premium?" Sandy asked.

"They are," Moon confirmed, "but there's a question of payment. The machine on Galatia is already paid for at the time it was ordered. The terraforming operation was part of the Alliance but became the United Worlds' responsibility after the surrender. They do not know if they still have access to their financial accounts or if the United Worlds might have plundered them."

"If they can guarantee cash payment, in advance, at triple the normal rate, we'll deliver it," Sandy said, somewhat boldly.

He didn't know why he committed the ship and his crew rather recklessly. After ending the call with Moon, he had second thoughts. He just agreed to take them all into what very well could be a war zone and didn't ask them. His rejection of Admiral Ketyungyoenwong's request still bothered his conscience, and he guessed that agreeing to take this shipment was his way of compensating. He'd talk to them when they arrived and back out of it if the others had cold feet.

He packed a bag, shut up his apartment, and then went to McAllister's yard and checked in with Tom. Sandy admitted to Tom that he could no longer bear inactivity. Tom chuckled and asked a worker to ferry Sandy over to the *Alice May*.

Entering the ship after it had been closed up for almost two months, it had the same sort of musty smell of uncirculated air that his apartment did after a long time away. It was also cold as hell. The life support functions were 'on-demand' systems. With no one on board, they had powered down to minimal levels. The ship would recognize that a human was back aboard and begin heating the interior to a more comfortable level and begin air circulation. He could sense quickly that the air was less musty. The heat would take a couple of hours.

He sent a quick message to Ali, informing her that their first planned stop was Galatia. He didn't mention the possibility of heading to Castor after that since he was worried the others might not want to go. Ali responded that she would try to meet them at Galatia. Transportation was uncertain at the moment, given the unrest in the United Worlds.

Mike Xie was the first to return. He asked Sandy what was going on, but

Sandy put him off. "If you don't mind, let's wait for the others, so I only have to tell you once. What did you do while you were away?"

"It was a great break, boss. I spent nearly the entire time rock-climbing. Providence has tons of amazing Class 5 climbs. I soloed on a 5.13 climb— by far the hardest I've ever done."

Mike was prepared to keep talking, but Portia returned. Boyle and Warburton followed her arrival closely. Sandy asked everyone to meet in the galley after they stowed their gear. When they had gathered, he explained about the cargo for Galatia and then the shipment for Castor.

"Castor is right next to where the HUWs are fighting, isn't it?" Warburton asked.

"Yes," Sandy replied. "It's possible we might run into some action as a result." Stick and Puss looked at each other with a gleam in their eyes.

"Mike? Portia? Does that bother you?" Sandy asked.

They both shrugged. "Sure, it's possible," Portia said. "I doubt the kids will be so lucky, though."

Mike nodded. "Same," he said.

"One other thing I need to mention," Sandy said. "Admiral Ketyungyoenwong contacted me and asked me to rejoin the navy. I told her I wasn't interested at this time. If any of you received a similar call and want to go, I'll buy back your share of ownership in the *Alice May,* and you can leave with my good wishes."

None of them said anything until Portia spoke up after having glanced at the others. "They contacted all of us. No admirals, though, just people we knew. We talked to each other after we got the calls. None of us are all that interested right now. What they're trying to do is no sure thing. Hell, they don't even know how they're going to pay for anything. You, on the other hand, just made all of us multi-millionaires. For me, anyway, the idea of going back to the navy, to my same rank and pay (if they ever get their hands on the budget) while facing the challenge of getting a retired ship up and running into a HUW attack group, it just doesn't interest me right now. Maybe down the road, I would be convinced but not as things stand now."

Sandy saw the other three nodding their heads slightly. "You agree?" he asked.

"Things could change, boss," Mike said. "But for now, I'm happier here than I was in the navy the last few years. You know I didn't want to get stuck in engineering, but that's all they'd let me do if I came back."

"The prospect of going to Castor doesn't bother you?"

"Nah," Portia responded. "Might be fun, especially if the kids get to blow something up on the way to or from."

Three hours later, the Manlius operatives arrived. Again, two men and two women. The men were brothers, Jude and Jerome Kearney: stocky, red-haired, possessed of booming laughs, and if the twinkle that seemed to be in their eyes was a clue, a sense of mischief. One woman, Emma, was of moderate height, with a gamine-like face and bright green hair. The other, Syd, was an Amazon come-to-life. She was the tallest of the four but not as bulky as Jude and Jerome. Her features were striking—not pretty, necessarily, but undeniably attractive.

After they came aboard, Sandy took the ship for refueling and to the station commissary to pick up the supplies he'd ordered. Stick and Puss argued over who would get to use the tractor beam to bring the container in the hold, finally settling the argument with rock-paper-scissors. Portia shook her head slowly, trying to hide her grin. Once the supplies were aboard, unpacked, and stowed correctly, Jude and Jerome volunteered to cook.

What they served to everyone about 45 minutes later astounded them all. Somehow, they had transformed the utilitarian ship food into a gourmet meal. Under questioning at dinner, they admitted they hoped to open a restaurant someday. They had come from Auriga in the United Worlds originally. Emma was raised in the Alliance, on Niobe, where Sandy was from. Her home had been on the opposite side of the world, though. Syd came from the non-aligned planet of Tyrol. She didn't talk much but seemed friendly enough.

The next day, they loaded their cargo and set off on the four-jump route to Galatia. Once they were released from traffic control, Sandy called the group together and reminded them that he would exit the tramlines before their terminus in case someone was lying in wait for them. Their cargo was worth a great deal of money, 135 million credits, and with the prospect of a civil war in the United Worlds and possible further disruption of trade, possibly even more.

They faced no challenges on the way. They arrived at Galatia Station eleven days later. Along the way, Bharwani & Minami had confirmed that funds were available if the *Alice May* would deliver the AI unit to the terraforming operation on Castor. Instead of cash in advance, as Sandy requested, they offered to put the money in an escrow account that would be released when the unit was delivered. Sandy agreed.

While they were taking on the cargo, Ali sent a message, asking if they could delay departure by a few hours. She was en route to Galatia Station. When they loaded the cargo, Sandy maneuvered into a spot designated by traffic control to wait. Ali arrived by taxi. After she stowed her small bag (in Sandy's cabin, he noticed), she went to the galley. Sandy gathered everyone. He introduced Ali to the Manlius people.

She changed her appearance during her time away. Her hair was now white, while her eyebrows were black. She had a beauty mark on her left cheek. Portia was the first to comment.

"You got your hair done, I see," she said drily.

"It looks good, Aunt Ali," Puss chimed in.

"Really good," Stick mumbled, then turned red when he realized he'd said that out loud.

Sandy didn't say anything but agreed with the boys. Ali was attractive to begin with, but now her appearance was jaw-droppingly sexy, he thought. Her face seemed slightly flushed. Sandy knew it wasn't because of the comments. She seemed excited about something. Sandy wondered what it was but figured she'd tell them all soon enough.

"You have all seen my updates (except for you guys—she addressed the Manlius people in an aside) and so know what's been going on. Things have changed again in the last couple of days. The man the Loyalists appointed as Group Captain of the newly constructed ships, Mataneice Feng, left the Nereus system about the same time you left Providence. He first reappeared in the Umbria system, a former Alliance planet. Feng declared he was forming a new government, centered on Umbria, that would also control the former Alliance planet of Eboracum, the United Worlds planets of Isolde and Garumna, and the non-aligned planet of Ammon. He calls the new multi-system group the Umbrian Confederation. Feng's ships are the least damaged of all the HUWs at this point. All the other attack groups have taken some moderate damage to some of their capital ships.

"Speculation is running rampant that the other two rebellious Group Captains, Mannbarschwein and Noyes, may attempt the same thing as Feng. Feng served as Noyes' XO about ten years back, so might become allied with Noyes and Mannbarschwein. The Loyalists don't have the numbers to go after the rebels if the rebels have agreed to coordinate. The rebels could defeat the Loyalists, but it would be costly, leaving them all vulnerable. While this has been happening, the Alliance Navy is in the process of reforming and has re-established control over seven Alliance planets so far, beginning with Valkyrie. Once they get their ships back in service, the Alliance will be slightly stronger than the HUWs but not enough to attempt any sort of offensive action. If the HUWs rejoin with the rebels, they could trounce the Alliance. Any questions?"

There were none. Since everyone was gathered, the Kearney brothers wanted to cook. Again, they took the mundane ingredients and made a savory meal. Ali was amazed.

Later, when Sandy's sleep period came, Ali entered his cabin and his bunk. She didn't say a thing, just backed herself into him and pulled his arm over. They both slept soundly. She woke before his alarm, and her stirring brought him out of slumber.

"Your information is incredible, Ali," he commented.

She paused as she was headed to the tiny shower. "What?" Sandy asked.

"I thought you were going to ask me how I got it," she remarked.

Sandy shook his head slowly. "Don't want to know. I went on a field trip in grade school to a sausage factory. As a boy, I loved sausage. Haven't been able to eat it since. I figure what you do is a lot like that."

Ali choked with laughter. "Closer than you'd believe," she acknowledged.

When she came out, she toweled off in front of him, seemingly not modest. She saw Sandy trying to keep from ogling her. It was her turn to say, "What?"

"Your new look is very... striking," Sandy said, after searching for the right word.

"Oh? You like it?"

"Yeah," he answered as calmly as possible. "A lot, actually."

"Good," she replied with a wink.

When Sandy came out after his shower, Ali was sitting on the bunk. "By the way, she's not mad at you. She didn't think you'd come back—I told her you wouldn't—but she wanted to ask."

"I have to say I was surprised to see her on the call," Sandy admitted. "I thought about it pretty hard."

"Of course," Ali affirmed, "that's who you are."

"The others were contacted as well," he said.

"As was I."

"As you can see, they're all still here. I worry that — "

"You worried that they stayed out of loyalty to you?" Ali finished his thought but with a slightly sarcastic tone. "Get over yourself, Sandy. I'm sure loyalty was a part of their decisions but not a deciding factor. Do you think I came back to the ship out of loyalty to you?"

Sandy shook his head, chuckling. "No."

"Remember what Darnell said when he learned his assignment on the *Ali Kat* was over?"

"Something to the effect that it was the most fun he had in the navy," Sandy recalled.

"Exactly. Each of us is getting something we want from this. For Portia, it's more money than she ever dreamed of, with her only irritation the occasional adolescent behavior of the boys. For Mike, it's the chance to learn everything about running a ship and managing people. For Stick and Puss... well, who the hell knows what motivates them, but they wouldn't stick around just for you. And it has been pretty low-stress. I think all of us appreciate low stress. Rejoining the Alliance Navy for you guys or ONI for me wouldn't be low-stress."

"What are you getting out of this, Ali?"

She sighed. "It's like my nest. I'm like a little bird—not ready to fly away on my own yet. But I'm thinking about it. I'll make it happen eventually," she explained.

"What do you want to do?" he asked.

"I'm going to set up my own freelance intelligence service," she stated.

"You'll be good at it," Sandy attested.

"Thanks. I think so, too. For the last two months, I've been testing my wings a little."

"Why did you come back?"

"You want the truth or the lie?"

"I'm like Stick and Puss. Give me the lie first."

"Oh, Sandy," she gasped, with melodramatic emotion, "I missed you with the passion of the burning of a thousand suns."

"Good one," Sandy chuckled. "And the truth?"

"I had some fun and excitement, but I was ready to come back."

5

The trip to Galatia was routine. They took precautions, but no ships were lying in wait for them. On the third leg of the trip, Sandy bumped into Syd as she was leaving Mike's cabin. When he mentioned it in a whisper to Portia, she simply nodded. Seeing Mike and Syd together was interesting. Syd was 10 centimeters taller than Mike. He asked about Emma, wondering if the two younger men were competing for her.

Portia laughed. "No. They've been teaching her how to play with the combat sims, and she's learning fast. She adores them, but more like a little sister to big brothers. Plus, those two and the Kearneys are thick as thieves. I'm sort of surprised they haven't started pulling pranks yet."

"Should I say something to warn them off?"

"Hell, no! That would just egg them on!"

When they reached the station, they were there for less than an hour. They offloaded their cargo quickly and took on the small box containing the artificial intelligence for Castor. Sandy received a message from B & M as they were leaving the system. There was a load waiting at the non-aligned planet of Noricum, bound for Providence if they wanted to pick it up on the return trip. Of course, Sandy replied that they would.

From Galatia to Castor was a five-jump trip. The direct route would take them along the edge of HUW-controlled space, adjacent to their Rutulius system. They entered every system cautiously. Sandy was more concerned that they might encounter a HUW frigate on picket duty than a competitor trying to steal their cargo.

They arrived at Castor after eighteen days. The huge terraforming ship was in a lazy orbit above the inhabitable planet. Sandy maneuvered the *Alice May* close to the mammoth vessel, and they transferred the cargo in open space. The Kearney brothers shoved the box containing the AI unit out into space. Someone aboard the terraforming ship captured it in a tractor beam and pulled it over.

From there, the *Alice May* headed for Noricum. Their planned route would take them past Excelsus, the site of a terrible loss for the Alliance in the war against the HUWs. Sandy's ship, the *Driscoll*, had been disabled and mostly destroyed in the fight at Excelsus, and he and the crew were forced to evacuate the ship in escape pods. When Sandy flashed back on his recollection of waking after being in the escape pod, he shivered. He had never felt so cold.

It would take seven jumps to reach Noricum. Their route took them in between the Excelsus system and the HUW's Marsyas system. Again, Sandy was more worried about a stray HUW frigate than any other sort of threat.

They were two systems short of Noricum when Ali came to the bridge. "You're going to want to avoid Noricum," she warned.

"What's happening?" he asked.

"Mannbarschwein's attack group has just claimed they control a group of systems centered on Vermilion, including Noricum."

"What other systems?"

"Marsyas, Excelsus, Noricum, Vermilion, Aquila, Dasypus, and Buteo, from what I gather," she replied.

Sandy activated the holograph of the astrographic charts. A blinking green dot indicated the *Alice May*. He keyed in the systems that Ali had just listed. The *Alice May* was currently near the middle of the blob of space containing those systems. The display only showed two tramlines in their current location: the one by which they entered and the one they planned to use to leave. He searched for tramlines in the next system. There were again only two: the one they were headed for, by which they would enter, and the one leading to Noricum. He backtracked to the previous system. It had three tramlines: the one they had used, one leading back to Castor, and one to Excelsus.

"We're in a bit of a pickle," he cracked, understating what his true feelings were when he really wanted to shout obscenities.

"Looks that way," Ali confirmed.

"Can you find out the locations of other forces that Mannbarschwein would consider a threat?"

"Like?"

"The two Loyalist attack groups and the two other attack groups?"

"I'll do my best," she replied, "but it will be rumors—not one hundred percent trustworthy. Why?"

"I'm going to assume he's competent," Sandy stated. "All I have to go by is that he blew my ship up in Excelsus and later led the attack on Freia, so it's safe to say he knows what he's doing. Any smart Group Captain will establish picket ships in the systems from which he feels an attack is likely. He has only a limited number, even though we don't know how many that is."

"You need this information quickly, right?"

"Yesterday would have been good," Sandy said with a weak smile. "If you have to pay for it, use company funds."

"I'll do what I can," Ali said as she left the bridge.

Sandy rubbed his face with his hands. He checked the Noricum system for its tramlines. It had three, other than the one they would use to enter. Two led towards HUW-controlled space, one led to the Karkinos system in what had been the Alliance. He got up, needing to ask Ali something else. Puss was sitting outside.

"Trouble, boss?" he asked.

"Why do you ask?" Sandy was curious.

"You look stressed out," Puss said somewhat hastily.

"Yeah. Well, I'll tell you all about it once I know more. Sit tight," Sandy assured him.

Finding Ali, he asked, "What are the planets where the Alliance has regained control?"

"Valkyrie, Arete, Niobe, Aurora, Neoterra, Caledonia, Hesperia and recently Inverness. Why?"

"Just trying to find a way out of here," he said, already heading to the bridge.

He entered the information in the computer, asking it to plot routes to the Alliance planets Ali had listed, to Providence, and to any system in the control of the Free Republics. It took the computer less than a minute to grind out the answers. It showed the routes on the display. Most of the routes followed the path from Noricum to Karkinos. Four of them involved doubling back and going through Excelsus. One involved returning to Castor and proceeding to Inverness. Sandy didn't like any of the choices the computer was giving him. Heading into Noricum seemed a bad idea. If Mannbarschwein's force had just assumed control of the system, they would want to stop his ship and likely had enough escort vessels that he could not evade them. Once they examined the *Alice May*, they'd undoubtedly seize her. Sandy reversed course, engaging full standard thrust. He didn't see the sense in plunging onward without more information.

Portia relieved him on the bridge. He was heading to check in with Ali to see if she'd learned anything when she appeared in the corridor. "You're going to want to stay away from Karkinos, too. Group Captain Noyes just announced he has taken control of Karkinos and six other systems."

"Time to share what we know with the others," Sandy said.

He returned to the bridge and asked Portia to set their course for Castor, then join everyone in the galley. It was Mike's sleep period, so he knocked on the hatch and gave him the same information. Ali rounded up Stick, Puss and Emma. Sandy found the Kearney brothers already in the galley. Mike and

Syd were the last to arrive, looking slightly disheveled.

Sandy activated the console on the table and projected the astrographic display he'd been examining recently. He pointed out their current location and then turned things over to Ali. She explained about the Group Captains' recent declarations of sovereignty over multiple systems. Sandy highlighted these as she listed them. After that, Sandy eliminated the routes that would take them through those systems. Only one was left—a return to Castor and from there to Inverness.

Sandy then focused the display on that route. He selected the Excelsus system and all systems linked to it. Their planned route from Castor to Inverness would take them through one of those adjacent systems.

"Why are you showing us all this?" Puss asked.

"Because it's somewhat likely we'll run into a picket ship out of Excelsus," he answered.

"From what you and Ali explained," Mike commented, "it's not like we have a choice."

"No, we don't. I just want to make sure everyone knows what we're getting into," Sandy explained. "And with all the smart people we have aboard, I'm hoping someone might come up with an idea. No hurry—we have more than a week before we get there."

It took nine days for them to reach the tramline that would take them into system SA 054, the system where they might encounter a picket of Group Captain Mannbarschwein's force. Stick had begun using the name "baby HUWs" to describe these three new multi-system governments, and it was so apt that Sandy had begun to think of them that way. No one had come up with any brilliant ideas. Ali could not uncover any further helpful information, so they were just planning to forge ahead.

When they emerged, three light-minutes short of the tramline terminus, they immediately brought up shields. There was no ship near the terminus, but there were two ships in the system. The information they had was nearly a day old due to light-speed lag. Both of the other vessels were frigates. The computer identified one as a HUW frigate, the *Grenko*, and an Alliance ship, the *J. O'Hare*. As the *Alice May* closed the distance, the information sped up, and they could see a battle unfold. It appeared as though the *Grenko* had been on picket duty, heading to position itself near the tramline leading to Inverness, when the Alliance ship had entered. The two ships had exchanged fire.

"Ali," Sandy called from the bridge, "can you contact someone and get us a kewpie link to the *O'Hare*? I'd like to help them out if we can."

A few minutes later, Ali entered the bridge and brought up a link to the bridge of the *O'Hare*. She activated the connection. Not recognizing the contact, *O'Hare*'s computer requested identification. "Sandy Pike. FT *Alice*

May. Do you require assistance?"

The connection went through immediately. Christine Weed appeared on-screen, wearing the insignia of a lieutenant commander. Weed had been a lieutenant on PAS *Chapman* when Sandy had taken command. It had been her complaint of sexual harassment that had brought the sorry state of the ship to the attention of the Office of Naval Investigation and resulted in the arrest of several of the senior officers and non-coms when Sandy boarded. She had been instrumental in helping turn the crew of the ship around. She had displayed grit and courage in the near-disaster that followed in Ilex.

"Not to be rude, Commander," she said, "but we're in a jam. So I'm sending you our current plot. Take a look and tell me how your FT can help."

Ali pulled the plot Weed sent up. Because of light-speed lag, the *Alice May* had not yet seen that another HUW frigate, the *Thomas Hardy*, had entered the system, but it showed on the plot Weed had sent. The *Thomas Hardy* was currently pursuing the *O'Hare*, and close enough that if *O'Hare* tried to change course, the *Thomas Hardy* might close within range. The initial HUW frigate, the *Grenko*, was trailing behind.

"What's your effectiveness?" Sandy asked.

"Here," Weed replied.

The damage control report for the *O'Hare* came through the link. Ali brought it up on the display. Shields were gone on the front half of the *O'Hare*. One of her two 75mm photon cannons was out-of-action. There were several hull breaches. Fortunately, her drives were still intact. Sandy absorbed the information quickly.

"Again, Commander," Weed asked, "how can an FT help?"

"I'm just Sandy, not commander," Sandy replied, "and this isn't exactly a normal FT. We have a 105."

"What?"

"The *Alice May* has a fully functional 105mm photon cannon," he reiterated. "The cycle time is a hair slower than on a *Ferlise*-class light cruiser but not by a lot. We're also fully shielded."

"What?" she said again in disbelief. Sandy began to repeat himself, but she waved him to silence. "I heard what you said. I'm just having a little trouble processing it."

"What sort of damage did you give the HUWs?"

Weed sent another report with sensor readings. Ali looked at it and summarized it aloud for Sandy. "Shields are gone on most of the front half of both ships. A couple of hull breaches. Guns on both are still functional."

"Christine, you're currently heading right for us. Keep coming. We're going to max boost to close the gap but reduce once we're close to range. When we reach cannon range, veer hard to port. The first of the HUWs will follow, and we'll take out their drives. Then we'll figure out what to do about the second one."

"No offense, Comman... Sandy, but that's a tough shot."

"Christine, have you ever heard of Stick and Puss?"

"Who?" she said, her face cracking slightly at the names. "Hang on... I haven't heard of them, but one of my lieutenants said they're supposed to have mystical powers or something... said the instructors at Gunnery School talked about them. So here, hang on."

Weed swiveled her console to show a young female lieutenant. "Um, hello, sir. Are Stick and Puss real people?"

Ali started to laugh, and Sandy couldn't stop himself from joining. "Yes, Lieutenant," he said, still chuckling, then started to laugh again.

The lieutenant looked uncomfortable, waiting for Sandy to regain his composure. "The reason I ask is the instructors talked about them like they were some sort of legendary figures with supernatural powers. We all thought they made it up."

Sandy began laughing all over again. His sides were starting to hurt. Ali had tears rolling down her cheeks and was laughing so hard no sound came out, just her gasping for breath occasionally.

When he finally gained control of himself, he apologized. "Lieutenant, I'm sorry. They're very real, and they are part of our crew. The reason I find it funny is... well, you just have to know them. I'll make sure you get to see them once we get through this."

"That would be awesome, sir," she replied. Sandy then heard her say to Weed, "They can hit the drives, Skipper."

"Good enough for me," Weed told her. "We'll stay on our current heading. Once we reach cannon range, we'll veer to port. Anything else?"

"Yes. Do you have any help on the way?" he inquired.

"Affirmative. There's a light cruiser about two days away," Weed replied.

"Great. We'll talk in a few hours after we deal with the first ship. *Alice May* out."

"Please tell me there's a recording of that," Sandy asked Ali.

Ali giggled. "Yup."

"Let's get everyone in the galley and tell them what we're doing. We can show the recording."

Five minutes later, they had all gathered. Sandy explained the situation and instructed everyone to strap in following the meeting since they would engage max boost for a couple of hours. Then he had Ali play the video, beginning with Sandy asking Lieutenant Commander Weed if she'd ever heard of Stick and Puss.

Portia reacted first. "Lord! That's Christine!"

As the video played, Sandy laughed all over again. Portia was clutching her sides, about to fall out of her chair. Ali was shaking and gasping. Mike's face screwed up as he tried to control himself. The four Manlius operatives laughed because the others were laughing so hard it infected them. Stick and

Puss beamed. Sandy had never seen two people look so smug and happy.

When everyone had recovered, Puss said self-righteously, "Aunt Ali, a couple of years ago, you said the same thing, but you said it was a lie." He wagged his finger at her. "Now we know it's the truth!"

Sandy shook his head and asked everyone to strap in. He gave them five minutes to get ready. As he was walking back to the bridge, he heard Stick say, "Dibs on the lieutenant. She's cute!" Sandy began laughing once more.

They went to max boost and stayed in that uncomfortable mode for two hours. The computer showed the time to engagement spooling down rapidly. Finally, after another two hours at standard thrust, they were nearing cannon range. Puss had control of the gun. He claimed Stick had forfeited his rights by claiming dibs on the lieutenant.

When they reached cannon range, the *O'Hare* veered off. The *Thomas Hardy* turned to follow. Further behind, the *Grenko* made the same course change, hoping to cut the *O'Hare* off if she escaped the *Thomas Hardy*. Sandy turned the *Alice May* hard to starboard, giving Puss a clean shot at the *Thomas Hardy*'s drives.

Less than a minute after Puss began firing, Ali, reading the sensors, commented, "They've lost thrust."

"You want me to take the guns out, too?" Puss asked.

"Sure," Sandy replied.

"Forward shields are brown," Ali cautioned. "C'mon, Puss."

When defensive plasma shielding absorbed more energy than it was able to dissipate, it changed color. The usually invisible shields would turn a dark yellow or light brown color. If brown shields were hit by more photon energy, the energy build-up would overwhelm the shield generator, causing it to fail.

A minute later, Ali declared, "They're not firing. We lost one shield generator. The others are shedding the energy build-up and should recover," she reported.

"Recover—in how long?" Sandy asked.

"About thirty minutes."

"Good." He then adjusted course to intercept the *Grenko*. In less than forty minutes, they would be within range. "Can Mike replace the shield generator in a half-hour?"

"I'll ask," Ali answered, getting up from the co-pilot seat.

"Commander," Lieutenant Commander Weed's face appeared on the comm screen. "My sensors officer tells me you took out their drives *and* their guns. I sure wouldn't have bet on it. Thank you. We're lucky as hell you showed up."

"You're welcome," Sandy replied. "We'll take care of the *Grenko* when we close the range. You're going to need to send your Marines over to take control of the ships while you wait on that light cruiser."

"Will do," she replied.

"There's someone else here who wants to say hello," Sandy said. He left the bridge and waved Portia in. Even through the closed hatch, he could hear Portia's excited voice, at least an octave above her usual tone.

"Nice shooting, Puss," he commented.

"It's all because of the supernatural powers, boss."

"Don't make me hit you," Sandy said, taking a swipe at the back of Puss's head. Puss ducked just in time.

A few minutes later, Portia came out. "You promised the lieutenant she could see them."

Sandy turned to find Stick and Puss already there. "Go ahead. Keep it short."

Puss exited the bridge after only a minute. Sandy raised his eyebrow. "He called dibs," Puss said with a shrug.

Sandy waited five minutes, then barged in. "Gotta go," Stick said hurriedly. "The boss is back."

Sandy heard the lieutenant giggle as Stick relinquished his seat. Christine Weed appeared on-screen again. "Any other surprises?"

"Mike Xie's with us, too," he answered, "but I just sent him out to replace a shield generator."

"Wow. I wasn't that close to Mike, though I thought he was a good guy," she explained, "and I've already done enough damage to my dignity talking to Portia, so I'd better close this. I've gotta say, Comm... Sandy, this was shaping up to be a terrible day, but instead, it's maybe the second-best of my life so far. Thanks."

"Just curious," Sandy inquired. "What was the best day?"

"Boarding and capturing an enemy ship in just body armor. Duh," she grinned.

"We were two jumps from Noricum when we heard the announcements from Mannbarschwein and then Noyes," Sandy explained. "We were worried as hell that we'd run into more than we could handle, but things worked out just right, thanks to you being here. As lucky as you feel you were, we were just as fortunate. Are you on picket duty?"

"Yes," Weed replied. "They were waiting for us at the terminus. Thankfully, someone taught me to be cautious when entering an uncertain system, so we dropped out two light-minutes early. It gave us enough time to be ready. We took most of our damage from the second ship—they dropped out of their terminus right on top of us and were able to head us off."

"Well, you brought them right into our laps, so that worked out pretty well. We're coming up on the *Grenko* now, so I'll sign off. *Alice May* out."

Ali reappeared. "Mike's back aboard," she said.

They slid behind the *Grenko*. Puss again disabled the drives quickly, then eliminated her guns. The *Alice May* took some fire and lost two more shield generators. Sandy resumed course for Inverness and asked Mike to replace them.

Once in the Inverness system, Sandy contacted Bharwani & Minami to see if there was any cargo they could pick up. Kevin Moon, their agent, apologized for putting them in a bind, sending them to Noricum. Sandy reassured him he had no way of knowing. An hour later, Moon sent a message that there was cargo on Valkyrie to go to Niobe. When they reached the Valkyrie system, Ali told Sandy she'd be hopping off the ship and would catch up with them in a month or two. Sandy made a motion like flapping tiny wings, and Ali smiled slightly in response.

Sandy asked everyone if they minded staying a couple of days on Niobe. He would arrange for them to all stay at a resort near his mother's house, and they could get some time in the sunshine and fresh air on the beach for a couple of days. When Moon contacted him to let him know of a load on Niobe, Sandy asked if the shipper would mind if he delayed the departure by three or four days. Moon replied a few hours later that the shipper didn't want to wait, but there was another job available four days later. This one would take them back to Edda.

Katherine was his mother's name, though he never heard anyone call her anything except Kitty. Sandy informed her about his impending arrival. He asked if she'd like to see his ship and meet his crew. She responded that she didn't really care to travel up to the station and back since he'd sent her pictures of the ship but that she would be delighted to meet his co-workers.

When they landed on the planet, it was morning on a mid-summer day. The resort had a shuttle that picked everyone up, but Sandy's mother had sent a driver to collect him. Sandy watched them go, assuring them he would meet them for dinner where they were staying.

When he arrived home, his mother gave him a hug and a kiss. Once he'd dropped the small bag he'd brought, she ushered him into the kitchen. "I want you to tell your friends that they're invited to a party tomorrow night. Of course, they don't have to come since they won't know a soul. You do, though."

Sandy groaned. "Mom," he whined, "why do you always do this?"

"Said the frog to the scorpion," his mother replied. "Because you don't come home very often. I'm quite proud of you. My friends who have known you are also proud of you. They enjoying seeing you. My newer friends like to know what all the fuss is about. What are your plans?"

"I'm going to see them all for dinner this evening at the resort. Then, tomorrow, I'll need to buy a suit for your party."

"A blazer will be fine, dear," she counseled.

"I'll offer the others a ride into the city if they'd like to join me. There's your party tomorrow night. After that, I imagine we'll just hit the beach for a couple of days. We just had a bit of excitement, so I think rest and relaxation are in order."

"Really? Tell me."

Sandy told his mother an abbreviated version of the encounter in SA 054. When he reached the point where the young lieutenant spoke about Stick and Puss, his mother pressed him for more. Sandy ended up telling her the entire story about the two when they were first posted to PAS *DeLuca*. His mother, who typically tended to lose interest in navy-type things, was actually quite interested. Of course, it was a fun story to tell.

Dinner that evening was a relaxed affair. Sandy brought his mother, who told them they were invited to a cocktail party the following evening. None of them expressed an interest in attending. He mentioned he'd be going into the city to buy some clothes. But, again, there was no interest.

The following day, Sandy took his mother's ground car into the city. Ground cars enjoyed a resurgence once humans spread from Terra Nova. Population density on the newly colonized planets was much less. Building public transportation systems at massive expense for a widely scattered public made little sense. Personal transportation, like electric ground cars and small flitters, was the logical alternative. A traffic control system guided the ground cars, even parking them.

Sandy went to his father's usual clothing shop. He hadn't needed to worry about civilian dress clothes while he was in the navy. The store he remembered going to with his dad would be an excellent place to start.

It took Sandy no time at all to buy what he needed. He took the blazer and slacks to the car and then visited the Kruppen office around the block. Though he didn't have an appointment, once he verified his identity with the receptionist, the office manager came out and introduced himself as Sergei. He and Sandy reviewed Sandy's portfolio of investments, and Sergei had some recommendations to help reduce his taxes.

Sandy asked him what he knew about the breakaway Group Captains and found Sergei amazingly well-informed. When Sandy expressed this, Sergei smiled, saying they had just had an exhaustive company briefing on the situation. He told Sandy that Kruppen's 'official' view was that, once the actual borders became established over the next 30-60 days, further outbreaks of violence were unlikely for several years. "It should be a very lucrative time for your business," he stated. "Most businesses are quite worried, given the upheaval to the status quo, and will be happy to pay a premium for security. On your end, in another month or two, things will be calm—though your customers will not realize that."

Sergei's comm buzzed. "I'm sorry, Mr. Pike. I do have an appointment scheduled. It has been a pleasure to meet you. I enjoyed our discussion."

Sandy left the office and returned to his mother's house. Earlier, he'd told the group he would come to join them on the beach when he returned. The car returned to the garage; Sandy went inside, hung up his purchases, changed into swim trunks, and found his mother. He asked to borrow the car again. She requested he return no later than 5:00 pm to get ready for the party. Sandy immediately translated that in his head to 17:00. Then, kissing her on the cheek, he headed out.

When he reached the resort, he checked in with the concierge and then headed out to the beach. The beach was not crowded, but plenty of people were out enjoying the weather and the sea. He spotted the group at a distance, thanks to Emma's bright green hair. When he reached them, he noticed Mike and Syd were missing. He asked, and Portia responded, "Clothing optional beach."

Sandy made a face, thinking of Amazonian Syd. Emma giggled, seeing his face and reading his thoughts. "It's a sight to behold," she cracked.

Sandy spent an enjoyable afternoon on the beach. Portia stayed mainly in the shade of an umbrella but did venture out to go swimming with Sandy twice. The Kearneys, Emma, Puss and Stick seemed to be on their feet or in the water the entire time, though the latter two drifted away. They were in friendly conversation with some young women.

Sandy returned home, showered, and changed into his new clothes. His mother was just finishing with the caterers. She sailed away to get dressed, telling Sandy to entertain anyone who was uncouth enough to show up on time. Sandy shook his head and smiled, remembering conversations he'd held with his father about the same subject.

As expected, the doorbell chimed with the first guests before his mother reappeared. Sandy introduced himself to them and engaged in conversation. A half-dozen people had arrived by the time his mother came sweeping out.

Sandy made the rounds, as he had been taught to do years earlier by his father. While Sandy was engaged in a conversation with some friends of his mother's, he felt a hand on his shoulder and a booming voice say, "Welcome home, Sandy."

He knew from the voice it was Bob Wilson, the next-door neighbor, and Leezy's father. He turned and shook hands. Bob Wilson was a lot like his father. He hadn't seen the Wilsons arrive. After saying hello, Sandy went to the bar to get a glass of water and saw Mrs. Wilson, Bettina. She stopped during her conversation with Kyra Khatri and came over to Sandy. He had not seen the Wilsons since their daughter had broken things off with him after the Battle of Excelsus. Bettina hugged him in a way that he knew she was trying to communicate how sorry she was. It made his heart clench, and he hugged her back in much the same way.

She stepped back and held him at arm's length. He could see tears welling in her eyes and had to look away. "How are you, Sandy?"

There were so many ways Sandy could answer her. It took him a few seconds to sort and find an appropriate response. "Prosperous," he replied.

She looked him in the eye as though she could read all the things he didn't dare say. She gave the briefest of nods. "Good."

She released him. "There are so many things I'd like to say," she sighed, "but none of them would do any good."

Sandy gave her a sad smile in response. Kyra Khatri saved him from needing to say more by coming to say hello to him. Sandy continued to circulate, and soon enough, the party wound down.

Sandy spent most of the balance of the remaining two days at the resort with the others. During the day, they didn't see Syd and Mike but met up with them for dinner. Stick and Puss were nowhere to be found. Portia explained they were with the young ladies they'd met the day before.

After three days, they returned to the ship, all feeling better than when they arrived. Stick and Puss were the subject of much teasing but didn't say a word about how they'd spent their time. They picked up the cargo bound for Edda and set off. The load was of transparent aluminum, rare and costly material. It was bound for Edda Station to replace some materials that had been recently damaged.

There were five systems between Niobe and Edda, requiring six jumps. The direct route between Niobe and Edda was not much traveled. Still, they kept their eyes open, anticipating danger that so often didn't materialize. When they entered the fifth system, sensors indicated a fast transport near the tramline they would take to Edda. That information was nearly two days old due to light-speed lag.

The computer identified the ship as the *Lucinda Gayle* out of Edda. She seemed to be waiting near the tramline terminus. Sandy sent a message to Ali, asking if she could learn anything about the ship. It was fourteen hours later before she responded, also in a text message.

"They're bad people. Wanted by the Alliance for possible human trafficking. What are they doing?"

"Waiting by the terminus of the tramline to Edda," Sandy keyed back.

"Possibly waiting for a pick-up," Ali replied. "Keep an eye out for a small ship, a yacht perhaps."

Sure enough, less than three hours later, the gravimetric sensors noted the entrance into normal space of a small vessel. Gravimetric sensors, within their range, had no light-speed lag but could only show the mass of a ship entering normal space from hyperspace. An hour after that, the gravimetric sensors indicated the small vessel had re-entered the tramline and left the system. It would be another three hours before the light from that action reached the *Alice May*.

Puss relieved Sandy on the bridge as his watch was on. "Puss, that FT is a slaver," Sandy stated. "As soon as you know which direction they're heading, I want to cut them off from whatever tramline they're aiming for. I don't want to spook them, though, so wait until the last minute to change course. Understood?"

Puss nodded his agreement. Sandy left the bridge and headed to his bunk for his sleep period. Of all the criminals in the galaxy, he hated those who engaged in human trafficking the most. Criminals would kidnap children, usually on the cusp of puberty, and sell them to deviants who used them for sexual purposes. The criminals would usually make their captives into drug addicts and use torture and the addiction to condition their prisoners to subservience. Sandy never encountered one, but his friend Monty did. Monty told Sandy what he saw aboard the captured ship. It was a horrifying story.

Sandy was unable to sleep. He gave up trying after a couple of hours and returned to the bridge, taking the co-pilot's chair. Puss pointed to the display.

"Nothing yet, boss."

Sandy decided to grab some coffee. He went to the galley, only to find Mike sitting on Syd's lap with their arms around each other. They broke apart quickly, their faces guilty. Sandy, preoccupied, simply muttered, "Keep it in your cabin." The two left while he was making coffee.

When he returned, Puss pointed again to the display. "This is what the gravimetric sensors logged a few hours ago. A small ship entered from Edda and is maneuvering to the FT."

Sandy watched the display. Since the *Alice May* was traveling up the light path, the sensors updated in a way similar to watching a video on fast-forward. He watched the smaller vessel approach the *Lucinda Gayle* and an umbilical tube extend from the FT, then retract. The smaller craft re-entered the tramline and headed back to Edda. The *Lucinda Gayle* was heading to a tramline on a heading 92° by -26° from the *Alice May*'s current course.

Puss was busying entering data into the computer. He finished and sat back. "We can wait another two hours before changing course and still be able to cut them off from either tramline," he informed Sandy.

"Good," Sandy grunted.

He then contacted Manlius and Tom McAllister, notifying them of an impending pick-up. Before making the course change, the watch ended, and Mike replaced Puss on the bridge. Sandy stayed in the co-pilot's seat while Puss brought Mike up to speed on the impending course change.

When Mike moved to intercept the *Lucinda Gayle*, Sandy watched to see whether they would try to continue on their current heading or attempt to double-back and return to Edda. The *Lucinda Gayle* was heading to a tramline that led to a system with nothing special but the system after that had six different tramlines that the *Lucinda Gayle* could use. She could reach over fifty settled systems from there.

The information the sensors could read was an hour old by the time it reached the *Alice May*. Fortunately, the *Lucinda Gayle* had the same handicap. Sandy entered different scenarios into the computer to see if the *Lucinda Gayle* could escape. He was pleased to learn they could not. Then he remembered the necessity of retrieving the captive or captives from the *Lucinda Gayle*. That was trickier. He must at least match course and speed in order to get the Manlius people across. Then there was the problem of captives—how to get them aboard the *Alice May*. He had no intention of putting them to sleep in the escape pods.

The information the computer provided spurred Sandy to jump out of the chair. "Mike, we need to engage max boost as soon as we can. I'll go tell everyone but be ready to punch it once I'm back."

Sandy scurried through the ship, warning everyone to strap in immediately. He woke the Kearney brothers, who were in their sleep period, but they responded quickly. Sandy lingered to make sure everyone was strapped in before he returned to the bridge. When he finished buckling the safety harness, he told Mike, "Hit it."

Through gritted teeth and the strain of nearly 4G, he explained why he needed max boost. Breathing was hard enough. Talking was worse. "Do same when they see course," he grunted. The 'ess' sound was particularly difficult, coming out as 'th'. "Can't outrun uth to tramline. Not good enough. Gotta get the captiveth back to our ship. Gotta before they freethe. Tight window."

Mike grunted back, "uh-huh."

"Dunno how retrieve captiveth," Sandy grunted.

Mike responded two minutes later. "Thlickth," he mumbled.

"Uh," Sandy grunted in affirmation.

Sandy focused his attention on the screens. As the distance between the two ships closed, the information from the sensors grew closer and closer to 'real-time.' After 87 minutes, he told Mike, "Flip. Thtay makth."

They stayed at max boost for another 79 minutes. Watching the displays, Sandy ordered, "Cut bootht, no thrutht."

Mike disengaged max boost. He and Sandy both gasped, the weight on their chests released. The display showed the *Alice May* slightly ahead of the *Lucinda Gayle*, traveling at nearly the same speed. However, the latter was continuing to accelerate.

"Shields up," Sandy told Mike.

Sandy punched the intercom. "Gunnery station, send them a missile once they fire at us."

Stick replied, "Got it, boss."

Just before the *Lucinda Gayle* pulled within cannon range, Sandy grabbed the microphone and broadcast a message. "*Lucinda Gayle*. Heave-to and prepare to be boarded."

When the range closed, the *Lucinda Gayle* opened fire with her 40mm photon cannon. Stick responded by firing an EMP missile. The powerful pulse disabled the ship. Her acceleration ceased. Sandy quickly scanned for life forms. There were six in the forward half of the ship and four in the hold.

He punched the intercom.

"Portia, make sure all four of the Manlius folks go across and take four slicks with them—there seem to be four captives in the hold. I expect trouble. These are bad people—slavers."

Syd responded to Sandy directly through her suit mic. "Are you authorizing the use of deadly force?"

"I am," Sandy confirmed. "Ship's scans read 10 life forms with four in the hold. I strongly suspect the four in the hold are captives. I'll keep you posted if they move. If they do, I'm guessing they might try to threaten the captives. Convince them, by whatever means necessary, that their only hope of survival is if the captives receive no further injury. Bring the captives back using the slicks."

"Affirmative," Syd answered.

Two by two the Manlius soldiers exited the airlock in their combat armor. They flew across to the *Lucinda Gayle*. As they did, Sandy saw one of the life forms heading to the hold. He informed Syd. Two-by-two, the Manlius soldiers entered the airlock on the *Lucinda Gayle*, Syd and Jude first. Sandy accessed the camera feed from Syd's helmet.

"If any of the captives suffer further harm, your lives are forfeit," Syd growled. The voice filter on her suit was intimidating as hell, Sandy thought. "Summon your crewmember who went to the hold."

One of the crew yelled, "Stan, come back. Now!"

Sandy watched the scanner. "He's using a captive as a shield, Syd."

Syd grabbed one of the crew and cupped his jaw with her armored glove. "If you want to have teeth, tell him to release the captive *now!*"

"Stan! No funny business! I mean it! Let the slave go!"

"Fuck you!" came the voice of the man struggling up the companionway with a captive in front of him—no simple task in zero-G.

"You," Jude pointed at another. "Tell him what's about to happen."

"Stan," the second man said, clearly scared, "they're about to crush Joe's face."

By now, Emma and Jerome were aboard.

"Probably be an improvement," came the voice from the corridor.

Emma calmly replaced the magazine in her fléchette pistol with one containing tranquilizer darts. The man with the captive was nearing the bridge. Emma pushed off and floated into the companionway.

Sandy saw the two bodies separate on the sensors. He saw Emma's form glide over the two bodies and head into the hold. Only Syd's camera was linked to the ship, though the Manlius armor could communicate from suit to suit.

"Escape pods, *now!*" Syd's voice barked. She roughly shoved the one she had been holding. "One of you collect the dumb shit."

Sandy watched through Syd's camera as the six crewmates entered (or were shoved into) the escape pods. Syd activated the pods but did not eject them. Jude and Jerome went to the hold.

"Mr. Pike," Syd said, her voice hoarse, "We have all four captives and will put them in slicks to bring them back. I'm turning off the camera now. You don't want to see what we see."

"Syd, they probably have them hooked on 'shiver' or 'sneeze.' Find it and bring it with you. I don't want to force them to detox just yet. That's better handled by medical professionals."

"Understood," Syd replied.

Minutes later, the Manlius soldiers exited the airlock on the disabled ship. Each was carrying one captive. When all were back aboard, and the course was entered to continue to Edda, Sandy rose to go see the captives. Emma stopped him in the companionway.

"Not now, Mr. Pike," she said firmly, holding her hand up in a stop gesture. "They're in awful shape. We're treating their injuries as best we can, then we'll clean them up. They need sleep and food. They also need clothing. Do you have any coveralls or jumpsuits aboard?"

"I don't know. Portia would know if we do and where to find them."

"I'll ask her. She's helping with first aid. We're putting them in our bunks for the time being—we'll sleep on the deck. We want to monitor them full-time. Once we get them cleaned up, we'll have pictures for you to send to the authorities so they can find the parents."

She shivered. "I knew people like this existed," she said quietly, "but I've never encountered anything like this. I'm glad I was able to save these kids, but I wish I'd never seen it."

Emma turned and went back to her cabin. Sandy suddenly felt the lack of sleep as his adrenaline from the encounter wore off. He went to his bunk and passed out.

He woke to the smell of coffee. Syd was sitting in the chair, facing him. She held out the cup of coffee. Sandy sat up and took it from her.

"Three girls and a boy," she said. "Physically, they'll recover. Emotionally?" She shook her head sadly, then blew out a sigh. "I don't know. It all depends on the family support they'll get."

"How are you guys holding up?" Sandy asked.

"Shaken," she replied, "but functional. We all saw something we can't un-see. It's a good thing we put those guys in the pods before I went back to the hold, or I'd still be taking it out on them."

Sandy sensed she wanted to say something more, so he waited. Tears welled up in Syd's eyes. He could see her fight to control her emotions.

"They addicted the kids to 'sneeze.' They raped them repeatedly and beat them regularly. Then they tied the 'sneeze' to sex—the kids couldn't get the next hit until they begged their captors to abuse them. They were begging

Jude and Jerome to — "

She fell silent. A deep sob wracked her frame. Tears rolled down her cheeks. Sandy wanted to comfort her but wasn't dressed. He reached over and took her hand instead. She clasped it so tightly he almost winced. After a couple of minutes, she realized. She released his hand. "Sorry."

"It's okay," he assured her.

"Anyway, we had Portia send pictures ahead to Edda so the authorities could locate the parents. She also found us something for the kids to wear. Jumpsuits—huge on them."

"I'd like to meet them," Sandy asked. "Let them know we're glad we found them."

"That'll be fine," Syd replied. "Actually, if you get up and get dressed, now is good. They're due for another hit of 'sneeze' in a couple of hours—in about an hour, things will get ugly. You don't want to be around for that."

When they arrived at Edda Station to unload, police met them at the dock. Jude and Jerome had been moving the cargo and called Sandy to the dock to meet them. Sandy saw three men in uniforms. Cautious, he asked to see identification.

"Sure," the one in front replied, reaching into his jacket. His hand exited his coat quickly, holding a fléchette pistol. He shot Sandy. His companions shot Jude and Jerome.

Mike was on the bridge, only paying vague attention to the camera feed. He saw Sandy slump to the ground like a puppet whose strings have been cut, and Jude and Jerome do the same a split-second later. He knew what needed to be done but couldn't remember the keystrokes.

"Computer!" he shouted. "Shut the hatch. Disengage. Emergency."

Before the three men could board the ship, the cargo hatch slammed shut. The *Alice May* withdrew her docking couplers. Sensing this, the station's dock door slammed shut before the huge opening was exposed to the vacuum of space. Mike activated thrusters, pushing the *Alice May* away.

"What the hell is going on, FT *Alice May*?" came the voice of freight control.

"Three of my people were just shot at dock A-15," Mike stated urgently. "Notify the police."

"Shit!" the freight control desk replied. "I got no eyes on that. Don't go far, *Alice May*. They're gonna want to talk to you."

"Affirmative," Mike answered. "I'll look forward to hearing from them."

He clicked the mic off and switched to the intercom. "Syd, we have a problem."

"What's going on? Did we undock?" she asked.

Mike accessed the camera feed and played it for her. "Fuck!"

Syd left the bridge hatch and began striding towards the hold. "Emma!

Suit up, stat!"

Once Syd had donned the helmet of her combat armor, she accessed the Manlius Military net. "Protocol Romeo Echo Delta. Code 30. Code 53. Corporal Kooluris. Edda Station."

"What is the nature of your emergency?" came the voice of the dispatcher.

"Three down, including client. Unknown assailants. Edda Station, dock A-15. Currently shipboard, disengaged from dock."

"Client?"

"Ship is FT *Alice May*. Client is Alexander 'Sandy' Pike. Contract on file," Syd stated.

"Stand by."

Opening another channel, she asked, "Mike, shoot me a copy of that camera feed. Then, link me in when the authorities contact."

The connection to the Manlius net reopened. A dark-skinned woman wearing the oak leaves of a Major appeared. "Corporal. What do you have?"

Using the optical register in her helmet, Syd accessed and sent the video she'd just received from Mike.

"Edda Station is a problem," the Major stated. "We have no presence in the Edda System. So we're going to transfer the operation to Gonzales Corp. I'm staying on until we get connected."

A new face appeared three minutes later—a pale man with black hair and a pencil-thin mustache wearing the silver eagle of a colonel. "Colonel Calderon," he said, introducing himself. "Thank you, Major. Corporal Kooluris, I'll be taking command. I'm also connecting with law enforcement on the station. Thank you for that camera feed. The freight terminal's cameras were disabled, so that's the only eyes we have on the scene."

Calderon stopped speaking, tilting his head slightly. "Law enforcement has just arrived on the scene. Two bodies. Here's the picture."

Syd looked. "Both ours, not the client."

6

Sandy woke in pain. He was lying on his back. His mouth was forced open with some sort of spreader on his upper and lower jaws. He tried to move his head, and sharp pains in his temples and on the back of his skull spiked. Something he couldn't see held his head immobile. It felt as though it had been screwed into his skull. His arms and legs were immobilized.

"Ah," came a voice. "When the student is ready, the teacher will appear."

Sandy looked toward his feet. A kindly looking older man with a fringe of white hair was there. He approached and sat on a stool next to Sandy, busying himself with items on a tray that Sandy couldn't see. They clinked.

"You have something that belongs to me," the man said. "I want you to give it back. Shh—don't try to talk. You'd only say no. I'm going to attempt to change your mind. These," he gestured at the tray, "are dental tools. They haven't been needed for over a thousand years. They are still quite useful, however. Let me show you."

The man picked up one and pressed a button on the side. A high-pitched whine came from it. He leaned forward, hovering over Sandy's face. Sandy could tell the man had inserted the device into his mouth, then felt it on the first molar on his left lower jaw. The tone of the instrument dropped to a lower register as it bit into the enamel of the tooth. Suddenly, Sandy felt incredible pain from that spot. Hearing Sandy yell, "Augh!" the man withdrew the drill. The hurt lessened but did not disappear.

"Yes, quite useful," the man commented. He picked up another device, this one connected to a tube. He pressed a button, and a puff of air hit the spot where he had drilled. It triggered the intense pain again, pulling another shout from Sandy. The man waited patiently, watching Sandy's face to judge when the agony had subsided. He released another puff of air. Another yell from Sandy, and tears streamed from the corners of his eyes. The man continued. Sandy lost track of how many times the man hurt him. Though his head was held fast, he'd jerked involuntarily. He could feel a trickle of blood on his temples, and the pain where they'd connected the restraint to his skull was worse, sharper. A hand that did not belong to the old man appeared in Sandy's peripheral vision. The sharp pains on his head heightened in intensity.

"Thank you, Jorge," the old man said.

The muscles in Sandy's arms and legs were strained by his fight against the straps holding him down. His throat was raw. His neck muscles were clenched.

"Just a small breath of air. What do you think this would feel like?" The man held up a dental probe with its thin curved end. "Would you like to see?"

The old man inserted the probe into the hole he drilled. The pain was far more intense. Sandy was on the verge of losing consciousness.

When he felt Sandy had recovered, the old man commented, "That looked painful. Let me cool things off for you."

He picked up a device attached to a blue tube. He sprayed ice-cold water into the hole he'd drilled. It was the worst of them all. Sandy lost consciousness.

"Corporal Kooluris," Colonel Calderon ordered, "bring Private Rudd and come to our ops center. Location should be on your heads-up."

Syd finished locking her armor. She looked, and Emma was doing the same. They crossed to the airlock and activated it. They exited the ship and used the thrusters on their suits to follow the display. It led them to another airlock about a quarter of the way clockwise around the station ring. They entered and crossed the corridor into the Gonzales facility. Syd and Emma were waved through, entering a warehouse area. They saw a dozen soldiers in combat armor and Colonel Calderon.

"Corporal Kooluris, Private Rudd, welcome," the Colonel greeted them, waving them forward. "Sergeant Backhoff, step forward so they can link to you."

One soldier stepped forward and faced Syd, holding out his hand. Syd reached with her armored glove. When the two touched, their communications synched. Emma then did the same.

"I'll be in command once we jump off," Backhoff said through his suit mic.

"Unfortunately," Calderon interrupted, "we are in the dark as to where Mr. Pike is. We have identified the people who took him and shot your comrades but have not found them yet. The police are also looking, and sharing information with us. They'd prefer if we took over for the actual capture."

"Mr. Pike, I hate to tell you but fear I must. There is no help on the way.

Local law enforcement either has no idea who I am or is on my payroll. Your friends will not find you. There will be no *deus ex machina* to save you. There is just you and me. And pain. An inexhaustible supply of pain, I fear. Even though I know it is too early, I will ask. Will you return my merchandise to me? Blink once for yes and twice for no."

Sandy quickly blinked twice. Despite the horrible pain, he would not surrender those children to this monster. He pictured the bruises on their cheeks, the bandages covering their wrists where the manacles had cut their skin, the hollow look in their eyes—he would suffer what he must.

"Not surprising," the man said calmly. "Some more incentive, then."

He picked up the drill. The high-pitched whine started. He attacked the next tooth, the molar behind the first. Agony, when the drill reached the nerve. Sandy's shout announcing the pain sounded like a sob.

"Jorge, please make sure our guest is tightly restrained," the old man asked.

Sandy felt the screws tighten on his skull. It hurt but compared to what was happening in his mouth, it was almost bearable. He could feel a new trickle of blood on his temples.

"Thank you, Jorge." Looking at Sandy, he said, "Jorge is so reliable. He's been with me for decades. He's simply a blessing. Good help is so hard to find these days. Shall we see what a puff of air feels like?"

He grasped the device and released a breath of air over the two teeth. The pain was no sharper but was far more profound. Sandy could almost imagine his jaw vibrating from pain. His eyes rolled up.

"There you are," the old man commented as Sandy regained consciousness. "Had a nice rest, did we? It was really quite impolite of you to nod off like that. You simply must pay attention, Mr. Pike. If you don't, I may give in to Jorge's entreaties. He very much would like to have a chance to convince you. I would warn you, though, Jorge does not like delicate tools such as these. He prefers more brutish things, like welding torches."

"We have a lead on two of the three," Calderon stated. "Sergeant Backhoff has their location. Go."

Syd and Emma jogged along with the Gonzales soldiers. They entered a huge airlock. A door shut behind them, then the outer door opened onto the inner diameter of the station's ring. They launched their suits into space. The destination was highlighted on the heads-up display. They flew not quite halfway across the ring to an airlock, where they were forced to enter two-by-two.

When Syd and Emma entered the station, Backhoff took off at a jog. Again, the destination was shown on the heads-up. They went up the corridor, then left at the first intersection, passed three more intersections, then right. Once they'd turned right, Backhoff slowed them to a walk so the thudding of the armor would not give away their presence. He paused at a door. Noting it was already open, Backhoff burst through into another corridor. His suit registered four heat signatures around the next corner: two standing and two lying on the floor.

Backhoff sprinted the last few steps to see two men holstering fléchette pistols. "Don't need you tonight, Gonzales," said one man. "We got 'em ourselves."

Backhoff signaled one of his team. Together they seized the two. "Hey, asshole! What do you think you're doing?" cried the first one. "We're station PD."

Backhoff contacted Colonel Calderon. "Sir, the two suspects are dead. These two shot them just before we arrived. Say they're station PD. I thought you said station PD wanted us to handle this."

"They did. I've got facial recognition on them. They're station PD. Shit. Hang on to them. I need to call this one in."

Calderon's mind was racing through its gears. His contact at station PD had stated quite clearly that they wanted Gonzales Corp. to arrest the suspects. Yet, these two men, identified as Detectives Weber and Karolya, had shot and killed the suspects. Was it a case of overzealousness, or was the station PD compromised? He decided to start with his contact.

He picked up his comm. "Bob," he said when his police contact answered, "my guys are at the scene. One problem. Two of your guys killed the suspects right as we got there."

"Who?"

"Detectives Weber and Karolya."

"They aren't supposed to be anywhere near there," Bob spat. "Plus, I ordered my people to stay out of your way."

"Bob, I've got a subject who might be the captive of someone associated with the two dead bodies. Can you swear on your mother's honor that Weber and Karolya are squeaky clean?"

"What are you talking about, Colonel?"

"I'd like my guys to question them. The clock is ticking, Bob, so we're going to use RR714. What they say won't be admissible in court, but if they're dirty, it will point you in the right direction so you can gather other evidence."

"What if they don't know anything?"

"Then I'll apologize, humbly and profusely. Gonzales Corp. will make it right, and I'll probably get busted down a couple of ranks."

"As long as it's your head on the block, question away. I don't know if they're dirty, but I wouldn't swear that they're clean."

"I'll let you know what we learn. Calderon out."

As Colonel Calderon ordered Backhoff to interrogate the two suspects using RR714, a truth drug, Syd received a message from Mike. "Syd, there's a yacht that is edging closer to us. I'm going to need to pull away from the station. I'm not leaving you in the lurch, am I?"

"No. We're okay. Stay safe."

Syd communicated to Colonel Calderon about the yacht approaching the *Alice May*. He contacted Mike and learned the registration of the yacht. While this was taking place, Sergeant Backhoff's interrogation was producing results. Weber and Karolya were spewing forth information. Calderon had linked the police captain into Backhoff's camera feed and had shared the registration of the yacht trying to approach the *Alice May*.

Weber and Karolya shared the name of the man who had initially approached them and paid them to look the other way. It was a lawyer, obviously a middle man. The registration of the yacht linked to a leased dock on the inside of the station's ring. Ownership of the yacht was a dead end, leading to a corporation with no other known assets. The lawyer could be linked to the lease.

"Leave two men behind to hold the detectives," Calderon ordered his sergeant. "Head to the dock. It's all we have."

Backhoff detailed two of his men to detain the police detectives and ordered the rest of the group to follow him. Another destination appeared on the heads-up display. Syd and Emma joined the rest of the group, forced to exit the airlock by twos. When all were outside, Backhoff activated the thrusters on his combat armor and flew to the destination, a dock a third of the way along the inside of the station ring, in a counterclockwise direction.

The old man was tapping the probe into the nerves of the two teeth he'd drilled. He was alternating between them, stopping when he felt Sandy was about to pass out. Sandy was in agony. Tears streamed from his eyes. The muscles in his neck, arms, and legs were cramped from having convulsed within the restraints.

A tall, thin man with hollow cheeks and deep-set eyes appeared in Sandy's field of vision. He leaned down and whispered in the old man's ear. The old man frowned.

"I hate to leave a job half-finished," the old man said to Sandy as he rose from his stool, "but I'm afraid our time here is ending. So until the next time, Mr. Pike."

Sandy was left alone in the chair. He didn't know how long he'd been left alone when he heard the thudding of combat armor approach. He heard a door open. A figure in combat armor leaned over him. The visor rose, and he saw Emma's face just before his eyes rolled up, and he blacked out again.

When he woke, he noticed from the stark white walls and machinery around the bed that he was in a medical facility. His arm, leg, and neck muscles were sore. He felt throbs of pain in his temples and the back of his head. His throat felt raw. Surprisingly, his teeth did not hurt. He cautiously explored with his tongue and felt nothing unusual. An orderly entered, noted he was awake, and departed immediately. A few minutes later, a pale, thin man wearing a green uniform entered.

"Mr. Pike, I am Colonel Calderon with Gonzales Corp. Manlius Military engaged us since they have no presence in this system."

"Your people are the ones who found me?"

"Yes. And the two Manlius operatives."

"Is my ship safe? My crew? The children?" croaked, his throat hurting with the effort to speak.

"Yes, to all three. The children have been taken to our medical facility down-planet. We have not released them to the authorities yet, for reasons I will explain. Two of the Manlius operatives were killed when you were abducted. Your ship is safe, though not docked at the station. Your crew, and the two Manlius soldiers, are safe aboard your ship. You are in our medical facility here on the station. We repaired your teeth, as I'm sure you have noticed, and have treated your other injuries."

"Who was that guy?" Sandy rasped.

"A slippery and somewhat mysterious figure," Calderon replied. "Mr. Alfred Mendele, a retired teacher. He has been suspected recently of human trafficking, but this is the closest the authorities have come to establishing a direct connection. He is, regretfully, still at large. He left the facility where you were found just before we arrived."

Calderon allowed Sandy a few moments to process the information, then continued. "This incident has kicked over a whole hornet's nest of problems, not the least of which is that the police here on the station are compromised. Law enforcement down-planet appears to be involved as well. The uncertainty of political control since the Alliance's surrender has created an environment where someone like Mr. Mendele can operate with relative impunity. The very people who were responsible for investigating crimes like his were on his payroll. We are assisting law enforcement with the investigation since they are unsure of who is involved. It is, quite frankly, a mess. As far as the children go, Gonzales Corp. is committed to their recovery and safety. We do not feel comfortable surrendering them to the local authorities until our investigations are complete."

"What can we do?" Sandy asked.

"Not a thing," Calderon answered. "It might be best if you left Edda and stayed away until we can clean things up. Now that you're awake, we're going to take you to your ship. It's the safest place for you."

Less than an hour later, they helped Sandy get out of bed and dress. Then, feeling weak and wobbly, they escorted him to a small shuttle. The shuttle delivered him to the *Alice May*. When he arrived, Portia gave him a hug.

"You look like hell," she said.

"Feel like it," he responded.

"Right. Off to your bunk, then," Portia ordered.

"But — " he started to protest.

"No 'but' just do as I say. We're heading to Providence. We can figure out the next step once we're there."

The next day, Sandy emerged. He felt better. His muscles were less sore, and the places where they had anchored the head brace only transmitted a dull ache instead of the previous sharp pain. He had a message from Lieutenant Colonel Tumperi at Manlius.

"Mr. Pike," Tumperi said when Sandy contacted him, "I'm glad to see you. First, a Gonzales ship is on the way to retrieve the crew from the *Lucinda Gayle*. Based on what I have learned from Colonel Calderon, I would suggest that we deliver them to a planet currently under Alliance control and not Edda."

"Colonel," Sandy replied, "I'm sorry about the Kearneys. As far as the animals on the ship, take them wherever they will suffer the most. What else can you tell me about this Mendele person?"

"What happened to the Kearneys is unfortunate," Tumperi admitted, "but not your fault. As far as the criminals, the best chance for justice to be served is in the Alliance. When they are convicted, their stay in prison will be highly unpleasant. Without any other evidence, the camera feeds tying them to that ship will be enough to put them away forever. As far as Mendele, believe it or not, it could be far worse."

Sandy began to protest, but Tumperi cut him off. "Mendele is a monster, no question. He's also small-time, as these things go. Most human trafficking is handled by large criminal organizations. If you ran into one of them, you would not be alive, and there would have been little we could do about it. Mendele has only been operating in the Edda system, so far as we know, though his customers are spread through settled space. His influence and resources are limited. He's a small-time bottom-feeder. He has been under suspicion for several years. It is believed that he began with one victim at a time. The political upheaval following the surrender of the Alliance and the United Worlds' failure to establish firm control of the Edda system provided him with an opportunity to expand because law enforcement down-planet fell apart. That allowed him to expand his business by providing him with extra cash that he used to buy protection by corrupting members of the station police. Thus, he was able to expand further."

"Do we need to be looking over our shoulders?"

"His reach is limited," Tumperi explained. "I'm not saying you have nothing to worry about, but, compared to the Graz Syndicate, the risk is several orders of magnitude less."

"How are the children?"

"According to Colonel Calderon, their recovery will take time. Physically, they are on the mend. The mental and emotional side will take much longer. They have to be weaned off the drugs first, and then therapists can address the conditioning they received."

"I feel horrible about the Kearney brothers," Sandy remarked.

"Don't," Tumperi replied. "If they had done their jobs as they were trained to, you would not have been abducted. Their deaths are unfortunate, but ours is a business with inherent risk. When you reach Providence, are you planning on resuming business?"

"I need to speak with the rest of the crew. My preference would be to resume."

"If that is your decision, we will assign a new team."

After speaking with Tumperi, Sandy sought Syd and Emma. He found them in the hold, sparring. When he entered, they stopped.

"Yes?" Syd asked.

"I wanted to stop by and see how you're doing," Sandy explained. "I'm sorry about Jude and Jerome."

"I'm okay," Emma responded.

"I'm good, too," Syd added. "We're sorry about them as well, but they fucked up."

"At least three different ways," Emma included.

Sandy raised an eyebrow, questioning.

"First, when unknown personnel approached the dock, they should have taken defensive positions. They didn't," Emma explained.

She turned to a console and brought up the video from the ship's camera. "As you can see, they didn't move. They accepted the uniforms as real. They did not act as we have been trained. When the 'policemen' approached, they should have moved here," she indicated one spot just inside the hatch, "and here," pointing to another similar location. "They should have asked the people to stop."

"Then, they should have called us to join them," Syd continued. "Finally, once we came, they should have asked to verify identity. Only after that had been done should you have been called to the dock. If they'd done their job, you would never have been in danger."

"We let you down, sir," Emma stated, her eyes downcast.

"You didn't let me down, Emma, or you, Syd," Sandy replied. "You kept your heads and coordinated my rescue. I didn't see the video of what happened until now and probably wouldn't have analyzed it the way you do. But, I know you were both there when they found me. I can't ask for anything more."

"Still," Syd said, "it shouldn't have happened."

"Hey buddy, you doing okay?" Monty Swift asked on the comm.

"Well, I've been better, to tell the truth, Monty. How did you know?"

"Portia. I asked her to let me know when you get in trouble."

"Huh," Sandy replied, making a mental note to talk to Portia. "What did she tell you?"

"That you intercepted a slaver, freed the captives, got attacked on the loading dock, tortured and rescued. Did she miss anything?"

"That pretty much sums it up," Sandy sighed. "What's going on with you, butthead? How's retirement?"

"That's Commander Butthead to you, Mr. Pike," Monty replied.

"You rejoined? Good for you."

"Yeah. Well, I thought I had something going with this beautiful redhead. We'd been seeing each other for a couple of months. So I was about to ask her if she wanted to move in with me."

"And?"

"Before I asked, she informed me she was getting back together with her old boyfriend, who had just proposed. See ya, Monty. It's been great. Bye!"

"Ouch," Sandy commented. "Sorry."

"Meh," Monty remarked. "You know me. Love 'em and leave 'em."

"You love them. They leave you."

"You say to-mah-to — "

"How is it, being back?"

"Strange," he said. "In a good way, though. The admiral has only asked the good people to return. No more Slocums. I genuinely like my peers—knew most of them already—and my officers and crew are awesome. I have the *Boxford*, a *Piqua*-class heavy cruiser. We're close to having all the remaining ships fully manned. Gotta say, your name was all the rage in the rumor mill a couple of months back."

"Me? Why?"

"Something to do with you showing up like a white knight and rescuing Lieutenant Commander Weed. People thought you'd come back after that."

"Don't know what you heard, old buddy, but that was pure luck."

"Did you or did you not disable two enemy frigates?" Monty asked.

"Well, we did, but she brought them right to us, and they thought we were just a regular FT. If it had just been us trying to get through that system, we wouldn't have made it. They were focused on her ship and ignored us until it was too late."

"Still, pretty impressive," Monty commented.

"Maybe it would have been impressive if we'd done it with a normal FT. With what the *Alice May* is packing, not so much."

"So, did you think about it? About coming back?"

"Not for a second," Sandy replied.

"Sorry to hear that," Monty commented. "I understand, though. Besides, you seem to keep finding ways to stay in trouble."

Later, Sandy received a message from Tamas Takada, the office manager at Kruppen with whom Sandy had been doing business. "Mr. Pike, an unusual deposit landed in your corporate account. I'm contacting you to see if you can explain."

"How much?"

"Just over 45 million credits," Takada stated.

Sandy was stunned. "Was there any information regarding the depositor?"

"None that I can share."

"I have no idea what it is," Sandy admitted.

"Well, it's highly unusual, sir. I need to know more so I can classify it properly for tax purposes. For example, if the corporation sold some assets, that would be handled differently from, say, earned income. Will you please let me know if you get an idea of what it's for? I will query back-channel, but don't expect to learn much."

"I'll do that, Tamas, but right now, I'm just as baffled as you are."

The next day, Sandy gathered the crew, minus Syd and Emma. "If it's acceptable to you, I'd like to make our stay in Providence short. I understand if you're feeling a bit shaken after what just happened, but, personally, I would like to stay busy."

"Pay up, suckers," Portia said, turning to the other three. Mike, Stick and Puss groaned and reached for their wallets.

"I told them that you'd want to press on," Portia said. "They thought you'd want a break. We had a bet. They lost."

"You're good with moving along?"

"Heidi and Cheyenne can't get leave, and Syd is being reassigned," Portia said, "so they have no reason to want some time off right now. I'm as happy on a ship as I am anywhere, so I'm fine."

"Besides," Stick commented, "maybe we'll have some more excitement."

"Speaking of excitement," Sandy added, "a deposit of 45 million credits showed up in our corporate account. Anyone have a clue what that could be?"

After a pause, Puss ventured, hesitantly, "Prize money? For the two frigates?"

Mike quickly ran the numbers through his head. "If it's prize money, it's about half of normal."

"We're also not navy," Portia remarked, "so if that's what it is, the Alliance was under no obligation to give us anything. I'm sure as hell not planning on bitching to them about it."

"I'll ask Ali to check into it," Sandy said, "but you might be right, Puss."

When they arrived at Providence Station, they stopped briefly at Tom McAllister's yard to pick up a replacement for the missile they'd fired. McAllister confirmed that the FT they'd disabled was on its way back and asked if Sandy wanted to 'spruce it up' before auction. Sandy agreed. B&M

had a cargo for them, bound for Corbulo, but it wouldn't be ready for two more days. Emma and Syd were joined by three other Manlius employees. Syd reminded them that their personal protection was part of the contract. Sandy left the ship and went to his apartment, accompanied by a Manlius soldier introduced as Cliff.

Sandy took care of minor errands for the next two days, accompanied everywhere by a Manlius operative. It was disconcerting. Sandy wasn't used to having a shadow. He was relieved when it was time to board the *Alice May*.

The other members of the crew arrived, each with his or her own shadow. A group of four combat-armored soldiers then appeared. This group was three women, Tina, Joanne and Bette, and one man, Don. Any of the four could have posed for a recruiting poster.

Sandy piloted the ship to the loading dock, where they picked up the cargo bound for Corbulo. As they were about to close the hatch, Tina alerted them to someone approaching. Portia looked at the camera feed and said, "Stand down. It's Ali."

Ali's hair was now a becoming shade of auburn, with her skin darkly tanned. She looked terrific. Sandy told her so when he saw her.

He stayed at the controls. They eased away from the station and followed the instructions given to them by traffic control. Ali took the other seat on the bridge.

"I heard I missed some excitement," she said. "Tell me all about it."

"Which part?"

"I've already heard about what took place in SA 054. Tell me about Edda."

"You don't want to hear about visiting my mom?" he teased.

"Heard about that, too. Everyone had an enjoyable time. I'm sorry I missed it."

"What do you know about Edda?" he asked.

"I know a lot more about what's happening there right now than what happened with you," she admitted.

"If I tell you what happened to me, will you share?"

"Of course."

Sandy started with intercepting the slaver. He explained about the condition of the children they rescued, though not in graphic detail. He told her about his abduction from the loading dock and Syd and Emma's opinion that the Kearneys had screwed up.

"They did," Ali commented.

She wanted to know what happened after that. Sandy told her about the old man, what he did to Sandy's teeth, and about how the old man's assistant supposedly like to use welding torches more. Ali nodded thoughtfully.

"Dental nerves are among the most sensitive in the body," she explained, "and they only register one thing—pain. Other nerves are differentiated to feel heat or pressure. Dental nerves aren't. Heat or cold causes pain. Pressure or agitation causes pain."

"It was astounding that a small puff of air caused so much agony," Sandy remarked. "But when he stuck the probe in — " he shuddered.

"It's actually quite clever," Ali pointed out. "I've never heard of that approach. In contrast to the welding torch approach."

"Honestly, the welding torch sounds more horrific," Sandy admitted.

"It is. The welding torch is used to heat implements, which are then applied on or in the victim's body. So besides the pain, there's also the awareness of injury and disfigurement. That's actually counter-productive," Ali stated.

Sandy's eyes widened. "You haven't — ?"

"No," she assured him, patting his hand. "Training only, I promise. The way it was explained to me, if the victim can resist the first couple of—let's call them, procedures—he or she realizes that he has no hope of surviving the ordeal. The damage is too great. A trained operative can use that knowledge to hold out, despite the pain. If you know you're going to die regardless — "

"That's horrible," Sandy gasped.

"On the other hand, targeting a tooth is not disabling or disfiguring. Other than the scabs and underlying bruises you still have on your forehead, you show no trace of your experience. Because the injury is so small, the victim might believe that he or she could possibly survive. That would make it harder to resist in a prolonged or repeated session. Tell me. What was he like?"

"He was older, with white hair," Sandy began.

Ali shook her head. "What was his demeanor? His attitude?"

"He was calm," Sandy recounted. "Very matter-of-fact. Not enraged. He seemed to understand that it would take time, and he seemed prepared to wait as long as he needed to. His calmness made me realize what a monster he was, but, at the same time, his patience was unnerving."

"Hmm," Ali remarked. "It must have been horrible. I'm sorry."

"You said you'd tell me what was going on there now," Sandy reminded her.

"Right. The Alliance is re-establishing control of the system. The Navy is now at a point where they can include Edda under their protection. Edda was one of the systems left in limbo by the surrender and then the HUW civil war. Essential services—power, safety, waste disposal—fell apart. The HUW governor had not yet put her people in place when the civil war broke out. News of war spurred widespread unrest across the planet. When the HUW Navy left, the governor fled and absconded with all the money she could. Edda Station was the only part of the system that continued to function somewhat normally. Down-planet, the remnants of the old Alliance government tried to re-establish control but had no financial resources. They restored basic services to two-thirds of the population based on not much more than promises, but the rest of the planet remained in chaos. Different people or groups seized power in different areas. In an environment like that, someone like your slaver can operate.

"With the Alliance returning to the system, the government will be able to re-establish control over the rest of the planet. The work that Gonzales Corp. started, in terms of rooting out corruption within law enforcement, will serve as a firm foundation. They will continue to be involved for the foreseeable future."

"Have they caught Mr. Mendele yet?"

"No."

"Speaking of the Alliance," Sandy mentioned, "a deposit of 45 million credits just appeared in our corporate account. Would you know something about that?"

"I would. It's prize money for the capture of two frigates. It's half the normal amount because, well, the Alliance is strapped for cash right now."

"Portia thought it was because we aren't part of the navy," Sandy stated.

"Nope."

"It's damned generous of them, regardless," Sandy remarked.

"Your timely appearance saved their frigate and bagged two of the enemy. So I'd say it was fair."

"That frigate brought the enemy right to us," Sandy explained. "We wouldn't have made it past two enemy frigates by ourselves. It was good timing all around."

The conversation turned to the topic of the baby HUWs. Ali informed him that the situation was stable in terms of boundaries being established and that the threat of further fighting seemed to be diminished. As far as what was happening down-planet in those systems, the new rulers had no difficulty with the former HUW planets. The former Alliance planets were in much the same situation as Edda. In all three breakaways, the military had quickly reinstated the former Alliance government as long as it pledged loyalty. That brought affairs under control rapidly.

"Within a couple of months, look for a resumption of normal economic activity," Ali predicted. "Right now, I'd keep my distance. Other, safer markets to serve."

They would transit four systems on the way to Corbulo. The first three passed without incident. The fourth contained something none of them had seen before.

Puss was at the controls. "We have a contact, boss. The computer identifies it as Free Republics *Calliope*-class destroyer—at least 300 years old. She's positioned to intercept us at the Corbulo tramline."

Sandy and Ali were in the galley, eating. Upon hearing the description, Ali snickered. Some of her sandwich escaped her mouth. Sandy looked at her.

"I know this guy," she explained, once she'd swallowed.

"And?"

"Up to you," she replied. "I can warn him off, or you can have Puss or Stick take him down. I'd prefer to warn him off. Plus, I don't think we'd get much for his ship. It's too... unusual."

"Who is it?"

"Jean LaFoute." She pronounced his name 'Zhawn.'

"An absolutely charming, devilishly handsome man who lives just on the other side of the law. The kind of guy where you check your pockets if he bumps into you and count your fingers after you shake hands. He's mostly a smuggler but has been known to indulge in a bit of piracy now and then. But, unlike every other pirate I've ever heard of, he is scrupulous about not harming his captives. In fact, he treats them like honored guests until the ransom is paid."

"Sounds like you have more than a casual acquaintance with him," Sandy remarked.

Ali blushed, something Sandy hadn't seen before. "It was on an assignment," she explained. "I was his, uh, prisoner for a couple of weeks. He had some information we wanted. I obtained it."

"Not the most unpleasant assignment you ever had, I'm guessing, based on your reaction," Sandy smirked.

"Um, no," she admitted. "Not unpleasant."

"Go ahead and warn him off," Sandy suggested. "You never know when you might need a friend... with a 300-year-old ship."

"Don't think about the ship," she requested. "Think about having a source of information... and an ally."

"An ally I could probably count on to run away at the first sign of trouble. Go ahead, Ali," Sandy said. "I'm just enjoying seeing you look so uncomfortable."

She pulled her comm out of her pocket. She looked up the address. "I'm going to need to use a console for this," she explained. "I need to access one of my other selves."

"Other selves?" Sandy inquired.

"You know me as Ali Lynch. Other people know me by different names."

"Go ahead. I don't know whether I'd like to be a fly on the wall for this conversation or not."

Ali thought for a moment. "Actually, having you on the call could be useful," she said. "You'll have to act like I'm your girlfriend."

Sandy raised an eyebrow, questioning.

"Like this," she said, scooting next to him, lifting his arm around her shoulders and tucking herself into his side, transforming herself into a winsome coquette. "Just look smug and confident."

Sandy laughed. Ali glared at him.

"As long as you promise not to punish me for it," Sandy said.

"We'll see," she warned.

She tugged him up and to his cabin. She adjusted the console on the small desk so it would show them sitting on his bunk. Then she rumpled the sheets to make it look slept in. After that, she looked in the mirror and mussed her hair. Looking down, she undid buttons on her shirt past the point of decency. When she was satisfied with her appearance, she ruffled Sandy's hair and unbuttoned his shirt to the waist. Turning to the console, she keyed in some complicated instructions. Eventually, the communications screen appeared. She keyed in the number, then hopped onto the bunk and tucked herself into Sandy. He put his arm around her possessively.

A man with video-star good looks appeared on the screen. "Melanie, my darling," he said. "How nice to see you again. To what do I owe the pleasure?"

"Hi, Jean," she replied in a flirtatious voice Sandy had never heard her use. "Sandy was nice enough to let me call you. I had to beg him and beg him."

"Really?"

"Yeah," Sandy said gruffly. "We're the FT that you may have noticed just dropped into the system."

"Oh, and you wish to negotiate?" LaFoute suggested.

Ali giggled. "No, silly. I asked Sandy if he would let you go."

"Let me go?" LaFoute looked incredulous, then laughed.

"Listen, LeFlic," Sandy began, sternly.

"It's LaFoute, sweetie," Ali corrected.

"Whatever," Sandy growled.

"Jean, you have to listen to me," Ali said with a pout and a flounce, in the voice of a woman who is not accustomed to having people take her seriously. "His ship is not what you think. He's got a really big gun."

She looked down at Sandy's lap then and, as if realizing what she'd just said, clapped her hand over her mouth and giggled. "Oops."

"A really big gun, eh?" LaFoute remarked.

"Look, pal," Sandy countered. "I'm only talking to you because the little honey begged me. But yeah, my ship is fully shielded, and we've got a 105. You do what you want. No difference to me. I don't know that I'd take anyone's word on it myself. When you can read our power signature in a few hours, maybe that'll help you make up your mind. Just remember, I gave you fair warning."

Turning to Ali, Sandy asked, "You happy now?"

She nodded up and down slowly and solemnly, like a child.

"See ya, LeFlic. Or not," Sandy said as he closed the connection.

Ali started to laugh, and Sandy couldn't restrain himself either. "A really big gun?" he commented, laughing.

"She's... uh... different," Ali admitted. "Melanie was the daughter of an industrialist on Dryope. LaFoute captured her yacht and held her for ransom. Melanie likes," she switched to her Melanie voice, "big, strong men," she said, rubbing Sandy's chest. Then changing her voice back, she continued, "So, it's only natural she would become LaFoute's plaything until the ransom was paid."

"How could you stay in character all that time?" Sandy asked.

Ali shrugged in response. Privately, Sandy's question made her uncomfortable. She had a gift for becoming these different personalities and still maintaining her objectivity. She also felt it was a curse—that the flip side of that skill was her inability to develop friendships or deeper emotional ties.

Later, she crept into his cabin during Sandy's sleep period and slid into his bunk with an uncharacteristic giggle. Sandy guessed she was playing at being Melanie for him. "Well, hello there, little honey."

Her giggle in response told him he'd guessed correctly.

When Sandy woke, Ali was already gone. He accessed his console and saw that LaFoute's ship was pulling away from the tramline. Perhaps LaFoute would spread the word, and the *Alice May* would face less interference in the future.

They continued on from Corbulo to Amiens, on the border between the Free Republics and the HUWs, to Dryope, Freia, Aurora, Raetia, Nemea, Galatia, and Lares. They had encountered two more ships who tried to intercept them and dealt with both easily. From Lares, they were headed to Noricum, assured by Bharwani & Minami that the way was clear and they should face no interference from the baby HUWs. They had just about reached the spot where they had turned around the year before when Ali asked to talk with him.

He sensed it was significant from her tone. He followed her to her cabin. She sat on the bunk and waved at the chair.

"What's up?" he asked.

"I want you to buy me out," she said.

"Huh?"

"I want you to buy me out—buy my shares of the business," Ali explained. "I'm ready to leave."

"What are you going to do?"

"Set up my own shop on Dryope," she replied.

"Freelance intelligence service?" Sandy asked.

"Yes."

"Is it — ?" Sandy began.

"It has nothing to do with you and me," she interrupted, anticipating his question, "and our friendship. We talked before about this, remember?"

"Yes, I do," Sandy agreed. "What do you think is a fair offer for your twenty percent?"

"When we agreed on the twenty percent, that was based on adding my courier boat to the company's assets. Since we've been in business, it has pretty much sat idle at the McAllister yard. I've used it on a couple of my 'excursions,' but the company has never needed it. So sign it back over to me and throw me another ten million, and I'll be happy."

"Are you sure that's enough?" Sandy asked.

Ali laughed. "You've already paid that much in profit-sharing, Sandy. It's plenty."

"Okay. When do you want to do this? Right now? Or can it wait until we get back to — "

"I'd like to have it done and jump ship in Noricum," she replied quickly. "I've already contacted the lawyer. She has everything ready to go if you're okay with the ten million."

"Wow," he said softly. "Sure. Have Sarah send it to me, and I'll sign off on it. How do you want the funds?"

"It's in the documents. You'll need to make a transfer to my personal account at Kruppen."

"You have it all wrapped up in a neat package, Ali," Sandy commented drily. "Tell me. Am I the last to know about this?"

Her mouth tightened slightly. "Yes."

"That stings a bit, Ali," he said quietly.

"I know. I couldn't talk to you about it. It would have been too complicated," she explained. "I'll have Sarah send you the documents."

She rose, a signal to Sandy that the discussion was over. Sandy stood up. He looked at her, trying to discern if there was any expression on her face. There was nothing he could detect. Sandy left, closing the door behind himself softly.

By the time he crossed to his cabin, his comm had chimed, indicating he had received a message with attachments. He woke his console and saw they were from the corporation's lawyer. He authorized his approval with his thumbprint without reading them. He then contacted Tamas Takada at Kruppen. The receptionist stated he was busy but would contact Sandy as soon as he could.

Takada contacted Sandy a few minutes later. "Is this about the transfer, Mr. Pike?"

"Ten million to Ms. Lynch from my personal account," Sandy confirmed.

"Oh. I thought it would come from the corporation," Takada stated, slightly surprised.

"No. I wish to purchase her shares myself," Sandy instructed, "not return them to the corporation."

"I understand, sir. There is one slight problem with that."

"What?"

"You don't have ten million in cash in your account, sir. Certainly, you have far more than that in your account in terms of assets, but we will need to liquidate some of your investments."

"Tamas," Sandy said with a calm seriousness. "I would like this to happen today. If you need me to authorize a letter of credit against the proceeds of whatever assets we liquidate, do it."

"Sir, if I may—are you sure you want to use your personal account? I can prepare alternative — "

"Tamas," Sandy interrupted, "which is the best performing asset in my portfolio?"

"The corporation, sir."

"With this transaction, I will now control an additional twenty percent of the corporation. You would try to talk me out of that?"

"When you put it that way, sir... but, there are — "

"Tamas, please do as I ask. Liquidate the poorest performing assets with an eye to minimizing tax liability."

"Yes, sir. I understand. I'll get the documents to you within hours, Mr. Pike."

"Thank you, Tamas. I will approve them as soon as I receive them."

Seven months after Ali left the ship, they were on another run to Noricum. Also on the same route, about 90 minutes ahead of them, was the aged destroyer belonging to Jean LaFoute. Sandy smiled, remembering the airheaded heiress Ali had pretended to be but otherwise was unconcerned. They followed LaFoute through two systems. When the *Alice May* dropped out of the tramline (two light-minutes early) into the system bordering Noricum, they were immediately alerted to a firefight taking place nine light-minutes ahead. Two frigates were engaged, and it looked as though LaFoute had flown into the middle of it.

The computer identified the two frigates as belonging to two of the baby HUWs: one Vermilionese and the other Karkinosian. The Vermilionese controlled Noricum, so the Karkinosian ship had likely been scouting and probing their defenses. Both of them were now targeting LaFoute as well as each other.

Sandy sent a quick message to Ali. He had no idea where Ali was or what time she was keeping but hoped she was awake and able to help. "Your friend LaFoute is in the middle of a skirmish. If you give me his contact info, I can help him out."

To his surprise, a response came back moments later with the information. "Remember, to him, I'm Melanie."

Sandy punched the contact address into his console. Since LaFoute's comm did not recognize the sender, it asked for identification. "Sandy Pike on FT *Alice May*. Want some help, LeFlic?" he growled.

LaFoute responded quickly. "Pike, I hope you weren't lying about your weaponry. I could use some help—we're getting hammered right now."

"Break at 90° to the tramline," Sandy instructed him. "We'll cut the corner and get there as quick as we can."

LaFoute's ship made an immediate course change, rising above the ecliptic of the system. The two frigates followed. It was clear from what Sandy could see that LaFoute had no chance of outrunning the frigates. His three-century-old ship didn't have the power to accelerate quickly enough to shake his pursuers. He was lucky that they continued to fire on one another even more than they targeted him.

Sandy hit the max boost alarm, warning everyone to strap in. Stick stuck his head in the bridge. "What's going on, boss?"

"Strap in," Sandy told him. "We're going to go help a guy out."

Stick took the co-pilot chair and buckled up. He accessed the console and read the information. He opened the intercom. "Dibs on the gun," he called.

"Damnit," Sandy heard Puss curse from outside the hatch.

Sandy engaged max boost, and they were thrust into their seats uncomfortably. He kept them at that rate for over twenty minutes before dropping back to standard thrust. They had closed the distance considerably and were nearing cannon range. Stick unbuckled and went through the hatch to the gunnery console.

"I was here first," he heard Puss complain.

"Tough. I called dibs," Stick responded. "Move it, or you'll get the boss mad, and he'll let Mike or Portia do it."

"Okay," Puss sighed with a hint of a whine.

Sandy could tell from sensor readings that LaFoute's shields were gone. The two frigates had shield damage but were in much better condition. The 75mm cannons on the frigates were more powerful than the 57mm guns on LaFoute's aged ship. Sandy figured that the damage they had taken was from each other rather than LaFoute.

"LeFlic," Sandy called through the comm. "We're going to hit the Karkinos ship first. Noricum belongs to Vermilion, so maybe they will lay off you if we help them out."

LaFoute appeared on-screen, his slick deployed, the hood covering his head and face. There had been a hull breach that exposed his bridge to space. "Karkinos is in better shape. Vermilion has taken more damage. I tried contacting the Vermilionese captain, offering my help, but he's not responding—except to fire at us."

"We might be able to get his attention," Sandy replied with a grin.

The *Alice May* was easing into range, coming up behind the three ships.

"Stick, hit the Karkinos ship. Stay off the other. Drives, then guns if you can."

Two minutes after closing within range, the Karkinosian ship lowered its remaining shields in surrender. Stick had hit both drive nacelles, leaving the frigate without propulsion. The Vermilionese ship stopped firing as well.

Sandy opened a broadcast channel. "Attention, Vermilionese frigate. This is FT *Alice May*. Do you require assistance?"

"No," was the only response.

"Are we and Captain LaFoute's ship cleared to proceed to Noricum?"

"You are. He's not," came the response.

"May we render assistance to Captain LaFoute?" Sandy asked.

"No."

"Chatty, isn't he?" Stick remarked, sliding back into the bridge. "LaFoute must have pissed them off. Either that or the guy is just a jerk."

"Former HUW," Sandy commented.

"True," Stick acknowledged. "That explains it."

Sandy contacted LaFoute. This time when his face appeared on-screen, Sandy could see the hood of the slick collapsed around LaFoute's neck. He'd obviously been able to exit the bridge into a compartment with atmosphere.

"You heard all that, right?" Sandy asked.

"Yeah," LaFoute sighed. "I was trying to help the asshole, too. That'll teach me."

"You gonna be okay?" Sandy asked.

"Yeah. I got people replacing the Alcubierre generators right now. Once they're done, I'll move on. I figure jerk face won't follow. He'll have his hands full with his 'prize.' You know where I can get a ship like yours?" he asked.

"It's one-of-a-kind, pal," Sandy commented, "like yours."

"Well, I think she's about all used up," LaFoute sighed. "I sure don't have the money to put her back in order. But, hey, is Melanie still with you?"

"Nah," Sandy answered. "I sent her home a couple of months ago."

LaFoute smiled. "She's a fun girl but not one who is hard to leave behind."

"Agreed. Well, good luck, LeFlic. Maybe I'll see you again sometime."

"It's LaFoute—but you know that already or you wouldn't keep busting my chops. See ya, Pike."

Arriving in Noricum, the *Alice May* was allowed to drop her cargo, but while at the dock, officers from the Vermilion security force appeared. The Manlius operatives took charge of the situation, verifying their identification before calling Sandy to meet with them. Before Sandy did, he contacted the Kruppen Financial office on Noricum Station. He warned them that he might be taken into custody. He established Portia as a point-of-contact. She would inform Kruppen if that happened, so an attorney could be sent to deal with the authorities.

As he'd expected, the officers arrested Sandy. When they reached the security office, they put Sandy in a cell. He waited a brief period before a guard came to inform him that his attorney had arrived. They also wanted to question him, but he was allowed to have his attorney present.

What followed had to have been one of the most fruitless interrogations Sandy could imagine. They moved Sandy into a small, windowless room with a long mirror on one wall. Sandy knew there were observers behind the mirror. He met his lawyer for the first time when she arrived. She was a sharp-featured woman in a severe-looking suit. She activated the field suppression unit on her comm and placed it on the metal table.

The police interrogator asked, "Why did you help the other ship?"

Sandy's lawyer said, "Don't answer."

"Were you aware the commander of the other ship, Jean LaFoute, is a known criminal?"

The lawyer again said, "Don't answer."

"How long have you known LaFoute?"

Sandy looked at the lawyer. She shook her head.

Sandy leaned close to his lawyer and cupped his hands around her ear. He whispered as softly as he could, "I don't know the guy. If anything, I helped them capture the Karkinosian ship. What's their problem?"

The lawyer shook her head in response.

"If you're not going to answer our questions, we'll inspect your ship. I don't need to tell. you that angry police tend to be a bit rough during inspections of this type."

"There are at least five different legal precedents I can cite off the top of my head that establish your lack of authority. You may not inspect his ship without his explicit approval. He does not approve," the lawyer stated.

"Fine," the interrogator spat. "Then we'll impound it."

"Section 5.29, Part A, Section 3, Paragraph 2 of the Civil Code of Vermilion says otherwise," the lawyer responded. "If you persist, and either inspect or impound his ship, you open yourself to a flurry of expensive lawsuits that will keep me, and several other attorneys, happily employed for years and make my client an extremely wealthy man."

"Why did you help LaFoute?" the interrogator demanded.

The lawyer shook her head. Sandy remained silent. The interrogator continued. At one point, he was shouting in Sandy's ear, and spittle from his mouth was coating Sandy's face. The lawyer used her comm unit to take a picture.

"Why did you do that?" the interrogator demanded.

"Uninvited exchange of bodily fluids is a form of assault and battery, according to Vermilion law. I'm documenting this for court and the lawsuit we will file," she replied coolly.

After nearly four hours, they finally gave up. Sandy was released. He thanked the attorney and returned to the ship. Bharwani & Minami informed him that their outbound shipment had been canceled. He suggested that Sandy stay away from the baby HUWs for the time being. Sandy had no problem agreeing.

Two months later, an alert from his comm woke Sandy during his sleep period. He rolled out his bunk and brought it up on the console. Ali was on-screen, pale-skinned, wearing heavy dark makeup, and changed her hairstyle to all black. The sides of her head were shaved clean, but the hair above was a regular length. Sandy blinked a few times—to get the sleep out of his eyes and take in her new appearance.

"Hey, Ali—what's up?"

"I woke you up," she observed.

"Don't worry about it," Sandy replied. "What can I do for you?"

"Nothing. I wanted to let you know I've been trying to track down your acquaintance, Mr. Mendele."

"Did you find him?"

"No. We were able to follow his trail for a bit, and then everything went cold."

"So, you were involved," Sandy clarified.

"Yes."

"Are you going to tell me about it, or do I need to drag it out of you, one question at a time?"

"I just wanted to let you know," she answered. "Do you need the whole story?"

"Well, you've piqued my curiosity," Sandy said, "so, yes, I'd like the whole story—or as much of it as you want to tell me."

Ali looked at him for a moment, considering whether to continue. Then, with a slight tilt of her head, she went ahead.

"Okay. After your encounter with him, I started poking around, trying to get some information on the guy. Not because of what he did to you, but because human trafficking disgusts me. What he did to those children, and others we don't even know about, is obscene. Listening to your story of how he tortured you, his calm, measured approach, and learning what he did to his captives, convinced me the guy was a monster—the worst kind of psychopath. That also interested me. You know I have my own personality flaws, but compared to someone like him… I wanted to know what sort of person could do these things."

"When I set up my own bureau, I won't be able to go in the field as much. I'll be the face of the business. This was one of my last opportunities to work undercover. I went to Edda and worked with Colonel Calderon. He shared the information they had learned about Mr. Mendele. Did you know he was a teacher?"

"Yes," Sandy responded.

"He taught science in secondary school for twenty-five years. Can you imagine having him teach children?" She shook her head. "During his teaching career, there were five children who went missing in the region where he lived. There was no link to him—they were not his students. They were from other communities. All of them had divorced parents, and one of the parents disappeared at the same time. Hence, police assumed the missing parent kidnapped the child in a custody dispute."

"Colonel Calderon and Gonzales Corp. had started the investigation and located the house where he'd lived during the period. They examined it thoroughly and found the remains of the missing children and parents. From the decomposition of the more recent bodies, they figure he killed the parents immediately and kept the children alive for one to three years."

"That's awful!" Sandy exclaimed.

"I know," Ali said with a tight-lipped grimace. "It's worse than that, though."

"How could it be worse?"

"He apparently allowed the man he called Jorge to torture the parents before killing them," Ali stated, "or Jorge tortured them until they died. The forensics people could not come to a conclusion then because of decomposition."

"Oh, Gods above," Sandy muttered.

"He retired from teaching about seven years ago," Ali continued, "and decided to make his hobby into a business. He moved to a different continent and started up again. He followed the same procedure, kidnapping children along with a divorced parent. In the residence he kept until recently, they found the remains of the parents but none of the children. When they found these bodies, the forensics experts determined that the last two victims were tortured to death."

"This is sick," Sandy stated.

"Yes. We turned over the evidence to the Alliance Investigative Service. They did not have any agents they could spare, so I stayed on the case. They did provide me with a psychological profile of Mr. Mendele. This helped us up to a point."

"What then?" Sandy asked.

"Guesswork," Ali replied. "I figured he moved again after almost getting caught on Edda Station. I guessed that he would stay on Edda but move as far away this time as he did before. I combed through real estate transactions to find him and narrowed it down to six possible locations. Since he'd addicted his previous victims to 'sneeze,' the AIS profile stated he would use the same drug again. So I insinuated myself into that segment of the underworld. We got a good lead on where he was and found the house he'd bought, but he wasn't there. It was completely empty. We did take down a drug ring, so it wasn't a total waste of time."

"Why did you take this on?" Sandy commented.

"You and I have talked, and you know I have my own personality quirks," she said. "ONI did a complete psychological profile on me when they recruited me. They diagnosed me as being asocial. I'm sure you figured that out already from what I've told you and from getting to know me. An asocial personality is in the same family of disorders as a sociopath or psychopath. Asocial behavior is one end of the scale, and psychopathic behavior is the other.

"I'd never met a true psychopath before. A part of me was always curious, with a 'there but for the grace of God' type of interest. Having gotten to know more about Mr. Mendele, I was even more curious. The evidence I've seen tells me he is a monster in human form. Plus, it bothered me that someone like him might escape justice. People get away with things all the time, but I don't know about them. I knew about this guy. So I decided to do something."

7

Four years had passed since Ali left them in the Noricum system. It was almost three years since they last traveled with any Manlius operatives aboard. Word spread about the *Alice May*. There were only two more encounters with hostile competitors after Ali's departure and the episode with LaFoute. Since then, they settled into a regular schedule of routes and established a reputation for being efficient, reliable, and secure. One of their regular runs was the shipment of rare earths from Providence to Galatia. It was their most profitable.

They were carrying a load to Cambria, an independent system bordering the Free Republics. Portia was on the bridge. She woke Sandy in the middle of his sleep period.

"What do we have?" Sandy Pike asked as he entered the bridge.

"Used to be an Alliance patrol boat," she answered, "PB 039. God knows what they call her now. Claims to be part of the Cambrian Navy. Didn't know they had one."

"They didn't. Last time we were here," Sandy agreed, sliding into the other chair in the bridge. "Was the contact video or just audio?"

"Video," Thompson confirmed. "Ran the face through the recognition programs. The system flagged her as wanted by the Alliance with a 25,000-credit bounty for stealing PB 039. Calls herself Captain O'Reilly now. Wants us to heave-to for inspection."

"Huh," Sandy grunted. He was assessing the situation. The astrographic plot showed the patrol boat was between his ship and the tramline to Cambria, on the far side of the ecliptic. So it was unlikely the patrol boat would be a threat to them unless he wanted to go to Cambria, which he did. As a matter of fact, he and his crew had a strong financial incentive to head straight to Cambria. Sandy sent a quick text to the Bharwani & Minami agent on Cambria. Bharwani & Minami were the shipping agents who represented the *Alice May*.

"Pat—since when does Cambria have a navy?" he sent.

It took five minutes before an answer came back. "They don't."

"We have a former Alliance patrol boat up here claiming otherwise. Used to be PB 039. Captain O'Reilly. System flagged her as having an Alliance bounty on her head."

"Oh," came the reply.

Sandy waited for more. Nothing followed. After two minutes, his patience wore out. "Oh—what?"

"Hang on," came the message. "You woke me up. Give me a minute."

Sandy waited, drumming his fingers on his leg.

"Sorry," Pat said, appearing on the console as a live connection was made. "O'Reilly is sort of freelance. She has that patrol boat. She contracts with non-aligned systems under a letter of marque to curtail piracy and smuggling."

"So, she's legit?" Sandy queried, puzzled.

"Not even close," Pat clarified. "As you know, most of the non-aligned systems don't have much in the way of a naval presence until you reach the planetary station. She approaches the governments with a slick presentation describing how much customs revenue they are losing to smuggling since they lack deep-space interdiction. She then obtains a letter of marque to act on their behalf, where she gets to keep all the contraband she seizes. She gives the governments a token amount of money which keeps them happy. It doesn't cost them a credit to engage her services, so they figure any money at all is better than what they had before."

"Sounds like a pirate," Sandy commented.

"Right. She doesn't limit herself to seizing only contraband. She's a pirate with a license to act on the government's behalf, at least until the government realizes what she's actually doing," Pat responded.

"What else can you tell me?"

"That's all I have. I'm just a shipping agent," Pat replied.

"Crap," Sandy muttered, almost to himself. "Okay, Pat. Thanks, I guess."

"One thing I forgot," Pat said before the connection was terminated, "she does business as Blackhawk Interdiction Services, and the ship is registered on Faunus as *Blackhawk*. Should I be worried that you won't be able to make delivery of your cargo?"

"Don't even go there, Pat," Sandy admonished. "*Alice May* will be there, on schedule." Sandy closed the link and leaned back in the chair with a sigh.

"That doesn't sound too great," Portia commented.

"No, it doesn't," Sandy agreed. "But it's just a patrol boat, so it won't be too awful."

He sent another text, this time to Ali Lynch. Ali had moved to Dryope and set up her own intelligence operation. She had been successful and had established herself as the prime source for intelligence on the non-aligned systems and the baby HUWs. If anyone could give Sandy more information on Blackhawk Interdiction Systems, it would be Ali. She'd charge him for the information, though, just as she did any other customer.

"At least she doesn't charge me extra," Sandy thought as he typed out a text to Ali.

"How do you want to handle this, Sandy?" Portia asked, waving her arm to indicate the situation with Blackhawk.

"Send 'em a message and tell them we will comply. We're a couple of days away from them, so plenty of time to figure out how we'll deal with them."

"I can send you the file I have on Blackhawk Interdiction," Ali said when she contacted Sandy, "for 500 credits—the going rate. It's a standard deep-dive credit report type file."

"Would that file include information relating to the current condition of her ship and the size of her crew?"

"Ah. No," Alison answered. "I have some information on that, but I'm gonna need to charge you extra."

"How much extra?" Sandy asked.

"Another fifteen hundred credits," Ali replied. "It's specialized information and more expensive to obtain. I gather this type of stuff on all sorts of different operators. It doesn't often get requested, but when it is needed, it's usually somewhat necessary."

Sandy explained his situation, hoping that Ali would let a clue slip that might save him 1,500 credits. Instead, Ali grinned at him in response—not a warm, friendly grin, more a predatory one. Sandy knew she figured out what he was trying to do. She had always been able to read him.

"Sounds like you really need this information," Ali smirked. "It's a good thing I like you, or I'd charge extra now, knowing how much you need it."

"Goddamnit," Sandy muttered, angry at himself. "I set myself up. Again. I can't even blame Portia for not making me shut up since she's off duty. Okay, 1,500 it is."

"Nice try, Sandy," Alison smiled. "The whole package is 2,000."

Sandy groaned. "Alright. Gimme a sec."

He entered the transfer of funds into the system. Ali nodded when she received notification. A few seconds later, he received two files from her.

"A pleasure doing business with you, Sandy," she said, closing the connection to prevent him from responding.

Sandy accessed the 'normal' file first. As Ali said, it was an analysis of the financial health of the company, describing briefly what sort of business they did ('interdiction'), assets, outstanding loans, payment histories, a bio of Jennifer O'Reilly, and a competently written summary on the advisability of hiring them as a vendor. She did not recommend it.

Sandy opened the smaller, more expensive file next. According to the file, O'Reilly had been a master chief petty officer in the Valkyrie shipyard, where the patrol boat was being refitted when the war ended. About six weeks after he and Portia had left to retrieve the *Alice May*, during the confusion following the Alliance's surrender, O'Reilly and a group of yard workers took possession of the patrol boat and left the yard.

She and the ship, now named *Blackhawk*, reappeared almost a year later as Blackhawk Interdiction Systems. Their first contract was with Altius, a non-aligned world. It lasted seven months. In the last six years, they had six different contracts. None of the contracts lasted an entire year. As each planet learned precisely what sort of interdiction O'Reilly was conducting, they forced them to leave.

O'Reilly moved along quietly until about 8 months ago. When the Dagmarr system rescinded their letter of marque, O'Reilly attempted to stay. However, Dagmarr then hired Manlius Military Bureau, the same mercenary company with whom Sandy had done business, to force O'Reilly to move along. O'Reilly traded fire with the Manlius ship before being forced to leave. Reading this, Sandy shook his head. He could have saved 2,000 credits. He had been doing business with Manlius Military since the *Alice May* returned to service, though not much lately.

According to the file, *Blackhawk* was not able to make repairs following that engagement. Manlius was confident that their fire had breached *Blackhawk*'s hull in at least two places. Given that the crew of *Blackhawk* contained former yard workers, they might have been able to make the structural repairs themselves. The critical information in the file was that *Blackhawk* was trying to obtain plasma shield generators on the black market since that encounter. Their most recent inquiry was a month earlier, and they were not willing to meet the seller's price. This told Sandy that a portion of *Blackhawk*'s hull was unshielded.

Even better, *Blackhawk* was estimated to have no more than ten crew members aboard, in addition to O'Reilly. Reading on, Sandy learned none of the original members who stole the patrol boat from the yard remained other than O'Reilly. O'Reilly replaced them with the sort of people you'd expect to find on a pirate vessel. Sandy surmised that perhaps she was not able to make the hull repairs so easily. According to Ali's file, O'Reilly was not a pleasant employer. Most of the attrition occurred with crew members jumping ship when they docked at a station. Still, O'Reilly was rumored to have sent a couple of the crew who disagreed with her methods on one-way trips out the airlock.

Sandy sent a couple of quick messages. The first was to Tom McAllister, the other was to Manlius Military. In both cases, he heard back quickly.

"What's up, Sandy?" Tom asked.

"Hey, Tom—how soon can you get a salvage tug to — " he paused, checking the astrographic chart, " — system KR 056? Next to Cambria."

"How big a tug?" he inquired.

"Big enough to bring in an Alliance patrol boat," Sandy answered.

Tom looked at him skeptically. Sandy returned his gaze coolly, looking as though butter wouldn't melt in his mouth.

"An Alliance patrol boat?" Tom asked, shaking his head with a smile. "By now, I'd have thought you couldn't surprise me anymore. But I'd be wrong." Checking his console, he said, "I have to reach out to someone on Cambria but I could get a tug to you in three or four days max—likely quicker."

"Good enough," Sandy confirmed. "Make it happen."

"I thought you were done with that kind of business?" Tom asked.

"We certainly don't go looking for trouble," Sandy answered, "but when it gets in our way — "

No more than two minutes after he closed that connection, he received a call the system identified as coming from Manlius Military. An imposing-looking dark-skinned man with a shaved head was on the line. Sandy brought him on screen.

"Captain Pike," the man greeted him, "Major Darius Jenkins. What can I do for you?"

"Major Jenkins. Nice to meet you."

"Likewise."

"Are you now my point of contact with Manlius? I dealt with Lieutenant Colonel Tumperi before."

"I'm just filling in for him while he is on leave, Captain," Jenkins replied.

"Does Manlius have any presence on Cambria?"

"Not at the moment," Jenkins answered. "If it's something you need right now, we can contract with another firm. If it's longer term, we can get some assets moved."

"It's for right now," Sandy clarified.

"What services do you require?" Jenkins asked.

"I'm about to take down a former Alliance patrol boat belonging to Blackhawk Interdiction Services," he explained, "in system KR 056. I need someone to offload their crew, keep them on ice, and provide security for the ship until a salvage tug arrives in a couple of days. The ship will be mine. Disposal of the crew is negotiable."

Jenkins accessed information on his system. "There are bounties from the Planetary Alliance on Jennifer O'Reilly and her crew," Jenkins informed him. "25,000 credits for O'Reilly and 5,000 for each of the others. How many in the crew?"

"My latest report shows ten, plus O'Reilly," Sandy stated.

"How soon?"

"They've demanded we heave-to for inspection. I can stretch it out to 57 hours, but I have a deadline to meet at Cambria Station."

"So, we need to scramble an op PDQ," Jenkins summarized. "The terms of our previous contract no longer apply. Off the top of my head, I'm going to figure that we'll split the bounties with you 70/30, though depending on what I hear back from the other firm, I might be able to improve that to 65/35. That will cover the cost of the operation, so there would be no charge to you."

"Don't bother whittling it down," Sandy responded. "70/30 is fine. I'd rather have you guys fat and happy in case I need you again down the road."

Jenkins smiled for the first time on the call. "Understood, Captain. From reading your file, you've always taken that approach and kept us fat and happy. It tends to make any request from you an urgent priority. Let me reach out to some folks, and I'll get a contract to you within the hour."

The contract Sandy received included the name of the mercenary outfit coming from Cambria—Berlioz Associates. He signed the contract with his thumbprint and then reached out to the contact for Berlioz. He was slightly surprised when Tina Berlioz, the owner of the firm, replied. Berlioz already scrambled a ship. After sharing course and speed information, they agreed that the Berlioz ship would exit the tramline from Cambria a few minutes after Sandy planned to disable Blackhawk. It would then be another two hours before Berlioz could take possession of *Blackhawk* and offload its crew.

A couple of hours later, Puss Boyle came to relieve Sandy on the bridge.

"What's up, Skipper?"

Sandy explained briefly about *Blackhawk* ordering them to heave-to. Boyle raised an eyebrow at this. Sandy nodded with a slight smile.

"It's under control, Puss," Sandy stated. "Nothing to worry about. You'll notice I've adjusted course and speed as though we aim to comply. I have other plans, though."

"Care to share those, Skipper?"

"I will, at the appropriate time, Puss. But, in the meantime, if they try to contact us, just put them off until you can get me on the line."

The hours went by, with the *Alice May* seemingly maneuvering to heave-to within easy shuttle distance of *Blackhawk*. The necessity of slowing to a stop dragged things out. Sandy always found these last few hours before an encounter to be the most agonizing. As the *Alice May* approached, *Blackhawk* did not bring defensive shields up. The report he purchased from Alison indicated their shields were not working. He hoped that was the case. It would make things easier.

Patrol boats were used by most planetary systems for customs enforcement—preventing smuggling. They were typically armed with a 57mm photon cannon and very light plasma shielding. The shielding was just enough to absorb a handful of shots from the 40 mm cannons found on most smuggling vessels (and pirates).

Sandy was on the bridge with Tim Warburton. "Okay, Stick," he asked, "once they fire, it's time to earn your pay."

He looked at him quizzically. "We haven't needed to do this for a while."

"It's like riding a bike. Toss a missile at them. Their shielding is gone. Can you do that?"

He snorted. "Are you kidding? This close, moving this slow? Even Puss could do it, Skipper."

"Well, Puss isn't lucky enough to be sitting here right now, so you get to unless you're afraid you'll miss. I know it's been a couple of years since the last one. I'll see if Puss wants to do it."

"Oh, stop," Stick said with an exasperated sigh. He accessed the console, made some adjustments, and entered some information.

"Go ahead and bring our shields up and see what they do," he asked.

Stick activated the plasma shielding. Within seconds of this, the patrol boat began firing at them. "Okay," Sandy said, "they asked for it."

Stick accessed his console. The missile bay opened on the ventral quarter of the *Alice May*. The missile flew straight and true, detonating just short of *Blackhawk*'s hull, overwhelming every electrical system on *Blackhawk* and burning its circuits out. Sandy checked the damage control screen. The 57mm photon cannons on the patrol boat had hardly strained the *Alice May*'s robust shielding.

"Easy peezy, boss," Warburton cracked. "They're fried. What now?"

"Thank you, Stick," Sandy replied. "Now, we head to Cambria and make our delivery."

"You aren't just going to leave them there, are you?"

"Nope. Got some folks coming to take charge even as we speak. Should be dropping out of the tramline any minute. They'll offload the crew before they run out of air or freeze, and a salvage tug will get the ship in a day or so."

"Manlius?"

"No, they don't operate around here. Another group they lined us up with."

"We haven't done this for a couple of years," Stick commented. "I miss it—a lot."

"That's because we eliminated all the stupid people," Sandy cracked. "Still, there's always room for new stupid people, I guess. Folks who haven't heard about Stick and Puss, the Scourge of Pirates."

"Is that the lie or the truth?"

"The truth, so far as I know," Sandy assured him, lying.

At that moment, the gravimetric sensor noted a ship re-entering normal space from the tramline. "That will be our friends," Sandy commented.

The commander of the Berlioz ship, Captain Jurevesic, contacted Sandy. Once again, they went over the details, with Sandy confirming the information about the salvage tug that Tom McAllister hired. "We tagged them with an EMP charge," Sandy explained, "so every system on the ship is toast. You'll have to operate the airlock manually—and please use the airlock. I really would like to avoid cutting a hole in the hull." The conversation over, Sandy stood and stretched.

"Let's have a team meeting," he suggested. "Time to let everyone know how rich I've just made us."

Stick accessed the ship's 1MC and announced a 'team meeting' in the mess. After checking the ship's course and speed, confirming they were headed for the tramline entrance, he rose and followed Sandy.

When the whole crew had gathered, Sandy began. "Some of you know pieces, but I wanted to go over the whole thing. I know we haven't done anything like this for a couple of years. We just disabled a former Alliance patrol boat that had been acting like a pirate, more or less, since just after the end of the war. We contracted with a mercenary outfit to collect the crew. They just arrived and will collect the prisoners before their air runs out. A salvage tug is on the way to collect the ship. There are bounties on the crew, of which we will get a portion. After that, the ship is all ours. Unless some of you object strongly, I think our best plan is to sell her back to what's left of the Alliance. Portia and I still kind of owe Admiral Ketyungyoenwong. We might be able to work out a deal to stock up on some of the hard-to-obtain spare parts that will help Portia keep the *Alice May* in tip-top shape for another decade or so."

"How much are we talking, Skipper?" Puss asked.

"Even at the most bargain-basement, sweetheart-deal rates?" Sandy commented. "Millions. That's an Alliance patrol boat. I'm sure it needs some work to be brought back into pristine condition, but the Alliance needs ships. The cost to buy her from us and refurbish her will be less than half of building a new ship. Last I knew, patrol boats cost in the neighborhood of 65 million credits."

When the *Alice May* exited the tramline and entered the Cambria System, a message was waiting for Sandy from Captain Jurevesic. Sandy contacted him.

"Captain Pike," Jurevesic said in greeting. "We have the prisoners in custody and are keeping watch on the ship. The tug is due to exit the tramline in a few minutes."

"Any problems?" Sandy asked.

"None on our end," Jurevesic reported. "We used the airlock as you requested."

"Did they resist?"

"Having a squad appear in full combat armor when you have only sidearms, no gravity, your air supply is running out, and the temperature is dropping fast tends to cut down on argument. Have to warn you though, sir, the interior of that ship is a mess."

"Not entirely unexpected, Captain," Sandy replied. "Is O'Reilly among the prisoners?"

"Yes. She tried to give us a different name, as did a couple of others, but we did DNA swabs, so that didn't wash."

"Very well, Captain. Thanks for handling everything so smoothly. I've never worked with your outfit before, but you're making a good first impression."

"Thank you, Captain Pike. I'll pass that along."

Sandy then contacted Ali but left a message when she didn't connect, asking for a direct contact method for her aunt, Admiral Ketyungyoenwong. Ali buzzed him back an hour later. "Why do you want to contact the admiral?" she blurted, skipping any sort of greeting.

"Hello to you too, Alison," Sandy answered affably. "Your information was worth every credit, as always."

"Why do you want to contact the admiral?" Ali asked again, with an exasperated tone.

"We disabled and captured that patrol boat," he explained. "I thought I'd give the admiral the chance to buy it from us at a discounted price before we put it on the open market."

"Oh," Ali replied, clearly thinking Sandy was asking about the admiral for another reason.

"What did you think I wanted her contact for?"

"Not that," Ali said grudgingly. "I won't give out her contact, but she has yours. I'll let her know you want to talk."

"Um — " Sandy started to interject.

"Don't worry, I won't spoil your surprise."

"That will work," Sandy agreed. "Is everything okay?" he asked. "You seem — "

"Don't worry about me, Sandy," she said flatly. "I'm a big girl, and I handle my own problems."

It took another two days for the admiral to contact Sandy. Naturally, she caught him during his sleep period, shortly after they had offloaded their cargo of transplant organs at Cambria Station. He asked her to give him a chance to wake up, and she agreed to call back fifteen minutes later.

"Thank you, Admiral, for giving me a few minutes."

"No problem, Sandy. What can I do for you?"

"Nothing, Admiral," Sandy said with a sly smile. "There's something I can do for you, though."

Admiral Ketyungyoenwong raised her eyebrow, indicating Sandy should continue.

"Admiral, I have just come into possession of a ship formerly known as PB 039. We're willing to make you a pretty sweet deal if you want to buy her back. Interested?"

Ketyungyoenwong opened her mouth to say something, thought better of it, and closed her mouth. She opened her mouth again, then closed it once more. Finally, "Yes," is all she said.

"We hoped you would be. Portia and I owe you, and we haven't forgotten. We'd prefer to deal directly with you, Admiral, if that's acceptable."

"What sort of 'pretty sweet deal' are you talking about, Sandy?"

"We were figuring we'd let you have her back for a third of what it cost you to build a new one. Of course, if we sold it on the open market, we could easily get twice that, but money isn't everything. We also want to be able to buy certain components from you at your cost."

"We're not a hardware store, Sandy," Ketyungyoenwong admonished.

"Understood, Admiral," Sandy replied quickly. "It would be a one-time purchase, not an ongoing obligation if that helps make it more palatable."

"I'm going to need to get other people to sign off on this," she cautioned.

"Yes, Admiral. We would prefer to negotiate only with you, however. We don't necessarily know the other people, but we do know and trust you if that makes sense."

Ketyungyoenwong nodded in agreement. "Sandy, what would it take for you to come back?" she asked after a moment. "If I knew what a mess this whole thing would turn into, I would never have let you go."

"If we'd known, the Alliance would never have surrendered," Sandy suggested. "But we didn't. With all respect, Admiral, I can't imagine wanting to trade my current situation to put on the uniform again. That said, things can change quickly, so I'll say I'm flattered by your interest, and I promise to stay in touch."

"You're continuing to prosper? I used to get regular updates from Alison until — " her voice trailed off.

"We're continuing to prosper," Sandy confirmed. "I hope Ali is as well, though she sounded a bit stressed when we spoke a couple of days ago. We bought some information from her, which was first-rate, as always. It led to this opportunity."

"She would disown me as her aunt if I shared any information about her with you," Ketyungyoenwong said, "but I will tell you I'm concerned about her as well and leave it at that. I will get back to you on your offer."

"The sooner, the better," Sandy suggested. "The salvage tug has already picked her up and is on the way to Providence. The first two legs of that route are the same as heading to Valkyrie, so I have about four days before I need to order her to change course to come directly to you."

"Understood, Sandy, but it's a fair amount of money that's not in the budget, and the Alliance, as it now stands, doesn't have much in the way of additional resources." Holding up her hand to forestall his objection, she continued, "It's a bargain at twice the cost, I'll admit. I just need to sway some other people to my way of thinking."

Three days later, Admiral Ketyungyoenwong contacted Sandy. "I have authorization to negotiate with you," she stated after exchanging greetings, "for PB 039. Why don't you tell me what you want?"

"How does 20 million sound?" Sandy replied.

Ketyungyoenwong was clearly surprised at the lower-than-expected number. Sandy could sense the gears turning in her head. "Is the ship still in one piece?" she asked.

"Still in one piece," he confirmed, "though her electronics are fried. We disabled her with an EMP shot. Her shields need replacing, and the interior needs to be cleaned, but other than that, she's in good shape, according to the report I received from the tug captain. I'll be happy to forward that to you."

"What's the catch, Sandy? I know you could probably get about double what you're asking on the open market. Wait a minute. I remember. You once asked me for twenty million."

"I did, didn't I? This is unrelated and based on the cost of a new patrol boat. But, as I said, we owe you," he replied with a shrug. "It's never been about money."

"If that's the case, why can't I convince you to come back to the Alliance?" she inquired.

"Ah… well, you do have one thing that I think I can live without," Sandy responded. "Politicians."

"But, Sandy — "

"Admiral, once I got away from the navy, I had the chance to think clearly. It occurred to me that the worst situations I encountered in my career all had one thing in common—politics. Politicians almost cost me my life a couple of times, and they did cost me the best relationship I've ever had. Politicians are responsible for the current, messed-up state of affairs. Politicians prevented us from being ready for the HUWs when they got restless. Politicians made an already bad situation worse afterward.

"With what we do now, we work for ourselves, Admiral. We have customers, certainly, but if their demands are unreasonable, we don't take the contract. That isn't an option in the navy, as you pointed out to me once. The civilian masters call the shots, even when what they demand is unreasonable and unethical. As much as I respect you, I don't know if I could do it again."

Admiral Ketyungyoenwong was silent for a bit, mulling over what Sandy had told her. "I wish we had this talk a few years ago, Sandy before you left the service."

"Admiral — " he began.

"Please, Sandy, call me by my name. My friends call me Letty."

Sandy smiled slightly. "Letty, it took being away from the service for me to realize the common denominator. If I somehow stayed, I think I'd be unhappy and not understand why. That would make me a bad person to have around, and then the high regard you seem to have for me would have dissipated."

Letty sighed. "I wish I could argue with you. I'd tell you that since Al Dorsey was re-named Head of Council, the navy has enjoyed the government's full support, but that doesn't change the past. I would suggest you talk to Monty Swift to see how he's doing, but I know you two still talk anyway. I would tell you that I have more problems than I have answers and could use your help, and I would tell you we have new construction in the works and that I need someone to command those ships, but I suspect you already know that, too. All I can do is appeal to your sense of duty and loyalty."

"I did my duty," Sandy said bitterly, "and it cost me my best chance at happiness. Right now, I'm exercising my second-best chance, and I don't want to lose it as well. As far as loyalty goes, I didn't have to give you the chance to buy back this patrol boat — "

"Understood, Sandy," Letty interrupted, seeing his anger grow. "I understand. I wish I could change the past, but I can't. I'm just trying to safeguard the future. I appreciate that you contacted me and the generous offer you made. We will be delighted to take you up on it. As part of the negotiation, I'm authorized to allow you to buy certain components from us at cost. This was agreed to by the Head of the Council himself, who I can say understands your feelings better than you would ever guess."

"Letty, I apologize for getting heated. I appreciate your kind sentiments. As I've told you before, I can't envision changing my mind about coming back, but I will keep the line of communication open."

"I will appreciate that, Sandy. I'll send a purchase order to you for PB 039. Please send me a list of the things you'd like to purchase."

"I'll get that to you soon," Sandy promised.

"One last thing," Letty said hesitantly. "If you hear from Alison, please ask her to contact me."

"Is something wrong?"

"I can't seem to get in touch with her. When she was on an assignment, it used to happen, but I didn't think she still went in the field the way she used to. It's probably nothing — "

"If I hear from her, I'll let her know," Sandy assured her.

8

The last request from the admiral disquieted Sandy. Ali seemed unusually tense when they last spoke a few days earlier. Still, she left him and the company and made it clear since then that she preferred to be on her own. It stayed on Sandy's mind. He was never in love with Ali, nothing like what he had felt (and still missed) with Elizabeth Wilson, but she was an integral part of getting the business started and a good friend and comrade. He respected her desire to be on her own but was worried even so.

The following morning, he sent messages to Major Jenkins at Manlius Military and Tina Berlioz at Berlioz Associates, asking them to keep their eyes and ears open for any unusual news about Ali. Sandy figured the mercenaries were as well-informed as anyone and might have information to which he had no access. Moreover, they were likely customers of Ali's as well, so they had an interest in her wellbeing already.

He mentioned it to Portia, seeking affirmation that he was doing the right thing. Portia thought about it for a minute. "What's the last thing Ali told you?" she asked.

"That she was a big girl and could handle her own problems," Sandy replied, cringing a little.

"Mhm," Portia commented.

"But the admiral — " he protested.

"No 'but' Sandy," Portia corrected. "You know you stepped across a line she drew, and that's why you're talking to me."

Sandy met Portia's steady gaze. "You're right," he said at last, with a sigh.

Portia reached over and patted his hand. "You're a good man, Sandy. The best. It's nice to know you care about our people."

Sandy raised his eyebrows at this.

"Even though she left, she's still one of us," Portia explained. "I care, too, and what you told me has started my wheels turning, but she has made it clear that she wants to be on her own, one hundred percent. So even if Ali is in trouble, don't expect her to be grateful if you step in. Let me know if you learn anything," she said as she rose from her seat.

He didn't hear anything for five days. In the meantime, they had taken on new cargo in Cambria, arranged for the salvage tug to deliver PB 039 to Valkyrie, and transmitted an order for every military-grade component Portia thought might wear out on the *Alice May* over the next 20 years. The next destination was Cartagena, a planet in the Free Republics. Sandy had only been to Cartagena once when he was in command of the *Ali Kat*, testing whether the concept of a stealthily armed freighter would be able to curtail smuggling and piracy.

Upon emerging from the tramline, Sandy's comm pinged with a message from Major Jenkins at Manlius Military. "Captain Pike: Alison Lynch has vanished. Her office on Dryope has been dark for several days, but it does not seem that she is closing her business. Her ship is still parked at Dryope Station. We are attempting to make discrete inquiries to learn what she might have been working on that might have led to her disappearance, but, as you know, discretion and speed do not often come in the same package."

Sandy passed the information along to Portia. "She's likely in the field, doing what she does," Portia counseled. "She was a field agent for ONI. She's done this before. You know she used to disappear. No need to panic."

"Do you believe that?" Sandy asked.

"I have to," Portia stated, "even though she hasn't done that in a couple of years. It doesn't mean anything other than she found a compelling reason to do it."

"How do you know she hasn't done it in years?"

"We stay in touch," Portia smirked slightly. "That said, I have no idea what she's up to."

Reassured by Portia, Sandy tried to put it out of his mind. Unfortunately, it kept creeping into his thoughts, and he chastised himself for it. They offloaded their cargo in Cartagena and picked up a load bound for Agnus, a non-aligned planet.

After leaving Cartagena Station, Sandy received another message from Major Jenkins. "Lynch was investigating the Graz Syndicate according to what little information we've picked up. No other information."

Sandy had heard of the Graz Syndicate but didn't know much about them. Ordinarily, he would contact Ali to buy further information, but that was, obviously, impossible. "What information can you share about Graz?" he replied.

It took several hours before Jenkins answered. "Information we have is proprietary, so not at liberty to share. Where are you now?"

"On the way to Agnus," Sandy replied.

"Contact Matt Bruns on Agnus. We use him, and he should be able to provide you with more information," Jenkins stated. "I'll send you his contact information. You know Agnus has become sort of wild and woolly, right?"

"I didn't," Sandy replied.

"Agnus always had a bit of a reputation when it was in between the Alliance and the Free Republics," Jenkins said. "Now, the two former Alliance systems it neighbors are members of different governments, and customs enforcement is a joke. Agnus Station operates under the golden rule—if you've got gold, you get special rules. Pretty much everyone in a government job there is for sale, at least temporarily. Funny enough, residents of the planet are blissfully unaware of what is happening in the space above the planet. They know only that their economy is booming and are content with that."

"Whoa," Sandy remarked. "The sort of place where you keep your head on a swivel and your hands out of your pockets?"

"You got it," Jenkins confirmed. "Again, Matt Bruns is your contact."

Sandy didn't know Matt Bruns. He guessed Bruns was a freelance intelligence source, similar to Ali. He mulled it over and decided to talk about it with Portia before he did anything else.

He shared the brief message he'd received from Manlius Military with Portia. When she read the name 'Graz,' her lips pursed. "These are bad people, Sandy," she said.

"I've heard the name," he allowed, "and know they're an organized crime group, but that's all."

"I don't know much more," she said, "but what I do know isn't good. Graz is all about drugs and human trafficking."

"Should I contact this Matt Bruns?" Sandy asked Portia.

"Seeing as how you've already stuck your nose in," Portia retorted, "you might as well."

Sandy gave her a look.

"Okay, okay," she admitted, lifting her hands up in surrender. "I admit that now I'm curious."

"Curious? Or concerned?"

"Curious, but the mention of the Graz Syndicate gives me a bit of... trepidation. As Ali said, she's a big girl and can handle herself, but... these people are evil."

"If they're involved in human trafficking, they're pure evil," Sandy commented.

Thinking of Ali in the hands of similar monsters horrified and frightened Sandy.

Sandy heard back from Bruns the next day. Surprisingly, it was on a video connection and not merely a reply text. When his face came on screen, Sandy thought he recognized him from somewhere.

"You're thinking we've met before, aren't you?" Bruns chuckled. "We did. I introduced you to Tyria LeBeau."

The pieces clicked into place in Sandy's head. Matt had been the ONI agent on Agnus when he arrived on the *Ali Kat*. Sandy gave a sheepish smile.

"Ordinarily, I wouldn't be so indiscrete," Matt explained, "but since our paths have crossed — "

"That's fine," Sandy allowed. "It would have bugged me until I placed it, so you just saved me some time."

"What can I do for you?"

"I'm told you are the person to contact if I want information on the Graz Syndicate."

Matt frowned.

"Is that a problem?" Sandy asked when Matt did not respond further.

"It's an unusual coincidence," Matt said tensely. "I provided information on them to a mutual friend about two months ago. I don't like coincidences. Coincidences are usually bad."

"Would this mutual friend have been present back when we met?" Sandy asked.

"Mhm. What's going on?" Matt asked.

"I honestly don't really know myself," Sandy replied, "and I'm probably interfering in a way that would piss Ali off if she knew. The last time I spoke to her, about three or four weeks ago, she sounded stressed about something. When I asked her, she told me to mind my own business. Ali's aunt also mentioned something seemed wrong right about the same time and then told me she couldn't reach her. I had some friends check up on her discretely after that, and they reported back that her office had been dark for some time, but she hadn't moved out. Her ship is still at Dryope."

"She and I trade information from time to time," Matt explained. "We have some of the same customers but specialize in different astrographic areas. She asked me for what I had on the Graz Syndicate, and I didn't ask why. Of course, she wouldn't have told me even if I had asked, at least, not the truth. Now that you show up asking for the same information and tell me that she's disappeared, I'm a bit concerned. As I said, I don't like coincidences."

"One of my colleagues suggested she might be out of contact because she's in the field," Sandy offered.

"Bullshit," Matt answered quickly. "There's no more fieldwork for the likes of us. Once we hang a sign out with our name on it, we can't go back out and act like agents the way we once did. We'd be recognized immediately. Instead, we hire that out to people who won't be recognized—folks who stayed undercover. Graz is trouble with a capital T, Captain, and nice people like you should stay as far away from them as you can."

"Well, I've already stuck my nose where it doesn't belong—in Ali's business—so I might as well keep going. She can only kill me once."

"With the Graz folks, killing might be a mercy. So I'm going to hold off on sharing any information with you, Captain. At least for now. Let me check with some people and get back to you."

Sandy shared what he had heard with Portia when they changed watches. Puss Boyle overheard the last part of the conversation. "Is something going on with Aunt Ali?"

Puss and Stick had been lowly but brilliant ensigns when assigned to the *Ali Kat*. The cover stories for the crew were that of a family: Sandy and Ali were supposedly married. Puss and Stick were their irresponsible nephews. Nevertheless, the two younger men had continued to call her Aunt Ali when they rejoined Sandy and Ali in the crew of the *Alice May*. While Sandy guessed that they did it as a weak joke at first, it developed into an actual term of endearment.

"Damn your ears, Puss," Portia exclaimed. "You should know better than to listen in when the grown-ups are talking." Puss and Stick were two of the brightest and most talented young officers either she or Sandy had seen. They could also be annoying, especially when they were together in the same location. As a result, Portia often adopted a testy attitude with the two.

"Sorry, Mama, I couldn't help it," Puss said.

"Don't you 'mama' me, boy-o. If I were your mama and knew what you'd turn into, I'd have drowned you at birth," she replied.

"You say that, Mama, but we know you really love us," Boyle said, sticking his head into the bridge. "Seriously, is something up?"

Sandy shrugged. "I don't know," he admitted, "but I do know that your Aunt Ali would be mighty pissed off at me if she knew I was checking up on her. So you won't tell her, right?"

"Probably not," Boyle said with a shrug.

Sandy rolled his eyes.

Boyle looked from one to the other, waiting for an answer to his question. "Are you going to tell me or not?"

"Best tell him, Sandy," Portia counseled with a sigh. "Otherwise, he and Stick will start digging to try to learn something, then that'll get Mike curious, and they'll make a big mess."

Sandy turned to him. "First of all, we don't know that anything is wrong. Second, I'm sure to make Aunt Ali mad as hell at me by even asking any questions. Third, if something is wrong, it's probably not something we can fix. Got that?"

Puss nodded. "Okay."

Sandy then brought Puss up to speed and what they knew.

"Now that you've told me," Puss admitted, "I kind of wish I hadn't asked. It might be nothing, in which case Ali is going to chew you up one side and down the other, and I want to sell tickets to the show, or if it's not nothing, it could be pretty bad."

"More than the five of us could handle, that's for sure," Sandy remarked.

When Boyle left the bridge, Portia shut the hatch and turned to Sandy, hissing, "Liar."

Sandy snapped his eyes back to her. "What?"

"You heard me," Portia whispered urgently. "You don't even know what's going on or what sort of odds we might face if it's as bad as it could be, but you're already talking yourself into going after her. You might be able to fool Stick and Puss, though I doubt it. I've seen you this way before, and I know what you're thinking. Just promise me that you'll give me a chance to talk you out of it and, if we do go through with it, that you'll get enough help because whatever it is, for damn sure the five of us won't be able to handle it by ourselves."

"I promise," Sandy said meekly. "But I swear — "

"Like I said, you're already talking yourself into it," Portia responded, lifting her hand up to stop his reply. "Maybe you haven't quite gotten there yet, but you will."

Matt Bruns contacted Sandy the next day. His grim expression communicated plenty before he even began to speak. "They have her, Captain," he stated flatly. "They nabbed her on Dryope a little over three weeks ago. One of my sources confirmed he saw someone matching her description being loaded a few days ago onto one of the freighters they control. She reported that the person was not in good shape and considerably older than the usual 'passenger' boarding a Graz ship."

"Where is that ship now?" Sandy asked.

"On its way to Agnus Station."

"When is it due in?" Sandy asked.

"Three or four days. They're not in-system yet, so haven't checked in with traffic control. Once they do, I'll know better."

"We're due at Agnus Station in four days," Sandy stated.

"Captain, I would strongly advise you not to do anything," Bruns cautioned. "I know you and Ali have history, but the Graz Syndicate is one of the top three most powerful organized crime operations. They have their fingers everywhere. If you tangle with them, they'll ruin your life."

"Understood. Matt, just confirm when they check in with traffic control. We're going to jump into hyper in about twelve hours, so we'll be out of touch for about a day."

After ending the conversation, Sandy checked schedules. Puss was the only one who had a scheduled sleep period, but since he'd already stuck his nose in, Sandy didn't worry about waking him up. Sandy called for a team meeting. They gathered in the galley/mess. He shared what Bruns had told him.

Portia shook her head sadly, as though she knew the answer wouldn't be one she liked, even before she asked the question. "What are you thinking of doing, Sandy?"

"Well," he began, "it would be great if we could take them in open space, but — "

Portia gave a snort of disgust.

" — but," Sandy repeated, "we can't."

Portia looked at him quizzically. Sandy shrugged his shoulders.

"I'm sure we could disable their ship but, then what? We don't have combat armor. We don't have enough people. Even if I were to try to contract Manlius or some other mercs, they'd never agree to take a ship in a planetary system because it goes against their contracts with the different systems. They'd be out of business and, quite frankly, so would we."

"Are you thinking of hitting them while they're at the station?" Mike Xie asked.

"Can't," Sandy replied. "Same reasons."

"Then what are we going to do?" Portia asked, now curious.

"All we can do is watch and wait," Sandy answered. "I'll hire some people to watch to see if Ali comes off their ship. If she does, we'll have to figure it out from there. If she doesn't, I suggest I hire some extra help from Manlius, and then we shadow their ship and disable it when we're in another system. Then we can get Ali. That's if Manlius is willing to take on the contract. They might not. The Graz Syndicate is an enemy they might not be willing to make. For that matter, I've considered what it might do to us."

"What do you mean?" Puss inquired.

"If we attack their ship, they'll eventually learn who did it, probably sooner rather than later. After that, it will only be a matter of time before they come after us, individually or as a group."

"This doesn't sound good at all, Sandy," Portia commented. "Do you have any other ideas? Ideas that don't end up with all of us dead?"

"Only one that's come to mind," Sandy said with a frown. "If Ali is still alive, maybe I can buy her from them."

"You mean, *we* don't you?" Stick asked.

"I wasn't going to ask," Sandy said. "I'm willing to cover it. Just had a windfall, after all."

"I'd like to contribute," Stick protested.

Mike, Puss and Portia both nodded at this.

"How much do you think it will take?" Portia asked. "Not that it matters."

"I have no idea," Sandy admitted. "I think it will depend on what she was doing that irritated them. I was planning on using a cut-out to try to keep our names away from them."

"Much as I would like to blow them up," Mike stated, "I think this is a better idea."

"Then, it's okay with you if I pursue this? Set it up?" Sandy inquired.

The other three nodded.

Just before entering the tramline to Agnus, Sandy contacted Matt Bruns.

"I still don't have word from traffic control," Matt opened.

"Matt," Sandy said with a wave, indicating he wasn't interested in that topic, "I'd like to run something by you. I'll need your help but it should minimize risk."

"I'm all in favor of minimizing risk."

"There's simply no way I can figure out how we could take her back by force without ending up in worse trouble," Sandy offered. Bruns nodded in agreement. "What about buying her from them?"

A thoughtful look came over Bruns' face. "That might work," he responded. "What are you thinking?"

"Could you set it up with someone like Tyria LeBeau and have her be the go-between?"

"Actually, Tyria might be perfect for this," Bruns replied. "Plus, it would help me mend fences with her. You realize she's going to charge you a fee?"

"No doubt," Sandy stated. "Let's structure her fee to give her incentive to drive a hard bargain, though. And keep our names out of it if you can."

"She won't want to know," Matt assured him. "That's why I think she'd be good for this."

"How much do you think it will cost us to get Ali back?"

"Depends on what she was doing to make the Graz folks angry in the first place."

"That's what I thought," Sandy confirmed.

"What form will the money be in?" Matt asked.

"I was thinking bearer bonds," Sandy said. "When we get a price, I'll have my broker code a chip in the exact amount and tell you where you can pick it up."

"That will work," Bruns confirmed.

"Good. We're about to enter the tramline," Sandy stated, "so I'll hope to hear from you when we drop into the Agnus system."

Twenty-seven hours later, and five hours after they had dropped out of hyperspace and into the Agnus system, Sandy heard back from Matt Bruns in a text message.

"I just got confirmation of your arrival time from traffic control. You'll arrive a few hours after the Graz ship is due. I've spoken with LeBeau, and she's apparently done these sorts of transactions with the Graz people before. I had a lawyer draw up a contract with a sliding scale fee structure with bonuses for LeBeau if she keeps the number down below certain thresholds. Bearer bonds are fine as currency. After discussing it with her, I think we'll set a ceiling of 10 million credits. She's never had a transaction exceed that. I'm going to transmit the contract for LeBeau. When you get back to me, I'll start things in motion."

The proposed contract was attached to the message. Sandy downloaded it and scanned it. He then accessed a directory for Kruppen Financial and got the 'net address for their office on Agnus Station. As he had learned over the last few years, the bank officer in each station office was also a lawyer. Sandy instructed the bank officer to review the contract for LeBeau. He asked the banker to create a new dummy corporation that would then contract with LeBeau, with no way of tracing ownership of the dummy corporation back to the *Alice May*. Sandy also informed the banker that he would need a chip created for bearer bonds in an amount to be determined, with that chip to be picked up by a third party. The banker was unphased by these instructions, as though he handled requests like this as a matter of his daily routine.

Less than two hours later, the banker sent Sandy the files with the contract for LeBeau, which he approved, and the incorporation papers. The banker informed him that the security protocol for the third party to obtain the chip would be shared once he knew the amount of the bonds. Sandy indicated his approval with a thumbprint and his personal alphanumeric codes.

Sandy sent the contracts to Bruns, and Bruns contacted him immediately. "Captain, I have the documents."

"Good," Sandy affirmed. "Go ahead and set everything up, but I'm willing to increase the ceiling on the offer to 20 million."

"From what Tyria told me," Bruns replied, "that shouldn't be necessary. She seems to think it will be less than 5 million. How do you want to handle the actual transfer?"

"The less personal involvement either of us has, the better, correct?"

Bruns nodded.

"Does Manlius Military have any presence in this system? I haven't checked."

"They do," Bruns confirmed. "They have an office on the station and a larger operation down-planet."

"Do they have medical facilities there?"

"I believe they do. Hang on. I'll check," Bruns said. After a moment, he declared, "Affirmative."

"I'm going to set that up through Kruppen," Sandy said. Bruns nodded.

Sandy contacted the banker and authorized him to use the dummy corporation to hire Manlius Military to handle the transfer of the data chip in exchange for Ali and to provide Ali with any needed medical services once she was in their custody. The banker quickly confirmed the details, stating that he could contact Manlius directly to handle them picking up the data chip with the bearer bonds on it. After a half-hour, Sandy received a contract between the new dummy corporation and Manlius, which he approved with his thumbprint. After that, Sandy had nothing to do but wait.

Sandy had always hated the waiting. In his navy career and even in the early days of the *Alice May*, there were situations where conflict was inevitable. Still, the laws of physics mean that hours and sometimes days would pass by before a brief yet furious encounter would decide the outcome. At least in those circumstances, he would be able to influence the terms of that brief encounter. Here, he felt powerless. He paced through the *Alice May* like a caged lion, annoying Portia, Mike, Puss and Stick. They all demanded he calm down since he was driving them nuts. He would sit for a bit but then, without thinking, would find himself pacing again. Finally, after the third time, Portia ordered Sandy to go to their cramped exercise facility and not emerge until he was exhausted.

Sandy did as he was told. When he emerged, he took a shower and ate, then went to sleep. He figured that would help the time pass as well as anything. When he woke, he was disappointed but not surprised to see that there was no news. It was his watch on the bridge, so that kept him from resuming his pacing.

When he was relieved by Mike, Sandy was still keyed up. He went to the galley, the biggest open space in the crew quarters, and began to work through his Tai Chi. He was having difficulty clearing his mind, preventing him from doing the exercises correctly. He needed to stop and restart a couple of times. When he finished, he felt more able to withstand the waiting.

He was in the middle of his second watch on the bridge when the message came from Matt Bruns. "Negotiations complete. Final price is 3.5 million credits. Transfer to take place before your slotted arrival time. Will confirm once transfer is finished."

Sandy contacted Kruppen with the amount and authorized payment to Tyria LeBeau once the transfer was complete. Kruppen again requested his authorization codes and thumbprint. That done, Sandy had another seven to ten hours to wait. While still full of nervous energy, he was better able to control himself since things seemed to be heading in the right direction.

With two hours to go before the *Alice May* docked at Agnus Station, Bruns sent a message. "Transfer complete. Package in transit down-planet. Goods are damaged."

Sandy immediately tried to contact Bruns but got no answer. He forwarded the message to his banker, asking for an update from Manlius as soon as possible. He then passed along the message to Portia, Mike, Stick and Puss. Portia came onto the bridge moments later.

"Does 'goods are damaged' mean what I think it means?" she inquired.

"Well, the person on Dryope who reported Ali was taken aboard the Graz ship mentioned she was not in good shape. We'll have to wait until we get word from Manlius before we know more."

"Unacceptable," Portia spat.

"Unavoidable," Sandy replied, more calmly. "Look, I've tried my best to make sure no one can trace any of this back to us. If we continue to work through the bank, frustrating though it is, we make it very difficult for the Graz people to circle back to us. Right now, things stop at the bank. Kruppen Financial should be a dead-end for anyone trying to find out more. If it's any consolation, I'm frustrated, too."

"We paid for her release," Portia stated. "They took the money and gave her back. Doesn't that put an end to it?"

"In the normal world, it would," Sandy conceded, "but this isn't the normal world we're dealing with here. We have no idea what Ali was doing that provoked their reaction. They might feel that, with whatever they did to her, that they've sent a message to her and people like her not to interfere with their business."

"Right. So — "

Sandy held his hand to stop Portia and continue. "They might also have let her go to see who else she is associated with, so they can eliminate any loose ends."

"Oh — "

"Once I get the report on her condition, I'll have Kruppen contact the admiral and let the admiral take responsibility from that point. Maybe someday we can talk about it, but certainly not now. I need to make sure Mike, Stick and Puss understand that as well."

Portia cocked her head and looked at Sandy. "Since when did you become such a grown-up? I thought you'd want to go after them and blow them the hell up."

Sandy chuckled softly. "I've been around you too long, maybe. Trust me, I do want to go after them and blow them to pieces, but not if it's going to end up with us getting blown up as well. If and when the opportunity presents itself, I'll remember and take appropriate action."

When Portia took over the bridge, Sandy explained things to Puss and Stick, and then later to Mike. All of them understood the importance of keeping this a secret. Though Puss and Stick acted like teenaged boys sometimes, particularly regarding their shared sense of humor, they were both quite mature and responsible. Mike always behaved soberly and intently.

The report Sandy received from the Manlius medical staff through Kruppen was horrifying. It included a psychological evaluation. Ali had been beaten, sexually assaulted, and addicted to 'shiver.' Her captors had used all of these jointly. They had conditioned Ali that her next dose of the drug depended on her willingness to degrade herself. The doctors planned to keep her on the drug while her injuries healed and she regained weight. Once her body was healthy, the doctors planned to put her through a detox program.

Unfortunately, it would likely take many months before they could release Ali from care.

Sandy waited to read the report until he was off watch. He sequestered himself in his cabin and was later glad he did. He broke into uncontrollable sobs before he reached the end and could only finish reading it with difficulty. He instructed his contact at Kruppen to send the report to Admiral Ketyungyoenwong. He then shared the information with the rest of the crew, warning them to read it when they were off duty. He remembered to send a quick message to Matt Bruns, thanking him for his help.

Sandy then contacted his shipping agent and asked him to cancel the load they were to pick up on Agnus. He needed a break and decided they would return to Providence. He told the shipping agent that they needed to make some minor repairs but figured they could all use some downtime.

When he told the others that he'd like to take a break, heads nodded. Mike Xie said, "I was actually going to suggest it. I think we've all been through the wringer with this, and I know I could use some time away."

They reached Providence eight days later. Sandy went to the apartment he kept on Providence Station. It smelled musty from weeks of being closed up. After staring at the walls, he decided he'd see if his mom were up for him visiting.

Since leaving the Navy, Sandy had been able to travel home more regularly. One advantage to this was he could make his stays shorter, which helped him avoid getting bored. His mother was always happy to see him and learned not to throw a party every time he visited.

He checked the time to make sure his mother would be awake and perhaps in the house. It was nearing the middle of the afternoon where she was, so he placed a call. As always, his mother was delighted to hear from him. When he suggested coming home, his mom pressed him for when he'd arrive. Sandy quickly checked schedules for the inter-planetary liners and saw that he could be there within a week.

"That sounds wonderful, dear," his mother confirmed. "Please bring a suit home."

"You're not going to throw a party for me, are you?" Sandy whined.

"No," she replied quickly. "I'm not going to throw a party for you. There's a new restaurant that opened, and I've been dying to check it out. It's pretty dressy, so you'll need your suit for that."

"Okay," he replied, appeased.

Sandy returned home every year since leaving the navy. In all those visits, he had not encountered Leezy Wilson, the daughter of the next-door neighbors. Despite the end of the war, leaving the navy, and establishing a less-risky way of life, Sandy did not try to contact her. She left it that she would contact him. She didn't. She made him promise to move on with his life.

He was not able to do that, regardless of his promise. Though he and Ali were lovers for two years, that was more of a 'friends-with-benefits' relationship than any deep emotional attachment—actually, using the word 'friend' to describe his relationship with Ali might have been an exaggeration. Ali was always a lone wolf.

His mother never shared any information with him about Leezy, nor did his sister. On a couple of occasions, he saw her parents, and they kept the conversation clear of her as a topic. He never met anyone who affected him the way she had. He engaged in a couple of dalliances since Ali left. When he realized how poorly they compared to what he felt for Leezy, he ended them as gracefully as possible. He booked his tickets for home and packed for the trip.

After a week, he arrived on Niobe. His mother had a car and driver waiting to pick him up since it was the middle of the night when he arrived. He let himself into the house and quietly went to his room to sleep. He always found it easy to sleep when he was on a planet. Being surrounded by night and darkness simply felt 'right' to his body. On ships and stations, there never was really such a thing as 'night'—only designated sleep periods.

With his late arrival, he slept late. When he woke, it was already light out. After stumbling out of bed and showering, he wandered into the kitchen. The local time was near 11:00.

"Good morning, sleepyhead," his mother greeted him, ruffling his hair. "I was afraid I was going to have to wake you so you could take me to lunch."

"I'd be delighted to," he said.

His mother made him drive, not that it required him to do anything other than telling the computer where to go. They went to a restaurant overlooking the ocean. They sat outside on a patio. After they had placed their orders, she took a deep breath. "I have a confession to make, Sandy," she said.

He looked at her quizzically.

"When I said I wasn't throwing a party for you, it was only technically true."

"What does that mean?" he asked, almost groaning.

"I am throwing a party tonight, but it's not for you," she said.

"Then what's the occasion?" Sandy asked, a bit of a whine creeping into his voice.

"Elizabeth's engagement," his mother answered meekly, peering up from her downcast face.

Sandy was stunned. After a moment, he quickly rose and went inside the restaurant. He barely made it to the restroom before he vomited into the sink. He could not catch his breath. He stood, leaning with his forehead on the mirror, gasping. He wanted to sob, but his body would not grant him that release. After some time, a tentative knock came on the door.

"Sir, is everything okay in there?" came a voice he didn't recognize.

Struggling to gain control of himself, Sandy replied in a voice like a gravel truck emptying, "Uh, yeah. I'll be out in a minute."

The interruption helped Sandy gain control of his breathing. He turned on the taps to wash away his puke, then cupped his hands to wash out his mouth. He finished by splashing some water on his face. After wiping himself dry with a towel, he looked in the mirror. He looked like a haunted caricature of himself. He closed his eyes and breathed as deeply as he could, then unlocked the door and returned to his mother.

Seeing him, his mother rose and embraced him in a hug. Then, patting his back, she said, "I'm so sorry."

"Why didn't you tell me?" Sandy said quietly, in a low, rumbling voice. "I would have come some other time."

"I thought about it when you called," she answered. "Then I decided to talk to Bettina before I told you."

Pained puzzlement came over Sandy's face. His mother reached over and clasped his hand. "I don't understand," he said.

His mother looked at him with as loving and kindly expression as he could recall. "I think you do," she explained. "Neither one of you has been able to get over the other. I know you best, and it's obvious to me. Bettina has said the same about Elizabeth. I know you haven't attempted to contact Elizabeth—it's been up to her to reach out to you. I also know she hasn't contacted you because she's been afraid you would reject her and, well, she's stubborn."

"How do you know that?" Sandy growled.

"Because Bettina, Bob and I talk from time to time, wondering if you two will ever see sense—mostly Elizabeth," she stated. "Don't worry," she giggled. "All of our conversations are not about you. Just every so often, it comes up."

"I guess I'm glad to hear you haven't been wasting all your time, then."

The server came with their orders. When she left, Sandy growled, "I really don't want to see her. Especially if she's engaged."

"And that's precisely why Bettina, Bob and I think you must see her or, more importantly, she must see you," she said, giving his hand a reassuring squeeze.

"You think that one glimpse of me and the heavens will part, the angels will sing, and we'll live happily ever after?" he asked with dark sarcasm.

"Not right away," his mother teased. "It's clear to her parents that she is not in love with her fiancé. They can't even figure out why she accepted his proposal, other than to guess that her loneliness has made her desperate."

"Mom, do you know how painful this is?"

"I do," she hissed sternly. "Do you think I don't miss your father? Have you ever wondered why I haven't taken up with someone else in all these years? I miss him every morning when I wake, and he's not beside me. I think of him countless times throughout the day. I keep myself busy, so I don't have time to wallow in what I lost. Don't you try to tell me I don't know what it's like to lose the love of your life. I wouldn't wish that heartache on my worst enemy, and I'll be goddamned if I want it for my son. The two of you have spent the last six years in misery, which is five years, eleven months and twenty-seven days longer than it should have lasted. I saw an opportunity possibly to put an end to it, and I've taken it. I won't apologize, no matter how painful it might be for you right now."

Sandy's eyes opened as if he'd been slapped. He sat up straight. His mother noticed the change.

"Good. You're starting to think," she commented.

Sandy thought for a moment and then gave a snort. "You think that merely seeing me will cause Leezy to have second thoughts?"

"It will remind Elizabeth of what she lost," his mother answered. "I suspect it is just as painful for her as for you, compounded by her fear of rejection and her stubbornness. I'm sure she has kicked herself many, many times for not calling you back a day or two later to say she was wrong. The more time passed, the harder it became for her to do it. Heck, I wouldn't be surprised if she barfs, like you did just now. How long it will take before she talks to you, I can't predict."

"So, what do I do?" Sandy asked.

"First, eat your lunch. It's getting cold. As far as this evening, focus on the positive and not the negative. Behave properly but remember the joy and the depth of feeling you shared. It will show on your face. I'm absolutely certain you'll be disappointed in her fiancé. Try to be polite and hide it from him, but count on the fact that she'll see it. That's all it will take."

Sandy nodded in agreement, trying to figure out how to demonstrate what his mother had said. He took a deep breath. Suddenly, he realized he was hungry and finished his lunch before it got cold.

On the way home, she asked about work. He explained that they had recently undergone a stressful time, and everyone needed a break. His mother started to chuckle.

"You needed a break from stress, and I threw you into this?" she cackled. "Great timing," she added sarcastically.

"You didn't know," he explained.

"Oh, I still would have done it," she countered. "I just would have taken a softer approach perhaps, instead of ripping off the bandage."

The afternoon wore on. The caterers arrived, keeping his mother busy from 3:30 pm on. Sandy tried to prepare himself mentally to see Leezy again. Even with the forewarning he'd been given, it would still be upsetting. He was darkly amused at what an unpleasant surprise it would be for her, if she did not know he would be there. He thought about going for a walk on the beach to gather his thoughts, but didn't want to give her the chance to see him before the party.

As was typical, his mother fussed with the caterers until nearly the last minute, then scurried off to get dressed. Sandy was already dressed in a conservative dark suit. She called out that he was to entertain anyone who was uncouth to show up early. A slight smile creased his face. His father used to complain about this habit of hers.

Guests started to arrive. Most of them he did not know well. There were a few he remembered from growing up, and he always looked forward to seeing them. His parents always had nice friends who were always kind to him. He imagined the newer people, the ones he didn't know, were likely just as pleasant. His mother sailed out of her bedroom and into the party after nearly a dozen people had arrived. She was only 30 minutes past the time the invitations had stated.

Sandy positioned himself so his back was to the door and made sure he was engaged in conversation. He found Kyra and Benil Khatri, old friends of his parents. As he approached them, he saw Kyra whisper in her husband's ear with a sly grin. He guessed she already figured out what his mother and Bettina Wilson were up to. Though not quite as close as his mother and Bettina were, she was still a close friend of both. Both she and her husband had always spoken to Sandy as an adult, even when he was a teenager, and that put them among his favorites.

He kissed her cheek and shook his hand. Kyra's eyes danced with amusement. Benil had a more worried expression. She leaned into Sandy.

"You do know the reason for the party, right?" she asked in a whisper.

Sandy pulled back and nodded. "Mom dropped it in my lap over lunch. I didn't take it well."

"She didn't tell you before you came?"

"She didn't want to."

"Oh, my!" Benil exclaimed. "That must have been quite a shock."

"It was," Sandy answered with a small smile. "I barfed."

Kyra started to giggle. Benil's bushy eyebrows rose. "I'm sorry," she gasped as she recovered. "It's not funny, is it?"

"I'm beginning to see the humor," Sandy admitted.

"Does Elizabeth know you're here?"

"I don't think so," Sandy shrugged. "But Bettina and Bob do."

"Oh, my!" Benil exclaimed again.

"You said that already, dearie."

"I know. But it's more polite than *holy shit!*" Benil retorted.

Sandy chuckled at that.

"I'm so glad you talked me into coming tonight, dear," he added. Then, to Sandy, he explained, "I was not looking forward to this party. I've heard that her fiancé is a loser. But now it might turn out to be much more fun than the book I left at home."

"You both are showing me a wicked side of yourselves I don't think I've ever seen," Sandy quipped.

"Well, our brand of wickedness pales in comparison to what Bettina and your mom have set up," Kyra said. "Oooo—here's the guest of honor."

"Please keep talking to me," Sandy asked. "I don't want to look for her. I'd rather she sees me first."

"Of course," Kyra said quietly. "Hahehehe! Bettina just said, 'Look who is here!' That's so nasty of her. Oops! There goes Elizabeth."

"Where?" Sandy asked.

"She headed in the direction of the bathroom," Kyra said with a smirk. "Quickly, too."

"From the speed of her reaction and the suddenly green tint of her face," Benil added, "I'm guessing she's having a similar reaction to the surprise as you did. Here comes Bob."

Sandy felt a hand on his shoulder. "Sandy," came Bob Wilson's booming voice, "what a nice surprise to see you here!"

Sandy turned as he said this and caught the quick wink in Bob's eye.

Bob greeted the Khatris. "Bob, you are an evil, evil man," Kyra whispered in his ear as they kissed each other's cheek, "and a horribly mean father. I think I love you. Run away with me."

"Only if it's okay with Benil, darling," Bob replied.

"Not just yet, darling," Benil suggested. "This is fun. Let's wait and see what happens. Do you think she'll come out or climb through the window?"

"The window is too small," Sandy answered, "and too high."

"Is Bettina talking to her through the door?" Kyra asked.

"I'd better go check," Bob answered.

"I'll come with," Kyra offered.

"I guess you're stuck here with me," Benil said.

"I wouldn't put it that way," Sandy said. "Is it safe for me to turn around yet?"

"Um, not really. About half the people at the party, the ones who understand what just happened, are bouncing their eyes between you and the hall where the bathroom is, like at a tennis match," Benil informed him. "The fiancé is standing there by himself, really confused, and no one is talking to him."

"Well, we can't have that," Sandy commented. "What sort of a host would I be to leave a guest all alone. I'll go chat him up. Nod in his general direction."

Benil nodded over Sandy's shoulder. Sandy shook Benil's hand, turned, and strode across the room. Two dozen eyes followed his progress.

Imitating what he remembered of his father's bonhomie, Sandy walked right up to the confused man, stuck his hand out, and boomed out affably,

"I'm Sandy Pike. Welcome to the party."

"Um, Kevin Bumgardner," he replied meekly. His handshake was soft, his hand slightly clammy.

"What happened to Elizabeth?" Sandy asked innocently.

"Um, I don't know. She sort of gasped and then bolted. Should I go see what's wrong?"

"That's probably a good idea," Sandy agreed with a sympathetic smile, knowing it was probably a very bad idea.

Sandy returned to Benil. Benil had an enormous smile on his face. As Sandy approached, Benil tried to smother his laughter. "Much better than my book," he whispered to Sandy.

Bob and Kyra returned a moment later, both trying to hide their grins. "Honey," Kyra told her husband, "as evil as I thought Bob was, Bettina is worse."

"What did she do?" Benil asked.

"The fiancé finally came over to see what was wrong, and Bettina said, quite loudly, 'Here, Keith, you talk to her!' She said his name wrong on purpose. She does that to make Elizabeth angry. When Elizabeth heard her fiancé's voice, she started to bawl. After he tried to talk to her and got nothing but wracking sobs in response, Bettina told him, loud enough so Elizabeth could hear, 'Keith, I think she's just disappointed to have taken sick at your engagement party.' The sobbing turned into almost howling at that."

"You really don't like this guy, do you?" Sandy asked Bob.

"Can't stand him. Can't understand… oh, never mind," he sighed.

"Hi, Bettina," called Kyra, looking over Sandy's shoulder. "Is everything okay?"

"Not in the slightest," Bettina said with a twinkle in her eye as she approached, "and I couldn't be happier."

She gave Sandy a big hug. "I know this can't have been entirely pleasant, Sandy dear, but there's a method to the madness." Stepping away from Sandy, she told her husband, "Bob, she doesn't feel well and wants to leave. Should we take her home and then come right back?"

"I hope you do return," Benil said. "This is the most entertaining party I've been to in ages."

Bettina and Bob left. They brought Elizabeth from the bathroom. She scurried out, covering her face. Sandy noticed she was wearing the aquamarine necklace and earrings he had given her years before. Thankfully, everyone was looking at her and did not see his reaction. Merely seeing her felt like a gut punch. Well-wishers called out that they hoped she felt better soon.

Once the door closed behind the Wilsons, the noise level from conversation doubled. So many people were casting furtive glances at Sandy that he began to feel uncomfortable. Sandy's mother swooped by and gave

Sandy a hug and held him, patting his back gently in a comforting manner. "Thank you," was all she said.

"Do you think they'll really come back?" Sandy asked the Khatris.

"Oh, yes," Kyra stated confidently. "Bettina is so evil she's probably told the fiancé to take care of Elizabeth." She started to laugh. Benil joined in.

The Wilsons returned after about twenty minutes. The noise level dropped as guests realized they were back. Bettina went to find Kitty, Sandy's mom, while Bob drifted off to talk with others. Sandy felt increasingly uncomfortable. He knew people were talking about him, based on the sly glances, but no one seemed to want to talk with him. He drifted into the kitchen and then out the back door. His mother found him there later, leaned over, gripping the railing.

"Come back inside, dear," she said. "People are leaving, so it would be nice for you to say goodbye."

Sandy stood straight and turned, following her in. It was only slightly less awkward than it had been before. The hugs he received from Kyra Khatri and Bettina Wilson helped him feel better. When the last guests departed, Sandy went to his room. After hanging up his suit, he climbed into bed, staring at the ceiling with his hands behind his head.

His mind was awhirl. He long ago gave up hope that Leezy would reach out to him. Even so, every woman he met since then he compared to her, and they all fell far short. He didn't know whether he should allow himself to hope again. He did resolve that he wasn't going to mope around the house waiting for something that might not happen.

9

The following morning, he woke early. He took a run on the beach and then performed his Tai Chi. After showering and dressing, he asked his mother to borrow the car for the day, promising to be home in time for dinner. She agreed, and he left before she had a chance to engage him in a recap of last night. He had only a vague idea of what he was going to do but wanted to be out of the house.

He drove into the city. He decided his first stop would be the local office of Kruppen Financial. He knew the manager casually from previous visits. Sandy did not pay much attention to his investments. He understood in the abstract that he was wealthy enough to never need to work again, but he was doing something he loved, so that thought was no temptation. He never handled down time well, anyway.

Even though he didn't have an appointment, Sergei at Kruppen was available. He made time to review Sandy's portfolio of investments. He recommended some minor changes, which Sandy approved. Sandy watched Sergei carefully to see if he betrayed any knowledge of the recent events surrounding Ali, but if he did know anything, he was careful not to stray in that direction.

Upon leaving the office, two men in navy blue suits approached him. Sandy's hand immediately went behind his back, where he would have carried a sidearm if he had one. His immediate thought was that the Graz Syndicate tracked him down. Seeing his quick movement, both men stopped. One held up his hands in a calming gesture.

"Captain Pike?" he said, "We're ONI. Nothing to worry about."

Sandy looked puzzled. What would the Office of Naval Investigations want with him?

"The admiral would like to speak with you over a secure line," the agent explained. "We were supposed to find you and bring you to the office to make that happen. We were instructed not to bother you at home but to try to find you if you ventured out."

"What if I never went out?" Sandy said, feeling a bit testy. This encounter had his adrenalin flowing.

"Then we would have seen you at the shuttle port and done it then," the agent said calmly.

"Have you been following me?"

"No, sir. Facial recognition software picked you up from Kruppen's security camera."

"Can I see some ID?" Sandy asked.

"Certainly." Both agents reached very slowly into their suit jackets. They retrieved their ID chips, holding them out for Sandy to scan with his comm to verify they were legitimate. Sandy's comm chirped twice, indicating they were indeed ONI agents.

"I'm not getting in a car with you guys," Sandy cautioned.

"No need, captain," the second one replied. "Our office is only a couple of blocks from here."

This was still highly unusual, and Sandy's fight-or-flight brain was running hot. "Go ahead," Sandy suggested, "I'll be right behind."

The men set off, and Sandy followed them a few feet back. He was prepared to bolt at the first sign of anything else unusual. After walking two blocks down the street and turning right, there was an Alliance Navy recruiting office. The two men entered, one holding the door open for Sandy. The other continued past the reception desk and down the hall. He stopped at the third door.

"There's a console on the table," he instructed. "The admiral should link in shortly if she's not already on."

Sandy entered the room, a small conference room. There was a console on the table, already awake and displaying Admiral Ketyungyoenwong. For the first time since the two men approached, Sandy relaxed. He sat down.

"Hello, Sandy," she said, "I apologize for this, but I wanted to speak with you on a secure line, and this is the best way I came up with."

"I must admit," Sandy replied, "having two strangers approach me on the street was pretty uncomfortable. This must be important for you to put all this in motion."

"It is," she stated. "I wanted to call you personally to thank you."

"Thank me? For what?" Sandy replied, pretending ignorance.

"For rescuing Ali," she stated.

"I don't know what you're talking about," Sandy said, putting a puzzled look on his face.

"Of course not," she replied. "But since there is absolutely no possible way of linking you to it and all ONI's inquiries reached the same dead end, I have no idea who to thank. I just picked you as being the most likely to know who it is since I know you a little. I have no proof, and I don't want any. That's why we're talking over a secure and scrambled connection even though you have no idea what I'm talking about."

"Right," Sandy said, feeling less uncomfortable now that even ONI wasn't able to trace anything back to him. "For the record, I don't know what you're talking about, but if I did, I'm guessing that I would be interested in how she is."

"In bad shape," Letty stated. "Her recovery will take months, perhaps years. Still, she should recover eventually, and for that, I'm extremely grateful to whomever it was that arranged and paid for her release."

"It's a shame I had nothing to do with it," Sandy lied. "Especially since you made ONI go to all that trouble to scare the pants off me. I'm sorry to hear she's in such bad shape but glad to know you're optimistic about her recovery."

"Well, I'm sorry to have given you such a fright, particularly since you had nothing to do with it. However, if you happen to learn who was responsible, please make sure they know that I owe them a huge debt of gratitude."

"I'll be sure to do that, admiral," Sandy replied.

After the conversation, Sandy resumed the errands he'd come up with to kill time and keep him away from the house. He found a café and ate lunch, then went to buy gifts for his crew. When he finished shopping, he returned home. It was late afternoon. His mother greeted him. "They sent Caspar Milquetoast home this morning," she informed him, "after you left, and the engagement is off."

"Who is Caspar whatever-his-name-is?" Sandy asked.

"The boyfriend," his mother answered. "Bettina, Bob and I have been calling him Caspar Milquetoast. His real name is Keith or Kevin something-or-other. I don't think he's a boyfriend anymore, come to think of it."

"Mhm," Sandy grunted noncommittally, pretending he wasn't curious.

"Bettina and Elizabeth had a blazing fight all day. Bob made himself scarce, though I understand he weighed in last night when they returned home. Caspar tried to butt in, not understanding what was happening, and Elizabeth told him to shut up and stay out of it. He persisted in wanting to know more—I guess she never told him about you. That's when Bob told Caspar he was a poor second-best to you, and he didn't understand how Elizabeth could ever seriously entertain marriage to a loser like him when all she had to do was apologize to the man she still loved."

"Wow," Sandy commented softly. "So, if they've had a blazing fight all day, how do you know this?" Sandy inquired, teasing his mother a little.

"Elizabeth retreated to her room to cry and sleep, I think. That's what Bettina told me before she went to take a nap herself. Bettina was exhausted," his mother reported. "How was your day?"

"Dull," Sandy said, which was mostly the truth. "I went to visit my broker and made a few adjustments, ate lunch, and then went shopping for the guys. If it's okay, I'd like to take the car again tomorrow—maybe play some golf at the club."

"Staying away from the house, eh?" his mother commented.

"Keeping myself busy," Sandy replied. "Idle hands are the devil's playthings, don't you know?"

The following day, Sandy woke early and went for a run on the beach. On his return, he saw someone sitting on the sand where he'd left his towel. He guessed it was Leezy. As he drew closer, that became evident. She looked too thin—her elbows and knees looked too large and knobby. Her eyes were puffy and bloodshot, and her nose was red.

"Hullo, Elizabeth," Sandy said dully as he slowed to a walk.

Hearing him call her Elizabeth made her flinch ever so slightly. Sandy noticed it because he called her that on purpose. She stood.

"Can we talk?" she asked, not looking him in the eye.

"I guess," Sandy said without enthusiasm. He wanted to make her work for it just a little. "Here?"

"As good a place as any, I suppose," she said, her voice strained.

Sandy unfolded his towel and spread it on the sand. He sat down cross-legged at one end, facing the middle. She sat down on the other end with reluctance. She still would not look at him.

"Elizabeth, look at me," he insisted.

She shook her head.

"Elizabeth, you were able to look me in the eye when you broke things off with me. You should be able to look me in the eye now. I don't think it's possible for you to hurt me that bad a second time, so you should be able to do it."

She looked up, a perfect picture of misery, tears streaming down her cheeks and her lip quivering. It made Sandy want to hold her and comfort her, but he managed to restrain himself. He waited.

"I was wrong," she choked out. "I was wrong, and I've regretted it almost ever since." She paused, taking an audible gulp of air. "I'm sorry," she concluded, looking down again.

Sandy leaned over and lifted her chin with his finger. "What do you want, Elizabeth?" he asked gently.

"I want you back," she whispered, then began to cry. She kept her head up, though, and looked at him in despair.

A thousand different things to say popped into Sandy's head, many of them cold and cruel. None of them seemed right. "Okay," he said softly. It was enough.

She wriggled over and sat on his lap, burying her face in his chest. She was sobbing. He held her in his arms, rubbing her back gently and stroking her hair. He murmured nonsense sounds softly, trying to calm her. It took some time. He didn't know how long they sat like that, but one of his legs went to sleep. Eventually, she stopped and turned her face up to his. He leaned down and touched his lips to hers lightly.

The same magic he felt when their lips first met was still present. A sense of rightness that he didn't know was missing crept back into his soul. He started to permit himself to hope that things would work out.

They did not have time to resolve all their issues before each of them needed to return to work. Still, he and Leezy were together again, and that was enough for Sandy. The rest would work itself out, he felt. He boarded the liner back to Providence in a renewed state of mind. Once he settled into his cabin, he contacted his shipping agent. He requested that the agent find some work that would take the *Alice May* to the planet Arete regularly. Leezy was still living there, in the city of Corniferra, and had advanced in her company. She was now a Vice President of Damara Mills, overseeing five different lines of breakfast cereal.

Mike Xie noticed a change in Sandy soon after Sandy boarded the *Alice May*. "What happened to you, boss?" he asked Sandy, curious.

"What do you mean?" Sandy replied, puzzled.

"Did you have some rejuvenation surgery while you were away?"

"No," Sandy answered, somewhat irritated. "Why would you even think that?"

"The lines on your face are different—not so deep."

"No way," Sandy protested.

"Yeah. Up here," Mike said, drawing his finger across his forehead, "and here." He skirted his mouth with his thumb and forefinger. "Not as pronounced."

"Huh," Sandy grunted. "I hadn't noticed."

When Portia returned to the ship, she noticed it as well. She didn't accuse Sandy of having rejuv surgery but commented that he looked really well-rested. Sandy looked closely in the mirror but didn't see what they were talking about.

When Stick Warburton and Puss Boyle came aboard a few hours later, Stick immediately cracked, "Skipper got laid while he was away."

Sandy barked at him harshly, "I did not! And my personal life is none of your business even if I did!"

Portia sat up at this. Normally Sandy never reacted to either Stick or Puss when they uttered some juvenile comment. She looked at Sandy carefully. She thought about teasing him but held her tongue. She figured she'd get it out of him later.

After three runs, just over a month later, Sandy's shipping agent contacted them with an opportunity to take a cargo to Vermilion, with a load there that needed to go to Arete. Sandy was excited about the chance to see Leezy again. His more than customary enthusiasm did not escape Portia.

"We've never done business in those systems before, Sandy," she commented, "and yet you seem awfully excited about it."

Sandy quickly scrambled to come up with a plausible excuse. "Well, uh, it's a chance to establish some new customers… and, uh — "

Portia laughed, shaking her head and saying, "Bullshit. You hate opening up new routes and going through the whole charade with the terminal managers and shipping agents. The only reason we went to Cartagena and Agnus on the run when Ali was missing was that your shipping agent on Cambria also handled those two systems, and you didn't have to schmooze anybody. Other than that, we haven't been anyplace new for three years."

"Well, I was thinking it's about time we moved into new areas and — "

"Even though we turn away profitable business in the areas we already service? Sorry, not buying it, Sandy. Does your excitement at going to Vermilion or Arete have anything to do with how happy you looked when we all came back to the ship?"

Sandy began to deny it, but the blush that rose on his cheeks betrayed him. Portia interrupted him simply by crossing her arms and shaking her head. He slowed to a stop and said, "What?"

"Your face is so pink right now, Sandy," she chuckled. "Who is it? C'mon, you can tell Aunt Portia."

Sandy shut the bridge hatch. "I'll tell you, but you can't tell the others—especially the kids."

"I promise," Portia said. "Unless it's really, really good and I can't help myself, or really, really bad, and I need to slap sense into you."

"Well, I think it's really, really good," Sandy began.

Portia's hands flew to her mouth. "The one who got away?" she asked, almost fearfully.

Sandy nodded, then paused. "Wait a minute. How did you know about that? I never told any of you. Ali knew, but I doubt it was her."

"It wasn't Ali," Portia allowed, "and that's all I'll say. I refuse to tell, under threat of torture," she stated, miming zipping and locking her lips closed.

Sandy went through a quick process of elimination. Then his eyes narrowed. "That rat! That's a major violation of the Bro Code! Tell you what… I release you from your almost, sort-of promise and grant you permission to tell him and only him. Hearing it from someone else is his punishment."

"I don't have any idea who you're talking about," Portia said with feigned innocence, the twinkle in her eyes giving her away.

"All the proof I need will be when he calls to complain that I didn't tell him myself."

The hatch to the bridge flew open. Stick Warburton stuck his head in. "My watch," he told Portia. Then, to Sandy, he said, "Congrats, Skipper."

"Congrats?" Sandy asked. "For what?"

"For getting back together with your old girlfriend. She's the one in that kissing picture, right?"

"What the hell?" Sandy exclaimed angrily. "Were you listening at the hatch or something?"

"Not exactly," Stick said, backing away from the hatch as Sandy rose with a thunderous expression.

"Not exactly, my ass," Sandy growled, advancing towards him menacingly.

"He didn't need to," Portia said with a slight giggle. "Didn't I tell you that Puss and Stick hacked the bridge mic the first day they were aboard?"

Spinning back to Portia, Sandy snarled, "No. You didn't."

"Hey, congrats, Skipper," called Mike Xie from outside. "That's really great news!"

"Oh, God!" Sandy moaned, his face flushing pink again. "So much for keeping things quiet." He buried his face in his hands.

"Oh, c'mon, Sandy," Portia said, laughing. "It's awesome news. Tell us what happened."

Sandy sighed. "Okay," he said after a moment, realizing there was no point in trying to keep something secret that clearly wasn't anymore. "Go wake Puss up. I don't want to have to tell the story twice."

"I'm already up, Boss. Stick told me a second ago."

Sandy started to laugh, shaking his head. "We might as well go to the galley and be comfortable," he suggested.

When they all sat down, Sandy told them the story of his visit home. They nodded in sympathy when he told them of his reaction to hearing that Leezy was engaged. They laughed as he told them what happened at the party. Portia 'awww-ed' when he told her about Leezy waiting for him on the beach.

"And yes, Stick. It's the woman in the kissing picture."

"That's so cool, boss," he commented. "That picture is incredible, by the way. How could you guys ever split up?"

Sandy then had to tell them about what had happened after he had left them on the *Ali Kat*. He told them about Robur and Ilex, about the contract for his murder, and then about the Battle of Excelsus. "I think what pushed her over the edge was learning that she might have been in pretty serious danger the whole time after I got shot because ONI was trying to keep things quiet. I don't know, though. We didn't get around to talking about it. No point. It's over and done with, and we're moving on."

"Gotta say, Sandy," Mike commented, "that contract thing would have pushed me a bit too far."

Stick and Puss both nodded at this. Puss added, "Too many times getting almost killed for my liking. We had that time on *DeLuca* but weren't around for the other stuff."

"The thing in Ilex was worse if you can believe it," Portia remarked.

"I didn't blame her," Sandy admitted. "I wasn't mad. I was just — "

"Lost, and incomplete," Portia finished for him. "And that's the change we all noticed in you when we returned. So, does she live on Vermilion or Arete?"

"Arete," Sandy responded. "I asked our agents if they could get us any loads to Arete so I could visit her. Sorry I didn't tell you. I would have, at some point. But now I've gotta ask. Why the hell did you hack the bridge mic?"

"We wanted to have advance warning if our sense of humor was going too far and you were going to push us out the airlock," Puss answered calmly.

"Oh," Sandy said, nodding. "Makes sense. As a matter of fact," he switched to a low growl and began advancing on Puss, "that's seeming like a really good idea."

Puss started to back away, saying, "Sense of humor, Boss. Sense of humor," repeating what Portia often told Sandy when the two pulled some stunt that irritated him.

"Besides, if you get rid of us," Stick added as he too edged away from Sandy, "who would you get to do the crappy stuff that you, Portia and Mike don't want to do?"

"I'd find some vagrant off the streets," Mike snarled in mock fury.

"Boss, why now? It would make all the other times you've put up with us just a waste," Puss protested.

Portia and Mike were laughing at this exchange. Sandy stopped. "Good point," he said calmly as he sat back down. "I invested so much time and aggravation, I would hate for it to have been wasted."

"Hey, Captain Cupid," Monty greeted him two days later on a comm.

"Well, if it isn't my former friend and betrayer of confidences."

"Ow! So that's why I had to learn from Portia," Monty replied. "You mad, bro?"

"I'm not mad," Sandy said with a sigh. "I'm just… disappointed."

"Good one. Sounded just like my dad," Monty commented. "Still stings, though."

"Good. It's supposed to. I should turn you in for a major violation of the Bro Code."

"You can't."

"Why not?"

"Statute of Limitations," Monty explained. "That was over five years ago, so I'm in the clear."

"Bullshit on your 'Statute of Limitations.' That was a major violation—

like murder or something. There shouldn't be a time limit."

"Nope, the Statute of Limitations applies because it was work-related. The Bro Code is quite clear on such things, Sandy. Article 6, Section C, Paragraph 3, Item 2 states: There is a five-year Statute of Limitations in effect when betrayal of a confidence by a confidee to a third party relates to the confidor's work performance and said work performance is deleteriously affected by the subject of said confidence."

Sandy chuckled. "It sounds like you're actually reading it instead of pulling it straight out of your ass."

"I am actually reading it, butthead," Monty countered heatedly, compensating for the lie he was telling. "Seriously, back when you guys were first on Providence, Portia noticed something was different with you from when you served with her less than two years before. She didn't notice it until you guys started carrying cargo. She called me and said they all picked up on it and wanted to know why it seemed like a piece of you was missing and whether they should be worried that you'd do something crazy and get them all killed."

"I was never that bad," Sandy protested.

"Eh—you got kind of dark there, bro," Monty commented. "How's bidness?"

"Pretty good, actually. Just had a bit of a windfall."

"That's what the rumor mill said," Monty agreed. "You captured an Alliance patrol boat that went missing and sold it back pretty cheap."

"It was still a lot of money, and I owed the admiral a favor. How are you doing? Are you still with... is it, Ellen?"

"Yeah, Ellen," Monty confirmed the name, "and no. I broke things off about a month ago."

"I'm sorry."

"Don't be," Monty replied. "She had a bad habit—a nervous laugh that sounded like a horse nickering. Started to drive me nuts."

Sandy laughed. "Any prospects for a replacement?"

"Yes, but it's early days. Too soon to talk about. Back to the matter I called about. I'm really happy you and Elizabeth are working things out. Portia told me the story you shared with her. Have the two of you talked it out yet?"

"Not really," Sandy admitted. "I think we were just so happy to reconnect that neither of us wanted to get into the heavy-duty stuff."

"You know you're going to have to, at some point," Monty warned.

"I don't know."

"I don't think it will hurt, and it might make things better," Monty offered.

"Listen to you... giving me relationship advice," Sandy cracked.

"I have a lot more practical experience than you," Monty retorted. "You've had... what? Two relationships in the last ten years? I've had five times that many. Ergo, I have way more knowledge of such things."

"If you say so," Sandy said, laughing and shaking his head.

When they arrived at Vermilion Station, Sandy met the representative from the shipping agent and one of the terminal managers at the dock. As he had learned to do, Sandy invited the terminal manager to join him for a cup of coffee and slipped him a 50-credit bill in the process. The terminal manager left without touching the coffee. Sandy had a brief chat with the shipping agent before returning to the ship.

A week later, they arrived at Arete, where Sandy performed the same ritual. He asked the shipping agent to plan for a three-day layover at Arete so he could see Leezy. She cleared her schedule as well and came up to the station to spend the time with him. The rest of the crew stayed aboard the *Alice May,* but Sandy booked a room in the best hotel on the station.

The second day, she insisted he take her to see the *Alice May* and meet his partners and crew. The ship wasn't docked at the station, so they needed to hire a taxi. Sandy asked the taxi pilot to turn on his lights and take a spin around the ship so Leezy could see the outside on the taxi's video feed. "It's prettier than I thought," she commented. "I always thought cargo ships were big and boxy."

"The bigger ones are," Sandy replied. "The *Alice May* is different, in that she's a fast transport. We carry smaller things that are more time-sensitive or high-value where security is critical. We generally take half the time to go from point A to point B than the bigger ships—less than half, the more systems that need to be crossed."

When they entered through the hatch, the entire group was waiting to greet them. Sandy hadn't called ahead to warn them, so he was a bit puzzled. Portia pulled him aside later and explained Puss figured it out when the taxi took the slow circuit of the ship.

Puss and Stick surprised Sandy by being utterly charming. Mike acted shy, and Portia enveloped Leezy in a big hug, as only she could. The two younger men took Leezy on a tour of the ship.

Two days later, they left Arete Station. Sandy and Leezy spent the time reconnecting, this time on a more physical basis. It was as though no time had passed. Neither of them wanted to delve into the reasons for their long separation—both were happy it was over. Sandy even began to contemplate marriage again.

The *Alice May* took on a load bound for Vermilion. There was a cargo waiting for there to go to Cygnus, a planet in the Karkinos group of systems. Like Vermilion, Karkinos was made up of former Alliance and Hegemony systems, controlled by one of the Hegemony's former group captains.

The trip to Vermilion took only five days. The *Alice May* was docked for less than two hours. They quickly unloaded, then took on the new cargo. It was a three-jump trip to Cygnus from there that would take them just under ten days. The first two tramlines were short, but the last took twenty-five hours, thirty-two minutes, making it one of the longer tramlines they'd ever used.

The three legs of the trip were uneventful. They entered the long final tramline to Cygnus. When they emerged into 'normal' space at the end of the tramline in the Cygnus system, all hell broke loose. The *Alice May* was heading in-system at $0.23c$, the customary maximum speed to enter a tramline. The first thing that happened was a message from their shipping agent that came through on the ship's comm, warning them not to proceed to Cygnus. It was sent about an hour too late, after they entered hyperspace, where the quantum particle communication system did not function. The second thing was the sensor readings, showing two groups of warships approaching the tramline that the *Alice May* just exited.

The two groups of warships were on intersecting courses that would meet about thirteen light-minutes away from the tramline entrance. Even as powerful as the *Alice May* was for her size, there would be no way to change her momentum to prevent them from sailing right into the middle of what looked to be a hostile confrontation. Each group of ships was centered on a *Ruthless*-class battlecruiser. Each was accompanied by a *Kerris*-class heavy cruiser and two *Palmyra*-class light cruisers. While all the ships had been built by the Hegemony, the computer identified the group off to starboard as belonging to the navy of Karkinos and the group to port as belonging to Vermilion. Both of these were split-away, multi-system governments created by former HUW group captains during the civil war.

Sandy was about to begin his sleep period when they emerged, but now he wasn't leaving the bridge. Mike was scheduled on watch, so he took the other seat. Sandy activated the 1MC, the ship intercom.

"Hey everybody, we have a situation we just dropped into. Take a look at your consoles, and let's talk."

"Already have it up, boss," Puss replied, "and I accessed broadcast news feeds from the planet. They're nine hours behind, but apparently, the Vermilion ships attacked a day ago. They came on a different route from us. They destroyed Cygnus Station and are trying to escape. Looks like the Karkinos ships are going to catch them."

"From what I've been able to plot," Sandy replied, "we can stay out of firing range of one or the other, but we have to decide now, and we'll have to engage max boost. Otherwise, we fly within range of both groups, and I don't think we want to try that."

"I'm thinking we want to stay away from the Karkinos folks," Portia commented. "They're undoubtedly mad as hell and might shoot first and ask questions after."

"Plus, there's a tramline in the Vermilion ships' direction," Mike added, "current bearing is 137° by -12°."

"Where does it go?" Sandy asked.

"Checking," Mike answered. "Crap. Nowhere. It's a dead end."

"The next closest is -32° by 51°," Stick informed them. "It eventually leads to Alliance space after three jumps."

"Wrong direction, though, if we want to avoid the pissed-off locals," Portia said.

"Okay," Sandy stated. "Everyone, get a slick on and strap in. As soon as we're ready, I'm going to max boost. We need to get past these guys, and then we'll worry about the tramline. None of them will be able to reverse course and catch up to us."

Within two minutes, they all signaled they were ready. Sandy engaged max boost and implemented the course changes to keep the *Alice May* out of the range of the ships from Karkinos. Thirty-two minutes later, the fight between the two opposing forces began. From what they could see, the ships from Vermilion were not doing well. Puss called out why.

"The Vermilion *Ruthless* only has two guns firing," he said in a strained voice. "They're getting hammered!"

Shortly after his comment, the Vermilion battlecruiser lowered shields. Despite this obvious sign of surrender, the Karkinos battlecruiser continued to fire on her. Less than a minute later, the Vermilion ship disappeared, blowing up when a shot hit her reactors. Without the battlecruiser, the rest of the ships belonging to Vermilion didn't last long before they too were destroyed.

"Attention fast transport *Alice May*. Attention fast transport *Alice May*. Begin immediate deceleration. Heave-to and await instructions," came a broadcast message.

Sandy disengaged max boost. "What do you think, guys?" he asked. "Should we listen to the nice man?"

"Not a chance," Portia said.

"Nope," called Stick.

"No way," Puss chimed in.

Sandy looked at Mike. Mike just shook his head.

"Okay, I guess we're not listening," Sandy confirmed. He implemented the course change to take them to the tramline that would eventually lead them to Alliance space.

The broadcast message continued but changed its tone, threatening dire consequences for the *Alice May* since she did not comply. There were thirty-nine hours until they reached the tramline. Sandy unbuckled and went to his sleep period.

While Sandy was sleeping, their primary shipping agent spoke to Portia, informing her that the *Alice May* was in deep trouble for not heeding the orders they were given, and it would eliminate any future business they hoped to do in the systems controlled by the Karkinos government. Portia shrugged it off. A shipping agent, who rarely left the safety of his desk, was not qualified to give her or anyone on the *Alice May* advice about a situation like this. She informed Sandy when he woke, and he agreed.

In the middle of Sandy's next sleep period, worse news arrived. Gravimetric sensors indicated a ship with the mass of a *Palmyra*-class light cruiser just exited the tram line to which they were headed. Puss Boyle was on the bridge. He sent an alert to Sandy, which woke him.

Sandy came to the bridge quickly and quietly. Puss showed him the gravimetric sensor reading. It would be a few more minutes before they obtained any further information on the ship due to light-speed lag.

"Oh, that's not good," Sandy breathed. "Give me a chance to shower and get dressed and then let's all talk."

Ten minutes later, they gathered in the galley. "You all know a *Palmyra* just dropped out of our tramline," Sandy opened. "We've got two choices. We heave-to, like they've been demanding since the battle, or make a run for it. If we make a run for it, we'll be under fire for a minute or two—we don't have full sensor data yet, so I can't be more specific. I will say that we modified the ship for precisely this type of situation. I have complete confidence that we would survive pretty much intact. The only issue is if they manage to take out one or more of the Alcubierre field generators. If they do, we might not be able to make repairs by the time we reach the tramline. That would mean we would need to swing around and try again and that *Palmyra* might get another shot at us. I'm not making this decision alone, so let me know what you're thinking."

"What do you think will happen if we heave-to?" Mike asked.

"Hm. They'll likely throw us in jail for a little while and impound the ship. Once there's a trial, they'll fine us and charge us to get the ship back. I don't know for sure—that's just a guess," Sandy replied.

"How likely do you think it will be that we make it without losing any Alcubierre generators?" Portia inquired.

"I think we'll lose a couple," Sandy answered. "If we lose more than, say, five, or if there's significant hull damage where we had one placed, then we'll overshoot the tramline. But, again, that's just a guess."

"What do you think our odds are, boss?" Stick queried.

Sandy took a deep breath. "Maybe a little better than 50-50 on trying to make it past them. But if we do that and end up on the wrong side of those odds, we'll be in jail for a long, long time and never get the ship back."

"Skipper, what about fighting back? We have the 105," Puss commented.

"I don't know if that improves our odds of making it to the tramline, but it would surely piss them off something fierce," Sandy chuckled. Sobering, he added, "We saw that they didn't honor the surrender of the Vermilion ships. We don't know if they have other ships following that *Palmyra* and coming out of the tramline. I've seen what you guys can do, and you might well be able to disable that *Palmyra*. Unfortunately, one more unexpected wrinkle, and we're done for. Don't forget, one of their *Kerris* heavies is only about eight hours behind us. If I had better intel and knew whether we could expect any other ships behind the *Palmyra*, I'd give it a shot. We don't have any intel, though."

No one asked any other questions. "Think about it for a minute, and then let's decide," Sandy said. He went back to the bridge.

Sandy needed to make up his own mind, too. Ten years ago, he likely would have taken his chances and tried to force his way past the light cruiser, allowing Stick and Puss to do as much damage as they could on the way past. He wasn't as eager now. He thought about whether the recent rekindling of his relationship with Leezy influenced his decision, then decided it didn't matter if it did. He wasn't in the navy, and he wasn't at war. This ship and these people were his responsibility, and he didn't want anything bad to happen to them.

He returned to the galley. Portia and Mike were already there. Stick and Puss reappeared after a couple of minutes. "What did everyone decide?" he asked.

"You go first, boss," Stick requested.

"Much as it pains me to say it," he began, "I think our best option is to heave-to. I don't like it much, but in the long run, it has the least horrible outcome."

Portia and Mike both nodded at this. Stick and Puss looked at each other. Puss shrugged, then Stick shrugged, too. Sandy could tell they were both slightly disappointed.

"I'm sorry, guys," he commented. "I believe either one of you could disable that *Palmyra*—no doubt. We just don't know what sort of damage we'll take and whether there's anyone else coming along. I'm willing to throw you a bone, though."

They looked at him with raised eyebrows.

"I don't want those goons messing with our ship," Sandy stated in a low voice. "I want you guys to set it up so that if they try to hack into the ship's systems to gain control of her, that it's the last thing they ever do."

The two smiled. "Okay, boss," Puss replied. "You got it."

They left the galley with their heads together, already discussing what they would do. Sandy chuckled softly. Portia and Mike both looked relieved.

"If you said, 'Let's go!' I would have gone along with it," Portia said, "but I hoped you wouldn't."

"Same," Mike agreed.

Sandy implemented the course change to reverse thrust at 500G and bring the *Alice May* to a stop. He did this a few minutes before they received the first message, demanding that they do so. It was another six hours before the Karkinos ship reached them. They were ordered to assemble near the main hatch and bring whatever clothing and accessories they needed for a long, indefinite period.

They heard the thump of the shuttle's umbilical connecting to the hull outside the hatch. The hatch opened, and a combat-armored marine waved them through. An officer wearing the two bars of a lieutenant was waiting.

"Sir," Sandy said, "I give you fair warning that if you try to do anything with my ship other than close it up and tractor it back to wherever we're going, bad things might happen."

"Sit down and shut up, mister," the lieutenant snarled.

Once Sandy and the other four were seated and the armored marine returned, the lieutenant went through the umbilical aboard the *Alice May*. He returned, red-faced, a few minutes later. He glared at Sandy.

"Disable your security protocols," he demanded.

"No," Sandy replied calmly. "Under inter-planetary law, I am not required to do so. You are allowed to inspect my cargo and make sure it matches the manifest. You are allowed to impound my ship, subject to the fines imposed if I'm found guilty of violations of your laws. You are not permitted to access any of the operating systems without my express permission. The law is quite clear, I'm afraid."

The lieutenant glared at him but said nothing further. He ordered the marine to close the hatch on the *Alice May*. When he returned, he retracted the umbilical and returned to the bridge of the shuttle. Once inside the shuttle bay of the cruiser, the marine directed them to stand and exit. A marine corporal took their belongings, including their comm units, and placed them in sealed bags. They were then marched to the small brig on the ship.

Thirty minutes later, another marine came to the brig. "Which one of you is Pike?" he barked.

Sandy stood. The marine opened the cell and gestured Sandy out. "Come," was his order.

Sandy followed through the ship. The marine stopped by a hatch and knocked. "Enter," came from within. The marine opened the hatch, waving Sandy to proceed, then followed immediately behind, remaining positioned at the hatch.

Seated at a small table was a woman—at least Sandy guessed she was—wearing commander's insignia on a khaki uniform. What made Sandy uncertain was the complete lack of hair on the person's head. The commander did not even have eyebrows.

"Have a seat, Captain Pike," the woman requested. The voice seemed to indicate a woman.

Sandy withdrew a chair and sat opposite her, trying to display a relaxed posture. She looked at him carefully for a few moments. "The famous

Captain Pike," she said finally.

Sandy nodded in acknowledgment. "Didn't know I was famous," he shrugged.

"Infamous might be a better word," she clarified, "at least, in certain circles. I've seen you once before, you know, aboard the *Cornelia Guest.*"

"Oh," Sandy said. "And how is my old friend Group Captain Johara?"

"If you were her friend, you'd be the first," she commented. "I wouldn't know. She stayed with the United Worlds. No one else wanted her on their side."

Sandy tilted his head in acknowledgment. "Not surprising. And you are?"

"Excuse me," she said, "pardon my manners. I am Commander Regina Kiernan of the Karkinos Navy."

"I wish I could say I'm pleased to meet you," Sandy stated, "but I would have preferred not to. No offense intended."

"None taken. Why didn't you heave-to when initially ordered?"

"We just saw your ships destroy the ships from Vermilion. We just came from Vermilion. In addition, your ships continued to fire on the enemy even after they lowered their shields in surrender. We feared we would get the same treatment, even more so since we were eyewitness to that violation of the Terra Nova Convention. The safest and most prudent option seemed to be to attempt escape."

"My officer asked you to disable the security on your ship," she stated.

"Demanded. I refused, as is my right under inter-planetary law. Moreover, I feel it only fair to warn you that attempting to hack the system may result in loss of life and the destruction of the ship."

Kiernan smiled thinly. "As he reported. He reported the system informed him that two more unsuccessful attempts would result in the immediate self-destruction of the ship. He also reported that the system responded in a manner similar to a child's computer game. It taunted my lieutenant. He did not appreciate it."

Sandy smiled and swallowed a chuckle. "That would have been my employees' doing," he said with a shrug.

"Did you know that once we undocked and pulled away, the shields on your ship came up and a weapon deployed? It appears to be a 105mm photon cannon."

"I did not," Sandy admitted, "but am not completely surprised that they would have done that. I would also hazard a guess that access to the ship is now subject to the same warning about self-destruction."

"We have not attempted, since with your shields up we cannot use an umbilical connection and would need to board with an EVA. Would engaging your ship with a tractor beam engage some sort of automated response?"

"I don't know," Sandy stated. "I don't think so, but I'd have to check."

"Please do," she said politely. "Our tractor beam is currently non-functional, but there is a heavy cruiser due to emerge in a few minutes that will tow your ship into a stable orbit of Cygnus. You and your crew will be delivered planet-side to Cygnus, where you will await trial. So tell me, Captain Pike, what is a fast transport doing with military-grade shielding and a heavy cannon? Are you some sort of pirate now?"

Sandy smirked. "Not in the slightest. We modified the ship in the period between the Alliance's defeat and the civil war. Our goal was to establish ourselves as the best option to transport low-volume, high-value goods securely. We figured that a few years of lawlessness might follow while the Hegemony established control of the Alliance planets. The civil war extended and deepened the degree of lawlessness. We merely wished to protect ourselves and our customers' goods."

"Interesting business model," she commented.

"It's been quite successful until now," Sandy stated.

"Please confirm for me whether a tractor beam will not generate a hostile response. It has been quite interesting to meet you," she said as she rose from her chair, clearly dismissing Sandy.

Sandy confirmed that a tractor beam would not set off any counter-measures and told the marine guard to relay that information to Commander Kiernan. Boyle and Warburton had programmed the ship to raise shields and deploy the cannon after the hatch was closed and the umbilical withdrawn. Any attempt to re-open the hatch would count against the two remaining attempts they had programmed into the system. The ship was also programmed to fire back if fired upon and to deploy an EMP missile if it registered an opportunity to disable an attacker with one. Stick told him he and Puss developed these counter-measures years earlier. They were resident in the system and merely needed to be activated.

The five of them were split between three cells in the small brig. As Portia was the only female, they decided she should have her own space. Sandy was sharing with Mike Xie.

10

The following two days were dull. None of them knew what to expect or what might be waiting for them at the end of the journey. The first break in the monotony was when they were ordered to board a shuttle to take them to the planet Cygnus.

When they arrived, they were handed over to civilian authorities and taken to a civilian jail. They were not the only people being held—there were criminals of all types in the facility. They continued to be kept two to a cell. Portia was taken down the hall to the women's wing. Sandy asked and was told she would be given her own cell. He also inquired about access to a lawyer. He was informed that an officer of the court would be meeting them later.

It was the following day before a youthful man in an ill-fitting suit visited them in jail. He informed them nervously that they were being charged with several crimes, including not following lawful military commands in a theater of war, fleeing the scene of a crime, attempted smuggling, and possession of an illegally armed ship. He asked if they had legal representation. Sandy informed him that he would like to arrange legal representation through Kruppen Financial. The young man nodded his assent.

Another day passed before Sandy was summoned from the cell. He was handcuffed and taken to a small meeting room. Once there, his handcuffs were linked to a bolt on the table. The table itself was anchored onto the floor. After a few minutes, the door opened, and a thin woman with short gray hair entered and sat opposite Sandy. She pulled out her comm unit and activated a field suppressor.

"Before you speak," she warned, "remember to speak softly and try not to move your lips if possible. If you can't do that, you'll want to lean forward and try to cover your mouth with your hands."

She began by introducing herself as Sonya Tsaich, an attorney hired by

Kruppen Financial. She asked Sandy some questions to verify his identity for Kruppen. Satisfied with his answers, she informed him, "I regret to say that your ship, the *Alice May*, was destroyed yesterday. Four people were killed in the explosion, and they have added four counts of murder to the charges against you."

"Counselor," Sandy said through clenched teeth, trying to suppress his anger, "I gave them two warnings that attempting to bypass the security protocols and access the ship would result in its destruction."

"To whom did you issue these warnings?"

"To their lieutenant when we were taken aboard their shuttle and to Commander Kiernan aboard the ship that brought us here."

"Were there any witnesses?"

"In the first instance, yes. That exchange took place in front of my crew. In the second, we met in her office aboard ship. In addition, the ship's system itself warned that further attempts to bypass security would result in the ship's destruction. I also explained to both the lieutenant and the commander that inter-planetary law did not allow them to access any of the ship's operating systems without my express permission."

"The law is quite clear on that, but they have stated that neither you nor the ship gave them any warning," she stated, "and your lips are moving. Try to cover your mouth."

Sandy responded with a growl through his closed mouth.

"The testimony of your crew will be of little value in court, I'm afraid."

Sandy leaned forward to cover his mouth with his hand, difficult since he was cuffed to the table. "Please instruct Kruppen to contact my insurance company—they have the policy information—and have them file a suit against the government for the insured value of the ship. Have the suit filed on Terra Nova. I would also like to file charges of war crimes, in the Inter-Planetary Court on Terra Nova, against the Karkinos Navy. Shortly after we entered the Cygnus system, we observed the Karkinos ships continuing to fire against the Vermilion ships even though the Vermilion ships had surrendered."

"These are serious charges, Mr. Pike," she said, "and filing these suits will not make things easier for you. On the contrary, it will almost guarantee that you and your crew will be convicted. Karkinos still employs capital punishment. You will probably be sentenced to death and your crew to lengthy prison terms. Do you have proof of the war crimes charges?"

Sandy nodded. He leaned forward. "A complete log of all sensor readings on the *Alice May* was transmitted to a secure server on Providence on an hourly basis as backup. The records we have will also likely provide proof that the ship's systems did warn them against attempting to access the ship."

"Where are these records?"

"On a secure server owned by Kruppen Financial."

"That will work for Terra Nova, but the local courts might declare them inadmissible as evidence."

"What kind of court system is this?" Sandy exclaimed, exasperated.

"Since you and your crew are not citizens, you have no right to trial by jury. You will be tried by a judge, who was appointed by the current government. Said government is quite angry with you."

"From what you're telling me," Sandy said, again leaning down to the table, "it sounds as though the courts aren't exactly prepared to provide a fair hearing."

"That is indeed the case," Tsaich replied with a slight frown. "I'm afraid the best we can hope for is to cast enough doubt to earn a more lenient sentence than death, in your case. The filing of the lawsuits on Terra Nova will not make that easier."

"If I have a Kruppen representative meet with me, would that be covered by attorney-client privilege?"

"If the Kruppen representative is an attorney, yes," she replied.

"Would you please arrange for that to happen?" he requested.

"Do you wish to replace me as your legal counsel?"

"No," Sandy said, shaking his head vigorously. "I appreciate your forthrightness. It's just that there might be another option to alleviate the situation, but you are not the person who can help with that."

"I must warn you that trying to bribe the court will not work if that's what you are thinking," she warned.

"Nothing of the kind," Sandy assured her. "I will grant you permission to share with Kruppen everything you know of my predicament."

The guard returned Sandy to the cell shortly after. Covering his mouth and speaking as softly as possible, he told the three men that the ship was destroyed and four counts of murder were added to the charges. Boyle and Warburton, in particular, displayed mixed emotions. Proud that their security system did its job but dismayed at the loss of the ship and the addition of murder charges, particularly since Karkinos still used capital punishment.

"How can they claim it's murder?" Stick asked. "The system gave them fair warning."

"They claim it didn't," Sandy answered. "Though our backup logs would show that it did, my attorney believes they would not admit the log as evidence."

Mike looked at Sandy incredulously. "That's bullshit, Skip."

"I know. My attorney was pretty honest about letting me know that it wouldn't be a fair trial."

"I told you we should have taken our chances," Puss commented.

"Sorry, Puss," Sandy cautioned. "I forgot to tell you that a heavy cruiser was right behind the *Palmyra* that we surrendered to. We wouldn't have made it. We made the right call. I just didn't think they'd be so stupidly stubborn as to keep trying to hack onto the ship."

"What do we do now?" Mike asked.

"I have one more card I think I can play, but it might come at a pretty high cost—for me, at least."

"You're not going to let them kill you?" Stick protested.

Sandy laughed. "Not that bad," he lied.

A few hours later, the guard took Sandy back to the meeting room. Again, he was handcuffed, and then the cuffs were fastened to the bolt on the table. A thin man in a gray suit entered and sat opposite Sandy. Like the attorney before, he activated the field suppressor on his comm unit. Like Sonya Tsaich earlier, he cautioned Sandy not to move his lips or to cover his mouth when he spoke.

His first questions were to verify Sandy's identity. When Sandy responded correctly, he asked, "How may I be of service?"

"I need you to contact Admiral Ketyungyoenwong of the Planetary Alliance as soon as possible. Please inform her of my situation. Ms. Tsaich can fill you in on any details."

"She has already."

"Good. Please communicate to the admiral that the favor she owes to someone has been given to me to make use of, and that I would appreciate her assistance in freeing my crew from confinement and the dismissal of all charges against them. If she can do that, the favor is repaid in full. You might have better luck getting a timely response if you mention my name up front."

"Anything else?"

"This is a matter requiring the utmost of discretion," Sandy advised. "I do not know Ms. Tsaich. I do know the standards Kruppen Financial upholds."

"Very well, Mr. Pike. I will do as you ask."

When Sandy returned from such a brief meeting, the others quizzed him. He waved off their questions with a smile. "We'll have to wait and see if it worked," he cautioned.

The rest of that day and all the next few went by with no further news or meetings. The morning of the sixth day, a guard appeared with the man from Kruppen trailing him. "On your feet," the guard ordered. Sandy remained seated. "You, too," the guard demanded.

The Kruppen representative gave a brief nod to Sandy. Another guard came in from the women's wing with Portia. "Come," the first guard said to them.

He marched them to the front desk. Their belongings, still sealed in bags, were returned to them. The guard escorted them to a vehicle. The Kruppen rep accompanied them.

"Where are we going?" Portia asked.

"The shuttle port," the Kruppen rep answered. "We shouldn't talk in here," he warned.

They were escorted to a shuttle, still accompanied by the Kruppen rep. He shook his head aboard the shuttle, indicating that they still should not converse. Nonetheless, the others turned to Sandy with questioning looks. He indicated he didn't know what was happening, either.

An employee of the shuttle came to the hatch and appeared to be extending an umbilical to another vessel. When the indicator lights showed that a secure connection was established, he opened the hatch and disappeared into the umbilical. He returned a moment later and waved them through. The Kruppen representative extended his hand to Sandy. "It's been a pleasure to assist you, Mr. Pike."

On the bulkhead opposite the hatchway, the first thing they saw was the Planetary Alliance flag. All of them unconsciously relaxed at the sight. A steward was waiting for them. He directed them into different cabins where they could stow their belongings. Sandy waited to be the last aboard.

"Where are we headed?" he asked.

"Valkyrie," the steward replied. "Welcome aboard, Captain Pike."

"Thank you. I'm pleased to be here. What's your name?"

"Machonis. Justin Machonis, Petty Officer First Class."

"Thank you, Petty Officer Machonis."

"Captain, you'll find a console in your cabin. Admiral Ketyungyoenwong is waiting for you to contact her."

"Will do. What ship is this?"

"PAS *Aquilifer*, Captain. She's normally used by the Head of the Council. Fortunately, we were only a couple of jumps away from Cygnus when the admiral called. Otherwise, I understand she was planning on leasing a local vessel."

Sandy tilted his head and cocked an eyebrow at this. He went into the cabin that Machonis had pointed out and dropped his bag. There was a small desk with a console on it. He woke the console and accessed the directory, finding the admiral's contact.

Before he keyed the contact, he checked the time. While the local time in jail was mid-afternoon, it would be 08:30 on Valkyrie Station. He keyed the contact and immediately was connected to the admiral's yeoman.

"Captain Pike," he said. "The admiral is just finishing a call right now if you will wait a moment."

After a brief delay, the admiral's face appeared on-screen. "Hello, Sandy," she greeted him. "How was jail?"

Not the question he was expecting. "Hello, Admiral. I'd have to say it wasn't as bad as when I was in the HUW's custody, but I'm glad to be out of there just the same. Thank you."

"Don't thank me," she replied. "I had very little to do with it."

"To whom do I owe my gratitude then?"

"Mr. Dorsey."

"Mr. once-again-Head-of-the-Governing-Council Dorsey?"

"The same."

"Please pass along my thanks," Sandy said.

"You can do that yourself," she commented. "You have a call scheduled with him a little less than three hours from now. I understand you are now without a ship of your own?"

"Sadly, yes."

"Mhm. That is unfortunate."

"From the smile I see you fighting to keep from showing, I sense you don't really share my sense of loss," Sandy remarked.

"When one door is shut, another opens," she replied. "I just wanted to make sure you made it to the *Aquilifer* right now. I would like to chat with you after you speak with Mr. Dorsey, though."

"What is our status as far as criminal charges?"

"All charges have been dropped, is what I was told," she answered, "but Mr. Dorsey can tell you more."

"Were any promises made regarding my suits against the Karkinosian government?"

"As far as I know, those subjects did not come up," she answered, more of her smile escaping.

"Do you know what else Mr. Dorsey intends to discuss with me?" Sandy inquired.

"Yes."

"Care to enlighten me?"

"Not for me to share," she said, shaking her head, her smile broadening. "Until later today. I'll speak with you then, Sandy."

The screen went dark. Sandy took a deep breath. He suspected the Head of the Governing Council would try first to lure him back to the navy and, if that didn't work, might apply other pressure. With the *Alice May* destroyed, one of his reasons for not returning had disappeared. His rekindled relationship with Leezy, though, might stand in the way of the Alliance's wishes. If she didn't like the idea, no amount of wheedling, cajoling, or arm-twisting would make him go back.

He left the cabin and heard the hum of excited voices from the sitting area. When he entered the room, the rest of his crew was there. They all fell silent.

"Uh-oh," Sandy said. "You guys want me to leave?"

Portia smiled. "Nope," she said, patting the seat next to her on the sofa. "Sit right down."

Sandy sat down. All four were looking at him, then began looking at one another to see who would start. Mike gave a slight shrug, cleared his throat quietly, and asked, "Sandy, do you have a plan for what to do now that the *Alice May* is gone?"

Sandy suspected he knew where the conversation was headed. "No. The *Alice May* was a unique ship, created under unique circumstances, which I doubt will happen again in our lifetimes. There's no way to build or configure a new ship that would have the same capabilities, regardless of cost."

"Do you think you'll try to continue the business with a conventional ship?" Mike asked.

"I haven't thought that far ahead, to be honest," Sandy admitted. "I was more concerned with trying to get us freed."

"The reason he's asking," Portia stated, "is because each of us had a message waiting for us from BuPers. The Alliance Navy wants all of us back and has offered each of us some pretty generous terms. Incredibly generous, for BuPers. I can't speak for the others, but if you were determined to keep the business going, I'd probably stay with you—out of loyalty, if for no other reason. I mean, you've made me a rich woman, Sandy. I could retire right now and live a damned luxurious life."

"What Mama is trying to say," Stick Warburton interrupted, "is that the last couple of years have been pretty boring."

"Hush, child. Don't put your words in my mouth," Portia cautioned.

"It's true, though," Puss Boyle countered. "What just went down in Cygnus is the closest we've come to any danger in almost four years. It kind of reminded all of us of what we've been lacking. No offense, Sandy, but we've become as exciting as truck drivers. I mean, the first couple of years were a gas. It seemed like we could run into trouble on every run, even though it was only every third or fourth. People took their shots at us; we took them down—it was fun and exciting. Watching the business grow was fun. The last couple of years, though... boring: same routes, no challenges, just profitable business. Like Mama said, you've made us all rich. I'm not ready to retire just yet, though."

"Is this something you talked about before? As a group?" Sandy asked, not with anger, merely curious.

"Stick and I talked about it," Puss admitted. "But today is the first time we've ever discussed it with Mike and Portia."

"Sandy, we're all incredibly grateful," Mike said, "and none of us were planning on leaving. I'm personally indebted because you helped me become a complete officer, not just an 'engineering guy.' Now it seems I have the chance to show that to the Alliance Navy, to prove myself in front of my peers. With everything you taught me and what I learned from Portia and the kids, I know that I can compete with anyone."

"What did BuPers offer you guys?" Sandy asked.

"Command Master Chief," Portia replied, "with my time on the *Alice May* counting as service 'on assignment' in terms of seniority and pension, plus the ability to pretty much pick my own posting."

"Commander," Mike added, "command track—not engineering. The same deal with years of service. They offered command of my own ship or an XO slot on a capital ship."

"Lieutenant Commander," Warburton tossed out. "Same deal with the service, and command of a frigate."

"Same," Boyle agreed.

"Holy shit!" Sandy breathed, surprised. "It's like they knew exactly what each of you would want."

"That's what we were talking about when you came in," Portia confirmed. "I have a feeling they asked Ali."

"I don't think Ali is in any kind of condition to give them much advice right now," Sandy commented.

"I have a feeling they asked Ali before that," Portia clarified.

"None of you have any problems with going back to the Navy?" Sandy asked.

"Honestly, boss, the only reason we left is that we thought the navy was going to cease to exist," Boyle stated. "And it did. None of us could have foreseen that Admiral K would resurrect it so successfully. When they asked us a couple of years ago, they didn't offer anything, and their survival was uncertain at best."

Sandy looked at each of them with a kind expression. "I'm genuinely happy for each of you. If you rejoin the Alliance Navy, they'll be lucky to have you."

"What about you, Sandy?" Portia asked, putting her hand on his arm.

"They haven't offered me my dream job," Sandy said with a chuckle, "but I am supposed to speak with the Head of the Governing Council in a couple of hours."

"What if they — " Portia began, but Sandy stopped her.

"They've asked me before. At least, Admiral Ketyungyoenwong has, and I've always said no. We had the ship, we had the business, I had an awesome crew. Plus, in the last couple of years of my service, some bad things happened. You and Mike were there for one of them but there were a couple of others after that were just as bad or, in some ways, worse that I told you about. It cost me my girlfriend, and you all saw that I just got back together with her."

"You should ask her," Boyle blurted out.

"What?" Sandy asked.

"You should get on the comm right now and ask her—before you talk to anyone in the government," Boyle added. "She didn't really have a problem with you being in the navy, did she? It was just that a bunch of bad stuff hit in quick order."

"He's right, boss," Warburton agreed.

Sandy rose and returned to his cabin. He checked the time to try to make sure Leezy would be awake. He didn't dare wake her for this call. It was approaching 21:30 in Corniferra, where she lived. He placed the call. Since her comm did not recognize the contact link, he received an automated response: "Please verify your identity and nature of your call."

"Sandy. Personal. Important," he stated.

Leezy picked up quickly. "Sandy—is everything alright? I haven't heard from you, and I was getting worried."

"I'm sorry I caused you to worry. Everything is — " he paused, " — is… well, it just is, at the moment. This might take a while. Is this an okay time?"

"Sure," she responded. "I was just going to read for a bit and then go to bed."

Sandy launched into a chronicle of what happened after they left Arete. "To sum it all up," he concluded, "the ship is destroyed, the Head of the Governing Council apparently arranged my release, my crew have each been offered his or her dream job within the Alliance Navy and I'm scheduled to be on a call with the Head of the Governing Council in," he checked the time, "about an hour. I strongly suspect that he wants me to rejoin the Alliance Navy. I thought I should talk to you before I even speak to him."

Leezy was silent for a time, processing all he had told her. Finally, she looked up at his face on the screen. "We haven't talked about it yet, Sandy, and I'm almost afraid to—like we'd be opening Pandora's Box—but I think we need to touch on it. Did our break-up influence the way you felt about the navy?"

"Looking back, I'm certain it did, though I wasn't thinking about it in those terms—but it wasn't the only thing," he protested. "You know what happened on the mission I had before we had our vacation on Arete. That was frustrating because it was so unnecessary—it was all due to politics, internal politics in our own government because someone couldn't admit his or her idea turned out to be so stupid. Then I got shot. After you left, the Office of Naval Intelligence lied to me, saying that they didn't know why I was shot. When I found out later that they knew all along but didn't tell me because they wanted to sweep it under the rug, I was furious. When I figured out that you had been at risk the whole time, I was horrified. And the guy who had tried to have me killed was a political appointee—he wouldn't have made it as far in the service without protection."

Sandy then summarized the last few months of his navy career. Then he covered the resurrection of the *Alice May*. "That's about it," Sandy shrugged. "We repaired and refit the *Alice May* and started our business. Just after that came the HUW's civil war, but once that ended, our business took off."

"Hooooo," Leezy let out a deep breath. "I didn't think I could feel worse than I did on Niobe a couple of weeks ago. You never explained things to me that way, or if you did, I didn't have the perspective to understand. I'm sorry. I only looked at how the things that happened made me feel."

"It wasn't just you," Sandy claimed quietly as he watched tears flow down her cheeks. "I didn't share those thoughts and feelings with you, so you couldn't have had that kind of perspective. Our time together was so perfect and felt so right that I didn't want to share my negative feelings and frustrations with you. You seemed to think I was perfect, and I wanted to be perfect for you. I enjoy every moment I'm with you so much—I don't want to ruin it. I'm sorry."

"Wow," Leezy commented in a choked voice. "Gotta say, airing this out isn't really pleasant, but I'm thinking it's going to do us some real good."

"Yeah," Sandy agreed, his voice just as choked. "The thing that really sucks is that Monty told me it would. I hate it when he's right."

Leezy laughed. "How is Monty?"

"Still the same," Sandy answered. "He's on about his tenth girlfriend since the last time you spoke to him."

"So, you think Mr. Dorsey wants you back?" Leezy asked.

"Based on what they offered my crew, I'm going to guess he will ask," Sandy said. "I cashed in the biggest favor anyone has ever owed me, asking for them to help my crew. I didn't think they'd get me out of Dutch as well. He might demand my services, and I'd have a hard time arguing."

"Baloney, Sandy," Leezy said. "You're no good to them as some sort of indentured servant. Give them credit for not being that dumb. They'd only want you back if you want to do it. That's the big question. Do you want to?"

"I don't want to jeopardize us," he admitted. "I feel like I spent years in the wilderness and — "

"You have my blessing," Leezy interrupted, "if that's what you want to do."

"Leezy, I don't think you know this, but I have enough money that I never have to work again. Our children will never need to work for a living and likely our grandchildren, too."

Leezy laughed. "I like hearing you talk about our children, but I can't see you retiring, Sandy. You handle free time worse than anyone I know. I'm never going to let you retire because you'll drive me nuts." Then, more soberly, she added, "So, what do you want to do?"

"One of the kids said something a little while ago that made me think."

"The kids? Those two charming men I met?"

"Yes—them. They were on their absolute best behavior for you, believe me. One said that what we'd been doing the last couple of years was about as exciting as driving a truck for a living. It wasn't quite that bad, at least for me, since I've been the boss and I have a few more challenges, but his point isn't far off. I do miss some of the excitement of the navy. I don't miss the politics and politicians, though."

"Listen to what Mr. Dorsey has to say," Leezy instructed. "A part of me still fantasizes about my dashing navy hero who prevails against impossible odds. I don't get the same thrill picturing you as a truck driver. If you rejoin the navy because that is what you want to do, then I'll be happy."

Sandy had a bit of time to compose his thoughts before speaking with the Head of the Governing Council. Sandy did not pay much attention to Alliance politics since leaving the navy. When the Hegemony's civil war broke out, Admiral Ketyungyoenwong had issued recall orders to the Alliance Navy, despite having no government to back her and no money. She convinced people that they would get paid, eventually, but that they had to chase the HUWs away first. Once the navy had regained control of several systems, the planetary governments woke up, and then the Alliance government reformed.

Al Dorsey, who had been ousted as Head of the Governing Council after the debacle of the Battle of Excelsus, was reinstated. After Excelsus, Dorsey had taken responsibility for the failures. He offered an aggressive plan to address the problems that were exposed, but the rest of the Council was content to believe things weren't as bad as he had stated. Time had proven him correct and the rest of the Council wrong.

Sandy tried to think about what he wanted. He didn't know whether he had a dream posting the way the others did. Despite his frustration with politicians, he did not question the need for civilian control of the navy—the Hegemony's civil war showed what could happen when civilian control was thrown off. Finally, after allowing his mind figuratively to chase its tail, he realized it was time for his conversation with Dorsey.

He sat at the desk and woke the console. The appointment program came up, and he hit the link for the scheduled conference. The 'waiting room' screen came up briefly, and then Dorsey's face appeared.

"Hello, sir," Sandy said.

"Hello, Captain Pike," Dorsey replied with a grin, "It's a pleasure to see you again."

"The admiral told me I have you to thank for my freedom."

"You owe me no thanks, Sandy. May I call you Sandy?"

He nodded. "Yes, sir."

"I'd prefer Al, but whatever you're comfortable with."

"Yes, sir, Al."

Dorsey laughed. "Sandy, as I said, you owe me nothing. Consider it repayment of a debt of honor—an old-fashioned way of looking at things, I know, but it's how I feel. I don't want to overwhelm you with false praise, but there's no one else alive who has earned the Legion of Merit and a silver oak cluster. Hell, you'd have a second cluster if we were able to recognize what you did with those Robur idiots. In return, we treated you poorly. It wasn't by intention, I'm sure of that, but between Robur, that lunatic Tobin and Excelsus and—more important—how we as a government and the navy dealt with those situations... well, we gave you the shitty end of the stick, again and again and again. No one blames you for leaving when you had the chance."

"Thank you, sir... Al," Sandy responded. "If you don't mind my asking," Sandy said, "how did you convince the Karkinosians to let me go?"

"I threatened them," Dorsey replied in a matter-of-fact tone.

"The charges are dropped?"

"Yup."

"Was there any mention of my lawsuits against them?"

"I refused to discuss them."

"Again, thank you," Sandy said.

"Sandy, don't thank me. I'm trying to thank you," Dorsey said, "and I'm not done. I understand that those idiots at Cygnus caused your ship to blow up, which leaves you somewhat high and dry, as the old saying goes. If you'd like to build a new ship, I'm willing to offer you access to the navy yards and any materials you need, labor and materials at cost, to build a new one."

He looked at Sandy for a response. Sandy was stunned. Of all the things he had tried to anticipate, this hadn't been a consideration. "Wow," he managed to say, finally. "Sir, that was unexpected."

"That might leave you without a crew," Dorsey commented. "I'm not going to apologize for trying to woo them back to the navy."

"Well, seeing that you offered each one of them pretty much his or her dream posting, I think you may have succeeded."

"On the other hand, if you don't want to go to the trouble and expense of building a new ship, I have one that is due to begin trials in six weeks, and I'll even throw in a crew as well. It won't cost you a single credit either," Dorsey added with a chuckle.

There was a pause while he gauged Sandy's reaction. "I'm still listening, sir."

"Well, you haven't said 'no' yet, so you want me to plunge onward?" Sandy nodded.

"I don't know what your dream posting is, Sandy, but I'd like to tell you a bit more about our situation. I know you might have learned some of this from your friend Captain Swift, but — "

"Monty learned a few years ago," Sandy interrupted, "not to talk about the navy with me. I might have bitten his head off once or twice, plus I've been guilty of deliberately not wanting to know, so I'm not very well-informed. Please, continue."

"Okay. It starts with what happened after Excelsus," Dorsey began. "They replaced me and canceled the plans I had to address the problems in the navy. That led to the disaster that was Freia. You know all that. When the HUWs started their civil war, Letty Ketyungyoenwong's quick action saved what remains of the Alliance and we re-established the government. Since events had proven that I was more right than wrong, the other Speakers wanted to put me back in charge. I took the job with a couple of ironclad conditions. One was that the other Speakers must agree to rebuild the navy to at least its pre-Excelsus strength in terms of capital ships.

"We didn't have the money, especially with a reduced economic base, so we needed to commit to a program of deficit spending and massive borrowing. While no one was happy about it, they believed me when I told them that it was our quickest way to restoring the Alliance. If we did nothing, the remnant of the Alliance would continue to deteriorate. Most importantly, I was able to convince the bankers that, if we were successful, the planets we brought back into the fold would be able to share the cost when the bills came due.

"The new ships we started are just now nearing completion. In the next 18 months, we will have restored the number of capital ships to what it was before Excelsus. We hope to use those ships to clean up the mess left by the HUW's civil war."

"How many ships are under construction?" Sandy asked.

"Eight superdreadnoughts and fourteen battlecruisers," Dorsey answered.

Sandy whistled softly in response.

"We plan to start another group of six SDNs and eight battlecruisers immediately—beginning in six weeks once slips are opened up. In addition, we recalled a number of light cruisers and frigates from mothballs and have updated their powerplants and weaponry.

"As you know, ships are part of the solution," Dorsey continued. "The other part is staffing. One of the few good things to come out of all the bad that happened is that Letty was able to completely eliminate sub-standard officers from the navy. There simply aren't any people left in the navy whose main qualification is a political connection or the ability to do paperwork neatly and not cause waves. She called only the good officers and crew back to duty. With the reduced number of ships we had after Freia, that was enough. With all the new construction and refits coming, we've been building up our ranks in preparation. We have more officers and enlisted personnel than we have ships for them at the moment, so we've been rotating crews on and off to provide them all with some experience. When they're not aboard a ship, they do simulation training on Valkyrie. You still haven't said 'no' yet, Sandy, or stuck your fingers in your ears, so I'm taking that as a good sign," Dorsey commented.

"I honestly had no idea that the shipbuilding campaign was this aggressive," Sandy remarked. "I thought that the reduced number of planets would have limited it to less than half what you just told me."

"We haven't exactly been shouting about it from the rooftops," Dorsey admitted. "Quite the opposite. I'm sure the HUWs know that we're building, but they might not have an idea of how much we've committed. I do know from intelligence reports that they are not in as good of a position. Of course, this is all a big gamble," Dorsey continued. "If we fail to restore the Alliance, it will all be for nothing. I don't want to fail. I hate losing. If we can get you to rejoin us, I think that helps us push the odds more in our favor. If you want it, we have a ship for you. As far as the other specifics, I'll leave that to Letty to communicate. If you want to run your freight business, I'll support that, too. I only want you to join us willingly and eagerly. Does that make sense?"

"It does," Sandy answered.

"All I can ask is that you consider it," Dorsey stated. "I know you'll think it through."

Almost as soon as he closed the call with Dorsey, another call came through from Admiral Ketyungyoenwong. "How was your conversation with Mr. Dorsey?"

"Interesting. Illuminating. I've had some other discussions as well. I certainly have much to ponder," Sandy replied thoughtfully.

"I'm going to add to your list of things to ponder, Sandy," she said. "I have two *Mayfield*-class superdreadnoughts and three *Resolute*-class battlecruisers nearing trials. Trials for all five should begin in about six weeks. Then, at six-month intervals following those, in total, I have another six SDNs and eleven battlecruisers coming along. When the second group finishes trials, I hope to begin offensive operations about nine months from now. That, by the way, is about as much information as I can provide to you right now. As you're a civilian, I shouldn't have shared even that much, as I'm sure you understand."

"I do."

"Mr. Dorsey told me he would grant you the opportunity to build a new ship, at your expense, using our facilities and components. I'm offering a different opportunity—to rejoin us and be an important part of the restoration of the full Planetary Alliance. I only want you to consider this if you can do so wholeheartedly and without reservation. I believe Mr. Dorsey also was planning to touch on that."

"He did."

"You would be promoted to captain, with your time in rank dated back to the orders you received after Excelsus. Your service time would be uninterrupted, with the last six years shown as 'on assignment' for the navy."

"So, just as generous as the terms offered to my crew," Sandy commented.

"Yes. I don't expect an answer today, Sandy," she said, "unless you were to say 'no.' I hope you will think about this and talk to people about it and make the best decision you can."

"I understand, admiral."

"You're still a civilian, Sandy, and a friend. I asked you to call me by my name."

"Yes, Letty," Sandy replied, blushing.

"I'm sure Mr. Dorsey also explained that the series of unfortunate events that created our current situation also had an unexpected benefit, in terms of being able to clean house. You'll find that the navy now no longer has any Slocums or Tobins. We do still have civilian oversight, but our civilian masters are entirely united in their support of the service. I believe that will continue for the foreseeable future."

"He did explain that."

"Good. Well, that's all I wanted to say," she stated. "Unless you have any questions that have already bubbled up."

"Actually, Letty, I do have a couple," Sandy offered. "Would you be offering the same terms of reinstatement as were offered to the rest of my crew?"

"Yes, except I'm not willing to share any information about your posting until I receive a full-throated commitment from you," she responded.

"If that's the case, I'll be leapfrogging people who responded to your call and have been with you since. Will that be a problem?"

She laughed. "I must say, that is the type of question only you would ask. I don't believe so. Your return would be viewed as a positive, in my honest opinion. There's more I could say, but I don't want to feed your ego. You wouldn't believe me anyway. Anything else?"

"That's all for now," Sandy replied. "I have a lot to consider. Thank you."

"What's up, peckerhead?" Monty greeted him.

"A lot, actually, Monty," Sandy replied.

"Huh. No return insult. Must be serious," Monty commented.

"Yeah. Kinda."

"You getting married or something?"

"Not yet," Sandy chuckled. "I'm thinking of coming back. I wanted to sound you out."

"Coming back... to the navy?" Monty asked.

"Yeah."

"Whoa," was Monty's first response. "Really?"

"Yeah."

"Pretty dramatic change of heart, all of a sudden, buddy."

Sandy described what had happened in Cygnus. He told the story of their arrest, the loss of his ship, their release, the offers made to his crew. He shared some of the details of his conversations with Al Dorsey and Admiral Ketyungyoenwong.

"And you told Elizabeth about this?" Monty asked.

"Yes. She's supportive."

"And you're excited about it?"

"Getting there."

"What's the thing that changed your mind?" Monty asked. "I mean, you have the option of building a new ship."

"Puss made a comment about the job having become as exciting as being a truck driver," Sandy explained.

"Ha! One of these days, I need to meet those two. They remind me of us."

"They're worse," Sandy commented, "and better."

"Truck driver," Monty repeated. "Ouch."

"Yeah. It stung."

"He's mostly right, you know. Sticking with it? Waste of your time. I think I understand why you cut ties. They didn't screw me over near as badly as they did you, but I needed some time away, too. Since I've been back, all I can say is that things are different, in a good way. I don't think you'll regret it."

The next day Sandy tried to distract himself with other tasks. He used the console in his cabin to find the sensor data covering the continued attack by the Karkinosians after the Vermilion ships surrendered and the sensor data showing the automated messages generated when the Karkinosians tried twice to open the hatch of the *Alice May*. He sent both sets of files to Sergei at the Kruppen office nearest his mother's house. He requested a status update from the Terra Nova courts on the lawsuit he had asked be filed accusing the Karkinosians of war crimes and asked Sergei to forward the files showing the Karkinosian attempts to enter the ship to Lloyd's, his insurance company, and to follow up on the insurance claim. Of the two, the insurance claim was of more immediate interest to him.

He had worked very closely with the insurer to determine an accurate value of the cost to replace the *Alice May* as it was being modified years before. It had taken some effort, and Sandy had needed to climb through several layers of management finally to reach someone willing to take the ship's unique configuration into account. With some of the components being unavailable even in the most secretive black markets, it was difficult to determine a replacement value. When the cost of obtaining the best-available replacement components climbed over 200 million credits, the Vice President he was working with at Lloyd's was horrified. He offered Sandy a binder that capped their liability at 100 million credits, explaining that it was the best anyone could do. Sandy had taken him at his word and accepted it. He had paid the stupendous premiums Lloyd's demanded religiously and without complaint.

Sandy had no doubt that Lloyd's would honor the claim—the company had a centuries-old reputation to uphold—but he wanted the Karkinosians to pay for their arrogant stupidity and for trying to trump up charges against him and his crew. The insurance payout would be important if Sandy decided to rejoin the navy and dissolve the corporation. He and the others were all shareholders, as was Tom McAllister, so the insurance money would be split by those percentages. He checked on the company accounts. Some short-term investment accounts the company held amounted to just under twenty million. That would be split as well.

He paused and shook his head slightly in wonderment. A month before he would not have dreamed of dissolving the company. He was still torn, but the talk with Leezy had helped prepare him for the possibility of returning to the navy. He took a break and found the others chatting away. As on the day before, when he entered, they fell silent.

"C'mon, guys. You're starting to give me a complex," he whined.

"Sorry, boss," Warburton replied sheepishly.

"Have you figured out what you're going to do?" Mike Xie asked.

"Not quite, but I think you can help," he answered. He shared with them some of the information from his conversations with Dorsey and the admiral. When he mentioned Dorsey's offer to allow him to build a new ship, Puss muttered, "Holy shit!" They all laughed.

"Seriously, Sandy, if you decide to do that, let me give you some design ideas," he said.

When Sandy related that Dorsey had told him that there were no more political appointees in the navy, Stick and Puss looked at each other. "No more Smalleys?" Warburton asked.

Sandy shook his head. Both the younger men responded by saying, "Awwwwwww."

"Did they offer you the same sort of dream job as us?" Xie asked.

"The admiral didn't share any specifics," Sandy explained. "She did tell me that my service time would be treated the same as in the offers they made you, but she wouldn't tell me about what sort of posting I'd have until I made a commitment."

"Did you talk with Elizabeth?" Portia asked.

"Yes," Sandy answered, drawing the word out like a sigh. "It was difficult but also cleansing. We both saw where we made some mistakes, and now, we know how to avoid them."

"What was her feeling about it?" Portia inquired.

"She said she'll be happy with whatever I want, but that she always thinks of me as a dashing hero of the navy and not as a glorified truck driver, Puss," he responded, aiming the last comment at Boyle.

"Are you leaning one way or the other?" Mike inquired.

"One of my biggest hang-ups is that I'm worried about how others will feel about me coming back and possibly jumping over them in terms of seniority if my service time is treated like yours. Think about how your colleagues will feel in your situation and whether it might be a problem."

The four looked at one another. Finally, Mike spoke up. "Sheesh! Why do I always go first?" he muttered. "Skipper, while that might be a thing we should be wary of, I don't think it will be a problem for you."

"Don't get a fat head from this, boss," Stick chimed in, "but you're sort of a legend."

Puss nodded. "After what you did with *Teaford*, sacrificing your ship so the other two could escape, people knew I served with you and the first question they'd ask me, I mean, after wanting to know how Stick and I got to be so awesome, was usually about you."

Portia just waved Sandy off, laughing at Puss.

"If any of you come up with a solid argument why I should keep the business going and not return to the navy, would you please tell me? I'm going to sit on this for a day or two and talk with Elizabeth again. It's a lot to think about, but I should have it processed in my head in a day or two."

Sandy really wanted to perform his Tai Chi exercises, but the craft they were on simply had no room. However, he did find time to meditate, and that helped a little. He spoke again with Leezy a little later and shared what he could.

"Sandy, I think a part of what you're struggling with is your feelings about the navy are all mixed up with your feelings about what happened with us. I'm willing to bet that if I hadn't been so stupid as to break up with you, when the admiral contacted you the first time you would have flown straight to Valkyrie."

11

After two more days of wrestling with his thoughts, pacing back and forth as much as he could in the small common area (and irritating everyone to the point where they yelled at him), Sandy made up his mind. He contacted Admiral Ketyungyoenwong. He reached her yeoman, who informed Sandy she was in a meeting but would contact him. He returned to the sitting area to pace, but the other four chased him out. He retreated to his cabin and lay on the bed, staring at the ceiling. He'd made up his mind. Now he just wanted to get on to the next step.

It was more than two hours before she contacted him. He jumped up at the chime from the console and stumbled into the bulkhead, trying to get to the tiny desk. He woke the unit and answered. "Hello, Letty," he greeted her, feeling awkward using her first name. Still, he figured it was likely the last time it would be permitted for several years, so he might as well try it.

"Hello, Sandy. I'm returning your call."

"Right." He took a deep breath. "My biggest worry is about leapfrogging over people who have been with you the whole time. I want to make sure that it won't create hard feelings. You addressed this superficially in our last conversation, but my concern remains."

"Oh, Sandy," she sighed. "You should remember how close-knit the navy is. Your shipmates from *Driscoll*, from *Chapman*, *Teaford*, *DeLuca*, and before have all shared their experiences with their peers. I cannot guarantee that someone might not get his or her nose bent out of shape, but I doubt there will be many. They will be outnumbered by a huge and vocal margin."

Sandy listened. "Okay. If you want me, you've got me. No reservations."

Letty grinned. "That's great news, Sandy. I'll have my yeoman transmit some information to you shortly. You'll be here the day after tomorrow. Plan on spending a few hours with me. After that, I won't need you until Monday, May 4—a week before your new ship starts trials. That will give you a little more than 30 days to settle your affairs. Is that enough time?"

"It should be," Sandy agreed. "Admiral, can you share with me what my assignment will be?"

"It will be in the orders my yeoman is sending. I think you'll like it," she said with a sly smile. "If that's all, captain?"

"Nothing further, admiral," he responded.

"Then I'll see you when you arrive. Welcome back, sailor."

Within a few minutes, Sandy received several files. One was the schematic of a *Mayfield*-class superdreadnought. The first of the class had been laid down only 25 years before, and only two of them had been built, with the last having been completed eighteen years earlier. Another file was a personnel roster for PAS *Audacious*. A third file was entitled 'Battle Group Omega.' The fourth file was titled, 'Orders.' The last was 'Construction Status.'

He opened his orders first. There was something reassuring about the familiar language. "The Governing Council of the Planetary Alliance does hereby charge and require Captain Alexander S. Pike to assume command of the Alliance ship *Audacious* — "

Also included in the file were other documents. Like the rest of his crew, his official service record had been amended to show the last six years as 'on assignment.' His time in rank was dated back to Admiral Ketyungyoenwong's orders after Excelsus, when she intended to 'frock' him to the rank of Captain.

The file for Battle Group Omega was empty except for a list of un-named assets. The Battle Group would include four SDNs, six battlecruisers, five heavy cruisers, six light cruisers and two frigates. No ship names were listed.

Sandy then opened the personnel roster. Looking at the officers, he saw that Commander Bronwen Gupta would be his Executive Officer. He scanned the list of names but didn't see any familiar ones. Next, he opened the enlisted folders. The Chief of Boat, or COB, was Troy McCutcheon. McCutcheon served on *Driscoll* and survived its destruction in the Battle of Excelsus. Having a good relationship with the senior noncom would certainly help get a new crew up to speed.

The construction status report provided details and status on the new ship construction. A separate folder also showed refits of ships retrieved from the 'mothball fleet.' These were older ships, made obsolete by newer versions. The Alliance brought a dozen frigates and four light cruisers from mothballs and upgraded them with new power plants, drives, weaponry, and systems. While not quite equal to newer construction, the refurbished ships gave the Alliance flexibility it had not enjoyed during Sandy's time. The light cruisers and ten of the frigates were already complete and in service. The remaining two frigates were due to be completed in ten days.

Sandy wondered what Battle Group Omega was. With nothing but an org chart, he had little to go on. He figured Admiral Ketyungyoenwong included it for a reason that she would share with him later.

He spoke with Leezy and confirmed with her that he decided to rejoin the navy. She seemed pleased. She was even more delighted to hear he would have a month off. She told him she would arrange something fun. He shared the news with his mother as well. She was happy to hear it.

His erstwhile crew was excited to hear his decision. They had received updated orders. Stick and Puss were taking command of the two frigates just finishing their refit after being reclaimed. The two friends were being split up. Puss would be in Blue Fleet, under Admiral Horton. Stick would be in Red, reporting the Admiral Giersch.

Mike chose to serve as an Executive Officer on a capital ship. He was being posted to PAS *Redemption*, one of the battlecruisers Admiral Ketyungyoenwong commanded in the action in system RY 232 the same day as the Battle of Excelsus. He would be reporting to Captain Olivia Park. Sandy shared his high opinion of Park with him.

Portia elected to serve as Chief of Boat on PAS *Percival*, Admiral Horton's flagship. *Percival* was one of the two *Mayfield*-class superdreadnoughts built before the construction of her sister ships was sacrificed to budgetary concerns. She told Sandy she was looking forward to having a wider variety of people to work with.

"No offense—you guys have become my dearest friends, but I'm ready for some fresh faces," she stated.

Sandy made some calls about closing the business. He spoke with Sarah Simpson, their attorney, and Tamas Takada, the Kruppen office manager on Providence. It was surprisingly easy to wrap things up. He also contacted Tom McAllister and informed him that the business was ending.

"You'll be getting a final payout from Kruppen once the insurance settlement comes through. After that, the corporation is dissolved."

"It's been an interesting adventure to watch, Sandy. What do you want me to do with the components I have in storage?"

"Send them to Valkyrie," Sandy asked. "I made a promise when we started out that none of that stuff would ever hit the black market."

"Understood," McAllister replied. "You know you guys could make a killing — "

"It's never been about the money, Tom," Sandy stated.

"I know, I know," McAllister answered, his hands up in surrender. "I have to ask, Sandy. Are you willing to go back?"

"Why do you ask?"

"I'll admit, we never talked about it," Tom said. "You showed up with the ship and your crew, all clearly ex-Alliance Navy. I looked into your career, as much as I could. I have to say, it was pretty impressive. Your leaving was due to the Alliance's surrender, but why didn't you go back when they reformed the navy?"

"There were some things that happened that you wouldn't necessarily know from my record. Not black marks," he added quickly. "Before getting into all that, why did you leave the Free Republics?"

"You didn't have Ali check up on me?" Tom asked with a smile.

"I'm sure she did," Sandy chuckled, "but she kept most everything to herself. I just know you were in the Free Republics' Navy and left to run the yard."

"Huh. Well, I left the FRN at about the same point in my career as you," Tom began. "I didn't have a surrender to blame it on, though. I'd enjoyed a decent career, progressing upward. But, once I reached commander, things seemed to stall. I was passed over for promotion twice. I felt I had a better record and was a superior commander to the ones who made the list. They were, for the most part, people I didn't like and certainly didn't want to emulate."

Sandy, remembering conversations he and Monty had years before, suggested, "Paranoid pencil-pushers? Yes-men?"

McAllister tilted his head, squinting slightly, then nodded. "Exactly. They were 'strictly by the book' guys. Some had political connections."

Sandy laughed. "You just described half the Alliance Navy at the time of the surrender."

"From what I read in the news reports, it seemed like the head of your government was aware of the problem and wanted to fix it," Tom said, "but then he got canned, and I guess nothing happened?"

"Pretty much," Sandy confirmed.

"But when you go back, won't those same people still be there?"

"I'm told they're not—both by official and unofficial sources," Sandy explained. "From what I've heard, when Admiral Ketyungyoenwong reformed the Alliance Navy, she only brought back the good people."

"That would certainly make it easier," McAllister commented. "Well, good luck and Godspeed, as they say. It was a pleasure working with you, and I'm sorry that the *Alice May* is no more. She was one of a kind."

Over the course of the journey from Cygnus they had adjusted to navy time—the time standard of Sigrun, the capital city of Valkyrie. Sandy asked Petty Officer Machonis, the steward, if it would be possible for them to have a fairly sumptuous dinner for their last night aboard. He not only agreed but threw himself into it.

"Tonight," Sandy greeted everyone at the table, "is our last gathering as a crew—the crew of the *Alice May*. I felt it was appropriate that we celebrate before we split up and move on. It has been an honor and a privilege to work with you for the last six years. I will miss all of you and hope that our paths cross again frequently. With that," he raised his glass, "to the *Alice May.*"

The others joined him in his toast, murmuring, "the *Alice May.*"

They sat and enjoyed the dinner Machonis had prepared. They shared stories and reminisced about the adventures they'd shared. Portia teased Mike, Stick and Puss, asking if they had stayed in contact with the Manlius operatives with whom they had enjoyed relationships during the first couple of years. Stick and Puss admitted that they were no longer in regular contact with Heidi and Cheyenne. Mike blushed. His lack of verbal response drew stares from the rest.

"Syd and I are still involved," he admitted. "As much as we can be, given that we rarely see one another. What about you and Morgan?"

It was Portia's turn to be slightly embarrassed. "We, uh, stay in touch," she admitted hesitantly. Then, seeing Stick and Puss about to crack wise, she shook her finger at them. "Don't you start, boys. I see that look on your faces, and I'm telling you right now, you'd better think before you speak."

Both of them tried their best to put an innocent look on their faces, but their smirks couldn't be hidden. They did manage to choke back whatever comments they were going to make. Portia glared at them until Puss put his hands up in surrender.

Sandy informed them of some of the steps involved in dissolving the business and that their ownership shares would be paid out soon. He also passed along a recommendation for a moving service suggested to him by the Kruppen office if they didn't want to return to Providence and pack up their belongings. He shared that he planned to use the service.

He asked when they needed to report to their assignments. Mike and Portia would be transferring to a supply ship headed to Inverness, where PAS *Percival* and PAS *Redemption* were based. They needed to leave in less than 24 hours. Stick and Puss would be here on Valkyrie Station while their new commands were being finished.

They arrived at Valkyrie Station just after 05:00 Navy time. Sandy's appointment with Admiral Ketyungyoenwong was scheduled for 08:00. Sandy made good use of the time. He stopped by the outfitters on the station to obtain new uniforms. He caused a bit of consternation since his appearance was entirely civilian. They needed to look him up in the system to make sure he was allowed to buy official uniforms. Then, there was slight tailoring that needed to be done, and he paid a premium to have one uniform altered quickly so he could wear it to his meeting. The others would be sent to the BOQ on the station to wait for him.

After his meeting with the admiral, Sandy would be heading down-planet. Leezy had found a mountain resort on Valkyrie where it was currently autumn. She was arriving at Valkyrie Station in a few hours. Sandy planned to meet her at the shuttle terminal after his meeting. She accessed the feed from the resort the day before and reported to Sandy that the leaves were changing color right now and the views were breathtaking. She had two weeks she could spend with him before needing to return to work.

Sandy left the outfitters and found a store that sold the kind of shoes and clothing he would need for the climate. Leezy had indicated that hiking and rock climbing were on the program. Sandy was looking forward to the exercise in the fresh air. It would be even better with Leezy accompanying him. He also bought a duffel bag and a rucksack.

Stowing his new purchases in the duffel, Sandy returned to the outfitters. He only needed to wait a few minutes before his dress uniform was ready. He changed from his civilian garb into his new uniform. He checked to make sure all the decorations were correctly displayed. Looking in the mirror, he had to admit to himself that something about the uniform, particularly a dress uniform, made him feel different—energized in a way. He noticed his posture was better—his back straighter, his chin higher. He had not thought he would ever wear the uniform again, but now that he saw himself, he felt better. He stuffed his civilian clothes and shoes into the duffel and headed to the admiralty.

He arrived slightly early by design. He had no official identification. The SP manning the entrance would need to verify who he was and then issue him a new ID. Thumbprints, a retinal scan, and a DNA swab were taken. It took a few minutes to obtain the results. Sandy waited patiently. The SP manning the reception desk called him over and handed Sandy a new ID card with a lanyard.

He arrived at Admiral Ketyungyoenwong's office right on schedule, at 07:55. He gave his name to the yeoman, who betrayed a slight reaction to the name, his eyes widening. Recovering immediately, the yeoman informed Sandy that he would let the admiral know he was here. From the yeoman's slight start, Sandy figured he might have been a topic of conversation recently.

The door opened moments later. Admiral Ketyungyoenwong stood inside. She put her hands on her hips and gave Sandy a look of appraisal, up and down. She waved him in.

"I wasn't expecting to see you in uniform," she admitted as she sat in one of the armchairs away from her desk, "let alone a dress uniform. But, I must say, it suits you. And it pleases me, in a way you couldn't possibly understand. Thank you."

"I just felt it was appropriate," Sandy replied quietly as he sat.

"Welcome back, officially," she began. "Why don't we start with your questions? That will probably lead us into the things I want to cover this morning."

Sandy nodded. "What is Battle Group Omega?" he asked.

"Right to the heart of the matter," she commented. "Good. Battle Group

Omega will be formed once our current construction is complete. You will be the commodore. It's one of the reasons I assigned Bronwen Gupta as your XO. She's capable of running the ship while you manage the Battle Group. Your task will be to eliminate the rogue fleets formed during the HUW's civil war. Once that is done, we will allow the planets they have controlled to determine for themselves whether they wish to remain independent, join the Alliance or join or form any other multi-system government. We believe, based on intelligence reports, that the former Alliance planets will wish to rejoin us. Those planets that were not part of the Alliance may join us or may resolve to stay non-aligned. Our reports indicate that not all of their former planets would willingly rejoin the United Worlds. There seems to be a certain yearning for independence on some of those worlds."

"In addition to eliminating the rogue fleets, you will be expanding our defensive perimeter. You will need to provide protection to the liberated systems until they make a decision on their political future. During this period, I would expect challenges to be presented by the other rogue group captains or the United Worlds. The Alliance is promising self-determination, and it will be Battle Group Omega's responsibility to allow that to happen. It's a big job and, as far as capital ships, you will only have the resources listed in the organization skeleton I provided. It is likely that we will commit some additional frigates and light cruisers for those systems that decide to rejoin the Alliance."

"The organizational chart only included two frigates," Sandy pointed out. "That's not nearly enough if I'm to defend the new perimeter. I'll need pickets."

"I thought you would have heard from Captain Swift about that," she commented.

"Monty and I did not talk about the navy," Sandy said. "It was a sore subject for me until recently."

"There's an ancient saying, 'Necessity is the mother of invention,' and in re-establishing the Alliance, we had a tremendous need for pickets and not enough ships. Even if we had the ships, we had neither the people nor the budget to fly them," she explained. "The tech people came up with a low-cost solution that has proven effective. We have been using remote sensor drones as pickets. They're relatively cheap, almost undetectable (unless you know exactly where to look), and last for decades unless they get hit by something. They have only passive sensors and no ability to maneuver, so we park them in a stable orbit close enough to the center of the system that they can use solar energy to keep running."

"How do you get them in place?" Sandy asked.

"That's a job for the frigates. Lieutenant Commander Weed was delivering some of the earliest drones when you encountered her in SA 054. Thanks to your timely arrival, she not only made it back with two captured frigates but was able to accomplish her mission."

"I'm guessing there is more information to come about which of the baby HUWs to target first, their assets, etc.?"

"Plenty of time for that later," she stated.

"Will Battle Group Omega report to Red or Blue?"

"Neither. Directly to me," she said.

Sandy raised his eyebrows at this. The admiral merely smiled at him in response.

"Do you have any preferences for commanders you would like in the Battle Group?" she asked.

Sandy thought for a moment, then shook his head. "I've been away. You know your people, so I'll defer to your judgment."

"Do you want Monty?"

"Only if he wants to be part of it," Sandy replied. "We've always been peers. Having to report to me might be too weird for him."

"Do you think you could handle it?"

"I think so," Sandy said. "It would be nice to have someone with whom I could bounce ideas back and forth—as long as he knew he could disagree with me during the planning and discussion phase of things and not when it came to orders."

Admiral Ketyungyoenwong nodded. "I'll think about it," she allowed. "I see you got a new ID card. When we finish, you'll work with my yeoman to reactivate all your navy accounts, and he'll provide you with a new comm."

When he finished with the admiral and her yeoman, Sandy had two weeks to spend with Leezy. He would have another two weeks after she went back to Arete and her job, but he figured he could spend that time profitably in learning more about his new ship and crew.

He changed back into civilian clothing and headed to the shuttle terminal. He joined the queue at the security checkpoint with his duffle and garment bags in hand. He was about to contact Leezy with his new comm unit, so she would have the address. He also wanted to find out where she was, when he felt a sting below his right ear.

Admiral Ketyungyoenwong's yeoman knocked softly on her closed door, interrupting her meeting. He then entered. "Admiral, please pardon the intrusion."

"It's fine," she replied. "We were just finished."

Her visitor, a commander, stood, said goodbye, and left. When the door closed, the yeoman said, "Admiral, I just forwarded a bulletin from ONI to you."

Letty returned to her desk. She sat at her console and opened the bulletin.

> Man collapsed in security line at shuttle terminal. EMS took him away within minutes. Second EMS unit showed up in response to

call, claiming there was not another EMS unit for this section of the station. Abandoned bags taken by security. Upon search for possible explosives, they discovered Navy ID, newly issued to Captain Alexander Pike. Security contacted ONI per protocol. Cameras for area disabled. ONI attempted to contact Pike by comm. No answer.

Cameras further along concourse picked up 'EMS' unit. Four members of Shimano Brotherhood identified by recognition programs. Cart abandoned near leased dock where a private yacht had departed planetside, with flight plan for Macawber. Traffic control lost contact with yacht below 500 meters. Yacht did not follow filed flight plan and could be anywhere on Valkyrie.

Letty's face went pale as she read the bulletin. When she finished, she ordered her console to send a Priority Alpha message to the Director of ONI. A Priority Alpha message would find the director wherever she was. If the director was using her comm, it would break through all other messages or applications. It was a summons that could not be ignored or postponed.

When the director responded, Admiral Ketyungyoenwong jumped right in. "Sheila, we have an urgent situation. My yeoman just shared a report from your people about an incident at the shuttle terminal just under an hour ago. Captain Pike was just kidnapped. I need you to get on this immediately. If you don't have enough resources, call AIS in. Actually, I'm going to call AIS in, regardless. Share everything you have with them. This is urgent, understood?"

"Understood, admiral," she replied. "Let me see what we have so far, and I'll forward to my counterpart at AIS. Then, I'll have my guys start digging to see if they can pick up what happened on other camera feeds and to see if he's still on-station."

"Keep me apprised," Ketyungyoenwong said, then closed the connection. She immediately ordered her computer to contact the director of the Alliance Investigative Service on a Priority Alpha basis.

When she reached the director, she shared the same information. The AIS Director, Bob Robertson, grunted acknowledgment. "Let me get things moving," he said. "I'll have my team leader buzz you to get additional information shortly."

After closing the call, Admiral Ketyungyoenwong turned to her yeoman, still waiting. "Thank you, Jeff. If you hadn't spotted that, things might be worse than they are now."

Her yeoman nodded and rose. "Should I cancel your appointments?" he asked.

"Yes."

As the yeoman was leaving her office, her console indicated an incoming call from Agent Kasongo of AIS. She opened the connection. A thin-faced, dark-skinned man appeared on the screen.

"Admiral," he said, "Akil Kasongo here. I'm the AIS Agent-in-Charge of the situation. We're just getting started, but I wanted to introduce myself and ask a few questions, if I may."

"Thank you, Agent Kasongo. Ask away."

"Do you know of any reason someone might want to abduct Captain Pike?"

"Captain Pike just returned to the Alliance Navy," she related. "He was in private business for the last six-plus years. This might be related to some encounter he had during that period. Most recently, he had an encounter with the Karkinosian government. A few months before that, he was involved in ransoming a hostage taken by the Graz Syndicate. I don't think it's either of those."

"Why not, admiral?"

"To the best of my knowledge, none of the rogue governments formed by the HUW's civil war has been able to mount a clandestine operation in foreign territory like this. As far as the Graz Syndicate, I had ONI investigate thoroughly to find traces of his involvement, and they had no success whatsoever. The ransom was paid by an account at Kruppen Financial and delivered by Manlius Military. Manlius was hired through Kruppen as well."

"How do you know he was involved, then?"

"A hunch based on knowing him for over fifteen years."

"I'm not going to rule either one out," Kasongo stated, "though if Graz has been able to penetrate Kruppen, that would be a miracle. We can't even get in there."

"There might be other loose ends. I suggest you speak to his former crew. I'll send you their contact information immediately."

"That will be helpful. Thank you."

"Is there anything else?" she asked.

"Not at the moment, admiral. I'll be in touch."

Kasongo closed the connection. Admiral Ketyungyoenwong instructed her yeoman to send the comm addresses for the former crew of the *Alice May* to Kasongo immediately. She leaned back in her chair, her thoughts racing—wondering who Sandy could have irritated so much to bring this about.

Agent Kasongo quickly had agents interview the crew of the *Alice May*. While that was happening, analysts were examining security camera footage. Though the cameras at the shuttle terminal check-in area had been disabled, others at a greater distance picked up the vehicle that had taken Sandy away. They were able to track it to a dock, only to learn that a yacht tied up at that dock had recently departed the station and headed down-planet. Facial recognition software of the camera feeds identified the kidnappers as low-level members of the Shimano Brotherhood.

That helped Agent Kasongo to rule out the Graz Syndicate as a suspect. Graz would never cooperate with Shimano—it would be more likely they would start killing one another. One of his agents tried to get a track on the yacht from Valkyrie traffic control. Traffic control indicated that the yacht's flight plan was to Macawber, but it never arrived there. Once it dropped below 500 meters, traffic control's systems stopped following it. The yacht could be anywhere on the planet. They had traced the yacht's registration and were combing through databases, trying to find possible links on Valkyrie. To this point, they reached a dead end. The paper trail on the yacht stopped with a lawyer. Unfortunately, attorney/client privilege would prevent the lawyer from disclosing the yacht's true owner.

"Ali, I need your help," Admiral Ketyungyoenwong asked on the comm console.

Her niece, Alison Lynch, was on the other end of the call. She did not look well. She was in hospital scrubs. Her hair had returned to its natural light brown color. She had lost weight, and her eyes appeared to have sunk into her face.

"Hi, Aunt Letty. I'm fine. Thanks for asking," she replied.

Admiral Ketyungyoenwong winced. "Sorry. I'm in the middle of a crisis, and I think you can help. And you clearly don't look 'fine,' but we'll talk about that in a minute. It's about Sandy Pike."

"I thought everything was all set with Sandy rejoining the navy?"

"It was. We had a meeting a little while ago, and then he left to go on leave. He was kidnapped at the shuttle terminal. ONI and AIS are investigating and are interviewing his crew to ask them the same thing I'm going to ask you. Is there anyone out there that Sandy crossed who would want to capture him? Someone with the resources to hire the Shimano Brotherhood to take him?"

A troubled look crossed Ali's face. "Well, there are the owners of the ships he captured," she said, "but I doubt any of them have the money to hire the Brotherhood. I also don't think they'd want to kidnap him. A fléchette gun to the chest is more their style. Sandy didn't get in much trouble after I left the ship, so I guess I'm as knowledgeable as anyone."

She paused in thought. A distasteful expression came over her face. "There's one I can think of: Alfred Mendele. He was the science teacher turned human slaver on Edda. After I left the *Alice May*, I volunteered to try to help run him down. We were unsuccessful. I believe he managed to leave Edda but have no idea where he would have ended up. He might have the money to hire the Brotherhood and certainly have a motive for revenge. He's also sick and twisted enough to want to get that revenge personally and painfully. He captured Sandy before and tortured him, wanting his 'merchandise' back."

An idea came to Letty. "That's what started you investigating the Graz Syndicate, isn't it?"

Ali nodded, a wistful expression on her face. "AIS worked up a profile on the guy," she stated. "I don't know that the rest of the crew would single him out as the most likely suspect but, the more I think about it, the more it makes sense to me. You should also have AIS find out where Sandy's girlfriend is. Mendele is evil enough that he might have grabbed both of them."

"That's a horrible thought."

"He's a horrible man."

"Thank you, Ali. I'll ring back after I pass this along to AIS."

"That's okay, Aunt Letty. I was just teasing you earlier. Contact me when you've caught Mendele and have Sandy safe."

Letty passed along the information to Agent Kasongo, giving him information on Elizabeth Wilson and adding that Pike had planned to meet her at a resort of some sort on Valkyrie. Kasongo immediately ordered his people to find Elizabeth Wilson and put her in protective custody immediately. He also instructed his people to focus on Mendele as a possible suspect.

That was the first break they had in the case. Traffic control delayed the arrival of the liner carrying Leezy by three hours. Her original arrival time would have put her in the shuttle terminal at roughly the same time they abducted Sandy. With the delay, she would not arrive for another 40 minutes. AIS immediately began to run facial recognition software on the people waiting for the arrival of that liner. Within moments, the scanning program identified four members of the Shimano Brotherhood. Shortly after that, the camera feeds from that passenger dock's waiting area went blank. Station Security reported they had been hacked. Security was trying to bring the cameras back online but not having much success.

Kasongo contacted Kathy Leis, a special agent in the Organized Crime section of AIS. She was the resident expert of everything to do with the Shimano Brotherhood. He informed her succinctly regarding the abduction of Captain Pike and the possible connection to Mendele.

"What does that have to do with me?" she asked.

"We identified four of the Brotherhood waiting for the arrival of Pike's girlfriend at passenger dock 14B on Valkyrie Station before the security cameras went dark. We have a little less than 40 minutes before the liner begins to offload passengers. We will not allow them to take her. In addition, Mendele, if he's the one behind this, was engaged in human trafficking. I believe the Brotherhood dropped out of that business. I'm hoping that you use this information to our benefit."

"How?"

"Call the Brotherhood off. Prevent an incident that might turn violent. Try to find out where Captain Pike was taken. The Shimano Brotherhood has always followed a 'hands-off' policy regarding our military in the past. Their involvement in the kidnapping of Captain Pike changes that."

"I'm going to need to talk with the Director before I do anything like that," she explained.

"Go ahead," Kasongo replied. "He handed this assignment off to me, so he's aware of it. Please make it quick, though."

"Let's conference him in. Saves time," she suggested.

Kasongo initiated a Priority Alpha call to the director. He answered right away. "Robertson," he said.

Bob Robertson saw both Kasongo and Leis on the screen of his console. Kasongo quickly summarized the investigation: the dead-end they had reached on trying to find Pike, the involvement of the Shimano Brotherhood, and the imminent arrival of Elizabeth Wilson, with the four Shimano operatives waiting for her. He then mentioned his hope that Special Agent Leis would contact the head of the Brotherhood to call off their planned capture of Wilson and inform him that they had involved themselves in a military matter by abducting Captain Pike, hinting that there could be unpleasant consequences for the Brotherhood as a result.

Robertson absorbed the information rapidly. "Right. Kathy, go ahead and call Ricky. Akil has the right idea. We're offering Ricky a chance to keep four of his people out of trouble and fix a mistake without losing face. If he needs to talk to me, he'll hear the same message but delivered more harshly."

Robertson ended the call. Leis told Kasongo, "Give me a few minutes, and I'll be back in touch."

She then used her console to contact Riku Shimizu, the head of the Shimano Brotherhood. The two of them had never met but were certainly aware of the other. She knew a call from her would get to him quickly.

As she expected, she reached an assistant first. The assistant tried not to show his excitement at receiving a call from Special Agent Leis. He put her on hold briefly. After less than a minute, Shimizu's face appeared on her console. It seemed as though he were outside.

"Hello, Special Agent Leis," he greeted her. "What an unexpected pleasure to hear from you."

"Hello, Mr. Shimizu. I'm calling as a courtesy, with a matter of some urgency."

"Please, call me Ricky. What is this urgent matter?"

"At the moment, at least four of your operatives are waiting near passenger dock 14B on Valkyrie Station, hoping to intercept a woman named Elizabeth Wilson. I'm letting you know that they will not be allowed to succeed."

"I will neither confirm nor deny whether that is true," Ricky responded. "I will ask, why is this matter so important to you?"

"This matter came to our attention as a result of another abduction a couple of hours ago at the shuttle terminal on Valkyrie Station. An abduction carried out by members of the Brotherhood. They took Captain Alexander Pike of the Alliance Navy. Miss Wilson is his girlfriend."

"Go on," Shimizu instructed.

"The Brotherhood's engagement in the kidnapping of an active-duty officer of the Alliance Navy is unprecedented, Ricky. The director views it as an extremely hostile act."

"Again, I neither confirm nor deny," Shimizu said. "If it is true, I will agree that something like that has not happened before. We have never interfered with your military in the past."

"Ricky, I'm giving you a chance to correct a possible error," Leis said. "I will suggest that you recall your people from the passenger dock. In addition, if you provide us with information regarding the location of Captain Pike, perhaps the involvement of the Shimano Brotherhood in his kidnapping would seem less hostile."

"Or perhaps be forgotten?" Shimizu suggested.

"I doubt that we can forget the mistakes that were made here," Leis countered. "Kidnapping an officer on behalf of someone who was a competitor of yours — "

"A competitor?"

"In a small way. We believe your client is a man named Alfred Mendele. Mr. Mendele was engaged in human trafficking on Edda. He managed to evade arrest. Now he's hired the Brotherhood to do his dirty work for him. You pulled the Brotherhood out of that business when you took over. Someone on your end didn't do his homework on this one, Ricky."

Shimizu scowled. "If all this is true, then I suppose I should thank you for bringing it to my attention, Special Agent Leis. Human trafficking is abhorrent to me, and I would not wish to interfere with the Alliance Navy."

"I very much hoped you would see it in that light," she responded. "I should remind you that time is of the essence. Miss Wilson's liner is due very soon. Mr. Mendele already has Captain Pike. The man is a psychopath. Who knows what he is doing with Pike? If Pike is harmed in any way, I'm afraid the Brotherhood would bear responsibility in the eyes of our director."

"Someone will be in touch with you soon," Shimizu stated conclusively. "They will contact you presently. Thank you for the call."

Leis let out a deep breath when the call ended. She sent a message to both Kasongo and Robertson with a recording of the exchange. She waited, drumming her fingers on her desk. Kasongo sent her a text less than five minutes later. The Shimano people were leaving the arrival area for passenger dock 14B. Though the cameras had been disabled, as they were at the security checkpoint, an AIS agent who had already arrived spotted them leaving. She had just finished reading it when an incoming call from a number she didn't recognize came to her console.

Sandy woke in a brightly lit room. The intensity of the light made him blink and squint. His wrists and ankles were tied to a rectangular frame of metal tubing, with his hands above his head. He had no clothing on.

He could move his head. Looking around, he thought he was in an unfurnished room of an apartment or house. The walls were white. The floor was of some sort of tile. There was a plastic tarp underneath where he was bound. There was a similar frame with a plastic tarp underneath, opposite him, with no one in it.

He heard a door open, then footsteps. He turned his head in the direction of the sound. Alfred Mendele appeared, holding a stool. Sandy breathed, "You!"

Mendele chuckled. "It's so nice to be remembered. You remember Jorge, too, I hope?"

The tall, stoop-shouldered man shuffled in after Mendele. He carried a small folding table. He erected the table to the side of Mendele and then returned the way he came. Mendele sat, a faint smile playing across his face. Jorge returned with a satchel he placed on the table, then took a position behind Mendele.

"As you have not forgotten me, neither have I forgotten you, Captain Pike. You created great difficulty for me: danger, trouble, expense, and inconvenience. I knew that someday I would repay you for that. That 'someday' has finally arrived."

"What do you want from me, Mendele?" Sandy snapped.

"Pain. Suffering. Emotional distress," Mendele said calmly. "Make no mistake, Captain. I will see you break. I will crush your hopes and dreams, and by the end, you will beg me to kill you. I may or may not. I'll have to decide when the time comes which outcome is more pleasurable for me.

"You'll see I had Jorge bring his tools," Mendele said as he nodded at the satchel. "I'm afraid to say you won't be the same man afterward. It's entirely possible you won't be a man at all if you catch my meaning."

"Then what are you waiting for?" Sandy asked.

"I'm expecting another guest," Mendele replied smoothly. "Her arrival was delayed, but she should on her way here soon. I believe you know her? Elizabeth Wilson?"

Sandy felt a mixture of horror, rage, and sadness. Emotion overwhelmed him. He broke into a cold sweat and heard roaring in his ears. He felt dizzy and nauseous.

"The waiting doesn't bother me," Mendele resumed after seeing Sandy's reaction. "I find that anticipation often makes the experience sharper."

"You're a monster," Sandy hissed. "I know what you did to those children and their parents. How can you live with yourself?"

"Just fine, thank you," Mendele said calmly, "and I sleep soundly at night. I started because I had the urge to. Then, I found I could make a considerable amount of money from my hobby. You put an end to that. You and people like you forced me to hide. I can only indulge myself on rare occasions these days. I don't enjoy it the way I used to. No one knew about me or would have ever suspected me before. Now I have to worry about being caught. Fortunately, I made enough money from my hobby that finances are not an issue. I was able to afford to hire the men who took you from the station—and they weren't cheap. The same group will be bringing Miss Wilson along shortly."

"So, this is your revenge?"

"You ruined the one source of pleasure I'd found in my life," Mendele explained. "It will amuse me to ruin you. I've been looking forward to this for a long time."

Leezy was nearing the hatch to the gangway. She was in line with other passengers. As she drew closer, a group of four broke from where they'd been standing near the exit and approached her. There were two men and two women dressed in dark suits. "Elizabeth Wilson?" asked one of the women.

The four serious-looking people created an icicle of fear in her belly. She didn't know whether to be scared for herself or wonder if something had happened to Sandy. She nodded weakly.

Seeing her unease, one of the women said quietly, "Relax, ma'am. We're from AIS. We're here to protect you. Will you please follow me?"

Leezy whispered, "Yes," as she gulped. The group headed for the side corridor just behind her. Two were in front of her and two behind. They kept close to her. Shortly after turning into the side corridor, they stopped.

"Sorry for the scare, ma'am," the woman explained. "There was a plot to kidnap you once you left the ship. We believe that those plans have been called off, but we are here to guarantee your safety even so."

"Where's Sandy—Captain Pike?" Leezy demanded.

"I don't know anything about that," the agent answered. "We were instructed only to put you in protective custody. When the crowd at the hatch is gone and we receive clearance to leave the ship, we will be taking you to our office. I'm sure someone there will be able to answer your questions."

Leezy tried to contact Sandy on his comm. When he was issued a new Navy unit that morning, the yeoman had set the old one to forward to his new device. It didn't do any good since his kidnappers had destroyed the new unit almost immediately. Leezy heard the recording saying that the address was inactive.

After waiting a few minutes that seemed to Leezy to take forever, the agents escorted her off the ship and to a small vehicle. They completely bypassed customs and passport control. They drove about one-third of the way around the ring of the station before turning into a corridor and then into a garage. The agents brought her into the office and took her to an empty conference room.

"Wait here," one of them said, "someone will come to see you shortly."

As Leezy waited, the last of her emotional paralysis faded. Replacing it was the old feeling of dread she had experienced before when Sandy had been in danger. The uncertainty and the fear of losing him plagued her again. Along with it came anger. It was because of that dread that she had called it off with him before. She'd encouraged him to rejoin the navy and almost immediately, something bad had happened.

Had she made a mistake, reconnecting with him? Was she strong enough to deal with this? Was it worth it? She was so absorbed with sorting through her feelings that she did not notice the door open softly.

When the man entered her peripheral vision, she looked up, startled. She began to stand, but he waved her down. He then offered his hand in greeting.

"Miss Wilson? I'm Bob Robertson," he said.

"Mr. Robertson," she replied. "Can you tell me what's going on? Where's Captain Pike?"

"Our people are on their way to collect him," Robertson answered.

"Is he okay?"

"I don't know."

"Where is he? What is going on?"

Robertson took a deep breath. "We believe he was kidnapped by a man who engaged in human trafficking. Captain Pike and his crew had an encounter with him several years ago. They disabled a ship and freed some captives. The suspect kidnapped Captain Pike a few days later and tried to torture him, to return the captives. Local authorities were able to interrupt that and free Sandy, but were unable to capture the suspect."

"Following that, there was a hunt for the man. He managed to evade capture and has been in hiding since. Somehow, he learned that you and Captain Pike would be on Valkyrie station today and planned to abduct you both. We haven't had the chance to dig into this further to determine how he knew. We've only been on the case for a couple of hours, beginning shortly after they took Captain Pike."

"This isn't related to the navy?" she asked.

Robertson shook his head. "I hate to say it, but his rejoining the service was a benefit. If he were still a private citizen, his abduction would not have been noticed for hours or even days. But, as it happened, when his abandoned bag was turned over to station security, they found his navy ID and alerted the Office of Naval Investigation. Admiral Ketyungyoenwong had just met with him minutes before, and her yeoman saw the bulletin from ONI and brought it to her attention. She got us involved immediately."

Mendele continued to try to taunt Sandy. He mused out loud whether it would be more entertaining to begin with the woman or with Sandy first. Sandy tried not to respond. The horror and sadness he felt faded while his rage grew. Through it all, Mendele's assistant, Jorge, stood impassive and motionless.

From another room, Sandy heard a knock at the door. There were two raps, a pause, then two more raps. "Our other guest has arrived," Mendele said, smiling warmly. "Jorge, please bring her in."

Jorge left, crossing behind Sandy to the door. Sandy heard the door close. A few minutes later, he saw Mendele look up in surprise, then slump over. Two men entered his view. They began to unfasten the restraints binding Sandy to the frame. Then, two other men appeared and began to bind Mendele with his arms behind his back. Sandy opened his mouth to say something, but one of them made the 'sh' gesture, putting his finger to his lips.

When Sandy was freed, he shook his arms, trying to regain circulation. One of the men handed him his clothing. The one who had shushed Sandy said, "AIS will be here shortly. Stay put."

Sandy processed this quickly. "You're not AIS?"

The man shook his head. They had finished tying Mendele up. The man looked around the room. He nodded in satisfaction, and they left. Sandy quickly donned his clothes. He followed out the door, finding a set of stairs upward. He climbed the steps and opened the door. He was in a hallway. To his left, Jorge was tied up, unconscious. The men had departed.

Robertson's comm unit buzzed. "Robertson," he answered. "Good," he grunted. "Patch him through."

He handed the comm to Elizabeth. "Hello?" she said uncertainly.

"Leezy?" came Sandy's voice. "You're alright?"

"I'm fine," she answered, tears forming in her eyes. "Are you okay?"

"I am," he said. "And knowing you're okay makes me feel even better."

12

Sandy and Leezy's reunion was subdued—partly because of the AIS personnel around and partly since they were still processing the events of the last few hours. "Do you still want to be with me?" Sandy asked hesitantly.

She nodded.

"Still want to go on vacation?" he asked.

"I think we could use it after this," she answered, in a darkly humorous tone.

"Who is in charge?" he asked.

Leezy nodded at Robertson.

"Miss Wilson and I were planning on visiting a resort," he explained. "Do you need us here any longer?"

Robertson shook his head with a smile. "I don't, but the medical people want to make sure you're okay. Give them a minute to run whatever scans, then grab your bag, and I'll get an agency flitter to take you wherever you want. I will ask that you make an appointment for a full debrief when you return. I understand from the admiral that you'll still be on leave, but this isn't really a navy affair."

Leezy and Sandy did not have the opportunity to talk privately until they checked into the resort and reached their room. After Sandy tipped the bellhop, he turned to find Leezy sitting with an uncomfortable expression on her face. Her arms were folded across her chest in a defensive posture.

"What the hell just happened, Sandy?" she asked. Her tone was not angry—at least, her anger didn't seem to be focused on him.

Sandy crossed slowly, almost hesitantly, to the chair facing hers. "Something I never expected," he replied as he sat.

He told her the whole story: of stopping the ship with the children on it, of Mendele torturing him, of Ali's attempt to track Mendele down and bring him to justice, and of what he knew from today. He described how he woke up naked and bound and feared that Mendele would capture her. Now, sitting here, at a plush resort with her, it seemed surreal—as though it couldn't have happened. If it weren't for lingering soreness in his wrists and shoulders, he could almost talk himself into believing it was a bad dream.

When he finished, she sat back. "Okay. You had it worse. Again."

"What do you mean?"

"I was stopped by four AIS agents as I was leaving the ship. They explained there was a plot to kidnap me, but they thought it had been called off. They didn't know anything about your situation. I tried to call you, but it said your comm was out of service. They took me to an office where Mr. Robertson explained a bare-bones version of what you just told me. I was scared and a little angry. I have to admit, the whole thing brought back how I felt when I knew you were in danger."

"I'm sorry," Sandy apologized.

"About what?" she snapped. "You don't have anything to apologize for. The whole thing is a result of you freeing those children. I would want you to do that. If anything, I should be apologizing to you."

Sandy sat up in surprise. "Why?"

"Because I began to think I'd made a mistake getting back together with you. I'm mad at myself for thinking that, but the distress and panic I felt, thinking I might lose you again, took me back to why I called things off."

"I'm sorry — " he began.

"Don't apologize," she said.

"I'm sorry that you felt that way," he continued.

"It's not your fault. Like I said, I had it easier than you did. I didn't have some psycho string me up and threaten to torture his girlfriend in front of me. That must have been awful."

"It was, at first. Then, I got mad. My anger drowned out all my other emotions. That made it easier," he explained.

"I got angry too," she said. "I was angry with you, then angry with myself. I'm still angry, but it's unfocused right now."

She had unwrapped her arms from around her chest, but her hands were still clenched in fists in her lap. Sandy stood and crossed to her. He grasped her right fist and tugged to get her to stand up. She stood but looked at her feet, her hands clenched by her sides. He brushed her hair out of the way and kissed her forehead gently. She took a deep breath. He kissed her forehead again. She looked up and leaned toward him.

He thought she might be softening up. He was wrong. She leaned toward him to begin pounding her fists against his chest. He let her for a few moments, then clasped her wrists to stop her.

"That's enough," he said. "You're starting to hurt me."

She collapsed into him, sobbing and laughing at the same time. Her fists were still closed in between them. He wrapped his arms around her gently and began to rub her back. Tears flowed from his eyes. When she gained control of herself, she looked up. She saw his cheeks wet with tears.

"Oh, Sandy," she sighed, then hiccupped. That started them both chuckling.

"Sandy, why can't this be easy?" she asked when she settled down.

He didn't have an answer.

They were able to put it aside until morning. Leezy felt that the unexpected nature of what had happened threw her off. Sandy did not sleep well. The events of the day before woke him several times. Each time, he felt disoriented and panicked.

Over breakfast, she explained, "Before, I knew you when you were heading into danger because you generally gave me some warning. This caught me by surprise. I think I'll be okay with it, but I'm going to talk to a therapist when I get back to Arete. I need to learn to deal with it."

"I can almost guarantee that I'll be in the middle of some conflict," Sandy admitted. "It's a part of the job."

"I know, and it's an important part of who you are. Even out of the navy you managed to find someone who wanted to torture you and kill you."

He laughed.

"How are you feeling?" she asked.

"Not great," he admitted. "I didn't sleep well."

"I noticed."

Before they left the room, the front desk called, saying there was a package for Captain Pike. Sandy went to retrieve it, only to find it was a navy issue comm unit, replacing the one taken from him the day before. There was already a message on it.

"Glad you're safe. Enjoy your time away. Letty."

Sandy and Leezy went out on their first day's adventure, a 15-kilometer hike through the hills. Each day brought with it a new physical challenge. They went rock-climbing, canoeing and white-water rafting. They went to a ski resort that would be covered in snow in less than eight weeks and rode mountain bikes. They took hikes, had picnics, and even tried skinny-dipping in a lake. They discovered that only the top layer of water, less than a meter, was warm. Below that was icy cold.

The physical nature of what they were doing was a pleasant break for both of them and diverted their minds from what had just happened. They ate well and went to bed each night, feeling like they'd made the most of each day. On the eighth day, they had climbed a particularly challenging rock face, a Class 4, with minimal help from their instructor. Sitting on the top, Sandy turned to her.

"I have an answer to your question," he said.

"Which one?"

"Why can't this, us, be easy."

"What did you come up with?"

"Nothing worth having usually comes easy. Look where we're sitting. If we'd taken a flitter up here, it would still be a pretty spot, but it wouldn't be very meaningful. Instead, we climbed up and did it the hard way. It's still a pretty spot but knowing what we did to get up here makes it special."

Leezy sat quietly for a minute. Eventually, she leaned into him. She kissed his cheek and laid her head on his chest. "You're right."

That evening, while waiting to be seated for dinner, a man and woman approached them. The couple was well-dressed and attractive. Their features showed Asian ancestry.

"Excuse me," the man said, "but, by any chance, are you, Commander Pike?"

Sandy immediately felt nervous, given the events of a few days before. Leezy gripped his arm tightly, having a similar reaction. The man noticed and held up his hands in a peaceful gesture. "I apologize. I don't mean to make you uncomfortable, but my wife thought she recognized the two of you from a picture that was in the news several years ago."

Sandy relaxed. Leezy's hand on his arm loosened. "I am," Sandy replied, "or was. I just was promoted to Captain."

"Congratulations." Turning to Leezy, the man said, "Are you Elizabeth Wilson?"

"I am."

The man turned to his wife. She beamed in triumph at being proved correct in her guess. "Would you please join us for dinner?" she asked. "I'm Mei, and my husband is Ricky. We're so sorry for disturbing you, but there was a picture of the two of you several years ago that took my breath away. I've never forgotten it."

"It would be a very great pleasure to have you join us," her husband said, reinforcing the invitation.

Sandy looked at Leezy to see what she wanted to do. She looked back at Sandy and gave him a faint smile. Turning to the couple, she said, "Thank you. We'll be happy to join you."

Ricky signaled to the maître d', indicating that the two tables for two would now be one table for four. The maître d' nodded and gestured them forward. The two men followed behind the ladies, helping them into their seats before sitting themselves.

The waiter arrived and took their drink orders. Sandy asked for sparkling water, Leezy for a glass of wine. Ricky and Mei looked at one another and asked Leezy if she minded if they ordered a bottle of wine for the three of them.

"Go right ahead," she replied, "though I'm a cheap date—I'll probably make the one glass last all night."

"We're not much for drinking either," Mei explained, "but ordering the bottle means fewer interruptions, though."

"You said you were just promoted to captain?" Ricky asked. "I would have thought with your record of accomplishment that you would have been promoted years ago."

"After the Alliance surrendered," Sandy explained, "I left the navy and pursued other interests. They just recalled me to active duty. The promotion was waiting for me when I returned."

"What sort of business were you in?" Ricky asked.

"I had a specialized freight operation," Sandy answered, trying to be as vague as possible. "What do the two of you do for a living?"

Mei looked at her husband to see if he wanted to go first before answering. "I'm on the board of several non-profit groups," she said. "I spend the most time working with the SPAC—the Society for Protection of Abused Children. I'm very proud of the work we do."

Sandy and Leezy turned to Ricky. "Nothing so noble," he explained. "I work for a big multi-system corporation."

Leezy nodded in agreement at this. "And you, Elizabeth?" Ricky asked.

"A big multi-system corporation," she replied.

The waiter returned with the wine. He pulled the cork and presented it to Ricky. He poured a small amount into his glass for him to taste. When he nodded his approval, the waiter poured for Leezy and Mei.

When the conversation resumed, work was not brought up as a topic. Instead, Ricky and Mei asked what the two of them had been doing during their stay. Leezy gave them a list of the activities they'd enjoyed. It led to a discussion of which was their favorite, which they'd never do again, and similar things Ricky and Mei had done together at different times.

Two-and-a-half hours later, they said their goodbyes. Ricky had insisted on picking up the check. Despite the initial awkwardness, it had turned out to be a most pleasant evening. Sandy kept an eye open the remaining few days of their stay to see if they would encounter the other couple again, but they did not.

The day before they were to leave, lying in bed, Leezy kissed him. "This has been a nice break from reality," she commented. "I think I'd like to do this again if the chance came up."

"Agreed," Sandy replied, his arm around her. "All's well that ends well, despite the awful beginning,"

"Ugh. Don't remind me," she said. "You still have a couple of weeks before you officially report for duty. What are you going to do with the time?"

"First, I'm getting a new ship. Not just new to me, new as in just finished construction. She's a type of ship I've never commanded, so I need to learn a lot about her. She's bigger and likely more advanced than the other ships in her class, in some respects. In addition, there will probably be lots of other information that I'll need to know. I'll be in command of a group of ships, and we have a mission. I need to know who the other commanders will be, the scope of the mission, any information regarding what we will encounter, and anything else the admiral thinks is essential."

"How long do you have to get this done?"

"Between today and when I officially report for duty, I have two weeks and a day. Once I report, I have a week before my ship begins trials—the initial full-scale testing of all the ship's systems, with a full crew. All of the different components will have been tested before that, but only separately— not as an integrated whole. Between making sure I know my new ship as thoroughly as possible and the meetings and briefings that I'm certain to have to attend, that week will be packed. The more I can do between now and then will make it easier for me to be effective."

"You said your ship will be more advanced than others of its class," she mentioned. "I thought they made them all alike."

"The last ships of her class were built starting 25 years ago," Sandy explained. "I'm sure they found a few things they wanted to improve since then."

When their time came to an end, the resort took them to the nearest shuttleport. Sandy stayed with Leezy until she passed through security, boarding the liner to Arete. He remained on the station and checked into the BOQ in the navy section. He found the uniforms he'd purchased waiting for him.

The following morning, he had an appointment with AIS for debrief of the incident with Mendele. He showed up five minutes early and was immediately escorted to Director Robertson's office. Sandy did not realize until then that Robertson was the head of AIS.

When he entered the office, Robertson stood from his desk to greet him. Already seated was a red-haired woman. Robertson introduced her as Special Agent Leis. She offered a hand in greeting and indicated he should sit.

When Sandy sat, Robertson began. "The reason Special Agent Leis is here is there were that of some unusual circumstances involved in your capture, rescue, and afterward. She is a lead agent in our Organized Crime Unit and our chief expert on the Shimano Brotherhood."

"Captain Pike," Leis began, "the Shimano Brotherhood were the ones who captured you and, we believe, the ones who came to the house where you were held. They set you free and bound Mendele and his assistant."

"How do you know this?"

"First, surveillance video of the group that captured you," she replied. "They had disabled the cameras at the shuttle port, but other cameras further along their route provided proof. At roughly the same time, we received a tip from Admiral Ketyungyoenwong that Miss Wilson might also be a target. Fortunately, her liner was delayed in arrival, and we were able to forestall her abduction."

"She told me that she was met by four agents before she left the ship," Sandy said.

"That was probably unnecessary," Robertson interjected. "The threat was already gone. We didn't want to take any chances, though."

"Thank you," Sandy offered. "How did you eliminate the threat?"

"At the Director's request, I contacted the head of the Shimano Brotherhood and let him know he had crossed a line when his people kidnapped you. Up until then, the Brotherhood had never interfered with military personnel in the past. I also informed him that Mendele was our chief suspect and that he was involved in human trafficking. When Riku Shimizu took control of the Brotherhood a couple of years ago, he moved them out of that business. He is currently weaning the organization away from the drug trade as well."

"Regardless," Leis continued, "immediately after my conversation with Mr. Shimizu, their operatives departed passenger dock 14B, where Miss Wilson's ship was arriving. A few minutes later, I received an 'anonymous tip' telling me where you were being held. When our agents arrived, you had already been freed, and Mr. Mendele and his assistant disabled and bound, waiting for our arrival. Those events were more supporting evidence of the Brotherhood's involvement."

"I wondered who they were," Sandy admitted.

"Finally," Leis said, "Mr. Shimizu and his wife treated you and Miss Wilson to dinner a couple of nights ago."

Sandy's jaw dropped open.

Robertson chuckled. "We didn't think you knew who it was," he said.

"I had no idea," Sandy agreed. Then, after a moment, he added, "If I did, I would have — "

"Would have, what?" Leis asked.

"Until just now, I had no idea who he was. I had no idea that the Shimano Brotherhood no longer engages in human trafficking. If I had known, I might have asked for a favor. I certainly would have let the admiral know."

"Really?" Leis asked, amused. "What favor would you ask?"

"A few months back, Admiral Ketyungyoenwong's niece was taken by the Graz Syndicate. I have a feeling she was looking into their involvement in human trafficking. They caught her and treated her like all their other captives—as punishment for sticking her nose where it didn't belong. I bought her back from them, but she was not in good shape after being in their hands. The tip you received from the admiral was probably information she got from Ali, her niece. I think Ali is still in a rehab facility. They really messed her up."

"So, what would you have asked Mr. Shimizu?" Leis asked again.

"For revenge against the Graz Syndicate," Sandy said flatly.

"Wait a minute," Robertson interrupted. "You dealt with the Graz Syndicate?"

Sandy shook his head vigorously. "No, not directly. As I said, I did my best to make sure I *didn't* deal with them. I worked through my bankers, Kruppen. We set up a dummy corporation that hired Manlius Military to deliver the payment. I did not want the Graz people to come after my crew or me."

"All the same," Robertson said, "I'm going to have my people check into it, to make sure your tracks are hidden."

"I understand from the admiral that ONI looked into it and came up empty."

"That's good," Robertson agreed, "but we'll check, just the same. I have a feeling we'll get the same result—AIS has never been able to get anything out of Kruppen Financial. I don't think anyone can."

"If you were serious about wanting revenge," Leis asked, "how would you be able to point the Brotherhood in the right direction?"

"I wouldn't be able to," Sandy admitted. "Ali went missing. I had some people look into it. They provided the information that it appeared the Graz Syndicate had taken her. I arranged for some intermediaries to contact Graz to see if I could buy her from them. But, as I said, I didn't want Graz to be able to track it back to my crew or me."

"Probably for the best that you didn't bring that up with Ricky," Robertson mentioned. "The last thing we need right now is a gang war."

"Can you tell me what will happen to Mendele?" Sandy asked.

"He and his assistant will go to prison," Robertson replied. "Their sentences will be long, though I don't expect them to last more than a year or two."

"What do you mean?"

"Prison inmates don't like child molesters," Robertson said. "They hate slavers even more."

Sandy nodded soberly. "Will I need to testify?"

"I think we'll try to keep you out of it," Leis said. "There is plenty of evidence to convict Mendele without you. Bringing you into court might expose our interaction with the Shimano Brotherhood. That would serve no good purpose."

His meeting with AIS complete, Sandy's curiosity drew him to the shipyard, where his new ship, the *Audacious*, was. When he arrived at the slip, a woman stopped him. "Where do you think you're going?" she demanded.

"I, uh, just wanted to see the ship," Sandy answered, a little taken aback by her aggressive tone.

"Why?"

"She's going to be mine," he responded.

The woman smiled. "She's never going to be 'yours,' captain. You might be in command, but she will always be my baby." She stuck her hand out. "Sally Danforth," she said.

Sandy shook hands. "Sandy Pike," he replied. "Why is she yours?"

"Because I built her," Danforth answered. "I'm the project superintendent. I've been with her since she was nothing but drawings and schematics."

Sandy grinned. "I'll concede the point of ownership, then."

"Not ownership," Danforth shook her head, "parentage."

Sandy nodded in acknowledgment.

"Would you like a tour?" Danforth asked.

Sandy grinned. His eyes widened as they scanned the massive warship in the viewscreen. He turned to Danforth and answered.

"Hell yes!"

13

Seated around the table were Admiral Mataneice Feng, Admiral Dieter Manbarschwein, and Admiral Alfred Noyes. The three of them ruled the multi-system governments centered on Umbria, Vermilion, and Karkinos, respectively. Feng stood. "I'd like to request that we dismiss our aides."

Manbarschwein looked over at Noyes. Noyes nodded slightly. Manbarschwein tilted his head at Feng in acceptance. There was a bustle as their aides picked up their papers and collected their belongings. Once the last one left, Feng, still standing, resumed.

"Gentlemen. We have spent the last seven hours in childish bickering and finger-pointing—mainly between the two of you. If you think your most significant threat is in this room, you're an idiot. I served with both of you, and I don't think either one of you is that stupid.

"There was a statesman back on earth who once said, 'We must all hang together, or, most assuredly, we will hang separately.' He could have been speaking directly to us. Instead, we have been pursuing our own aims, looking to gain an advantage over one another. I am as much to blame as either of you. In the process, we've lost ships and crew. We haven't been able to repair some of the ships which took damage when we split from the Hegemony. Our intelligence operations have focused on each other, so we don't know what the Alliance is doing. We have better information about the Hegemony, if only because of our personal connections.

"It came to my attention that the Alliance is nearing completion of a massive building campaign. My intelligence service did not provide me with this information. I just happened to scan the newsfeeds. In less than two months, the Alliance Navy will be as strong as it was at the beginning of the last war. That means they will have the most powerful force in space. Considering that each of us has former Alliance planets under our control, shouldn't we be worried about the Alliance and not each other?"

"What are you proposing?" Noyes asked.

"We must join together and form a confederation. Our combined resources make us strong. But, separately, we are the low-hanging fruit the Alliance will pick first."